...es on a farm in Anglesey with her ...y lecturer husband, assorted pets who arrived as ...ys and never left, and sometimes one or both of her boomerang sons. When she's not writing she loves to be outdoors gardening, or walking on one of the beaches for which the island is famous—along with being the place where Prince William and Catherine made their first home!

When **Kali Anthony** read her first romance novel at fourteen she realised two truths: that there can never be too many happy endings, and that one day she would write them herself. After marrying her own tall, dark and handsome hero, in a perfect friends-to-lovers romance, Kali took the plunge and penned her first story. Writing has been a love affair ever since. If she isn't battling her cat for access to the keyboard, you can find Kali playing dress-up in vintage clothes, gardening, or bushwalking with her husband and three children in the rainforests of South-East Queensland.

Bromley Libraries

30128 80505 571 5

Also by Kim Lawrence

A Passionate Night with the Greek

A Ring from a Billionaire miniseries

Waking Up in His Royal Bed
The Italian's Bride on Paper

Jet-Set Billionaires collection

Innocent in the Sicilian's Palazzo

Spanish Secret Heirs miniseries

The Spaniard's Surprise Love-Child
Claiming His Unknown Son

Also by Kali Anthony

Revelations of His Runaway Bride
Bound as His Business-Deal Bride
Off-Limits to the Crown Prince
Snowbound in His Billion-Dollar Bed

Discover more at millsandboon.co.uk.

CLAIMED BY HER GREEK BOSS

KIM LAWRENCE

THE MARRIAGE THAT MADE HER QUEEN

KALI ANTHONY

MILLS & BOON

All rights reserved including the right of reproduction
in whole or in part in any form. This edition is published
by arrangement with Harlequin Enterprises ULC.

This is a work of fiction. Names, characters, places, locations
and incidents are purely fictional and bear no relationship to
any real life individuals, living or dead, or to any actual places,
business establishments, locations, events or incidents.
Any resemblance is entirely coincidental.

This book is sold subject to the condition that it shall not,
by way of trade or otherwise, be lent, resold, hired out
or otherwise circulated without the prior consent of the publisher
in any form of binding or cover other than that in which it is published
and without a similar condition including this condition
being imposed on the subsequent purchaser.

® and TM are trademarks owned and used by the trademark owner
and/or its licensee. Trademarks marked with ® are registered with the
United Kingdom Patent Office and/or the Office for Harmonisation
in the Internal Market and in other countries.

First published in Great Britain 2022
by Mills & Boon, an imprint of HarperCollins*Publishers* Ltd,
1 London Bridge Street, London, SE1 9GF

www.harpercollins.co.uk

HarperCollins*Publishers*
1st Floor, Watermarque Building,
Ringsend Road, Dublin 4, Ireland

Claimed by Her Greek Boss © 2022 Kim Lawrence

The Marriage That Made Her Queen © 2022 Kali Anthony

ISBN: 978-0-263-30098-7

09/22

This book is produced from independently certified FSC™ paper
to ensure responsible forest management.
For more information visit www.harpercollins.co.uk/green.

Printed and Bound in Spain using 100% Renewable Electricity
at CPI Black Print, Barcelona

CLAIMED BY HER GREEK BOSS

KIM LAWRENCE

MILLS & BOON

CHAPTER ONE

THE GLASS DOORS swished open silently.

Tilda Raven shook the raindrops from her rich brown hair, the damp, messy waves spilling down her back almost to her waist today rather than constrained in the usual sensible, sleek, fat ponytail on her nape.

Tilda didn't pause. She was a woman on a mission, a mission interrupted by a security guard who blocked her way with his bulk.

'Do you have an appoint…?' The smartly suited man did a comical double-take. 'Oh, sorry, Miss Raven, I didn't recognise you.'

Tilda smothered her impatience and out of deeply engrained politeness forced her lips into a smile of acknowledgement that didn't touch the wide green eyes hidden behind the rain-spattered, pink-tinted lenses of the unflattering heavy-framed glasses that covered a lot of her small heart-shaped face.

Her eyes strayed beyond the uniformed figure to the art deco clock on the wall above the sleek reception desk. Yes, she could still make it back for three if… Her rounded jaw firmed. There was no *if* about it; she *was* going to be back for three—non-negotiable.

It wasn't as if he could try to lock her in!

Although she could easily imagine her terminally selfish boss doing just that, if he could have got away with it.

How would he take it?

'Not well' was pretty much a given.

At that moment the coward's way out was looking very appealing—she had been tempted—but she owed him an explanation in person if nothing else. Her decision was made and there was no going back—though Ezio could be very persuasive.

She was pretty sure that he wouldn't be wishing her well, but she was prepared for him to kick off.

She didn't care. For once this wasn't about her brilliant billionaire boss; this was about her brother, Sam.

Sam was her priority.

Better late than never.

Tilda felt a kick of guilt as an image of her teenage brother's scared eyes above an oxygen mask flashed into her head... Her hand went to her throat, her chest tightened, the sound of her heartbeat filled her ears and she fought for breath the way Sam had... *He's fine now... he's fine now...* She repeated the mantra, her head fighting free of the panic.

Sam *was* fine. You'd never know, seeing him sitting glued to a computer screen playing a game, that last night he'd been blue-lighted to hospital. If anything did happen, Mrs Lowther—the elderly neighbour who had known them since they were children—was sitting with him, much to Sam's disgust.

She realised that the security guard was talking to her and she hadn't heard a word he had said.

'Sorry, James.' She interrupted him mid-flow. 'I'm... I'll catch up later.' She threw the suitably vague promise over her shoulder, knowing it was a lie as she hurried across the space designed to give anyone visiting the iconic Angelos Building for the first time a serious *wow* moment.

Tilda still got a little frisson of pleasure when she walked in, but today she was not interested in the eclectic art, the modern sculptures, the polished concrete floor or the clever use of light. Her eyes went again to the stylised art deco clock behind the elegant reception desk staffed by an equally elegant team of reception staff. It wasn't actually morning, but even though that didn't matter any longer she found herself quickening her pace.

A bit like a condemned person being in a hurry for their last meal… The image drew a frown. She was not condemned—this was her choice—she just hated being late.

It was a lucky hang-up, given who her boss was, that she was an uber-punctual person, because tardiness and being kept waiting were on the list of things that wound up Ezio Angelos. The list was not short and it included excuses.

Not that she was about to offer any today. The only thing she planned to offer was her resignation. Not because she'd had a better offer—well, not recently, anyhow—or because she disliked her job, because she didn't, despite the fact that her boss ticked a lot of boxes on Tilda's own list of undesirable qualities in a man.

Many people were willing to overlook those qualities because they came wrapped up in some pretty marvellous packaging. Had she been the sort of female that went for smouldering, lean beefcake with the odd billion in his personal account, she might have too. But Tilda had higher standards. And being the owner of ridiculously long eyelashes, sybaritic cheekbones and a carnal mouth that should have carried a health warning did not, to her mind, make it all right for him to be arrogant.

And he was arrogance on steroids!

He also possessed the empathy of a flint, a ruthless streak a mile wide and as for beautiful women... He went through more of them than he did disposable razors—and her Greek boss, who possessed a carved jaw and lean cheeks that were dusted with a shadow before midday, went through quite a few of those.

Despite all these faults, Ezio, who had made his fortune in AI, was a pretty good boss. He was demanding, sure, but fair, not patronising and the work was *never boring*. Breathless, sure, but *not* boring.

The man was an intellectual adrenaline-junkie who considered the word 'impossible' a challenge. It could be pretty exhausting just trying to keep up with him. Tilda usually failed but she loved the buzz she got trying.

Also, she had a level of autonomy that she could not imagine being granted elsewhere. And in Tilda's eyes it really went in his favour that there were never any of the sort of inappropriate remarks or looks that had made her feel uncomfortable in her previous jobs. Equally importantly, he had not once suggested she looked too young to be taken seriously. She was sure this was in part thanks to the glasses her twenty-twenty vision didn't need, a piece of stage dressing that in her estimation added a good five years to her baby-faced twenty-six. They were an inspired prop, even if she acknowledged she shouldn't have to prove her seriousness anyway.

A flicker of regret slid across her face. She would miss her job. Also, if she was honest, she would miss the expression on people's faces when she casually threw into the conversation she was Ezio Angelos's PA... Yes, *the* Ezio Angelos...

Levering her back from the wall of the lift as it arrived at the top floor, she felt a stab of guilt at the selfish and shallow thought. She straightened her slender shoulders and reflected wryly that there might be no need to resign. Maybe she was already sacked. Ezio was not exactly renowned for his patience and she was *extremely* late.

She glanced quickly at her phone just to check for messages from Sam but there weren't any. She was only partially soothed. There had been no messages from him last night when she'd thought he was at his chess club. It turned out that he'd actually been in the local hospital A&E department.

And she had only found out thanks to the owner of a corner shop who had been incredibly kind—considering Sam had just tried to shoplift a can of beer from him—and had gone in the ambulance with the would-be thief after Sam's efforts to be accepted by the *cool* older school kids had triggered an asthma attack. The worst one he'd had in years.

If it hadn't been for the actions of the shop keeper in being so quick to call an ambulance, and who wasn't pressing charges, Sam's future might be looking very different today.

She shuddered. He might not have a future!

They owed that man a lot... Tilda could have kissed him...she actually had. His well-meant advice on parenting was a very small price to pay for his kindness. *And, let's face it,* she thought, sketching a bleak, self-condemnatory grimace, *I need it!*

The lift opened directly into a large room that was dominated by her own desk. She could see the shadow of her assistant distorted through the thick glass partition. Even now, after four years, the novelty of having an assistant and not being *the* assistant hit her some days.

She reached the open door, beyond which lay the spectacular architectural award-winning office with the glass wall along with its outward-projecting glass-floored section that only someone with a head for heights would venture near—Tilda hadn't.

In her own head, Tilda had never thought of it as an office. Instead *lair* had always seemed a more appropriate description, fit for the sleek predator her boss of four years was.

She took a deep breath, stepped inside the *lair* and turned to close the door just as Rowena emerged from her office alcove, desperately mouthing, '*He's in a vile mood,*' as she dramatically mimed a cutting motion across her throat in a well-meant dramatic warning.

Tilda didn't need the warning. Even without Tilda seeing his face, Ezio's clenched body language said it all. His loose-limbed body was rigid and she could almost see the quivering tension in his broad shoulders as he stood facing the glass wall, oblivious to the dizziness of the drop visible beneath his feet, listening to the disembodied voice on speaker phone that she immediately recognised belonged to Saul Rutherford.

The image of the man frequently termed 'a silver fox', a legend in his own life time, flashed into her head. In his seventies, Saul still ran his successful IT firm, niche rather than revolutionary these days, but his name still carried clout.

'I would let my company go under before I would let Baros get his claws into it.' Tilda could hear the bubbling anger in the normally softly spoken man's shaking voice.

'There is no question of either of those eventualities coming to pass, is there, Saul?'

Nothing of the explosive quality he was exuding was evident in Ezio's measured response, which emerged cool and silky-smooth, giving no hint of the frustration she could see drawn on his lean, dark 'fallen angel' features as he swivelled round, looking exclusive and sleek in one of the gorgeously cut suits he habitually wore. He registered her presence with a narrowing of his black, dark-framed eyes—eyelashes like his were wasted on a man—and a sharp, stabbing motion of one long, elegant brown finger that she followed to the crumpled tabloid lying open on the desk.

Even before she saw the two-year-old, digitally altered photo, the fake headline above it drew a grimace. This represented a sharp escalation of the drip-drip of stories attributed to people close to the 'couple'.

Surely this was the moment for him to speak directly to Athena? Because ignoring her wasn't working… Maybe, she mused, it was the *ignoring* that was part of the problem.

Or maybe it was just revenge, spite or maybe…?

She gave her head a tiny shake and closed down the line of speculation.

It was hard to take on the new reality, which was that she was no longer totally invested in her boss's projects or problems. It was no longer her job to point out the options he didn't want to see and to quite often get her head bitten off for her trouble.

Focusing on the plusses somehow didn't make her feel any happier, but this wasn't about being happy; it was about being there for her brother.

Ezio was no longer her problem, but Athena Baros

was his. Tilda was actually amazed this sort of situation didn't occur more often, considering the callous way Ezio dumped the women in his life, but generally they seemed remarkably un-resentful. Certainly, none had previously planted a series of false stories which left the impression that their romance had been rekindled.

Sources close to the socialite *influencer* Athena Baros denied it. She had maintained a loud silence but her enigmatic smile had set names trending. According to an online survey, nine out of ten people were convinced that not only were the beautiful pair secretly engaged, Athena was pregnant.

Tilda wondered if Ezio had read the same survey. Being sane, she hadn't asked. It wasn't that, as far as she could tell, he gave a damn how many articles were written about his love life—which was just as well, as when your name appeared regularly in the top five eligible bachelors on the market the stories were par for the course. But this was different because this time it wasn't personal, it was business, and when it came to business Ezio was never casual. Focused and ruthless, yes, but not casual.

He had invested a good deal of time and effort in the Rutherford deal. Tilda knew it was part of his vision for the future of Angelos Industries. And if her boss was invested, he expected her to be too, and that was the problem. While she'd been giving her all to her job, what had been left over for the really important things? Her priorities had got seriously skewed, but that was going to stop right here, right now.

She might not a be parent but she was the closest thing to a parent that Sam had now.

The self-recriminatory groove in her forehead smoothed

out as she lifted her chin. Beating herself up over past mistakes would achieve nothing; her priorities had been redrawn. Ezio's billion-making deals did not even make the revised top hundred. She was about to focus all her energies on keeping her brother safe, stopping him from falling in with the wrong crowd and wrecking his life.

This had been a warning and she was heeding it.

'Even without us joining forces on this project, Rutherford has the respect of the industry and balance sheets to match. Of course, if you join us you will step into a different league...'

'You expect me to get into bed with you when you are in bed with Baros's daughter, that lying snake... He's been trying for years get his hands on my company.'

She watched as Ezio paused, no doubt swallowing an acid rejoinder on the tip of his tongue, and pressed a row of long fingers to his temple.

'Athena and I had a casual relationship several years ago.'

The muscle that was clenching and unclenching beside his mouth as he formed the words through bared white teeth held an unwilling fascination for Tilda, who knew how much the words must cost him.

She had learnt pretty soon after she'd come to work for him, first as an assistant to his assistant and then as his PA, that he never explained himself to anyone, and she could only imagine what being obliged to do so now must be doing to him.

Welcome to the real world, she thought, unable to summon a shred of sympathy for his dilemma in her present mindset. Ezio didn't realise how lucky he was... Oh, not because of his wealth or power—she didn't envy him that—but he didn't seem to possess a shred of self-doubt. He didn't pretend to believe in himself, he actually did.

'Baros is not involved, Saul, and never has been.' Nothing in Ezio's expressionless delivery suggested that he was starting to have doubts on this score himself.

Given the timing and the escalation, how could he discount the possibility that George Baros, Athena's father, was behind this somehow? Hell, the two old men had been playing a grudge match for the past fifty years... they certainly kept the animosity fresh.

Was Athena helping her father out using this non-romance as a way of killing off a deal that would benefit her father's old enemy?

Along with the most incredible legs, Athena did possess a rather twisted sense of humour, and no discernible conscience. That had not bothered him any more than the fact that he and the guy who'd replaced him in her bed had overlapped by several weeks... There had been no drama, no big romance, they had just drifted apart.

'Saul, I can—' The sound of the phone being slammed down in some distant office echoed around the silent room.

Tilda held her breath and fought the craziest urge to laugh... Someone had hung up on Ezio! A wicked part of her wanted to applaud.

The silence stretched until Ezio broke it by stringing together a volley of curses in his native tongue, with a few random languages thrown in.

'What does she hope to achieve by this?'

He dragged a hand through the dark hair that sprang from his broad, bronzed brow, and Tilda watched his eyes narrow to black glass slits, before he turned and adopted his previous pose, feet apart, rocking on his heels, spine straight, staring out at the panorama of the city far below.

This was the cue for Tilda to get on with something, but she wasn't in the mood to be tuned out.

Not today!

She was not in the mood to be dismissed.

She felt the outrage that she hadn't known was there tighten in her chest. She hadn't been late *once* in four years, and he hadn't even asked if there was a problem. But then it was always about Ezio, she thought, feeding the heated core of resentment.

'You seriously don't know why she's doing this?'

He spun back, pinning her with an incredulous, laser-like stare.

She didn't slink away into a corner. Instead she met his stare with one of her own, though it was hard to trade glares when her eyes were hidden behind the tinted lenses.

'Just thought you might like my input.' He was great at delivering sarcastic jabs, but she doubted he'd even recognise it when he was on the receiving end of one.

'Athena and I moved on two years ago.' About to turn away again, he paused when she spoke.

'*You* moved on…it's not actually the same thing.' Her disproval of his attitude to women was genuine; her sisterly solidarity with the other woman was more forced. On the handful of occasions she had encountered Athena Baros, the tall blonde had acted as though she'd been invisible. Her sweetness was reserved for people who were of use to her.

Tilda shrugged and bit back the apology on the tip of her tongue, reminding herself that, as a soon-to-be ex-employee, she was no longer obliged to polish his ego or say the right thing. 'Maybe she's trying to make you notice she's still alive,' she mused, half to herself, thinking, *good luck with that*. 'Just a thought,' she added, producing a faint half-smile.

His dark brows were knitted in a perplexed weave as his stare travelled the length of her petite, slim figure, moving from her face to her feet and back again as though he was seeing her for the first time.

'Athena does not connect sex with her emotions…' He realised that he had just come dangerously close to excusing himself to his PA, who was…late, which was a first, and…

If he'd been asked to describe Matilda Raven in one word, it would have been neat. She did not look neat, she looked…*different*, he decided, noting the heavy chunk of rich brown hair that fell against one cheek, the rest either tumbling down her back or stuck down the collar of a padded jacket that was fastened on the wrong buttons.

'You're late and…what the hell are you wearing?' He dismissed his own question without waiting for a response. What his PA chose to wear was of minor importance.

With a sharp shake of his dark head, he abruptly folded his long frame into the miracle of ergonomically designed blonde wood-and-metal chair behind the desk and directed his probing stare at the tips of his long, brown steepled fingers.

He heard her take a deep breath before she spoke. 'I'm sorry, I know this is a bad time, but I'm leaving.'

His eyes lifted as he expelled a long, sibilant sigh of irritation and fought to keep a lid on his frustration. In four years, Matilda Raven had only taken time off for a root-canal filling and had been directly back at her desk, though he'd sent her home because he hadn't been able to understand a word she was saying. Now she was calling him an unfeeling monster and absenting herself just when her presence as a sounding board would be useful.

'How long do you need?' He didn't ask for reasons. He was assuming something worse than a root canal. To his mind, his staff's personal life was none of his business so long as it did not impact their efficiency during working hours. His distracted gaze slid from her face and, though he was not a person inclined to question the staring-you-in-the-face obvious, he heard himself ask, 'Are those *jeans*?'

Matilda's eyes drifted downwards. 'Yes, and for ever… I'm resigning.'

'You choose your moment.'

She shook her head, seeming bewildered by his calm reaction.

Ezio felt the muscles along his jawline quiver. This was not the moment for Matilda to start negotiating for a rise. 'Shall we cut the drama? How much do you want? Actually, can this wait until later? Or, better still, contact HR and tell them I've authorised a pay rise…you decide what you're worth. I need to find out if—'

'No!' she blurted.

The frown playing across his broad brow deepened, digging out the semi-permanent frown line that was developing between his dark brows. She planted her hands on her hips and glared at him, the two red circles on her cheeks emphasising she hadn't even applied the discreet make-up she normally wore to the office.

He had never seen his PA wear anything but black, nor-

mally an A-line tailored skirt teamed with a white blouse.
There had been black trousers that had revealed details that
the skirt had not, but in jeans that went double…possibly
treble. Her legs were slim and disproportionally long for
her diminutive height and her behind was… Clearing his
throat, Ezio lifted his gaze, irritated it required an effort.

Admiration of feminine bottoms had its place in his
life but not in his work place. He maintained a scrupu-
lously clear-cut, unambiguous line between the personal
and private and he expected his staff to do the same. Re-
alistically, relationships developed, but when they did he
expected that line between professional and personal to
be observed.

It was perfectly possible to do so, just as it was possible to notice that his PA was good to look at, *despite*
her efforts to disguise the fact, without dwelling on the
fact she had a waist and one so slender he could have
spanned it between his hands.

He met the eyes looking back at him, the colour in-
determinate behind the pinkish-tinted lenses of a pair of
owlish spectacles. Her fashion sense was unimportant
to him; the important thing was he could always rely on
her sharp brain, cool head, her calm practicality and her
absolute, total discretion.

He clenched his teeth, then dug deep into his reserves
of patience and smiled. 'Look, Matilda, shall we start
this conversation again? Clearly you've had some issues
this morning.' *Though not as bad as mine*, he thought,
congratulating himself on being so tolerant.

Tilda pushed her glasses further up and folded her arms
across her heaving chest. He wasn't listening, he wasn't
hearing. 'The smile isn't going to do it.'

He looked bemused by the tart comment. 'And it's Tilda, not Matilda. Everyone else in the universe knows that!

'I thought Matilda was your name.'

'It is but that isn't the point—the point is, I'm re-signing.'

'*Resigning?*'

She nodded, taking a tiny spurt of irrational pleasure from the stunned disbelief on his face. 'And you know something? You're making it so much easier because you're just…just…' She scanned his face and closed her lips against the unwise but honest addition that was on the tip of her tongue.

Best left unsaid but true. He *was* the most incredible-looking man on the planet, and the irony was he was probably too arrogant even to have noticed. His confidence had nothing to do with his amassed billions or his painfully perfect profile—it was as much part of him as his fingerprints.

Dragging a few shallow breaths, she tried to regain some sort of sanity, and failed when his gaze zeroed in on her face. Her stomach dipped dramatically. She had seen that look before, seen the perfect symmetry of his face harden to ice and watched the dangerous smile that left his eyes cold…the moment before he went in for the kill in the financial sense.

'Just…?' Ezio prompted, the chilly edge of his voice making it clear, if she hadn't already twigged, that his anger had shifted from the ex-lover who was putting his business deal at risk.

Her chin lifted as she embraced her antagonism. After all, they were things she had wanted to say for four years, so why not?

'An entitled, selfish…' She stopped and swallowed a sob that was trying to fight its way out of her chest.

'Oh, don't hold back, this is fascinating.'

'I shouldn't have said that… I have liked working for you, but that doesn't mean you're a…a *nice* person. I know you're going to say I was late and you didn't bawl me out, but that's only because you know I'll make up the hours. You haven't asked me what's wrong because, the fact is, you're not even vaguely interested, you're the most selfish, self- absorbed man I have ever met.'

'A monster, in fact.'

A beautiful monster!

'Possibly you should have remembered that fact before you opted for brutal honesty.' He pressed the intercom on his desk. 'Rowena, call Security and have them escort Miss Raven and her belongings from the building.'

Tilda lifted her chin. *So maybe not the best time to ask for a reference.*

There was a long silence and then, 'You can't sack someone because they are late.'

The unexpected support from the disembodied voice belonging to her shy, nervous assistant brought an emotional lump to Tilda's throat.

'Oh, it's OK, I want to go, Rowena,' she said, resisting the impulse to applaud her assistant. The last thing she needed was anything else on her conscience and she certainly did not want to be responsible for the brave young woman losing her job.

Ezio threw up his hands. 'What is this, "bring your protest placard to work" day?' he wondered, incensed, dragging a hand through his dark hair.

'It's fine,' Tilda inserted, not fooled by Ezio's languid tone. She could take his moods but poor Rowena got flustered every time he spoke to her. 'Don't worry, Rowena, call them. I could do with some help to carry my things.'

Her face was filled with haughty contempt when she turned back to Ezio. 'Actually, I am quite capable of leaving under my own steam, thank you.' Mid-stiff-backed turn, she caught sight of the discarded tabloid on the periphery of her vision and made a detour to pick it up. 'If you want to kill the story dead, you could always marry someone else—another of the rejects you treat like rubbish, maybe?'

The words hung there… Another time, the look of sheer disbelief on Ezio's handsome face would have made her laugh, but instead she felt a stinging tightness in her throat and a burning heat beneath her eyelids.

She would not cry.

Teeth clenched, she turned her defiant gaze back to Ezio and flung the paper back down on the desk, not realising that the jerky action had dislodged the plastic hospital identity bracelet she had shoved in her jeans pocket after Sam had torn it off in the taxi. It nose-dived an inch in front of her feet and, before she could retrieve it, Ezio came round from behind his desk and picked the tag up.

'What is this…?' Ezio's dark eyes went to her pale face… he realised for the first time just how pale. 'You have been in hospital?' The tightness in his chest stemmed from a surge of emotion that he felt no desire to examine. 'Why didn't you say so?' he growled out. In light of this information, a quick review confirmed he had acted badly, but how the hell was he to know if she didn't tell him?

'Why didn't you ask?' she countered, totally abandoning the polite office voice he was used to as she yelled,

'Not me, my... Samuel!' She stopped, clearly just one quivering syllable short of a sob, and bit her lip hard.

She held out her hand for the bracelet but, instead of handing it back, Ezio read the name on it.

'Who is *Samuel*...?'

She had a boyfriend?

CHAPTER TWO

'YOUR BOYFRIEND?'

'My brother.' She wasn't against the idea of a boy-friend but she wasn't actively looking for one. According to Rowena—who would have chatted constantly about her own boyfriend if Tilda didn't stop her—that was a mistake, because they didn't come knocking on your door. Also Tilda, apparently—again, according to Rowena—didn't put out *signals*, or at least not the right ones for men to know she was interested.

Maybe she set the bar too high. Her assistant had tentatively suggested this before dissolving into confusion as she'd hastily assured Tilda that she was really very pretty, and a very nice person, which was what counted. She probably wasn't so nice, because she had been amused to watch the younger girl tie herself in knots, offering reassurance that Tilda did not need.

The fact was, she honestly didn't care. Romance was the last thing on her mind and, as for sex, what you'd never had you never missed. The celibacy had been a conscious choice. She had decided early on in her guardianship that she wasn't going to disrupt her brother's life by having a stream of random men drift in and out of his life.

Love might be different, but for the life of her Tilda

couldn't figure out how you were meant to know that attraction was something deeper. It made total sense that you had to kiss a lot of frogs.

She had a brother? Ezio felt some of the unaccountable antagonism that had climbed its way into his shoulders lessen.

Had he known she had a brother…?

Did he want to?

Annoyed at the scratch on his conscience, he handed her the plastic identity tag.

Tilda sniffed as she shoved it into one of her jacket's many pockets. 'I need to get home.'

'Your par—'

Big eyes behind her lenses flew to his face, and the memory of scanning her HR file in the past surfaced in his head. She had lost both her parents in a motorway smash; he must have read about the brother.

Was *that* why she had hadn't come to the job through the usual university route?

'So now you are his sole guardian?'

She nodded without looking at him.

'Was there no one else?'

'We are fine.' Her defensive prickles were on full show as she met his stare head-on. 'Sam is a good boy… He… he got in with the wrong crowd.'

'Ah…!' How many career criminal families said the same thing? He was thinking, quite a few.

Her chin snapped up as she fixed him with a glare, and behind the spectacles her eyes glittered dangerously. 'What does *that* mean?' she said, her tone daring him to say anything bad about her brother.

'Your brother is still in hospital?'

With no warning, the tears filled her eyes again. She blinked rapidly to disperse the warm moisture as her glasses steamed up. 'No, he's home now.'

'So it wasn't serious.'

'Serious,' she echoed, her nostrils flaring. 'I suppose it depends on what you call serious, but most people would think that an asthma attack that requires hospitalisation is serious. If he'd been alone... But he wasn't, luckily. I wasn't there because I was working late. I actually spend more time with you than my own brother and...' She gulped and stamped her foot for emphasis. 'And that ends here and now!'

'You need some time...?'

'I have all the time in the world. I'm sacked!'

'You resigned, as I recall.'

She paused. 'We'll be fine,' she said, more for her own benefit than his. 'Maybe I'll rent our house out and Sam and I could find a smaller rental somewhere cheaper... Cornwall, maybe?' she said, her expression lightening as she was struck by the option. 'We used to go there every year on holiday. It was quiet and Sam...' She stopped suddenly, pressing both hands to her mouth.

If she hadn't been projecting mute distress, Ezio would have pointed out the flaws in this plan. He would have pointed out that rental property was limited in Cornwall, where the popularity of the holiday hot spot had priced so many locals out of the property market, but she didn't look as though she could take even a gentle version of the truth.

A profound sense of helplessness crashed down on Tilda like a black cloud smothering her normally buoyant optimism. She simply couldn't see a way out that had a happy ending. There was just a series of brick walls blocking her way.

Their house was worth a lot and they owned it outright, which was lucky, because there wasn't much left of what little insurance there had been and she had set that aside for Sam's future. She hated the idea of selling the family home that held so many memories but recognised now that there might be no choice. But, even if they did move, it wouldn't matter where they went because Sam would always be the outsider, always trying to fit in, and for the life of her she didn't know how to help him.

'Take a sabbatical. Your job will be waiting.'

He looked as surprised as she felt at his words. She felt a sudden a glimmer of hope, along with a lot more wariness.

'Why are you being so nice?' There had to be a catch. 'And it doesn't matter, because I don't need a sabbatical, I need for ever!' Aware her voice had risen to a shrill level of panic, she made a conscious effort to lower it as she added, 'I can't work, you take too much, and…' The wobble was back but this time there was no way of stopping it morphing into a long wail of distress. In that moment it felt as though she would never be all right again… She was alone and she had broken the promise she made to her parents at the funeral that she would keep Sam safe.

The sound horrified her but it just went on and on.

Finally she made it stop, and rammed her hands across her mouth as though to retain the control that she was leaking from every pore. *Oh, God, just hold it together, you idiot.* To lose it like that in front of anyone was humiliating…but in front of Ezio it felt a million times worse.

She flashed a look towards the tall figure who had not moved a muscle during her meltdown.

Ezio watched her almost visibly unravelling—she looked *breakable*. He felt something he could not put a name to tighten in his chest. That awful wrenching, feral cry of anguish had stopped, though he could still hear it, *feel* it. She was still crying behind her hands; he could hear the muffled sobs.

Female tears did not normally affect him. In general he viewed them with cynical objectivity. He didn't have total immunity, but he was getting there. Normally he simply removed himself from any situation that involved them but this was different. This was not a generic female, it was buttoned-up, tight *Matilda*. And that visceral sound…

'Perhaps it might be wise to talk to someone?' His mother swore by therapy, and said that she would not have been able to cope with her undemonstrative, dogmatic, cheating husband without it. Ezio thought that leaving him would have been a cheaper option.

Matilda's eyes lifted. She didn't make the mistake of interpreting the comment as an invitation to share with him, more a push towards the door, and she offered him a frigid little nod.

'Could Rowena call me a taxi, do you think?' she said quietly.

He knew there would be tears behind the misted lenses, and with no warning he found himself thinking of another office and another woman with tears in her eyes.

The roles on that occasion had been reversed. The woman in question that day had been *his* boss, his older, beautiful, charismatic and—as she had told him very quickly—unhappily married boss. He had been a youthful romantic idiot determined to play the big, protective hero… The memory of that long ago humiliation was enough to quash dead any impulse he might have felt to supply a shoulder for Matilda to cry on.

Self-contempt thinned his lips as he recalled the pathetic chivalry that had made him fantasise about rescuing her from her abusive husband and becoming a father to her children.

Just as well he hadn't. Fatherhood and him were not a good fit. He was too selfish. He was, in short, too like his own father. In Ezio's mind, it was better never to have a child than see that child grow up and feel no connection.

His father—a fully paid-up member of the '*it didn't do me any harm*' school of parenting—had replicated his own father's parenting style, which had not involved spontaneous displays of physical affection. *He* had started at the bottom, sweeping floors, and nobody had known that he was the *boss's* son. He'd wanted to instil the same standards in his own son.

So Ezio had arrived straight from university, just an anonymous office junior. It had never occurred to him to question his anonymity or suspect his identity had been revealed to senior management.

He considered that he had been lucky in his first boss, a woman who'd put on a brave face for the world but had allowed him to see the vulnerability beneath, had let him see her tears.

Hard to believe that he had ever been that stupid, that he had wanted to protect her. The principle that had put a married woman off-limits—back then he had had a lot of principles—had lasted barely a week.

He'd been in *love*. Before the self-contempt that always came with the memory could capture him, the sound of Matilda's sobs dragged him back to the present. Now she was crying softly, making him think of a wounded animal.

'S-sorry. I'll be fine in a minute.'

Ezio looked down at her bent head and swore. She

looked so fragile, she looked so broken... Something
shifted inside him and he swore again.

Then, without knowing what he was about to do, he
heard himself growl out, 'Come here!'

Tilda lifted her head and looked from his face to his
arms, extended towards her palms-up. With an inarticulate little cry, she took the two steps that landed her head
on his chest. It didn't at that moment matter who he was,
she needed the human contact.

The cry caused something painful he didn't recognise or enjoy to move in his chest as he looked down at
the top of her glossy head, feeling her soft body shaking.
Responding to some dormant instinct, his hands came
up to her shoulders, even though he held himself rigid
while her trembling body curved into his.

When she finally lifted her head, she looked embarrassed and backed away, her eyes anywhere but on him.

'I'm sorry...so sorry,' she sniffed. 'I never cry...well,
hardly ever. I must look...'

She made him think of a shivering puppy. 'Sit down
before you fall down,' he said, his voice roughened with
an impatience he didn't attempt to disguise. What was
the point? She could hardly think more badly of him than
she evidently did.

It had never crossed his mind to wonder what any of
the people he worked with thought of him, but knowing
the thoughts that had been in his PA's head had touched
an unexpected exposed nerve.

Tilda's legs folded as he urged her into a chair, not the
designer one, but one of the soft leather swivels.

'Please don't be nice,' she begged, then remembered
who she was talking to and laughed, stopping abruptly

when she realised that she sounded borderline hysterical. 'I don't want to start crying again,' she explained.

'Neither do I,' he said.

His tone made her flush. 'Sorry, I'll be fine in a minute, it's just… You don't want to know this…'

He probably didn't. She was so close to disintegration that he could see no harm letting her talk if it calmed her down.

'It's therapeutic, so I have heard, and don't worry—I probably won't listen.'

The flash of dry humour dragged a small, choked laugh from her aching throat.

He did listen as she began to speak—not to him, really, more to herself, slowly at first, and then as if some sort of dam had broken inside her as it all spilled out.

The story had a lot of unnecessary details, and a vast amount of pointless hair-shirt self-loathing. But, picking out the salient points, the condensed version, even allowing for sisterly exaggeration, seemed to suggest that her brother was some sort of genius who had got in with the wrong crowd… 'Wrong crowd' got mentioned a lot.

'So everything that has happened to your brother is directly down to you?' This simplistic view stood out strongly throughout the jumbled narrative.

'Who else?' she snapped.

'Your brother is young but not a child. Don't you think he should take some responsibility for his own actions?'

'I knew you wouldn't understand. I have no idea why I told you any of this.' She shook her head. 'Oh, forget it!' she finished on a note of self-disgust as she got to her feet.

'So your brother is a genius…?'

'I don't know…probably. He's super smart, but I don't think labels help. But then, what do I know? I don't want to push him, I want him to have a normal life, a real childhood. He is desperate to blend in, but that's not easy when you pass your maths A-level at ten. I think that's when he stopped trying. I'm so afraid for him. I don't know what to do...'

Tilda put her head in her hands again. Well, stopping revealing her inner angst to a man who really didn't give a damn might be a start, but maybe that was the point—he didn't—and he wasn't going to feel sorry for her. How her independent nature hated it.

There had been a lot of that early on after the accident and her private nature had shied away from it. She had learnt to deflect pity, while practical help, which had been in thin supply, would have been much more useful.

Actually, Ezio's cold-eyed objectivity in some weird way acted as an antidote, or at least diluted her out-of-control emotions.

'Can I get you anything—a glass of water?'

Tilda shook her head. 'I'm fine.'

'Security has arrived.' The disembodied voice carried a chilly note of disapproval.

'What for? I don't need security! I need brandy.'

There was a nervous giggle on the other end of the line. 'How many glasses?'

He looked at his PA, the wispy curls that surrounded her heart-shaped face.

'Make that tea, some of the herbal stuff, for one.'

When the tea arrived, Tilda nursed the mug between her hands, looking at him warily over the rim. 'Aren't you having a cup?'

'I'll pass.'

'Look, I'm fine, I'm just...'

He sighed. 'About to fall down.'

This correct interpretation drew a glare from Tilda.

'Sit there a minute, I'm thinking…'

Her teeth clenched. 'I don't work for you any more. I don't have to do what you say.' She grimaced to hear herself sound so childish. Actually, he had never spoken to her so dismissively when they'd had a working relationship. If he had, she would have been looking for a new job a long time ago.

'You might have been right,' he mused slowly as he subjected her face to a narrow-eyed scrutiny.

'I usually am—you just don't notice.'

'I do, actually, you have a natural ability to think outside the box.'

'Is that a compliment?'

'It's a fact,' he responded without emphasis or warmth. 'You said that the best way to shut down Athena is to marry someone else.'

When it came to self-absorption, he really did run away with a string of gold medals.

'I might have said something along those lines but I wasn't being serious!'

'I am. I think it could work.'

An image of Ezio married, his arm around a glowing bride, flashed into her head. 'Well, that's great—problem solved.' Only a man as cynical and without any moral compass would have taken her angry words seriously.

She put down her mug on the top of his pristine desk. She had no idea if he was winding her up or if he was serious, and she told herself she didn't care.

'I'll look out for the marriage announcement,' she said, making her voice flat and disinterested.

'Sit down, will you, Matilda?'

'My name is *Tilda*!'

He accepted the correction with an expressive shrug

of disinterest. 'Six months... *Tilda*?' His lips quirked as he rolled the word around his tongue. 'What do you say?'

'That I pity the woman you marry unless she has as little moral compass as you.'

His lip curled. 'I think you have enough *moral compass* for us both.'

He made it sound like a bad thing.

'But I no longer work for you and now, if you'd excuse me, I'll get my things and leave you to—' She stopped as he held up a hand, asking her to wait. She sighed. 'Look, I recognise this is not convenient for you, but I have to put my brother first. I have to move him away from—'

'The bad influences, I know... Would Greece be far enough, you think?'

Confusion replaced her annoyance. 'Greece!' She had never been to the Athens office but she had seen the views from the board room during online meetings; they were stunning. 'Is Agnes leaving too?' Tilda had met the elegant, grey-haired half-Greek woman who held her own role in the Athens office.

Even if there was a vacancy there was no way she could move to Athens...could she?

'No, Agnes is not leaving, and I'm not offering you a job. More a *role*... You could think of it as a temporary contract...six months?'

'Is it a promotion?' She was in no position to dismiss it out of hand. Something with more flexibility would give her time to look for something more appropriate. But Greece? No, that was *too* crazy...too far away. Though maybe far away was good?

'That kind of depends on your viewpoint.'

She muted the dialogue in her head and decided there was no harm hearing him out. 'It's real?' Her history of being around him told her it was not likely to be an invention, but she had to check. 'I'm not a charity case.'

He sighed. 'I'm suggesting that we spend the next six months as husband and wife, so basically six months in Greece, long enough to make people think we gave it a try and you found me impossible to live with.'

Shock collided with disbelief in her spinning head. Her brain went into shock and closed down.

'Obviously there is a time factor involved. This has to happen… I'll look into how quickly this *can* happen. It probably won't be the UK. I don't think you are able to book a slot Vegas-style here.'

'I suppose you know that you make it sound as though you're proposing to me?' She felt stupid even saying it.

'I'm proposing a way in which you can remove your brother from people and an environment that have become dangerous for him, while killing Athena's rumours that are stalling the Rutherford deal…' He flashed a look at her pale, still face. 'So, win-win. Are you all right?'

'I think I'm the one that should be asking you that,' she responded hoarsely. 'Is there *nothing* you wouldn't do to win?'

His devil-on-steroids white grin flashed. 'I don't like losing,' he admitted. 'That's no secret. But I think the relevant question is, is this something *you* would be prepared to do for your brother?'

Having succeeded in making her rejection of the plan prove she was selfish, he tilted his head to one side, his stare making her feel uneasy. He was good, he was very good, but she had seen him use this tactic before—actually, that didn't help.

Ezio felt his impatience rise as she didn't react, then another reason for her reticence occurred to him. 'Is there someone?' Contemplating the possibility that his PA had a personal life, a sex life, brought a wrinkle to his brow. There was no reason she shouldn't, that someone should not be enjoying the lush, sensual promise of her mouth. 'I got the idea that if he were twenty years younger Saul might be a rival.'

'Are you suggesting that I flirted with…?' She gave a gasp of outrage. 'If anyone is being unprofessional here, it's you, not me!'

He opened his mouth to deny this claim and then re-alised that she was right…he sounded like a jealous lover. 'All right, I concede, you're probably not his type.'

'Or yours,' she added. 'And, actually, you've hit on the obvious flaw, beyond the fact it is insane, obviously.'

His dark brows climbed towards his ebony hairline. 'I have?'

'We both know that a billionaire of any age does not marry a woman like me.'

'You don't think you're attractive enough?' As he was sure it took her longer to disguise the fact she was attrac-tive than it would have done to moderately enhance her good looks, it seemed a perverse attitude to take.

Detecting his slight sneer and misreading it, her jaw tightened. 'My self-confidence is quite robust, thank you,' she told him crisply. 'It so happens my self-worth is not based on the way I look—though, actually, I scrub up pretty well.'

The huffy addition made his lips twitch.

'I am quite sure you do.'

'But my problem is, I don't want to devote twenty per cent of my life to the pursuit of polished perfection, the sort of gloss that can't be achieved without good lighting and a master class in make-up. I wouldn't do that for any man.'

'You think that's what I want in a woman?'

'I think that's what you and most obscenely wealthy men *expect* in a woman,' she countered.

'So basically I'm shallow.'

'You're obscenely rich.'

It was pretty obvious she had based this harsh judgement of the '*obscenely* rich' on him. It came as a shock to know how the woman he had worked with for four years had been silently judging him. The question was, did he deserve it?

Ezio brushed away the question. The only reason to find out would be if he wanted to change—and he didn't.

'I wasn't talking about you…'

She stopped digging. They both knew she was, and why should she worry? It wasn't as if Ezio was going to cry into his pillow because she wasn't giving him a five-star review.

'Shall we just say joke over…? It's crazy…?' The upward lilt on the last syllable that turned her statement into a question made him give a smug grin.

'Audacious and actually, when you think about it, totally logical. I know you like logic.' He knew she considered herself the voice of reason, and there had been occasions when she had been.

'I'm simply not a risk taker.'

'You're capable, smart and have no great opinion of… well, me, but I also believe you are pragmatic. This might not be a palatable solution to you but it is a solution,' he pointed out, appreciating the novelty value of having to sell a prospect that any number of women would have spent a lot of time and energy trying to bring about.

'You are proposing this seriously…it's not a joke?'

'You're not normally five steps behind.'

'No, just two.'

Her dry rejoinder drew a slow grin before it faded quickly as he continued, all brisk and business-like. 'Obviously we can come to some sort of severance agreement upfront which will give you and your brother financial security.'

'But I can't just transplant us. There are schools and...'

He smiled to himself. He knew that schools would earn him points. 'Actually, I know of a school within traveling distance of the villa. It has an international reputation and an...*eclectic* approach to education. It has a child-first policy, the ethos is—'

'You seem to know a lot about this place.' Comprehension dawned on her face. 'You went there?'

'Let's just say I was not thriving in the school my father and his father before him went to.' It was one of the rare occasions when his mother had defied her husband and insisted that there was a tradition in her family too, one that said children should not be unhappy. 'I spent my last three years in school there.'

'And that is a recommendation...? Sorry,' she said, instantly remorseful. 'That was below the belt.'

His smile was rueful. 'Do not worry, I can take it. I was simply pointing out that there is no need to see problems where there are none.'

'This place sounds expensive.'

'It is, but that will not be a problem for you now or in the future. In fact, money would never be an issue for you again. Or your brother,' he emphasised, watching her face, well aware that her devotion to her sibling was the edge he needed, and having no qualms about exploiting this weakness.

* * *

'Villa, you said. Villa…?' Am I *really* considering this?

'My home—'

'*One* of them,' Tilda interrupted, going through a mental inventory of his penthouse apartments in several cities, the estate in Surrey that she had seen photos of in a glossy magazine, and where she knew for a fact that he had never spent a night. She suspected he'd never even seen it.

It was an investment; he had no emotional attachment to it. He had no emotional attachment to anything. Did he even know what a home was? A home in her mind was what she shared with Sam—the place her parents had bought when they'd first married. It held memories and it was Sam's security.

'It has privacy, a view and is a short helicopter flight from the Athens office.'

'I thought you had a house in Athens… Never mind; I'm sure your villa is delightful, but I live here.'

'I thought you were planning to move to Cornwall.'

Her eyes slid from his. She was not quite ready to concede defeat yet. 'I haven't decided what I'm going to do.'

'I understand your reluctance—you don't want to drag Sam away from all his delightful friends.'

She flinched as if he had struck her, and there it was—he knew he had closed the deal.

He gave a slow smile of satisfaction. 'It should be champagne, really,' he observed, looking at the half-empty mug.

She ignored the mug and him. 'I need to get back to Sam. I said—'

'Fine. It will be a good opportunity for me to meet Sam and we can get into the details on the way back.'

She looked at him blankly. 'Meet Sam? No, you can't, you have a meeting at... Oh, and you're picking up Ellie Watts for early dinner before the premiere of her film.'

'I think I might cancel that, don't you?' he said softly.

'You can't! She... Well, she's *her*, and they say that she's the odds-on favourite for best actress.' And according to rumour the latest notch on his bedpost, or was *he* the latest notch on *hers*?

'And I just got engaged. Think of the optics when someone works out the dates.'

'But no one knows, and we're not *really* engaged. It takes a long time to get a licence and things sorted. I thought that...'

Actually, she had not thought at all, that much was becoming obvious. 'I haven't said yes.' But she hadn't said no either, and his expression said he knew she wasn't going to.

'You wish me to get down on one knee?'

She cast a withering look at his handsome, mocking face.

'It's happening too quickly,' she complained.

CHAPTER THREE

'IF SAM HATES YOU, it's off!'

He looked amused and a little contemptuous. 'You allow a *child* to dictate how you live your life?'

Explaining the concept involved to someone who had never considered anyone in his life but himself seemed a waste of time and energy to Tilda, so instead she closed the conversation down. 'Of course not!'

'My mistake,' he drawled sarcastically.

'And for God's sake, don't call him a child.'

'What do you take me for? I was fourteen once, you know, in the dim and distant past.'

She grunted. She found it impossible to imagine Ezio suffering the traumas of a normal teen.

'My phone, where did I...?' Irritated by the greasy smear on her glasses, she pulled them off and began polishing them vigorously on a tissue. She rubbed the bridge of her pert nose before she put them back on.

Ezio seemed to freeze for a moment, then blinked. 'You have beautiful eyes.'

The personal comment came from nowhere. Tilda, conscious of a shivery sensation that spread outwards from a centre low in her pelvis, brought her lashes down behind the lenses as a further layer of protection.

'Have you thought of contact lenses?'

The tension she had probably imagined dissolved as she laughed. 'Oh, when I do, you will be the very *first* person I will consult on the decision.' Behind her smile of mocking and fake sincerity, she was aware that her show of empowerment might have carried a bit more punch if she'd actually *needed* the glasses.

Rowena was hovering when they walked out of the office.

'We're going out.'

Rowena nodded and glanced at the box of Tilda's belongings on the desk.

'Shall I...?' she asked, her nervous glance flickering from one to the other.

'Leave it there,' Ezio responded at his most enigmatically distant as he started punching numbers into his phone.

Turning round as they approached the lift, Tilda gave a thumbs up to the younger girl and promptly backed into Ezio.

'Sorry, I'm...' He arched a brow and she stepped inside, taking a deep breath. She knew from experience that Ezio and enclosed spaces was not a combination that made for comfortable—*more crawl out of your skin.*

Ezio had very long legs, and she did not, but it didn't occur to him to make any allowances for the difference in their inside leg measurements, and by the time they reached the underground parking area she was breathless and very glad she was wearing trainers.

'Did you see Rowena's face?' she asked fretfully as she responded to his imperious nod and fastened the belt of the passenger seat in the limited-edition designer car he drove. It was not exactly inconspicuous but it was comfortable.

'Rowena's face?'

'No, you wouldn't.' His radar was very specific and Rowena had not been on it. Whoever he'd been texting, he had been on his phone since they had left the office.

If they were together in the real sense of the word she would have dumped him before they reached the underground parking area.

'I was setting things in motion. It's looking like New York state is our best option…unless you fancy a Vegas wedding? I've got a really good wedding planner on it, and she'll sort the options, but New York is sounding good to me. I have a few things that I could do with checking on at the office there.'

'I think that's what you call hitting the ground running but, before you go the extra mile, let me be clear—*if* we do this, it won't be in New York while you multi-task,' she responded, matching his cool with some of her own.

The car purred into almost silent life. 'Why not? It's a twenty-eight-day wait in the UK.'

'It's not the place, it's the entire concept.'

'Never mind. The next time you can do it right— white lace and orange blossom and a house in a district with the best schools—but just remember to keep the number of a very good divorce lawyer for when reality kicks in.'

'You are such a cynic!' His mockery was making her teeth ache.

'Realist,' he countered, sketching a grim smile as he pulled into the stream of traffic.

'I feel sorry for you,' she countered, almost meaning it. 'It's in this country or nowhere, and this time frame is all too…' Her head lifted. 'I need time to think.'

'You could think about it for weeks, months, but it wouldn't change the essentials. This will work for us both. Now, where am I going?'

She refused to be diverted; she'd given too much ground already. 'The UK.'

He glanced at her profile and sighed. 'I'll invite Saul to the wedding. That should get around the problem of the unnecessary delay.'

His immediate response made it clear to Tilda that he had always had Plan B in place. 'Oh no, I don't want anyone there!'

'Don't worry, he'll refuse. I'll make sure the date co-incides with his granddaughter's wedding. The point is, he'll know we are getting married.'

'You are so Machiavellian!'

'Thank you. So, which way?'

'Nice house.' It was a solid-looking Edwardian property in a quiet tree-lined road of other similar properties in North London. He probably didn't mean it but Mrs Lowther, who got flustered and giggly when she was introduced to the visitor, didn't know that. Once in the door, he charmed the old lady into her coat and escorted her home.

It was quite a master class in charm.

Sam was less impressed. 'What did you fetch *him* home for?'

'He fetched me home, actually.'

'I thought your boss was a selfish bastard who...'

She flashed him a warning look as the tingle between her shoulder blades alerted her to Ezio's presence.

'I've heard a lot about you, Sam.' Ezio had to make his remark to the narrow, hostile back of the teen he was meant to be impressing. Tilda doubted that Ezio could recall the last time in his life he'd tried to impress someone.

'I've heard more about you, I bet. Ezio... Ezio... Ezio...' Sam mocked, ignoring his sister's horrified expression as he added, 'She's always talking about Ezio this, Ezio that.'

'I am not, Sam!' Tilda said, shaking her head as Ezio's dark eyes skimmed her flushed face. 'That's not true.'

Or was it? The disturbing possibility brought a frown to her smooth brow.

'I called my goldfish Ezio when I was a kid.'

And now you're so old. 'I'm flattered. Good goldfish?'

'Dead goldfish,' Sam came back with a straight face.

The teen watched suspiciously as Ezio threw his head back and laughed. 'I hear you are smart, Sam.'

'Yeah, a lot of people are intimidated. Tilda is quite bright too, you know—well, above average.'

From where she had dropped into a chair Tilda, gave a laugh. 'Why, thank you!' she drawled sarcastically.

'But she's a bit of an innocent, people take advantage.' Sam shot Ezio a glare before adding in a guilty aside, 'Including me.'

Ezio took the warning from the skinny little fourteen-year-old with an appreciative nod.

'Fancy a game?' Sam said casually, nodding towards the screen he'd been crouched over.

Tilda's eyes flew wide as she shook her head emphatically. 'Sam, Ezio *doesn't*.'

'Ezio does,' her ex-boss and future husband contradicted, taking off his jacket before looping it across the back of one of the dining chairs, dragging it into position next to Sam's chair and straddling it.

Her last chance had been Sam hating him, but against

all the odds Sam *wasn't* hating him. After he beat Ezio at the computer game, they bonded some more over a game of chess, after which winner Sam declared it a *close* game…a massive compliment, coming from her brother.

'You're too good for me,' Ezio said, polishing his rusty humility.

'You must be hungry, Sam, and Ezio has to be… Somewhere to go…?' She sent Ezio a nod of encouragement. 'Didn't you say that you had to…?'

'I cancelled remember? And you are definitely too tired to cook,' he continued his lips twitching at the killer look she had slung him. 'How about take away?' The ease with which he had adopted a pattern of easy familiarity made her grit her teeth.

She resented that he was very much setting the pace, taking control, but her hands were tied.

After some debate, pizza was decided on, and her choice of pineapple on top was treated with universal contempt.

My God, she thought, listening as her brother and her ex-boss and soon-to-be husband bonded over their shared loathing of pineapple on pizza and love of chess. If this day could have got any more surreal, she didn't know how.

She knew it was all an act on Ezio's part, but she had to admit, the man he was pretending to be ticked a lot of boxes. If that man had existed, she would have been in love in seconds. The acknowledgment created a sense of unease that she couldn't shake.

It was still there when, midway through the pizza, Ezio dropped the bombshell without any warning or consultation.

'I asked your sister to marry me and she said yes,

Sam, but you have the casting vote. We'd be moving to Greece, which would be a big thing for you, so what do you think?'

'What? You're getting married? And... Greece?' Sam looked at his sister for confirmation. 'For real?'

She nodded, hiding her annoyance that Ezio had made a unilateral decision to move the situation to the next level. If and when Sam was told, it should have been her doing the telling.

'Would that mean I wouldn't have to go back to school here?'

She nodded again. 'It would mean a lot of changes,' she admitted.

Sam's grunt in response could have meant anything but there was no misinterpreting the sag of relief in his narrow shoulders, a measure of just how much he was dreading going back to school.

Tilda's eyes misted. She was making the right choice.

'We have schools in Greece, some good ones. I could email you links...?'

'I'd need to learn the language?' The prospect of the challenge brought a glitter to the teen's eyes, which faded as he added, 'It doesn't really matter. I'll still be a weird loser there. The freak!'

Lost for words to comfort him, it broke Tilda's heart to hear him voice fears she shared.

'I got called weird and worse a few times at school.'

Brother and sister both turned in unison to stare at him, varying degrees of disbelief in their faces.

'You!' It was Sam who expressed the doubts written on both Raven faces.

'Uh-huh. There is a good ending to this story, though.

You know what those boys who called me weirdo do when they see me now?'

Sam shook his head.

'They smile politely and call me *sir*... They work for me.'

Sam looked thoughtful for a moment, then his thin face broke into a smile. 'That is cool.'

'It is actually *extremely* cool,' Ezio agreed. 'It's also cool being the smartest person in the room, though I should warn you, you probably wouldn't always be in the Athens academy. Right, then, I'll email you and Tilda the school stuff, Sam.' He turned and delivered one of his best megawatt smiles to Tilda as he got to his feet.

She suddenly felt a little more understanding of the women at whom he smiled and meant it—it was not hard to imagine that smile becoming a recreational drug of choice!

'Like to walk me to the door?' He held out a hand to her.

Aware that Sam was watching, after a second she stretched her hand out and allowed it to be enfolded inside the cool of his long, brown fingers. The moment they were out of the room, she pulled it free. The tingling sensation didn't stop even when she rubbed her hand hard against her thigh, only stopping to open the door for him.

'That was kind of you.' She nodded her head towards the sitting room door and added huskily, 'With Sam.'

He gave a dismissive shrug. 'Not kind. It will help if he doesn't resent me and, yes, it was true... I know you're dying to ask.' The corners of his mouth lifted, matching the smile glinting in his eyes. 'The only slight deceit was not telling him that I was not so good at turning the other cheek...' One dark brow lifted to a sardonic angle.

'Humiliate a bully and word gets around and it takes the target off your back.'

'Or it puts a target on your back for anyone who wants to prove they're tough.'

'That is not my experience, so relax; I don't think Sam is the physical type.'

But you are, she thought. As her eyes drifted down his hard, lean body, she swallowed hard and veiled her shocked eyes, feeling the soft flutter that had resided low in her belly all evening get stronger.

Less butterfly and more trapped bird.

'I sincerely hope he isn't.'

'A defensive martial art might make him feel more confident.' He saw her expression and lifted his palms towards her. 'Just a thought.'

'One I'd be grateful if you kept to yourself. Violence,' she said primly, 'Is no answer to anything, and the idea of my brother's hands being a lethal weapon would not make me sleep well.'

As she spoke, her eyes got tugged towards Ezio's hands, one of which was braced on the doorframe, long, elegant fingers that probably knew their way around a woman's body.

The rogue thought sent a rush of shamed heat through her body. Where had that come from? She channelled her ashamed confusion, resurrecting her earlier annoyance.

'And, for the record, telling Sam about us—the us we are pretending exists—was *my* job, not *yours.* You don't know Sam and—'

'And you'd like to keep it that way…fair enough,' he agreed, his expression not matching his careless shrug.

'That wasn't what I was saying,' she said, annoyed he

was twisting what she *was* saying. It would have been helpful if she'd known what she was saying!

'I accept I'm uniquely ill-equipped to parent, but I actually like Sam.'

She could see the surprise she could hear in his voice reflected for a moment in his dark eyes.

'I *love* Sam, and he'll always come first for me.'

'And where does that leave you when you're no longer first for Sam? You might not think so now, but that time will come.'

'You think I don't know that?' Her amusement was genuine and her throaty laughter was extremely attractive, he realised. 'Sam is a teenage boy. I already come second to any number of things. I'm not clingy; I want him to be happy, to leave home…knowing he can always come back. You must remember when your parents stopped being the most important things in your life? But you remain the most important thing in theirs.'

She watched as an expression she couldn't put a name to drifted into his eyes but it was gone so quickly that she thought she had imagined it.

'How old were you when yours died?'

'Almost twenty.'

'That must have been…' He stopped. Saying '*hard*' seemed hopelessly inadequate.

'It's hard when you realise there isn't anyone you're the most important thing in the world for any more. I swore Sam wouldn't feel like that.'

A silence followed her words.

Tilda had never imagined sharing those innermost private thoughts with anyone before and, if she had, the last person in the world she could have imagined opening up to was Ezio.

'Well, goodnight,' she blurted when the silence got too uncomfortable to bear. 'Oh, and shall I come in the normal time tomorrow, or do you need me early for the meeting with—?'

'No, don't come in. You're not my PA now, you're my bride-to-be.'

She looked surprised. 'But…we don't have to tell anyone yet.'

'I have no intention of telling anyone except Saul.'

'Not your family?'

'My mother would ask too many awkward questions and want to meet you.' His expressive lips thinned in distaste as he observed, 'My father would probably make a pass at you.'

Before she could decide if he was being serious, without any warning he casually leaned in. Tilda felt corralled by his sheer physicality and panic nipped at her as she felt the warmth of his breath stir the fine hairs along her hairline. She stiffened and fought against the slow, dreamy feeling that was invading her body, the weird floating sensation accompanying the heavy thud of her heart.

'There, got it.' He straightened up, opened his hand and a moth fluttered into the night air. 'It got tangled in your hair.'

'Oh, right, yes. I…'

'Do you need the tint in your specs?' he asked.

Tilda pressed a finger to the dark plastic that rested on the bridge of her nose, dodging his stare. 'It's not a matter of *need*. I *like* them this way,' she lied. 'So sorry you don't like glasses.'

He looked surprised. 'Did I say that?'

'No, but…'

A flicker of a smile played across the sensual line of his lips. 'I think there is something quite sexy about glasses…depending on who is wearing them, obviously.'

'Well, I know I'm not,' she blurted.

'What, sexy…?'

'No, I… I'm not interested in what you think is sexy.' She already knew it involved endless legs and curves.

The erotic images that flickered through Ezio's head effectively nailed him to the spot for several humiliating, painful heart beats, so until his control reasserted itself he cloaked his eyes with half-lowered lids.

Ezio had spent years enjoying sex without commitment and, now this situation was about to be reversed, commitment without sex did not sound nearly so pleasurable to him at that moment.

They said you could get used to anything.

'I'm light-sensitive,' she said. 'I don't know how it works, but these—' she tapped the frame '—don't affect my colour perception. It's more, I can see you but you can't see me.'

'Convenient.'

Looking panicked, she gave a little shrug as their glances locked. The air was suddenly filled with a painful, nerve-scraping tension.

'Sorry!' she blurted out, breaking it.

He lifted a dark brow. 'Sorry for…?'

'Oh, well, sorry you missed out on your film premiere. Speaking of which, I know six months is a long time for you to…' She broke off, blushing wildly as she dodged his eyes. 'But I'm realistic. I'm fine with…you know… But because of Sam can you please be discreet if you understand what I'm saying?'

'Actually not saying.' She was skirting around the subject like some sort of Victorian virgin. But he understood all right and he had no idea why it made him so angry. 'Shall I save you the bother? You're giving me permission to screw around.'

Her head jerked back at the crudity and she glanced back anxiously towards the closed sitting room door. 'I know you don't need my permission,' she admitted. 'And I'm not trying to, I'm just asking you… Look, Sam seems to like you, and I don't want him thinking of women, relationships, as… I want him to respect women.'

'I didn't ask to be a role model,' Ezio rebutted, his sardonic smile forced as he thought of the role model in life—his father. His father who had never needed permission to screw around, or seen any need not to flaunt his numerous affairs.

'No,' she conceded. 'But you asked me to marry you and Sam and I…we are a package deal,' she reminded him with stressed, forced calm. 'I'm not asking you to take a vow of celibacy, not with your…er…appetites.' He could see her cheeks flaming again and she stopped and closed her eyes, clearly wishing that she had not started this conversation.

'Where are you going?' she called after him as he abruptly walked through the door.

He turned back and produced a fixed feral smile. 'Well, I thought I might live down to your opinion of me and slake my animal urges with a woman I don't respect while I still don't have to ask for permission.'

The retort brought an angry glitter to her eyes. 'She has my sympathy,' she snapped as she slammed the door.

Tilda took a few sense-cooling moments before she returned to her brother and the million questions he felt the need to ask. The one she found most difficult to answer being the gruffly delivered, *'I can see why you want to marry him, but why so quickly? Shouldn't you live together or something first? If this goes wrong you could get hurt, Tilda.'*

Tilda had done her best to counter his concerns, pointing out that they might not have been dating very long—luckily Sam didn't ask *how* long—but they were not exactly strangers.

She was actually very touched by the brotherly concern which brought into focus the elephant in the room that Ezio seemed determined to ignore—nobody on the planet would believe that the most gorgeous man on earth would choose her over the glorious Athena Baros, she of the endless legs and much-copied pout.

This 'married to the PA' scheme, it simply wasn't *believable*. Tilda couldn't understand for the life of her why *she* was the only one who could see that.

It wasn't about self-confidence; Tilda wasn't intimidated by the Athena Baroses of this world. She didn't feel envious…except *possibly* when it came to leg length.

She had a lot to offer a relationship when she found the right man, who would hopefully be looking for those qualities. The point was the things she had to offer were not the things that Ezio was looking for outside the work environment.

He was out there looking for that right now—*superficially sexy*. It was a deeply depressing thought.

CHAPTER FOUR

TILDA KNEW BECAUSE she kept his diary, or had, that Ezio had a crammed, wall-to-wall schedule in the month running up to the wedding, so it wasn't very surprising that she saw him only twice. On both occasions he had spent the majority of the visits focusing on Sam, playing chess, discovering a shared interest in philosophy and generally making her feel intellectually inadequate.

But her brother was happy so she was prepared to forgive Ezio a lot... Not that he was ignoring her, *exactly*, but he did seem to be keeping her at a distance. Maybe it was a subliminal message and he was just signalling the way he meant things to go on.

Oh, God, was she over-thinking this? He was just treating her the way he always had. Actually, no, he wasn't; she had never felt excluded before.

The time would have gone quicker if she had just gone back to the office and resumed her previous role until the wedding, but Ezio had been adamant that it wouldn't be appropriate for her to continue working for him under the circumstances. And she had to admit she couldn't quite imagine how that would have worked either.

So Tilda found herself in a bizarre situation of being

secretly engaged to a man she had been used to seeing most working days but now barely saw at all.

As for any influence she might once have had, now she had none.

She didn't miss Ezio's presence in her life, *obviously*, but she was conscious of a massive gap that had opened up—which was not the same thing at all. While she had been cast into the wilderness, he was probably fitting in a lot of pre-marital sex *to slake his animal urges* before he got lumbered with her.

If this was what the *now* was like, what were the next six months going to be like...and after? Quickly tiring of moping around aimlessly, she made herself think about the future. She needed a plan. Sure, when the marriage ended she would not be poor, but there was no way she was going sit around doing nothing.

There were things that she'd always thought she would like to do if she had either the time or the money and now she was about to have both.

In that awful time after their parents had died, and Tilda had been left trying to comfort her grieving brother and be a parent, there had not been a lot of time to think about what *she* needed and not a lot of accessible help out there.

There had been dark moments, lonely moments, but she knew there were people who had it a lot worse than she did. They had the house, the memories and the financial cushion of a small insurance pot that had supplemented her first pay cheques. Not everyone was so lucky.

A chance encounter at a bus stop as she'd helped a girl load her mum and the older woman's wheelchair onto the bus had brought home how much worse her situation could have been. The girl, barely older than Sam, had been acting as her disabled mum's main carer and going to school.

She remembered thinking how good it would be to be in a position to help all those people like that girl, and for that matter people in the situation she had been in—people in situations where they were isolated and alone. At the most basic, provide someone to talk to, or point them in the right direction to access to available funding, a support network.

She remembered thinking that if she had the money and the time she could have made it happen.

Well, now she had both.

As she put down the phone after hanging up on Saul Rutherford, she felt a glow of achievement. She'd taken her first step towards the future she had envisaged.

She hadn't planned it. She had rung him to thank him in person for the massive bouquet he'd sent her to congratulate her on her future wedding. But it was Saul who had turned the quick courtesy call into something else when he had proceeded to ask her straight out, with zero subtlety, if she minded that Ezio was cheating on her. Tilda had not been thrown. She had not worked with Ezio for four years for nothing; she could think on her feet.

She had assured him calmly that the stories circulating were malicious and untrue. Crossing her fingers, she'd felt only the tiniest flicker of guilt when she'd said she trusted Ezio with her life. She must have sounded sincere because he had apologised.

Well, it wasn't a total lie. If she were to be stuck in a burning building, or facing down a gang of knife-wielding, drug-crazed thugs, she wouldn't doubt Ezio's ability to rescue her...or that he would.

He was one of those men, the heroes of this world, who

best functioned, and in fact thrived in fact in, high-stress scenarios… They were rumoured to struggle with life in the real boring, mundane world, though Ezio seemed to have that under control too.

Trusting him with her life—yes. Trusting him with her heart was another matter. Luckily, hearts had not been mentioned in any of the copious documents she had read before she'd signed away the next six months of her life.

She had told an apologetic Saul she was not the least offended and then had asked him for his advice. He'd been generous with it, and equally generous when he'd offered not just useful contacts he'd made when setting up his own charity, but a very generous donation.

The upcoming marriage was keeping the lawyers busy. She had stopped envying them their workload. She was no longer adrift, she had a purpose and she had a future waiting for her when her six-month marriage secondment, as she liked to think of it, was over.

So, while she was immersing herself in her new venture, she was quietly crossing off the twenty-eight days on her calendar before the day ringed in red arrived, pretending she was totally cool with it.

Even though anything important to do with the wedding had been taken out of her hands, there were a lot of incidentals, and then there were the practicalities. If Sam settled and was happy at the Greek school, she planned to take somewhere small in Athens and become fully involved in the charity.

It might be an idea to learn the language, though harder for her than Sam. It was never an ego- enhancing idea to compare herself with her brilliant brother, who made things look easy.

The prospect of not going back to the local school meant Sam was looking happier than she'd seen him in an age. Considering she had worried about selling the idea to him, it was ironic that if she'd backed out he'd never forgive her—though that wasn't fair, as he had told her that if she changed her mind he'd be fine with it.

But his reaction when she said she wasn't changing her mind spoke volumes. She wasn't backing out and if she did there was nowhere much to go back to. She was committed, and the physical evidence of her commitment was sitting on her finger.

She held her hand up to the light. The engagement ring had been couriered over to her that very morning, a massive square emerald surrounded by black diamonds. It fitted perfectly.

She was the one who didn't fit!

'It's here!' Sam yelled, watching out for the limo that was taking them to the registry office. 'You should see the curtains twitching. Not really,' he added as Tilda walked up behind him, looking worried.

At the front door they both paused, Sam looking smart and scrubbed in his new suit and suddenly looking almost as nervous as she felt.

'You look very pretty,' he said awkwardly.

Smiling at the brotherly compliment, she glanced down, smoothing the fabric of her recycled dress. It had still had the tags on and hadn't even made it to the charity shop's racks when she'd caught sight of the hand-sewn label. She'd bought it on the spot, drawn not just by the designer credentials but the simple empire line lifted by the hand embroidery around the neckline. Apart from needing a couple of inches taken off the length, it had fitted perfectly. She remembered thinking as she'd twirled in front of the mirror that all she needed now was some-where to wear it.

Her sensitive tummy flipped. Now she did have some-where to wear her recycled bargain: her own wedding.

'Thank you, so do you.'

They had reached the car when Tilda stopped and gave a sudden decisive nod. 'Wait a minute.'

'Don't ask me, mate,' Sam said at the question on the driver's face as his sister dashed off.

A few moments later, Tilda returned. 'I had to tell Mrs Lowther and say goodbye,' she said as she slid into the limo. 'She's been so good to us. She said I look like Mum,' she added as Sam sat back, having fastened his seat belt.

'You don't.'

'I know that, but it was so sweet of her.'

He looked alarmed. 'You're not going to cry, are you?'

'God, no!'

'I wish Mum was here, and Dad…you know?'

Tilda squeezed his hand. She did know. 'Me too, every day,' she said softly. 'If they were, I wouldn't be here at all,' she began with wistful regret before making contact with her brother's questioning gaze. She made a swift recovery. 'Mum would have insisted on a full church white wedding with hundreds of guests and I'd be float-ing down the aisle in miles of tulle.'

'Yeah, I guess so. I don't really remember her as well as you do.' Sam turned his head to gaze out of the win-dow but not before Tilda had seen the moisture in his eyes. 'I've never seen the streets this empty. You're going to be married before the rest of the world is awake.'

'Mum and Dad would have been proud of you, Sam,' she said softly.

'I know I don't say it, but I am grateful for all the stuff you have done for me. I think this is us,' he added before Tilda could respond.

'Isn't it fashionable for the bride to be late?'

'You sound jittery. Perhaps I should get him to drive us around the block one more time.'

'Too late,' she murmured as the driver opened the door for her. 'Thanks,' she said as she squared her shoulders, took a deep breath and slid out, refusing to let panic take charge.

Bending down to adjust the heel strap on her suede sling-back that didn't need adjusting, her attempt to slow her heart beat failed when on the periphery of her vision she saw a tall figure crossing the road.

From the other side of the limo, she heard Sam yell out a greeting.

Tilda smothered the panic and pasted on a smile before using her posy as a shield as she turned to face him. The knot in her stomach tightened as she took in the details of his achingly perfect appearance.

Ezio was wearing a superbly cut formal dress suit, looking the epitome of style—not that anyone would be talking fashion; they'd be talking about the gorgeous, handsome man they were picturing minus the clothes.

Or is that just me?

He always carried himself with the careless confidence and grace of a natural athlete. The aura of command he projected sent a tingle through her body before he even got close enough to speak.

'You got the flowers.' Ezio took in the dress, noting it was none of the designer ones he'd had sent over, but it was the epitome of understated feminine elegance and it fitted her slim figure perfectly. Cut to a couple of inches above the knee, it showcased her stupendously shapely legs and narrow ankles in a way that sent a stream of searing heat down his body.

She'd looked composed but that illusion was ruined the moment he got close enough to see her eyes behind the new cat's eye frames she was wearing. Startlingly green and wary, they made him think of a wild thing likely to bolt if startled.

'Thank you, they are beautiful, and smell gorgeous.' She lifted the bouquet to her nose.

His eyes moved upwards with the action but only as far as the pale skin above the square necked bodice that fitted snugly over her small, high breasts, revealing the finest suggestion of a cleavage and the delicate angularity of her collar bones.

Aware that he had been staring for…well, actually he had no idea how long…he cleared his throat. 'Pretty necklace.' It matched the earrings, the small studs with a pearl inset he had noticed she wore every day.

'Thanks, it was my mother's. And the ring, it's very…' She held her hand at an angle to expose the green glitter on her ring finger. 'It really…'

'Not too much,' he inserted, predicting her next words exactly.

'It is very beautiful. I'll keep it safe for you,' she promised.

'Keep it safe?'

'It was a family heirloom…the setting looks antique.'

'It is antique but not an heirloom. But I thought it would match your eyes…'

As their glances connected, Tilda experienced a spike of panicky excitement which she fought to subdue. There was no subtext; there was nothing to read into his voice, baring the obvious fact he could have made an ingredient label on a soup can sound sexy.

'Sam and I inherited Mum's eyes, but she was a redhead,' Tilda murmured as her gaze moved beyond him as though she had discovered some fascinating architectural details in the still-closed art deco building. 'Are we early?' she said, frowning as she heard the over-bright, perky note in her voice.

'Not much. They agreed to open early for us, so we will not be seeing our photos posted online,' he observed with a degree of grim satisfaction. 'It should be a quick in and out.'

'Quick in and out…?' She wasn't looking for romance, but it was hard not to supress a tiny grimace.

She saw his glance sharpen and added quickly, 'Oh, that's good. Perfect.' Escaping his stare, she turned her gaze to the trio of men standing on the steps of the registry office across the road. 'Are they with us?'

Ezio, who had pulled his phone from his pocket and was glaring at it, was still frowning when he looked at her.

'They are our witnesses.' He offered the explanation readily enough but she could see his mind was elsewhere.

She assumed he was talking about two of the three men waiting on the steps of the building, the two in suits. It was the third she was curious about. It was hard to see how he fitted in. In faded torn denims and a tee shirt, with shaggy white-blond hair, it was easy to imagine him carrying a surf board, but actually he was carrying a canvas bag slung over his shoulder, so there remained a bit of a question mark over his role.

She waited until Ezio put his phone away and moved towards her.

'Legal department?' she asked, nodding without looking to the two suits.

'Thought I'd keep it in-house.'

'A need-to-know basis,' she mocked gently, wondering if she had broken his rules by telling Mrs Lowther earlier. 'Lawyers always look like lawyers,' she added, making an unashamedly untrue generalisation as she stared curiously at the third man.

'Our official photographer.' As if he'd heard, the guy pulled a camera out of the bulging bag and began fiddling with dials in what seemed like an expert way.

'Come say hello.'

Very conscious of the hand on the middle of her back as they crossed the road side by side, her thoughts skittered around in her head... How many couples had made this walk before them up these steps? Couples who'd loved one another so much it hurt.

The sadness that settled over her was so energy-sapping that she went through the introduction process on auto-pilot, not realising until they had moved a little apart from the two men that she had not retained their names.

'Is that your phone?' she asked when Ezio's phone rang, thinking, *for God's sake answer it,* as the trill went on and on.

'Yes, it is,' Ezio said, making no effort to take it out.

'It's stopped.' Realising she sounded relieved, she added politely, 'Perhaps they will ring back.'

'Oh, *they* will,' he intoned grimly.

'You said there would be no press,' she reminded him in a hushed undertone as they approached the third man.

'He isn't press. Jake is here at my request.'

'So you have your own personal photographer?' she joked, then thought the joke could be on her. Plenty of people in his position did like to present a carefully contrived image of their perfect personal life. But for starters she'd have known it, and secondly, to give the devil his due, Ezio did not number vanity among his many faults. And it wasn't as if he could be worried about anyone taking an unflattering photo of him because he had no bad side or bad angle—whichever way you looked at him, he was pretty perfect. *Boringly so,* she told herself without much conviction.

'Jake is doing me a favour.'

'He doesn't look like a friend of yours…but then I don't look like…'

One sable brow lifted to an interrogative angle. 'You don't look like…?'

Her eyes slid from his. 'It's just the window dressing.' Her gesture took in the dress and flowers. 'It feels so fake, so insincere. Wouldn't it be better to keep it low key? Given the circumstances.'

'How much more low-key can you get?' he asked, looking exasperated. 'Two witnesses… Yeah, that is really over the top.'

'Hush, he's coming over,' she hissed. The friend with the camera was strolling towards them, the tools of his trade slung over this shoulder.

Ezio introduced them and the other man responded with a smile and a warm handshake. If he thought the entire marriage thing, and more significantly Ezio's choice of bride, strange, nothing in his manner suggested it.

'So you are still happy to leave the choice to me, Ezio…just want the one distributed?'

Ezio nodded.

'Fair enough, but you know there will be an appetite for more… I think that's just the perfect spot… Hold on a minute; I just want to check out the light…' Eyes narrowed, Jake crossed to the green space opposite.

'Distributed to who, exactly?' Tilda asked when he was out of earshot.

'The usual suspects.'

Tilda didn't have a clue who the usual suspects were.

'Don't worry, Jake can make anyone look good.'

It took Tilda a few seconds and a little gasp of outrage and she rose to the teasing challenge.

'I thought I *did* look good!'

It was true. She was not glossy or polished to within an inch of her life like the women he was normally photographed with—that went without saying. But her hair had been co-operative this morning and the soft, natural air-dried waves that framed her heart-shaped face and fell loose almost to her waist were flattering, and her charity-shop-bargain dress looked good on its one-time outing.

Tilda was all for recycling but she rather doubted she would ever wear it after today. Unlike with a normal wedding, the memories would be ones she'd want to bury, not cherish, which was why she was surprised that Ezio wanted photographic evidence. But she supposed this was all part of this *narrative control* he wanted.

The upwards sweep of his heavy-lidded gaze from her feet to her face did not reveal if he agreed with her bold self-assessment, but the gleam in his eyes made her shiver.

'Did none of the outfits I sent meet with your approval?'

He *had* noticed. Tilda had been afraid he was going to kick up a fuss about the dress, but then the likelihood of him knowing the contents of the vanload of designer clothes that had arrived on her doorstep was remote. It had probably been a pointless gesture to refuse them but, pointless or not, it had seemed an important point to make. She had lost control of so many things but she was still in charge of her wardrobe.

'I'm sure they were perfect.' *As are you…* Her stomach tightened in self-disgust as she dragged her eyes clear of his sinfully sexy face.

She adopted an amused attitude. 'You make it sound as though you spent hours personally selecting them.'

She knew better than most that this task would have been outsourced. In the early months of her employment, he'd tried to task her with outsourcing a parting gift for one of his ex-lovers, but she had made it clear that she did not consider it fitted in with her job description.

She remembered holding her breath as she'd waited for his response, wondering if the principle was really worth losing her job over. Now she wouldn't have been surprised by his reaction, but she'd been shocked when after a few moment's consideration he had agreed with her. Now, of course, she knew that he liked a clear delineation between his private and work life.

What was she filed under in his compartmentalised brain now? Perhaps he'd created an entire new box: *Temporary Wife/Seen But Not Heard*.

'Actually, I wouldn't know, I refused to sign for them. I'm not pretending to be something I'm not for you. So sorry if I'm not up to your standard.'

'*Pretend…?* You *are* my wife.' He paused to allow the fact to bed in. 'Or you will be in about ten minutes.'

Shock and fear shot through her body and she stood frozen in a furtive 'fight or flight' pose.

'And as for my standards…' His dark gaze drifted across her face. 'You look very beautiful.'

From a point somewhere over his left shoulder where they had strayed to, her eyes swivelled back to his face, ready to react to the sarcastic smirk she was sure would be painted on his face.

No smirk, but instead there was something in his dark eyes that made her stomach knot.

For a full thirty seconds she stopped breathing, then looked away, pretending the shivery sensation in her pelvis and the tightness in her chest hadn't happened.

'Is that meant to be funny?'

'Get a room, you two.'

Startled, Tilda half-turned to where her brother was standing, scrolling through his phone.

'Just wondering, have I got time to…? I'm half through the next level and Ezio hasn't switched his phone off.'

'No!' she snapped, realising that to the casual onlooker, or her brother, their low-voiced interchange could have looked intimate. Ezio might even have *intended* this to be the case. She glanced towards Ezio, who was indeed on his phone.

'Fair enough, keep your hair on!' Sam sniggered, strolling over to take up a position on the steps with the two witnesses who also had their phones out.

Her brother threw her an injured 'I told you so' look that drew a smile from Tilda.

Jake joined them—or rather, her. Ezio had moved away and was in the midst of what seemed to be an animated conversation.

'I'm sorry I can't stay around for the service but I've got the launch for the charity book later. I can't really be a no-show, I need to press the flesh, and it's all for a good cause. You know I'm really grateful for Ezio's contribution, though it would have been even better if he'd have posed for me.'

She was desperately trying to think of a response that would not give away her total ignorance when Ezio appeared.

'Jake, I think I should warn you that my bride doesn't actually have a clue who you are, but she lives a very sheltered life, and we only allow her out at weekends.'

Tilda shot Ezio a look of simmering dislike and offered her best smile to the other man, who looked more amused than offended.

'I used to work for him, so actually, it was *alternate* weekends.'

'Workaholic?'

'Oh, I can tell you know him well.' Tilda gave a husky laugh.

Ezio found it amusing that his bride seemed not to recognise the man who had not only shot the front cover of *Life* magazine twice but had appeared on it. He watched his friend respond to her warm, sexy laugh. There was something tactile about the throaty sound; he was pretty sure that he was going to have to get used to seeing men react to Tilda, while she remained oblivious to the effect that she had on men. What the hell was wrong with the men she'd dated that she didn't already know how utterly bewitching and sexy she was?

If *he'd* dated her she would sure as hell know! Before this thought could develop, his phone began to vibrate.

'I think that… Sorry, got to take this,' he tacked on, glancing at the screen of his vibrating phone as he moved away.

He returned a few moments later. Jake was hanging

on to a smiling Tilda's every word and she looked relaxed, as she didn't with him. Ezio felt something move
in his chest.

'Sorry about that.'

'Hope you're going to switch it off for the actual ceremony,' Jake joked.

'Oh, the phone is going to the third person in our marriage.' And that was the best possible option. It was much
more likely to be a tall blonde... The depressing thought
sent her mood spiraling down to her boots.

'Right, guys, down to business... How about across
the road? I mean, shame to waste an orange blossom in
full flower, given the circumstances...? Jake smiled, not
seeming to notice that Ezio looked distracted. Tilda, who
had been reading his face for the past four years, did, and
wondered about his phone call, the habit of being his PA
being a hard one to break.

'Will you hang onto my glasses for me?' she asked,
sliding them off her nose.

'Why?' Ezio asked, looking at her outstretched hand.
For a nerve-shredding moment, their glances locked.

'For the photos.'

Her fingers responded reluctantly to the mental instruction to unfold and, careful not to get lost in his stare
again, she offered her palm, tensing against the deep little shiver when his fingers brushed the exposed flesh.

'Great bones.' The photographer approved, studying
her face with a clinical intensity. 'Classic. I'd love to do
a series of portraits of you,' he enthused.

'Had we better get on before the world wakes up?'
Ezio intervened drily.

'Sure,' Jake responded as he fell into step beside Tilda,

who was walking a few steps behind Ezio. He gave her an eye-roll and a silent whistle.

'I've never seen Ezio jealous before. It must be love… That is, of course it's love…' he tacked on hastily. 'I meant it about the portraits, though,' he added. 'I'll give you a call.'

Embarrassed by his misinterpretation of Ezio's impatience, Tilda gave a weak smile, even though she had zero intention of taking him up on his offer, which she still struggled to take seriously.

As she watched Ezio stride across to where she had previously been left standing alone, she debated mentioning to him that some of his behaviour could be misinterpreted. Before she realised that that had probably been his intention—the burning looks, the little touches and the flashes of possessive annoyance were all part of the act.

Relieved she hadn't made a total fool of herself, she responded to his concern that she was cold with a carefully managed, one-size-fits-all, meaningless smile.

'I'm totally fine. It's so pretty here. You could almost forget that in an hour it will be choked with car fumes.' At the moment there was only the distant buzz of traffic as a constant reminder that they were standing in central London.

'You're going to ruin those shoes.' He was looking down at the pale suede sling-backs, the heels of which were firmly embedded in the damp ground. 'Typical Jake, he'd do anything for a good shot—have you hanging off a cliff if it was a good angle.' Ezio's dark gaze flickers up to meet hers.

Tilda tried to say something but her lips wouldn't respond to instruction. Her eyes were glued to Ezio's and her heart was pounding, the air between them seeming to throb with a sexual pulse that nailed her feet to the floor.

'Right, then,' said the photographer. 'How about you just relax... Great, that's lovely, carry on with *that* look, guys...'

With a tiny gasp, she tore her eyes free and fixed them on the floor, the effort making her chest rise and fall dramatically under the silk.

'I'm up here,' Ezio said, his voice pitched in a sexy, uneven tone deeper than normal. 'But, yes, my shoes are new. Put a bit of effort into it, will you? Pretend I'm someone else and look happy.'

Her head came up with an angry jerk at the soft mockery in his voice, registering as she did the strain in the lines around his mouth that suggested he maybe wasn't quite as relaxed as she had imagined. 'I hate having my photo taken and I *can't* pose... And I'm not that good an actress,' she slung up at him, wishing that she was, that she could pretend he was someone else, someone who didn't make her *ache*.

'Relax!' encouraged the photographer, with no discernible irony that she could detect as he began circling them, snapping away.

If her jaw had been clenched less hard, she might have laughed at the impossible advice.

'You heard what the man said.'

'What? That I have got great bones?' she shot back, self-mockery flavouring her delivery. She was already sick of this. She had not signed anything that said she had to pose and look stupid, and when she could get her breathing sorted she was going to tell Ezio that.

'Right, I think...yes... Now move a little closer... That look of love, guys...'

Something flashed in Ezio's smoky eyes that made her breath catch. Did she stumble or did her knees just give? Thinking about the moment later, she was never sure, but one second she was on her own feet and the next she was plastered up against the warm hardness of a male chest, supported by a band of steel arm that was looped around her waist.

'You all right?'

'Thanks, fine…' Only she wasn't. His free hand had curved around her face, drawing it up to his as he stared at her like a starving man, making her melt from the inside out.

'You *do* have great bones,' he said, feeling ridiculous, because it was something that had taken him four years to realise and Jake, damn him, had recognised it within thirty seconds.

He also recognised that he *wanted* her. But he didn't need her; it seemed important to him to make this distinction.

'Oh, for heaven's sake, will you turn it off?' The heat was everywhere as she fought the urge to melt into him.

'What off?'

She compressed her lips and breathed out heavily through her nostrils. As if he didn't know *exactly* what this was doing to her. The warmth of his breath on her nerve endings caused the air to leave her lungs in one long, sibilant hiss as he cupped her chin.

Tilda had speculated but she'd had no idea what *in love* felt like. But, if it felt anything like this, she doubted it would be so popular, she decided as she fought for breath, horribly more conscious of his sheer male physicality in that moment than she had ever been before.

But then, other than the odd brushed elbow, she had

always kept a physical distance from him. It was only now that she realised that that hadn't been accidental, that at some level in her subconscious she had always known that it exposed her to the fact she was a million miles from immune to the raw sensuality of the man who broke hearts for a hobby.

'How many photos does he need?' She gritted her teeth, determined not to lose her grip....

What are you holding on to, Tilda?

Whatever it was, she was about to lose it.

'How long is this going to take? My face is aching from smiling. It's not my fault I can't fake it.' Struggling to bury the sensations bombarding her, she took refuge in anger. 'I told you, I'm not photogenic,' she said, the effort of not trembling making her voice almost inaudible.

'You pretended you were not a woman,' he grated, painfully conscious in that moment how *very* female she was. It was not just the warm scent of her that made his nostrils flare, but the female dip and curve of her soft, trembling body that was no longer hidden under sexless clothes. 'Four years you managed that, so pretend now that you're enjoying yourself. Imagine...'

His voice faded as his imagination kicked in big time. The image in his head collided with the green eyes looking up, and the encouraging remarks being made by Jake, who was circling them while adjusting his lenses, becoming a buzz of irritation that was drowned out by the thud of his heart beat.

Then one thing got through.

'How about a kiss, guys?'

Her glance centred on the sensual outline of his mouth, Tilda swallowed hard. '*I'm not* kissing you because someone tells me to.'

'No...?'

'No,' she whispered before, stretching up on tip toe, she grabbed the back of his head yanked his face down until she could reach his lips. 'I'm kissing you because *I* want to.' Want didn't really cover the way she was feeling. Need came close, in a 'need to breathe' sense.

She felt his lips cool under hers. It was the only cool thing. She was drowning in a hot sea of sensation. The world stilled and the crazy, marvellous moment went on and on as she drank in the texture of him, the taste... A tiny shred of sanity crept into her head.

'Oh, God!'

She would have fallen back on her heels had the hand pressed to the small of her back not slid around her waist and dragged her up and into him, while the hand curved around her jaw meant her lips were just at the right angle to allow his mouth to cover them.

The slow, sensuous, expert movement of his mouth across her lips drew a deep groan from somewhere inside her.

Then it was over.

'Oh, guys, that was...' Jake was flicking through the digital images on the screen, looking happy. 'You want I should send my choice over for your approval before I distribute them?'

Ezio locked the animal groan that ached to escape in his chest and exhaled through flared nostrils.

'No, we'll leave it to you.'

Ezio looked so cool that she hated him in that moment. All she wanted to do was dissolve into an embarrassed pool of misery on the floor when she thought about how she must have looked, grabbing him. How good it had felt to grab him, to press her breasts up against… She tensed, blinked hard and locked the door on this line of thought.

Tilda nodded at the photographer, who was making his apologies as he gathered his gear and headed for a vintage sports car parked a little way down the street.

Digging deep, she adopted a coolness she was several universes away from feeling. 'Well, at least that part is over with.' Just the actual wedding to go… She refused to think beyond it.

Over with…

Ezio glanced down at her, thinking she was right—she was a very bad actress—and she was wrong—it had barely even begun.

The innate carnality of her kiss had wiped away any self-delusion he had managed to retain that he was in control… He wasn't. He wasn't even sure he wanted to be.

He was about to marry a woman who kissed like a wanton, hungry angel and liked to be in control. He could work with that.

CHAPTER FIVE

WHEN THEY STEPPED out of the building it was not to a shower of rose petals and cheers but the distant sound of bad-tempered car horns.

While they'd been inside the sun had vanished, blocked by heavy grey cloud. Fine drizzle that was falling steadily had darkened the pavements and the sound of the steady stream of traffic moving past drowned out the bird song.

Shouldn't she be feeling different…? Tilda didn't know how or what she was feeling, but it wasn't married.

She risked a quick glance up at the man beside her, the uniform grey of their surroundings emphasising his vibrant warmth of bronze colouring.

He didn't appear to be feeling the chill that made her hunch her shoulders in an effort to retain some heat as she hovered just inside the shelter offered by the enclosed porch.

His eyes touched hers, a question in the dark depths. 'Are you OK?' Her green stare had a glazed quality that brought a frown to his brow.

Tilda gave a shrug. 'I'm fine.'

Before he could respond to her unconvincing claim,

his phone began to ring, he glanced at the screen and swore. 'Sorry. I need to take this.'

Of course you do, she thought. *Welcome to the rest of your life, Tilda—or at least the next six months.*

Jogging down the steps, Sam paused beside her as Ezio stepped out into the drizzle.

'Are you changing your name?'

'I haven't even thought about it,' she admitted but now she thought it was hardly worth the bother for six months.

'I don't mind if you do, you know…it makes sense he's famous and you're not.'

Well, that was inarguable.

The damp had already penetrated the thin fabric of her dress halfway to the limo when someone appeared carrying a massive umbrella. Under its shelter she reached the kerb, where the open-doored limo waited.

Glancing over her shoulder, she saw that Ezio still had his phone at his ear. He lifted it away briefly to respond to something Sam had said with a nod of assent.

'I'm riding upfront, I don't want to be a gooseberry!' Sam yelled, jogging past her and around the limo.

'You don't have to—' Her words were lost in the slamming of the door.

She slid in, adjusting her dress before the door was closed, immediately muffling the noise of the traffic which, despite the early hour, had built up to rush hour level. Smoothing the skirt over her thighs, the ring on her finger caught the light. She paused and looked at the gold band that lay snugly against the big square-cut emerald.

She was still staring at it when Ezio slid in beside her. 'You're trying to figure out if they're real. You've found me out.' He held his hands up in mock surrender. 'They're paste. I'm a cheapskate.'

'I wish they were! I don't feel comfortable walking around with a fortune on my finger.'

He stared at her for a moment and loosed a laugh. 'You are a very unusual woman, you know that?'

It was hard to tell from his expression if that was a good thing or a bad thing.

'What are you doing?' She nodded towards his phone.

'Switching it off… Oh, the storm has shifted its path, so there's no issue with the flight—got the news update just before we went in.'

'Good about the storm… Actually, I didn't know there was a storm.' Though, now that she thought about it, Saul had mentioned something about the weather during the phone call last night.

Saul was actually being extremely helpful. He'd looked over her mission statement, suggested a couple of tweaks and given her the names of some potential trustees.

'It's been on every news bulletin for the last forty-eight hours. The phone…' He hesitated before volunteering, 'My father has been ringing me non-stop since last night.'

'Your father?'

'You sound surprised,' he observed, tucking the phone in his pocket. The gesture was an empty one. He might want to take a break from his father, but it was not practical to cut himself off entirely. His fantasy version of a desert island was a week with his phone switched off— the desert island scenario stood more chance of actually happening.

Tilda conceded the point with a faint shrug. 'I suppose I had the impression that you weren't particularly close.' It wasn't so much what he'd said about his father but the fact he rarely mentioned him at all.

'You had the right impression, so don't worry, there

will be no dutiful visit for you to endure,' he drawled. 'We do the yearly dinner, though my mother and I do meet up through the year.'

Tilda, who remembered the dates being in his diary, didn't say anything. 'I wasn't thinking about that. I... Oh...' His meaning suddenly hit her and she felt stupid for being so slow. 'You mean that by then we will be divorced,' she said tonelessly.

In the act of sliding one arm along the back of the seat, he paused, something flickering in his dark eyes. 'I suppose we will be.'

'Has your father found out about the wedding? Was he angry?'

'My father does not have the right to be angry. If he knows we are married, I haven't told him.' She sensed a tension in his steely posture underneath his languid pose. 'Actually, my mother has left him...about thirty years too late, in my opinion, but she has.' He cast a knowing look over her face. 'Yes, it was an affair, or rather the last in a long list of affairs... As it turns out, one too many.'

'Oh.'

'He wanted to know if I know where she is. The man is falling apart,' he said, sounding not too unhappy about this.

'And do you? Know where she is?'

He rolled his neck, as if to the relieve the tension lying in his broad shoulders. 'Yes.'

'But you wouldn't tell him.'

He produced a wry smile and shook his head. 'I'd pay good money to see him crawl to beg her to come back...bare foot and hot coals involved in the equation works for me too....but I gave my word. And it will do him good to think she is with another man...which of course he does, because he judges everyone by his own particularly low standards.' He sneered, his mouth thinning in contempt. 'I'm not claiming mine are high, but at least I have enough self-awareness to recognise the traits I share with the bastard. I might have screwed around, but at least I never hurt anyone doing it.'

Despite the headlines about him, she realised that it was true—if he used women, they used him right back. And who could blame them? she thought, her eyes drifting to his irresistible mouth.

'Is that why you never got married?' she blurted, hastily averting her eyes.

In the act of running his finger around his collar, he paused, an expression she could not interpret sliding across his face as the silence stretched so long she thought he was not going to respond.

'In that way at least I differ from my father. I know I'm selfish, but I'd never put a woman I *half*-liked, let alone one I professed to love, through the sort of humiliation my mother has suffered.'

'You married me,' she said in a small voice.

He jolted in his seat, a look of contrition spreading across his face. 'Oh, Tilda, I…'

She gave a brittle little laugh. 'Oh, don't be daft, it's fine. I know our marriage is not the same and, heavens, *love* doesn't come into it.' She laughed again, ignoring the bleakness that had invaded her heart… *Think about that later.*

Or maybe not. Some things were better left.

Aware of his forensic scrutiny, she painted a look onto her face that suggested curiosity rather than hurt feelings. 'So where is your mother? Or am I not in the need-to-know loop?' He seemed to juggle a lot of loops; perhaps his right hand actually *didn't* know what his left was doing, though she knew better. He had a mind like a steel trap and, to use a chess analogy her brother would approve of, he was always thinking three moves ahead.

'She's taken an apartment in Paris and had enrolled on a post-graduate degree in Fine Art at the Sorbonne. I hope she does meet someone who appreciates her.' He sank his head into the leather head support and turned to look at her.

'I am not enough of a bastard to spend my wedding day on the phone to my lover.' But bastard enough to know that was what she had been thinking, he thought, self-disgust tightening like a fist in his belly at the recognition. And he'd let her carry on thinking it, just because he didn't like explaining himself to anyone.

'I was getting mad,' she admitted. 'It seemed...*rude*.' She wasn't asking for much, but basic good manners seemed a not unreasonable ask to her.

'It seemed...rude...' he echoed with a half-smile, thinking that her mouth was not made for looking prim. The attempt was sexy, though. 'How will I cope in the office without you to tell me when I'm out of line?'

Her emerald eyes flew wide. 'I... I never did, I just...'

'Suggested it...?'

'Subtly.'

One corner of his mouth lifted but his eyes... The expression glittering deep in the obsidian depths made her think of his mouth feathering across her lips... As the thought progressed, her breathing grew faster and shorter before she literally shook it away and pushed out a breathy observation. 'You know you're going to have to turn your phone on, don't you?'

'I know. I might block my father, though.'

'Ezio, you can't do that! What if there was an emergency?'

Ezio snorted, his fingers tapping the wooden arm-rest impatiently. 'This traffic is…' As he was speaking, the traffic started to move.

'It heard you and got scared.'

A half-smile glimmered as he leaned back into his seat and, loosening the knot on his silk tie, stretched his legs out.

'Lucky we settled on pre-wedding photos; it's really bucketing down now.'

Tilda flashed him a look and was tempted to point out that *she* hadn't decided on anything, but she didn't want to break the little lull in tension they were enjoying.

He patted his pocket and pulled out her new glasses. 'I forgot… You need these?'

'Oh, I forgot.' She was shocked by the admission. Not long ago the idea of appearing without glasses would have made her feel naked; they had been part of her persona for so long. 'Thanks.'

Ezio didn't immediately hand them over, instead he held them out, regarding them through narrowed eyes. 'Very pretty,' he decided, before his gaze shifted to Tilda.

For a split second she thought about telling him the truth but held back. This was *her* makeover, not his.

The difference was important to her and, she realised now, was part of the reason she had refused the delivery of designer outfits. Tilda had no ambition to be some sort of Cinderella. She was nobody's project, she was her own woman.

'No tints?' he observed.

She shook her head. 'I liked this pair.' And she had rationalised her purchase by telling herself that specs were a fashion accessory.

'Just *how* short-sighted are you?' He held them out, and for a split second she thought he was about to raise them to his own eyes.

'I can honestly say that the wedding was a blur.' It was true, just not in the way he thought she meant. 'In fact, this entire day feels surreal.' Maybe she would wake up any moment and say, *I had this really vivid dream.* She turned her head to look him in the face. 'Sorry for moaning...you hate this as much as me.'

'Oh, not *that* much,' he said drily, the irony not lost on him. 'You know, there are some women who might consider marrying me not a total waste of a day.'

Tell me something I don't know, she thought.

'Sorry, it's nothing personal—and I'll make the best of it, I promise. I'm not a whiner,' she added solemnly, in case he thought she was going to bleat about it constantly. 'I'm a realist. I know you made a better boss than you will a husband.'

'You thought I was a good boss?'

While it was noticeable he hadn't concurred with her initial statement, if she hadn't known that Ezio didn't need approval from anyone she'd have thought her admission had pleased him.

'No woman ever had to push through a glass ceiling, because you never had one—that's rare.'

'Thank you. I'm glad you think I'm an equal opportunities employer, but actually I just like to reward talent. And, like the man says, if you've not tried it yet, don't knock it. I might be an exceptional husband.'

Tilda, who fully expected him to be an absent husband, didn't respond to the teasing.

'I know today hasn't been easy, but the next six months don't have to be unadulterated misery.'

'Why, because I've married a sex god?' The moment the waspish words left her lips, she would have given anything to retract them. 'It's that damned article—and don't say you don't know *what* article.' Colour rose to her face as she remembered reading the kiss-and-tell article that had been liberally sprinkled with lurid details.

'I don't, but I intend to look for it now.'

Her cheeks were burning but she made a recovery and managed a disdainful sniff. 'I'll send you the link. But, although a lot of the comments thought she was just after some publicity, even allowing for a bit of exaggeration, I'm sure you're great in bed!'

A gleam of appreciation appeared in his eyes. 'You look like Matilda on a Monday morning, looking disapproving because I've done something wrong.'

'It's still me. Just think of me as the piece of office furniture who can talk back outside the office,' she snapped back, pretending not to be aware that he'd shifted his position and his thigh was now against her own.

It was a lot of pretending!

Irritated with herself for being aware, she blamed that kiss... It had made her feel excited, vulnerable, a dozen other things she couldn't put a name to when she thought of it. Thought of the taste of him, thought of the tangle of tongues, the feeling... *Oh, God!*

'What is it?'

She shook her head. Then, desperate to divert attention from her momentary blip, she glanced pointedly at Sam, whose head was nodding away to the music he was listening to via the ear buds pushed in his ears. The glass screen protected her from the audible boom of bass she knew would be pumping out, despite the headphones. She felt a stab of sympathy for the driver and hoped the poor man shared Sam's taste in music.

'He'll probably be stone deaf by the time he's twenty.' *And I'll be a divorcee.* But divorce was six months away and, thinking of that kiss…would she ever stop thinking of it?…six months suddenly seemed a very long time.

She'd jumped in without thinking this thing through. In her defence, she had worked closely with him for four years. She'd have thought if incapacitating lust was going to be a problem it would have reared its ugly head by now.

She took a calming deep breath. This would work… this had to work… She owed it to Sam and she owed it to her parents, and the silent vow she had made to them at the funeral.

She didn't have to enjoy the next six months, she just had to get through them. The logical part of her brain told her she should not have leapt before taking precautions, such as having her own lawyer go through the contract she had signed, or working out that Ezio should come with a 'once kissed never forgotten' warning.

But all it took was for the image of Sam lying in that hospital bed to come into her head and the knowledge that the next time he might not be so lucky…that the next time, he might end up with a criminal record that could blight his entire life before it had started…and she knew it didn't matter. She'd have done it anyway.

Ezio's voice made her start, which was ridiculous, because she really hadn't forgotten he was there. He didn't have a forgettable bone in his perfect body.

She turned her head slowly, delaying the moment their eyes made contact. He'd dominate an auditorium, let alone the plush, air-conditioned interior of a luxury limo. Maybe the air-conditioning wasn't working, or maybe it was her own air-conditioning...because, even though she felt hot, she was shivering.

Her green eyes had a bruised, almost blank quality. She looked so young...much younger than her years.

'You have something against those flowers?' Concern roughened his voice.

She looked from his face to the drooping flowers she had picked up in her white-knuckled hands, as if she couldn't even remember picking them up.

'Or are they a substitute for who you really want to strangle? I think the technical term for that hold is a death grip.'

Ezio watched as she released the choke-hold on the ribbon-tied posy and put them down on the seat between them. The flowers looked almost as sad and wilted as she did. Her heart-shaped face made him think of a flower, her graceful neck the stem that held it up.

He rejected the image. Tilda was tough and resilient. He had always admired the fact that she always rose to a challenge, she kept her head and did not respond emotionally—it was one of the reasons that he had stopped looking for a replacement.

His long-term PA Angela's departure had been sudden after she'd fallen ill, but she had been the one who'd recommended her assistant, asking him to give her a chance. *'She'll shine,'* she'd said.

Ezio hadn't imagined the scared creature whose main skill had seemed to be the perfection of the art of fading into the background shining, not even in a quiet way, but he'd humoured Angela. Typically, she'd felt guilty for leaving him in the lurch, and he had never anticipated the situation would become permanent. But it turned out that Matilda Raven had only been quiet because she'd been learning and, before he realised it, she had made herself an invaluable asset.

He remembered the first time she had stood up to him. He could see her now, standing there looking at him and saying quite calmly, 'I think that's a really bad idea.'

To say he'd been astonished was an understatement.

He had tried to remember the last time anyone had told him *any* idea he'd had was bad...and couldn't. He'd complained about boot-lickers but then, when he'd encountered someone who wasn't inclined to polish his ego, his first reaction had been to annihilate her verbally... and then he'd remembered someone, probably him, saying that if ideas were not open to challenge there was no progress.

So, instead of yelling, he'd sat on the edge of his desk and thrown out his challenge.

'So, tell me, *why* do you think this is a bad idea?'

She had, calmly and concisely, and when he'd asked her what she would have done she'd told him that too. A lot of those suggestions had been unworkable but there'd been a kernel of possibility in several.

That was the day their relationship had changed and, while he'd missed Angela, he'd got over it. But he'd missed Tilda's presence in his office more than he would have imagined. She was here in his life now, though, still provoking and challenging him.

For six months.

The glass partition between the front and passenger seat suddenly slid down.

'Phillip.' Sam nodded at the driver. 'He says we're here.'

'The clue is the sign and the planes,' Ezio retorted drily.

'I've never flown before, you know—well, I have, but I was small, and I know only because there are photos, and Tilda tells me I threw up all over Mum on the plane and it stank.'

'Well, I sincerely hope that you do not throw up on this flight.'

'I've been reading about jet propulsion and—'

'I hope you haven't been making a nuisance of yourself, Sam?' Tilda was worried.

'Of course not. Phillip was interested.'

'*Phillip* was a captive audience, and he is polite. I had the foresight to pack the parachutes.'

Tilda tensed and half-closed her eyes.

Sam could get defensive at even the slightest hint of mockery—probably because he had suffered merciless teasing at school over the years, despite his often dry sense of humour.

But, after a pause, Sam laughed.

If *she'd* have said that, he'd have sulked for a week!

CHAPTER SIX

ONE OF THE experiences Tilda wanted to take away from her short stint as a billionaire's bride was that of getting to fly in a private jet. Once would do; she had travelled on the odd occasion with Ezio, but never outside the UK.

She had seen Angelos private jets with the discreet gold logo on the runway on several occasions when Ezio had requested she meet him at the airport to fill him in personally on the way to a meeting.

She'd often speculated what they looked like inside, and the luxury and space in the private jet was not a let-down. While Sam was trying to con himself a place up front with the pilots, she took a seat. Baggage allowances were not an issue but Tilda had brought on board a small carry-on containing some fresh clothes.

She intended to enjoy the novelty of using the on-board shower room facilities, which she knew existed, because she'd asked about Ezio's wet hair on one of the occasions she'd met him coming off a flight.

An image flashed into her head of him immaculately suited and booted, his dark hair slicked back, striding through the foyer towards her, drawing every single eye in the place and seemingly totally oblivious to the fact.

She pushed away the image and didn't try to stifle her

yawn, partly to prove to herself how relaxed she was, but mostly because the tensions of the day were catching up with her and the creeping exhaustion was enveloping her like a blanket.

She stretched out her legs and pushed her shoulder blades into the seat, only to reverse the process abruptly and sit bolt upright when an attendant appeared with champagne in a bucket and two glasses. She nodded her thanks and smiled at him, wondering if this was simply normal practice when Ezio travelled with a woman, though she doubted many of Ezio's travel companions had come with a teenage boy in tow.

A drink was either a very bad idea or a very good idea but, as she sat there staring at the bottle, she decided that, bad or good, she was going to say yes… It had been a long day and it wasn't even lunchtime yet.

'Wh-what…? Wh-where…?'

Ezio glanced up as a deep sigh left Tilda's parted lips, her lashes fluttering like butterflies against her lightly flushed cheeks as her luminous green eyes opened. Her eyes darted back and forth, the unfamiliar surroundings deepening her panic until she encountered a face that anchored her.

'It's you…' She studied Ezio's starkly beautiful face and smiled.

Ezio caught his breath at the invitation glowing in her eyes. His physical response was instant and painful. Her mouth was just the most… He had no idea where he got the strength not to accept the invitation in those incredible eyes. He could feel his sense of time and place fade fast, along with his resistance, as she lifted a fluttering hand towards his cheek. His chest was heaving as he struggled to draw in oxygen through flared nostrils and he felt his control slipping through his fingers like sand grains.

Their mouths were inches apart when, just as unexpectedly as it had been offered, the invite was withdrawn, a light seemed to switch on in her head and the slumberous promise went cold.

He remained hot.

She sat bolt-upright, almost knocking heads with him.

Ezio straightened up in pain.

Theos... If Tilda ever learnt the power those eyes had, no man would be safe.

What man would want to be *safe*...? What was safety compared to the lush promise of the lips?

The thought surfaced out of nothing, or at least deep frustration, and once there fed on the oxygen of his need. Packing it away would take more focus than he could tap into at that actual moment so it stayed there at the back of his thoughts, bedding down, inviting him to rationalise the needs he was denying...asking *why*?

He focused on the *why nots*. It was not a cold shower but it was all he had.

How about we have great sex for six weeks but then what for the rest of the six months...? Sure, that is really a good idea.

How about six months isn't enough...? Tilda was not like any of the women who had drifted in and out of his life leaving no ripples in its smooth, efficient running.

What if he hurt her? There was no *if* about it. He was enough like his father to know that he would. This argument with himself was the clincher. He might be selfish but he was already using her, but to hurt her... He felt the rejection of that at a cellular level.

'We're here—why didn't you wake me?' It was less a question and more an accusation.

'You were exhausted and it's been a long day.'

'You snore.' This was Sam, who walked down the aisle with a back pack slung over this shoulder. Presumably his suit was crushed in it, as he'd changed into a pair of khaki chinos and a tee shirt. His comfort made Tilda aware that she wasn't at all comfortable—she was wearing a dress she had slept in, which no doubt looked it.

'Thank you, brother dear, I love you too,' she responded with a grin.

'I wanted to wake you but he wouldn't let me.'

'You do not snore... Drool a little...?'

'When did you become a double act?' A smile appeared in Tilda's eyes as she looked from one to the other and some of the tension slid from her shoulders. She was actually starting to feel a bit ridiculous for getting worked up about a searing, hot, hungry look when it had been a product of her sleeping subconscious.

It was connected to reality by her guilt, which was irrational. A person could not be held responsible for their subconscious, it was not real, but the *not real* had left the echo of it low in her belly in an ache of carnal yearning.

In the real world she was not yearning she was... A tiny pucker appeared between her feathery dark brows. She felt creased and crumpled, much like the old dish rag her dress probably resembled by now—a dish rag that had been slept in.

Rubbing away the frown between her eyes, she lifted her heavy, silky hair off her neck. The plan had been to tie it back before they landed.

Why was she worrying? There was no one to impress except... Actually, there was no need to impress Ezio, which was just as well; outside the office she wouldn't have known where to begin.

And she definitely wasn't going try and look stupid making the effort. Mouth set firm, she unclipped her belt and rose to her feet, shaking out the silky strands of hair as she did so.

She felt Ezio's eyes on her and turned her head, catching *something* in his eyes—a trick of the light, maybe. It was only there for a split second. Imagination or not, she was wide awake now, all her senses tingling, her stomach somersaulting.

'Am I holding everyone up? Sorry, I didn't sleep much last night.'

'I hope he wasn't a nuisance?' she said anxiously.

'I would tell him if he was,' Ezio responded with a deadpan look that broke into a grin as he added, 'Relax, he was fine. He ate a great deal... I had forgotten that teenage boys are never full. But fortunately, under the circumstances, he was not sick at all.'

'You don't know what you missed. There is a *chef* on board.'

'I'm sure you'll tell me what I missed.' Tilda put a hand to the back of her neck and rotated her shoulders to alleviate the burning ache of tension that had already taken up residence between her shoulder blades.

Push through the pain, she thought ruefully as she picked up her bag. 'I meant to change.'

Ezio's glance travelled from her feet to the top of her shiny head before he casually claimed her bag.

'I'm fine.' Her grip tightened on the handle and her jaw squared, the resistance only lasting a second before it occurred to her that disputing everything would leave

her with little energy for the fights that really mattered.
The ones that she was starting to think were inevitable.

'Thank you.' She forced the words out as she relinquished her bag.

He tipped his dark, glossy head in sardonic acknowledgment. 'You look fine like that.' The throw away remark was delivered with no particular expression, and
his eyes were hidden by the fringe of his lashes, but the
tension she sensed in him made her stomach lurch.

She hurried to fill the static silence before it became
impenetrable. 'I feel a bit creased and...' She broke off
as his eyes met hers.

'You look beautiful. Accept a compliment with grace,
Tilda.'

She fought the temptation to look back over her shoulder and carried on walking, making damn sure she didn't
stumble. Because it wasn't the compliment, it was the
source it came from, that had her feeling very unsteady.

Her reaction to his formidable physical presence was
a problem, but all she had to do was sit tight and wait...
She knew his schedule—Ezio rarely spent more than
three days a month in the Athens office, and on those
occasions he sometimes flew back the same day.

She noticed that Sam seemed quite subdued as they
went through the tedious but VIP-accelerated airport
formalities. Her anxiety was mixed with guilt. This was
happening because she wanted to prioritise Sam, but yet
again it was Ezio who occupied her thoughts...and not
in a way she had ever imagined.

The problem was she was imagining too much.

'Are you OK?' she asked, lightly throwing an arm
around her brother's shoulders.

Just ahead a senior official of some sort had attached

himself to Ezio's side. She knew his attentive attitude would not be to Ezio's taste, but what he liked or did not like was not for her to worry about. She found herself hoping uncharitably that the man was boring the pants off Ezio.

'Fine. Actually, if you must know, I'm regretting the last burger...' Sam admitted, pressing his stomach. 'But I mean, a chef and food on tap... I asked and no one said no.' He gave a '*go figure*' eye-roll of wonder. 'It was like a dream.'

Tilda's lips twitched. Sam dreamt of an endless supply of fried food and she dreamt of... Well, who was she to criticise?

'It didn't occur to you to say no?'

'I did but two burgers too late.'

The official peeled away before they reached a sparsely occupied private parking area. Ezio was speaking with a group of airport staff who were in the process of putting luggage in the boot of large shiny four-wheel drive with blacked-out windows.

It looked showroom-new. Tilda glanced at her brother, who was still looking interestingly pale.

'If you're going to be sick...'

'Got it covered. I'll open the window.'

Tilda grimaced. 'Thanks for that image.' And she watched as her brother climbed into the back seat. Ah well, if he did spoil the leather upholstery it would serve Ezio right for not realising that a teenage boy had to be told when he had had enough to eat.

'You worry too much.' He had not intended to say it but she looked so... Did the woman never put herself first?

'Do I?'

'About Sam.' He'd noticed Sam trudging along looking sorry for himself and, having seen the boy keep the on-board chef on his toes, he was not particularly surprised or concerned. It was the worried looks floating in Sam's direction that he somehow couldn't filter out.

Her raised brows went higher, her delicate nostrils quivery with the effort of not responding.

Her restraint lasted a good ten seconds before, with a smile heavy with sarcasm, she bit back through gritted teeth, 'I bow to your superior knowledge on the subject.'

'I watched him munch his way through half a cow, and I happen to know quite a lot about unrestrained indulgence.'

'I'm sure you do, but spare me the details of your sexual endurance.'

Laughter burst from his lips.

A drop-dead look was not quite as effective as she'd have liked when she knew her face was scarlet but she gave it a shot anyway. 'And, if you watched, why on earth didn't you stop him?'

'In my experience, saving people from their mistakes is less effective than letting them suffer the results. You only stick your hand in the fire once...' His eyes fell to her lips and he immediately felt the painful evidence that this was not always true; sometimes those flames were just too tempting.

'Well, I wouldn't know. I am not drawn to flames, and anyway, that is the most stupid thing I have ever heard!' she exclaimed with a scornful sniff. 'What would you do, let a toddler stumble into the path of an oncoming car to show that being hit by a big chunk of metal going at thirty miles an hour really hurts?' She snorted. 'Tough love is another way of saying "I don't give a damn"!'

She broke off, breathless after her impassioned outburst. Every inch of her slender, supple body was vibrating with outrage that had fired up out of nothing, basically. Things seemed to overheat at a very low temperature between them but, *Theos*, she was quite magnificent… He had never been with a woman who aroused him this much.

He had never been with her.

He stood there wishing that he could go back to a point in time when he could have confidently tossed back that he didn't give a damn and did not care what hurt his words caused.

That ship has sailed, mocked the sardonic voice in his head.

'Fine. I spoke out of turn.'

The sparkle of disdain faded from her eyes, replaced by surprise. Perversely, the instant he stopped defending himself, she wanted to make excuses for him.

'And I overreacted a bit,' she admitted. 'It's my job to worry about Sam. I don't always do such a great job and…well…it's been the two of us for so long…' She broke off, thinking it still *was* the two of them. 'And his life is changing so much he's bound to struggle.'

'Sam seems to be coping. He seemed resilient.'

'He's had to be. When Mum and Dad died, for a long time afterwards he had terrible night terrors. He'd wake up in the night screaming.'

Watching her face, Ezio wondered if Sam was the only one who'd had night terrors.

'He used to ask me if I was going to die and leave him too.' She gulped unshed tears, roughing the edges of her disclosure. 'He had some grief counselling…we both did,' she said quietly. 'But I get scared sometimes.

When things seem fine it all goes...' She gave a helpless little shrug.

'These boys he got mixed up with...?'

She nodded. 'He's sensible really, but he so desperately wants to belong...'

Her green eyes sought his for understanding and that look made him feel as though a hand had reached in his chest and squeezed.

When he'd been nailing the fine detail, treating this marriage like any other contract, he had failed to appreciate that even a temporary marriage would impact his life, especially one that came with a ready-made family... At least, not in the way it was. Just considering someone other than himself was a mind-bending change for him.

'You're very kind to Sam, and I'm grateful. He likes you.' She really hadn't anticipated Ezio becoming some sort of role model for her brother. 'It worries me...' she admitted.

'What worries you, Tilda?' It worried him that the sight of her nibbling nervously at her lush lower lips was exerting such fascination, and that the impulse to wrap her in his arms and tell her everything would be all right was growing more compelling by the second. 'Surely,' he added brusquely, 'It is good that he likes me?'

She nodded and cast a furtive look over her shoulder. 'Of course, but he doesn't know that this is...well, not real...temporary. I'm afraid he'll get *too* fond of you.'

'I wouldn't hurt Sam.'

Her eyes flew to his face. 'I know you wouldn't mean to.'

'There is no reason we can't stay in touch *after*.'

'Stay in touch with Sam?' She was startled by the idea.

'I meant…' In all honesty, he didn't have a clue what he meant. 'People remain friends after divorces.'

'But they were friends before, we are…'

'Not friends,' he supplied, a hard edge to his voice.

'I wasn't going to say that.' Even if it was true. 'We were, I suppose, well, *nothing* outside the office.'

'So is the enforced intimacy making you feel uncomfortable?'

She felt a sudden spurt of panic as his glance connected. 'There is no intimacy, enforced or otherwise. We aren't strangers but I don't *know* you…' He was constantly challenging her pre-conceptions in a way that meant she couldn't relax. 'Not in any sense of…' Her eyes slid from his dark, sardonic stare. 'For instance, I never realised that you didn't travel with security in Greece.'

His lips quirked at the obvious attempt to change the subject. 'I travel with security most places…visible if you want to draw attention, and less visible…' She watched as he lifted a hand, turned to his right and a car fifty yards away flashed its lights. He then turned left and the same thing happened before he swivelled back to Tilda. 'If you don't. You are perfectly safe. I would never allow anything to happen to you or Sam.'

'I wasn't worried, just surprised.'

'The moment we got married, you and Sam became potential kidnap targets.'

'Kidnap…?' She cast a glance at Sam in the back seat and shuddered. *Kidnap.* The word floated through her head, sounding more sinister with each repetition. It wasn't just the word it was the matter-of-fact way he'd said it. 'I'm stupid, I didn't think…'

'Why should you think?' The stricken look on her face

felt like a stab in his chest. 'This is not *your* normal, it is mine.' He gestured to the waiting cars, then placed a hand flat on the black paintwork of the gleaming monster they stood beside. 'Armour-plated cars with bullet-proof glass are my world, and while you are in it you will be safe. I swear on my life.'

'I know, I never thought otherwise... I trust you.'

His lashes came down like a veil but Tilda sensed another mercurial shift his mood.

'Well, if you are ready?'

He held the door open, holding out a hand to help her on the step.

'Thanks,' she murmured, not looking at him, afraid that contact with his dark eyes would shake loose the confusing cocktail of dangerous emotions swirling inside her. She could not predict which one it would be, but none would be relaxing.

CHAPTER SEVEN

SAM SEEMED TO regain form as they drove through the dust and congestion of the city, Ezio good-naturedly answering his constant flow of questions while negotiating the traffic, which in itself deserved a medal.

After they had been driving thirty minutes or so, the urban sprawl gave way to a quieter area. The streets they drove along were lined with palms and the sea, which she had only glimpsed at a distance through concrete, was now a dazzling blue backdrop against the beaches that lay along the bay.

'This is so pretty.'

'Vouliagmeni,' he said with a nod.

'Sorry, you must feel like a tour guide.'

'Familiarity breeds contempt. It is actually good to see these places anew through the eyes of visitors.'

The small smile curving her lips faded at the reminder of her status...*visitors.*

Oblivious to her abrupt change of mood, he expanded. 'Many well-heeled Athenians come here. There is a thermal lake and people bathe there even in the winter. I will take you there.'

'Before I leave, you mean?'

'Who's leaving?'

Tilda felt a stab of guilty panic.

'Are you looking forward to the school tour tomorrow, Sam?'

Successfully diverted, Sam earnestly began to discuss in detail with Ezio the computer facilities, which he couldn't believe were as good as the prospectus suggested. He was also extremely impressed by the calibre of some of the staff, many of whom had come to teaching from a diverse spread of interest and expertise.

'How much farther to go?' she asked during a lull in the conversation.

They had left behind the pretty beachside town fifteen minutes ago and turned off through two massive wrought-iron gates onto a private road. The loops, dips and sharp inclines meant they quickly lost sight of the lead vehicle, though occasionally they got a glimpse of a dust cloud. The one bringing up the rear hung back, putting more distance between them.

'You wanted to know *when*? Ten, nine...'

In the back seat, Sam joined in.

Tilda folded her arms across her chest. Did men ever grow up? 'With this sort of build-up...' she began. 'Oh, my God!'

Ezio brought the four-wheel-drive to a halt. The pause meant the blacked-out limo that had been following them came to halt too further down the road.

'Villa Amphitrite.'

'The goddess of the sea,' Sam said. 'Well, you can see why.'

She really could! Set in the midst of formal gardens that stretched down to the sea, with a mountain backdrop looking out over it, the dramatic main structure was snow-white, including the roof, it seemed, giving the impression it was floating above the sea like a cloud.

There appeared to be two adjacent wings. One had a soft blue tinge and a square tower that stood in one corner looked gold at this distance.

'That,' Tilda breathed, unable to take her eyes off the spectacular sight, 'Is not what I was expecting. When you said "villa" I was thinking something… I don't know… less palatial, more rustic, with maybe a pool. Less historical ancient…more old.'

'The original building was ancient but that fell into ruin many years ago. Some ancestor of mine bought the ruin because he liked the view.'

'He knew a good view when he saw one.'

'He was full of good intentions, so the family legend goes, the "mouth not action" type. He'd inherited money, so basically he just sat, looked at the view and drank a little—actually, a lot, by all accounts. By the time his equally languid sons had died, the place was a wreck and half the land that came with it was sold off.'

Well, nobody could say that Ezio had inherited the lazy gene! It was impossible to imagine his combustible energy ever slowing enough to allow him to relax, let alone laze.

'It passed to my grandfather.'

'And he was not lazy.'

Ezio's white grin flashed. 'No, that was the last thing you could call him.'

'Well, it's…' She threw up her hands, genuinely lost for words. 'I don't know how you can bear to leave it? If I…' She stopped, her eyes widening in self-reproachful dismay. She had almost done it again. It was only luck that Sam had stepped outside to take a million photos on his phone.

'We should be careful, Ezio, with Sam…'

'So what is your plan with Sam, so that we are reading from the same page when the time comes to tell him?'

'When that time comes, I'm hoping that he won't need telling. I know in some ways he's pretty immature for his age but in others… He'll pick up on the clues. I'm not saying he knows much about people in love but I think he'll soon cotton on that we aren't.

'And do you know a lot about people in love, Tilda?'

'More than Sam,' she countered carefully.

'From experience?'

She felt the anger move like a rash of prickly heat across her skin. 'I'd say that's none of your business. What are you smiling about?' she tacked on crankily.

'I was wondering how many times in the office you wanted to say that to me.'

'It *was* your business then, that is the difference— though if you'd have asked me that back then I'd have still said it was none of your business and punched you regardless.'

Ezio threw back his head and laughed.

'One of Tilda's jokes?' Sam said, climbing back in and waggling his eyebrows at Tilda as he teased her. 'He's only being polite because you're on your honeymoon.'

Honeymoon? 'We're not—'

'We're not going away at the moment. We're waiting until I can take a decent stretch of time off, though we might island-hop for the odd weekend. I have a boat.'

'Big super-yacht?'

'No, a sailing boat—a thirty-footer, cross-over cruiser-racer, comfortable but built for speed. She's a beauty.'

If this was an invention it was a good one. His enthusiasm sounded genuine but Tilda didn't actually remember any photos of his model-clone girlfriends lounging half-naked on a sailing boat of any size. For that matter, she had never seen any of them at Villa Amphitrite.

Her eyes flicked to the villa. It looked almost unreal from here.

'You ready?'

She had felt his stare but she hadn't turned her head and she still didn't. The answer to his question was a loud no, on *so* many levels.

'Yes. It looks original from here.'

'From this angle at this distance, yes; you'll see what I mean when we're down there. It is definitely not a legitimate restoration, but a lot of the original features have been incorporated into the fabric of the new building. According to family legend, Amphitrite is named for the temple to her that the white marble for the original building was stolen from.'

'This spot, it's just so perfect.'

'And safe.'

The soft addition drew her eyes to his face. 'I know I sound a bit over-protective at times but I promised Mum and Dad at the funeral that…' She felt her eyes fill and closed them, before pushing out a fierce, 'Sam is my responsibility and if I put him in harm's way I would never forgive myself.'

The image in his head of her, a younger, lonely figure by a graveside making a vow, had a heart-piercing poignancy. 'Such slender shoulders,' he said in a shiver-inducing undertone. 'To carry so much… You're both under my protection—you are safe. I'll keep the nightmares away.'

Tilda looked from his dark relentless eyes to the floating castle and didn't feel safe, but she did feel excited.

By the time she reached the villa she had run out of superlatives to describe it, though no doubt, had she asked, Sam could have helped out. When the infinity pool came into view, and the beach, being Sam he made time to assure his sister that swimming on a full stomach was not dangerous; it was an old wives' tale.

They pulled up on the forecourt where not only the pool was visible but the towering glass-paned extension that faced the sea.

'Wow, I take it that isn't part of the original building?' she said, unfastening her seat belt and sliding out, immediately hit by the pungent scent of lemon thyme that grew in the cracks between the terracotta paving.

Sam had run ahead and vanished round a corner.

'He'll be fine,' Ezio said, anticipating her anxiety.

'That is beautiful.' She stared at the glass extension, marvelling how it seemed to blend organically with the original stone. The arched roof and striking cupola were even more stunning close up than at a distance.

'The planners were quite sympathetic to a modern extension when they knew we were going to use traditional methods. The idea was not to replicate anything, just make something beautiful, and we employed local artisans. Of course, we borrowed a bit design wise. It is based roughly on a Victorian greenhouse, but we had modern techniques to draw on.'

'It reminds me of one at Kew!' she realised, spinning round to face him.

He nodded. 'We used similar materials—glass, cast-iron and wood. The supporting arches inside are decorative steel. I'm glad you approve of my extension. My father thought I was insane.'

'Didn't he try and stop you?'

His expression hardened. 'He couldn't. My grandfather left Amphitrite to me. This was for him, to his memory—he was a great collector, and when it came to endangered plants and ferns he was an acknowledged expert.' He looked up at the building, then back to Tilda and smiled. 'Here, let me show you around. You might want to freshen up?'

Tilda raised a self-conscious hand to her hair and nodded. 'Should we find Sam first?'

'I'm sure he'll turn up. The poor kid's been cooped up all day. Let him— Of course, that's up to you.'

'It's so massive,' she said, casting an awed look up as they walked past a row of fountains to a massive, metal-banded double door.

'Big rooms, but actually not that many of them. No endless long corridors, and once you get the hang of the layout it's quite easy to navigate. The main living areas are mostly in, well, this white marble section, and the bedroom suites in the blue wing, a less grand local stone with no goddess connections. The kitchens and utility area are on the ground floor of the tower.' He nodded to the square gold tower. 'And my offices are on the top floor.'

'You must have quite a view from up there. An eagle in your eyrie.'

'Quite cruel of you to draw attention to my beak of a nose but, yes, it does have quite the view.'

Her glance automatically slid to the blade of a strong nose that bisected a face that was by any standards stunningly perfect.

'I'd call it more characterful.'

His grin flashed as he invited her to walk ahead of him.

Her first impression as she stepped inside was of space…and light. Light shone off every surface, the palette of soft French grey and white that picked out the stone friezes on the walls soothing. The elaborate mosaic in the floor was a pattern of concentric circles, again pale with splashes of sea-blue and gold.

'Large', he'd said, and he wasn't exaggerating. The massive square space's cavernous proportions were accentuated by a high-vaulted ceiling with dark, curved elaborately carved beams. It was sparsely furnished, even though you could have held a ball in the room. Most of the furniture, which was basically a few beautiful chairs and tables, was set around the wall, apart from a few large eclectic items set in the stone niches spaced around the room, and some modern paintings on the wall that provided dramatic splashes of colour.

Sitting centrally was a round stone table with a large stone urn from which spilled a fragrant and natural-looking display of flowers and foliage. She could imagine the low, modern chandelier set above dramatically highlighting it when it got dark.

'The friezes and the table were rescued from the original building—actually the pigsties.'

'Your home is very beautiful,' she murmured as she gazed around.

'It is your home for the moment.'

She smiled, knowing she would always feel like a guest.

'You look sad…'

She shook her head firmly. 'No, just a little over-whelmed.'

'Shall we save the tour until later? I'll take you to your rooms. This way.'

She followed him through one of the arches. This space was narrower and forked at the end. Along one wall, windows looked out onto a courtyard similar to the one they had entered through.

'So we take a right, and our suite is at the end.' He turned to the left fork. 'Sam's down there, and I had the sitting room turned into a study. I thought it would be more useful.'

Tilda had not heard the 'study' part... She had not got past the *'our'*.

'We are sharing a room? Over my dead body.'

'Dramatic,' he drawled. 'And, ultimately, a solution which really does not solve one hell of lot. I, however, have a much more practical idea...are you going to ask me what it is?'

She slung him a narrow-eyed look.

'I'll put a pillow between us, and I warn you, if you touch me I know self-defence.' His mockery melted away, the expression in his dark eyes growing flat and hard. 'I said suite, not room—we have *rooms*, two bedrooms, two dressing rooms and bathrooms and a large sitting room in between. I can have locks put on if you fear that I will be overcome by lust.'

By the time he was finished, her face was so hot it could have lit up Athens. There was no face-saving, or for that matter face-cooling, way to get out of this.

'Well, I feel pretty stupid now.'

She didn't look stupid, she looked like a crushed flower at that moment. Young and a little lost.

'I'm starting think, Ezio, that you're a lot better at this "keeping up appearances" thing than I am,' she admitted ruefully. 'I hadn't thought what Sam might think if we have rooms the opposite end of the house.' She lifted her chin. 'You seem to have come up with a very... workable solution.'

'You're not built for deception—you are too honest.'

Coming from Ezio, she wasn't sure if that was an insult or a compliment, and his expression wasn't any help. The tension shivering along his taut, golden stubble-roughened jaw made her wonder if he wasn't as uneasy at the prospect of the next six months as she was.

Honest... He might think so, but Tilda couldn't make the same claim, especially when she felt like the big lie she was nursing was written across her face in neon—namely that it was her too-handsome boss who might need the lock on the door. Not *seriously*, of course, because she would never get involved with a serial womaniser. She had more pride.

You married him, Tilda!

She had no idea why she stood rooted to the spot with the shock of it. It wasn't as if it was news. She had spent the last month counting the days off on the calendar and now it was here.

She had walked into this with her eyes wide open, and she was married, but not *involved*. God knew what the distinction was but it made her feel slightly less of a hypocrite.

Standing within the blast zone of his pure, *male* mind-numbing force field, she struggled to pull free of the sensual web that she had spun around herself.

Luckily, help was at hand, in the shape of a tall woman who wore her grey-streaked dark hair in a smooth pleat.

Handsome rather than pretty, she wore a pair of wide-legged trousers and a pale-grey silk shirt. Tucked in behind her was Tilda's brother.

'I am so sorry I was not there to greet you,' she said, addressing her remark to them both. 'I have discovered this young man.'

Sam stepped forward reluctantly, and his wet hair told a story.

'Tilda, this is Sybil, the housekeeper here. Any problem, she is your go-to woman.'

Not for the sort of problems I have, Tilda thought, managing a forced smile.

'And, Syb, this is Tilda, my wife.' Now those were two words he had never thought to hear himself say, but at least he could say them without flinching. Tilda could not hear them without doing just that.

Tilda assumed, as the other woman didn't stand there open-mouthed or go into shock, that she must have been given some warning about their married status.

The two women exchanged smiles and nods.

'We were about to send a search party out for you,' Tilda lied as she turned to her brother, brows raised. 'You decided on a dip, I see?' She didn't really mind. Sam was a strong swimmer, and actually she felt quite envious; she would give a lot to immerse her hot and sticky self into cool water. Swimming was the only sport she had ever been any good at, and she had passed on the skill her father had taught her to Sam.

'I was just giving you two some alone time,' Sam responded virtuously. 'And, in case you're worried, I didn't skinny dip. I left my pants on, which are a bit soggy now.'

'Syb, would you show Sam to his suite? We'll all catch up in the Fern House later.'

'Is that what you call it? Wow, Tilda, there is a cool—'

Ezio cut him off mid-flow. 'Later, Sam. She can see for herself.' He floated a comment in Greek to the house-keeper over Tilda's head and the other woman nodded before gesturing to Sam to follow her.

'This way, Sam.'

'Sam seems to have made himself at home.'

'A bit too much at home,' Tilda worried. It had never occurred to her that him liking life here too much would be an issue. 'It will be a wrench for him to leave.'

'You have barely arrived and the only thing you can talk about is leaving?'

Hearing the annoyance in his voice, she glanced up at the tall, sleek, beautiful male creature she was strug-gling to keep pace with and felt her throat close... He really was utterly gorgeous, even with his jaw clamped taut in annoyance.

'Well, I have to think ahead.'

He took a step ahead and turned to face her, slant-ing a glittering look at her face as he continued to walk backwards...

If I tried that, I'd fall flat on my face, she thought.

She could simply not imagine Ezio doing anything that wasn't elegant and co-ordinated.

'Ever heard of living in the moment?'

'I did that once today...' The words were out before she could stop them and she was watching herself grab him and kiss him... That it had only happened today seemed impossible.

'And very nice it was too.'

His throaty murmur almost made her trip...before she sought a solution to the problem by removing her shoes.

Hopping from one foot to the other with a lot of swear words was a useful distraction.

'I've got flats in my bag,' she grumbled. At some point, her bag had vanished…was it in the car?

Ezio stared at her small, narrow elegant feet, the toe nails painted pale-pink. He had never in his life considered a woman's feet a turn-on. 'I could carry you. Don't look at me like that. I have not just made an indecent suggestion.' His thoughts were a lot less pure, and, had she known where his tongue in his hot ever-developing fantasy that began at the arch of her foot had reached, she would have looked a lot more outraged. *Or not…?*

'I'm fine, thank you.'

He tipped his head, accepting her lie. 'It's not far now, and your luggage will be in our…sorry, *your*…room.'

They reached the room and he paused to let her enter before him. Tilda found herself in a pretty, light room. The open French doors faced a terrace with brightly coloured flowers set against the backdrop of the blue sea.

'The sitting room.' He made an expansive gesture that took in the room. 'Your room is that side. Mine…' He nodded to the second door. 'Nothing so scary as an inter-connecting bathroom. We are standing in the neutral zone… Oh, and you will find some clothes in the dressing room. The ones you rejected and a few others—and before you protest,' he inserted in a bored drawl that made her close her open mouth with a snap. 'These are not an indulgence but a necessity. In order to play a role convincingly, get into character, you need to dress the part. You are my wife.' The possessive note in this autocratic pronouncement should have made her laugh, but it didn't; instead, the quiver low in her belly became a thrum.

'And you think clothes are going to convince anyone of that?'

'I'm hoping your lingering look of love will seal the deal, *glikia mou*.'

'You are so up yourself!' she cried, her face flaming at his mockery.

'You'll miss me when I'm gone,' he teased, walking to the door and leaving behind the echo of his deep, throaty laughter.

The horrible possibility his mocking jibe was not a million miles from the truth was why she was resisting getting into the role...as much as she wanted to deny the attraction she was feeling. She wasn't blind to the real danger of buying into the fiction, getting so deep into character that she couldn't find the exit.

She needed to keep that exit in sight and not let Ezio spoil her for a man who one day might come along... Even if he didn't, she didn't want to spend her life comparing every man she met to this complex, infuriating man.

She walked into her bedroom which was complete with far too many mirrors, a stunning chandelier of wrought-iron and cut glass and, of course, the bed...a fairy-tale four-poster piled high with cushions.

Pre-warned, she still got a little shock when she opened the dressing-room door. The sheer volume of clothes hanging on the rails that lined the room took her breath away. She pulled open a couple of the drawers. She wouldn't have been human if the luxury fabrics, soft silks and delicate lace had not made her sigh with pleasure...and the thought of them against her skin.

The thought of someone peeling them away from her skin... Aware of the moist heat between her legs, she closed her eyes against the images, but they stayed there and there was no mistaking *whose* fingers she was imagining on her...

She needed to cool down; she needed a shower.

The bathroom was another jaw-dropper—double-ended beaten-copper bath tub, a view through the slatted shutters that was breath-taking and glass shelves lined with bottles of luscious-looking oils that invited her to take the tops off and inhale.

Tilda didn't, she headed towards the shower, which was the size of her bathroom at home, and stripped off, letting her clothes fall to the floor in a heap.

The controls looked as if they belonged in an alien space ship but, after pressing everything on the touch-pad control, something happened and water came at her from all sides.

She supposed it was adjustable but, rather than try to figure it out, she settled for having her skin pummelled clean by the jets. By the time she emerged, her skin was pink and glowing. Pity the same couldn't be said for her mind, which was still firing on all cylinders.

She was in the living room when there was a knock on the door. She was tightening the belt on one of the beautiful silk robes from the Aladdin's cave dressing room when the door opened.

The sense of anti-climax was intense.

Her brother walked in, looking clean and scrubbed. She recognised his expression with a sigh.

'So what do you want?'

'Me? Actually, I came to tell you dinner is ready when you are... The thing is, Tilda—you know, as this is your wedding night and all—I thought I might let you two...

you know… You can do the whole candle thing and everything.'

'That's very considerate of you, Sam, but totally unnecessary.'

'I already asked Ezio.'

'And what did Ezio say?'

'That I had to ask you, but the thing is, there's this podcast I've been really looking forward to and this guy…a professor at… Well, you wouldn't know him, but he's really good. He makes astrophysics so *accessible*, you know what I mean? And a tray in my room would be good because I'm really exhausted and, quite honestly, if I have to watch you two *smouldering* at each other I'll throw up.'

'Sam, I… We… Oh, all right. But tomorrow,' she warned sternly, 'You eat with us like a civilised human being.'

'Oh, God, yes…of course. Oh, thanks, Tilda—and it's just down the corridor, a sharp right and the other side of the hallway. The rooms kind of flow… Yeah,' he said, pleased with the description. 'They flow, so you just follow—follow the smell, I suppose.'

CHAPTER EIGHT

THIS WAS GETTING out of control, Tilda decided, standing back, hands on hips, to view the pile of clothes on the bed. Also, it was giving her a headache.

She shook her head—a mistake—and growled out an impatient, 'Get a grip, Tilda!'

For a split-second, she was tempted to dress for dinner in a pair of jeans and sweater, and not one of the selection of lovely cashmere ones beautifully folded on the shelves, but that might be a provocation too far. She didn't want to poke that particular tiger, which could get a bit unpredictable when roused.

No, definitely a gesture that could backfire, she decided, abandoning the idea with some regret.

But this indecisive dithering was slowly driving her crackers. She had never spent more than five minutes deciding what to wear...

Anyone would think she had someone to impress!

But then, she had never had so much choice, she thought, looking at the stack of designer garments piled high. How was she meant to know what a billionaire's wife would wear? Even a temporary one.

A small, secretive smile curved her mouth as she experienced a light-bulb moment. Yes, she knew the *perfect* way to make an impossible decision.

Eyes scrunched tight, she stepped towards the pile of dresses on the bed and burrowed her hand into the pile of silks and satins, letting her fingers close around a slithery piece of silk.

She opened them and held the dress up, a bias-cut calf-length in deep emerald-green. It was the sort of bold colour she rarely wore. The demure neck contrasted with the dramatic and daring low cowl-back that reached almost to her waist.

She had previously discarded it as being too bold, too not *her*… She shrugged and thought why not? She wasn't playing herself. The idea was oddly liberating.

She didn't want to fade into the background.

The idea of being looked at did not bother her so much…or was it the idea of being looked at by one particular person? It was hard not to feel confident when a man who looked like Ezio, a man who all women desired, looked at you the way he had… She gave a sinuous little shiver and felt scared and excited all at once. She felt like someone about to step out into the unknown.

Half an hour later, in a pair of spiky heels the like of which she had never owned in her life, she walked down the corridor, still feeling not quite like herself, but enjoying the swish of heavy silk against her legs as she walked, her heels tapping on the terracotta underfoot.

The breeze, scented with salt from the sea, wafted in through the open windows, the softness caressing the bare skin of her back and neck.

As she got to the end of the corridor, she glanced at her reflection in one of the windows to check her hair

was still in place. A few soft, silky strands had escaped
the loose chignon but otherwise it was still intact.

Sam had been right about the flow of the rooms in the
living area. They did for the most part flow seamlessly
on from one to another, giving the impression of space
and light, each in its own individual way as beautiful as
the one she had just left.

The light was fading now. A few lamps were on and
several candles in the sconces had been lit, casting flickering patterns on the ceiling. She reached a massive living room, furnished, as the villa was throughout, with
a combination of modern pieces and antiques. The vast
sofas looked made for flopping in, but no one was.

The place was so quiet, she could hear a clock from
the previous room ticking.

Ahead, she could see the formal dining room, but
that too was empty. She sensed movement and turned
her head, for the first time seeing that beyond the floor-
length windows along one wall there was another space,
previously dark. She could now see the golden reflection
of light against the glass—the famous Fern House, she
assumed, as she walked to a set of doors.

She was inside the fernery, the massive modern glass
house. The echo quotient went up as her heels clicked on
the floor. Tilting her head, she took in the spot-lit carved
wood and curved metal rafters high above her head, the
whole curved structure appearing to be supported by
four massive metal pillars. The same scrolled carving
was repeated in the frames of the multi-paned wood and
ornamental steel-framed glass walls.

Uplighters set in the stone floor picked out artistically
placed groups of green foliage, and the raised pond that
filled the space with the trickle of water took central po-

sition. Sofas were grouped at one end around several low tables, and at the other end a dining table was laid, the candlelight leaving a glowing nimbus of light around the pretty pots of flowers and reflecting off the cut-crystal wine glasses.

The place seemed empty as she walked along the side of the raised sunken pool, lights revealing the fish swimming in lazy circles among the swaying green fronds of aquatic plants.

'Good evening.'

For a brief, insane moment, she thought he had materialised in front of her, but as sanity kicked in she noted the open door and the breeze blowing in that ruffled his dark hair. He carried the scent of the warm evening air and green vegetation on his clothes.

As she watched him walk towards her, moving with the silent grace of a big, beautiful, sleek predator, her stomach started fibrillating.

She realised that she had just been standing there staring, and she didn't have a clue how long, and he was just a couple of feet from her.

'Hi!' she said brightly. 'I am… I'm late. Early…? Have I kept you waiting?'

'None of the above.'

He held out a hand that invited her to precede him. She tipped her head in acknowledgment and felt very glad that she had not come casual to make a point, not that she knew what that point would have been.

That's me…the rebel without a brain cell who is about to fall off her heels.

Ezio's only concession to casual was that he was not wearing a tie. His pale shirt was one of those she knew he had hand-made in Italy and ordered by the dozen;

there were always a handful of unopened ones in his office. He wore the shirt open at the neck, the open-button arrangement enough to reveal the strong column of his neck and deep olive-toned skin along with a tiny vee of skin at the base of his throat, suggesting that he was that glorious toasty colour all over.

Clean-shaven, there was no trace of the earlier stubble on his sculpted face. His suit was silver-grey, but it was the power not concealed by the supreme tailoring that made her shiver, not the perfect cut.

'Do I pass?'

She sucked in an embarrassed little gasp. 'I just thought, you changed... I didn't hear you...'

'I caught up on a few things. I keep some fresh things in my office. I didn't want to disturb you if you were resting.'

'Oh I see, like in London. Well, not the me resting part.'

'No, I have heard your boss is a bit of a taskmaster.'

She flung him a look. 'The you keeping things in your office part... I mean...' Her voice trailed off before she could sound any more like an inarticulate idiot.

This really didn't feel like London. In London there was no background accent of lush greenery. In London there had been an invisible professional barrier between them. Like those barriers down the motorway, it had provided safety...no collisions.

What would it feel like to collide with Ezio?

She lowered her eyes but she couldn't hide from the pulse at the apex of her thighs.

'The view from the shower here is better.' It was nothing on the view he had enjoyed from outside when he had turned his head and seen her standing there.

This was not a 'butterfly unfurling' moment or an 'ugly duckling into swan' transformation. In her dull office clothes, she had always been a beautiful woman, but standing there, gracefully poised on some crazy heels, the vivid green dress hugging her body and pulling tight against the thrust of her breasts and slender waist, she was bewitching, breathing-taking.

Mesmerised, he was rooted to the spot with white-hot lust. It took several dramatic inhalations to batter his instincts into submission before he could trust himself to approach her without wanting to sink to the floor with her—actually, he still did.

Tilda was involved in a very tough fight not to see him in the shower, but the carnal image of steamy water sliding off his water-slick skin flashed into her head, reducing her shaky inner calm to jelly.

She really had no idea what was happening to her… It was as if her hormones were having their revenge for being ignored for so long.

'None of the above.'

Panic floated briefly into her mind for the duration of the amnesia; she didn't have a clue what question he was responding to. Her breath snagged in relief as the memory surfaced above the sensual fog that had taken up residence in her head.

'I thought you might need to sleep. I hope it doesn't offend your sensibilities as much as it did the cook—please do not call her a chef; she will be insulted—but I wasn't sure what time we'd be eating, so I asked her to pre-prepare and leave things warming, which caused a minor meltdown. She considers heated trolleys an invention of the devil—or it might have been the seventies. I don't think she cares much for either.'

Smiling down at her, he pulled a chair out at the table. After a fraction of hesitation, she walked forward, making him think of a leggy, skittish colt likely to break for freedom at the last moment.

Her gliding grace was as natural as breathing, and all the more attractive because she remained utterly unaware that the way she moved made men watch her.

Standing behind her, he fought the impulse to tuck a behind her ear a stray strand of hair that floated across her cheek. At least he was free to enjoy the scent of her shampoo and take in all the details of the lovely length of her neck, the delicate protrusion of her shoulder blades and the line of her spine. A ballet dancer would have been jealous of the supple strength in the fine network of muscles under the silky skin of her back.

'She offered to stay.'

'Your cook?' Tilda said, faintly trying to jolt her brain into active life, but at least able to breathe now he wasn't standing so close. She watched through her lashes as he pulled out a seat opposite her but didn't immediately sit down.

'She has her grandson visiting her. He's an undergraduate at Oxford and she doesn't get to see him that much.'

'Oh, no, that's fine…that's very considerate of you.'

He pushed away the stab of guilt. His motives had been far from altruistic; he had just seized on the excuse to have dinner with Tilda with no interruptions.

He was playing with fire and he knew it, but it didn't seem to matter. A kind of madness had taken hold when he had seen her standing there, and he wasn't fighting it very hard. He wasn't fighting, he was going with the flow, and it felt…dangerous…but danger always had attracted him.

Some inner sense told her that if she didn't break the spell now she never would. 'I should look in on Sam…' she said, half-rising. 'I wasn't sure where his room was.'

'I already have looked in.' On one of the several occasions he had stood outside their suite door, debating whether to go inside.

'Oh!' She sank back down, thinking, *at least I tried… though not so desperately hard.*

'He is stuffing his face again and talking astrophysics.'

'And how goes the hunt for a new PA? Have you considered Rowena?'

'The office again!' He sighed. 'History repeating itself…'

Tilda gave a mystified shake of her head. 'Sorry I don't…?'

'*Angela* persuaded me to give *you* a chance.'

Tilda smiled. 'Did she? I never knew. I wonder how she is.' Tilda really regretted losing contact with the older woman. 'It's tragic…she was only thirty-one.' On the last occasion they'd met, Angela had been coping with the hair loss from chemo with typical Angela humour.

'And now she is thirty-five, and she and her husband have started a business and have adopted their first child.'

Her eyes flew wide. 'She had the all-clear!' Her delight morphed into astonishment. '*You* kept in touch!'

'She worked for me for eight years—I am their child's godfather.' Probably not a very good one, but he had been touched to be asked, and little Arthur was probably the closest he'd ever come to parenthood. Actually, he thought, self-correcting his thought, there was no probably about it.

He remembered his godson's birthday, sent him Christmas gifts and had set up a trust fund for his education, but he didn't *know* the child; he felt no *emotional* connection—certainly not the sort that he felt for Sam. In a few short weeks the teen had made a big impression and Ezio liked to think he had actually been of some help to the kid too.

'Well, send her my love the next time you speak to her. So, does your housekeeper live in…and other staff…?' She had seen a group of men looking busy in the garden.

'Sybil has a cottage in the grounds and the head gardener, Nikos, lives in the gatehouse. A contractor comes in for the heavy-duty stuff these days, but he has a few men who help, and a youngster he is training up to replace him.'

'The garden here looks very beautiful,' she said, relieved to be talking about something normal. 'I can't wait to explore.'

'They are actually more upkeep than the house. Sybil makes do with a couple of locals who come in daily, and more as needed, but the place is empty a lot of the year.'

Processing this information in her head, Tilda came up with the information she had been fishing for in a roundabout way—the place was empty except for Sam, who would probably fall asleep over his computer screen.

'Wine?'

'Oh God, yes please,' she said with feeling. Then, catching the quiver of his lips, she added quickly, 'I'm quite thirsty.' Her eyes went to the water jug and she grabbed it and filled her glass, looking at him over the rim as she raised it to her lips.

'And you missed out on the champagne on the flight.'

'It's been a long day.'

Her heart hammering like a drum, Tilda watched him fill her wine glass. The tension in the air was so dense it had an almost audible static buzz…or was that in her head?

'This really is very beautiful.' She tipped her head back to look at the gracefully arched beams. 'The craftsmanship is very special.'

He retook his seat and raised his own glass.

The stem felt slippery when she picked up hers, then she realised it was her hands, not the glass.

'To us.'

She lifted her drink, steaming the glass with her breath as she held it there, looking at him over the rim, fighting the impulse to say there was no *us*.

'To our first dinner together.'

'It isn't.'

'What?'

'It's not our first dinner together. I flew up to Edinburgh that time because you'd forgotten those papers and your date had stood you up. You had booked at that posh French place and you took me, then she rang and said… Well, I don't know what she said, but it was obviously a pretty good offer, because you were out of there like greased lightning.'

A comical expression of dismay spread across his face. 'Oh God, I'd forgotten.'

'Oh, don't worry, you paid the bill before you left, and left money for my taxi, and I drank the whole bottle of that very expensive wine; it was actually really good.' Only just realising as she relayed the details that the memory still stung, she took a gulp of her wine. This was probably good too, but the truth was she was no judge.

He sat there looking stunned. He had blanked the occasion, and the memory of reacting to that phone call as if it was a lifeline, because it had rung at the same moment that he had acknowledged that taking his PA out of the office had been a mistake. He'd been *noticing* too much—her laugh, which was full-blooded and throaty, which he had never heard in the office. That her skin in the candlelight had looked quite astonishingly smooth.

'Shall I help myself?' she said, getting up and approaching the trolley. 'Wow, you should be very nice to your…cook. She is good,' she said, inhaling the scent of lamb in the rich, fragrant sauce.

She retook her seat with the plate and smiled across at him. 'You're not eating.'

'I was a selfish bastard,' he said, his voice harsh with self-recrimination.

She set her elbows on the table and looked at him. 'You won't get any arguments from me.'

'I don't remember her name…' he said, half to himself.

'Well, mine is down on a certificate, so that will make it easier.'

His frown deepened. 'Do not compare yourself. You're nothing like…' His dark eyes settled on her face. 'No man could forget you.'

She put her fork down, struggling to feign an appetite the tension had sucked away, her stomach churning with a strange mix of emotions. It felt raw…she felt raw… She felt suddenly incredibly angry.

'I did feel ridiculous, sitting there, but I mostly felt ridiculous because I'd been excited. That was the most expensive restaurant I'd ever been to, and when you left the snooty waiter looked down his nose at me all evening, and I didn't call him on it—I didn't even say a word and when I left, no actually I did, I said *thank you*… Can you believe it?' She came to a breathless halt, a look of horror spreading across her face. 'I have no idea where that came from. It was ages ago and—'

'Tilda, I am truly sorry.' He leaned forward towards her, the image of her sitting there alone driving a stake through his heart.

'Oh, I believe you mean it now, just like you probably mean it when you say *I love you* to the women in your bed, but—'

'No, I don't.'

'Don't what?'

'I don't say I love you. I've never said…'

She watched his expression change but, before she could interpret the look on his face, he veiled his eyes and leaned back in his seat.

'You never…?'

'I said it once…it was a long time ago. It's the sort of thing you say when you propose.'

'You were engaged?' She didn't laugh but she came close.

'No, she actually rejected me.' His lips twisted in a self-derisory half-smile as he recalled the events.

By the time he been brought to the point where he had declared his eternal and undying love in quite a dramatic way, as he recalled, Lucilla could finally afford to be honest about her feelings. She had by that point passed on the information she had been milking him for to the lover he later discovered she had left her husband for. The same husband whose supposed cruelty had filled him with vengeful fury. It was easy to see now why she had been so alarmed when he had announced his intention to confront the guy.

The memory of his younger in-love self, confiding all his hopes and dreams for a future he planned to share with her, made his gut tighten in self- contempt. For a long time afterwards, he'd tortured himself with the thought of her laughing with her lover over his sentimental drivel.

His big romance had been revealed as industrial espionage taken to an extra level. When Lucilla had not been not in his bed, she'd been in bed with one of the main rivals of the firm started by his grandfather and continued by his father—the firm that had been absorbed into Angelos Inc, but even then it had been worth three months seducing the boss's son.

'Don't get me wrong, I had fun. Not just the lovely information you gave me, I had permission to enjoy your youth and...enthusiasm... It has been an exhausting six months for me. I was actually prepared to put up with your sentimental rubbish and poetry for the sex.'

No matter how the memory made him feel, he wanted to remember, so that if he ever felt the urge to mistake sex for anything deeper it would be there to pull him back from the brink of making a fool of himself.

He had not needed the memory; he had not felt that way about any woman since. If the experience had killed off that part of him, he was glad of it.

He had learnt that day how to protect what was his— like chess, his father had said when he had confessed what he had done, you sacrifice your pawn to ensure you win... Play the long game.

His father had made his sacrifice and it had turned out to be Ezio himself.

The only way he'd learn from his mistakes, his father had told him, was if he wasn't there to clean up the mess. He'd had his chance and he'd blown it, he'd been told, and life didn't offer second chances. Or, his father didn't.

Tilda directed her gaze at her food but found her eyes tugged back to his face; his shuttered expression was hard to read.

'You were heartbroken, I suppose,' she tossed at him, stirring the food as she regarded him through her lashes, still waiting for the cynical punchline.

'Badly bruised, but I recovered,' he assured her, wondering what had possessed him to share this unnecessary information with her.

The half-smile faded and her lips flattened. It was this down-playing that made her realise that this wasn't a joke. 'You really... Oh, God!' She gulped remorsefully. 'I am so sorry, I didn't mean to...'

He gave a hard laugh, amazed that anyone could leak empathy this way. 'Open old wounds? You didn't,' he assured her. They were open because he had kept them that way, as a reminder. 'Anyway, I had my revenge.'

'What was that?'

'I got very rich, she let all that lovely money slip through her fingers and it was lovely money she was after.'

No one who had got over it, as he'd claimed, could sound that bitter. Who was the woman who had broken through the cynical shell of Ezio Angelos? And was the animosity a cover for the fact he still loved her?

Well aware of the danger of allowing her imagination full rein, she closed down the line of speculation but struggled not to feel empathy. The focus of her antagonism was for the faceless woman, until the irony of what she was doing hit her—yesterday she would have sworn that Ezio didn't have a heart to break and now, well, she was aching for him.

And she had to admit he didn't look much like a classic *victim;* actually, not any sort of victim. Conscious of pain, she glanced down where her hands lay on her lap clenched into white-knuckled fists. Flexing her fingers, she saw the deep red half-moons cut into her palm.

Tilda's tender heart ached. The idea that out there existed a woman who he had never recovered from left her feeling angry. The nameless woman had made him feel he had to guard his heart, had made him lock himself off from love.

Tilda didn't realise she'd physically shaken her head to clear the anger until she saw him looking at her, his head tilted questioningly to one side. She pushed away her plate, all appetite gone.

'So, were you together a long time?' she asked, casually wondering if the other woman had ever drunk from the glass she was holding... She put it down abruptly.

'No.'

Her lips tightened at the clipped response. She felt frustration well up inside her. His tight-jawed expression made it crystal clear she could fish as much as she liked but he was not opening up any more.

'You can sulk as much as you like, Tilda... Do *you* want to talk about previous lovers?'

'I am not sulking and I don't have...' She stopped dead and watched the expressions move like some sort of slide show across his face before settling into stunned disbelief.

She sat there folding her napkin with geometric precision before getting to her feet. 'I think actually I might... It's been a long day.'

'Are you saying you have never had a...? That you're a...?' He shook his head; even *saying* it sounded ridiculous.

'I'd say that's none of your business.' At least for once

she was looking down on him, and boy, did she need all the advantage she could get.

'And I thought *I* had problems.'

'I don't have a problem—well, except you. I made a choice some time ago that I wasn't going to expose Sam to a stream of uncles…and one-night stands are not my style.'

'Don't knock it till you've tried it,' he drawled. 'So weren't you worried when we got married that I might want to take it to the next level?'

'You mean sex? I'm a virgin… I can say the word, I don't have hang-ups…and I was not worried, because if that was what you wanted I feel sure you'd have included how many times and in what positions in the small print; you covered everything else!' she accused with breathless disdain.

His sloe-dark eyes glittered as he watched her lose it big time, the passion spilling from her… He watched the movement of her small breasts under the silk, making him think of them filling his hand—the perfect size. His heart rate slowed in time with the blood pouring in his throbbing temples and points south as he visualised those perfect breasts pushing up into him, her arms around him.

'No hang-ups,' he purred. 'No fun.'

'It depends on what you consider fun, and while we're being frank—' Some grain of sense slipped through the fog of fury in her head and she stopped dead.

'By all means.' His lean body rigid, he gestured for her to continue, and languidly crossed one ankle across the other as he pushed the chair back from the table with a loud scraping sound.

'Your bed-hopping strikes me as pathetic,' she flung

at him. 'It makes me shudder just to imagine anything so…so…empty.'

'Your prissy, judgmental, little virgin nose is quivering.'

'And, for the record, no, I wasn't even slightly worried because that…*sex*…would be *my* decision, not yours.'

His narrowed eyes gleamed and he smiled, looking lean and dangerous as he shook his head in reproach and murmured, 'Always polite to wait until you're asked, *glikia mou.*'

CHAPTER NINE

SHE STOOD THERE, fists clenched, and shook her head, her body trembling with anger. 'You are the most totally horrible man I have ever encountered!'

And once more with feeling, Tilda mocked the voice in her head. Nothing she said could make even the slightest impression on Ezio.

'What's the point?' she asked, throwing up her arms in an attitude of defeat as she delivered a final dirty look before swivelling away sharply on her heels, the action causing the fabric of her dress to flare, tighten then flare again around her legs as she began to stalk away.

Ezio knew that the image of her retreating bottom outlined by silk would would stay with him... The heaviness in his groin was not going to vanish any time soon either.

'Horrible...?'

Her teeth clenched as his mocking voice followed her. 'Can't you do better than that?'

'You are...' She twisted back and found he was no longer sitting down but standing, looking big, dangerous and beautiful, about six inches from her. The shock made her sway slightly.

His hands landed on her shoulders. The weight provided an anchor, the slow, sensual movement of his thumbs across her collar bones making it hard to keep her eyes open. Her neck felt too weak to support her head.

'I am totally desperate.' He moved one hand to her chin, bringing her face up to his so she could see the tension drawn into the planes and hollows of it. She could see the dark fire burning in his eyes. 'I'm asking, *glikia mou*, so what's your answer? Shall we add an amendment to that contract?'

Her lashes fluttered and she looked up at him. Need *ached* through her like a fever.

Feed a fever—wasn't that what they said? Tilda was pretty sure it was actually *starve* a fever, but she decided the situation warranted a little poetic licence.

'You're asking?' Her husky response was barely above a whisper. Her throat felt aching and tight.

'I am.' At this point he was so desperate beyond reason to shape her softness into him and sink into her, taste every delicious inch of her body, that he would have *begged* if necessary. The fact she was a virgin should have automatically put her off-limits. It was a responsibility that he should run from...or should at least have had had a 'cold shower' effect...but he was beyond cooling, beyond sense.

Tilda was shaking all over now, so hard her teeth were juddering as if she were someone with a fever; she was burning up from the inside out.

Like someone in a dream, she stretched up and took his face between her hands, her fingers cool against his warm skin. The warning voice in the back of her head was now the faintest whisper.

'My answer is yes please,' she whispered, staring upwards to his mouth, his really sinfully beautiful mouth.

Sin had never looked so good to Tilda.

He stood, body rigid. Fine tremors, like those of a racehorse held back at the starting gates, were running through his body as she moved her soft lips across his. He stood still while her tongue slid tentatively and then with more confidence into his mouth, and then his control broke.

A low growl vibrated in his throat and he took charge of the kiss, plundering the warm, secret recesses of her mouth with a ravenous, primal hunger that shocked and excited her more than anything she had ever known. Then when she was faint and breathless the hunger slowly transitioned to a slow dance of seduction, of strokes and probing, retreat and advance, until nothing existed in her world but the taste of him. All she could smell was him and all she could feel was the ache inside her.

When the kiss stopped she was plastered up against him like a second skin, her breath coming in a series of frantic, uneven gasps.

Fire flamed in his eyes as he wrapped his arms around her middle, picking her up so that their faces were level. Thrilled to the core by the display of casual masculine strength, she wound her arms around his neck, sliding her fingers deep in his abundant hair as she kissed the side of his mouth, then ran her tongue experimentally around the inner aspect of his lower lip. He jerked her back a little and, holding her gaze, slowly let her slide down his body, allowing her to feel his erection as the hardness pressed into softness of her belly the whole way.

Once on her feet, he pushed her a little way from him before he held out a hand.

'Come.'

She stared up at him, utterly mesmerised. Standing there feet apart, his face a golden mask of need, he presented a pagan image, wild and unrestrained, that imprinted itself on her retinas as she reached for him.

Walking backwards, his eyes not leaving her face for a moment, he led her to a large, low couch before drawing her to him and kissing her while his big, capable hands and clever fingers moved in slow sweeps over her body, caressing her curves through the silk and bare skin he discovered on her back, awakening every nerve cell in her body into tingling painful life.

Little soft, mewling sounds left her mouth and were lost in his as he kissed his way up the curve of her exposed neck. Her back arched as he lowered her onto the wide sofa, sweeping the cushions off in one movement. He removed her crazy heels one by one, throwing each shoe over his shoulder.

She watched, her lids half-lowered, as he rested one knee on the sofa and, bracing the opposite foot, he took hold of one of her feet. She let out a slow gasp of surprise as he ran his finger down the high arch of it before licking the places his finger had touched.

The other foot received the same treatment, and then his fingers and tongue moved higher, sliding under the silk of her dress, reducing her in a matter of seconds to a mass of inarticulate craving.

'I think,' he said hoarsely. 'We can dispose of this.' He took the hem of her dress, scrunching the fabric in his hands as he worked his way up. She gave a little wriggle, lifting her hips to let the silk slide up and over her bottom, and then after a couple of expert tugs it joined her shoes.

Then his fingers went to the back of her head and, finding the clip that secured the loose knot, he freed her hair, watching with an expression of satisfaction as it fell in a silky skein down her back.

'I've been wanting to do that since you walked in...
I've been wanting to do a lot of things.'

'Such as?' she murmured huskily, feeling bold and
womanly, feeling the power of her sex for the first time
in her life.

He smiled his slow 'devil on steroids' smile that made
her insides shake. 'You're in a such a hurry.'

He was not wrong; she was consumed by an urgency
to have to have it all right now.

Wearing the satin camisole and a pair of silk shorts,
the only thing the cut of the green dress had allowed, she
fought the urge to hide behind her hands, instead letting
them lie clenched at her sides, suddenly painfully conscious that she was not what he was used to.

He just sat there on the edge of the sofa looking down
at her, his eyes watching the rise and fall of her breasts
against the thin satin covering, the thrust of her nipples
pushing through the fabric.

'You're beautiful,' he groaned, bending forward to
cover the hard nubs with his mouth through the fabric.
Her body arched again and she sighed at the exquisite
burning pleasure of the contact, which left wet marks
against the silk.

He raised himself to take up where he'd left off on her
legs, stroking her foot as he continued his carnal journey along the inner aspect of first one thigh and then the
other. By the time he reached the burning wet apex of her
legs, she was making hoarse little wild sounds.

He took a few moments to shrug off his jacket and
then fight his way out of his shirt.

One hand trailing limply on the floor, Tilda watched
him, catching her breath as his bronzed torso was re-

vealed. She squirmed, the kick of lust low in her belly and the insistent pulse between her legs making her moan.

The sound brought his eyes to her face as he unfastened his belt and unzipped his trousers then, holding her eyes with a heavy-lidded, carnal stare, he kicked them aside before freeing his erection from his underwear then it too was slid down his long, lightly hair-roughened legs.

Tilda could barely breathe. The emotional constriction in her throat reduced her breathing to a series of shallow gasps. He was the epitome of everything male. There was not an ounce of spare flesh on his lean body to conceal the perfect musculature of his body, the strength of his shoulders, the muscular slabs across his flat belly.

'Now you, I think.'

An expression of purpose stamped on his lean face, he applied himself, first to her camisole, which was disposed of in one slick motion. He paused then for a moment, staring with a mixture of stark greed and reverence at her hard-tipped breasts, purring out a low, stomach-shuddering, '*Perfect*,' before removing her seriously damp shorts.

She was quivering as he then arranged his long length beside her and, with one hand between her legs, he pulled her up against him hard, his hand between them as he focused his carnal campaign on the wet aching folds between her legs.

The first skin-to-skin contact drew a shocked long, low moan from her parted lips and she pushed her small breasts against the solidity of his warm chest. Then, as his clever fingers slid over her slickness, teasing the delicate folds and tight, aching nub, she lost all sense of self. There was just the pleasure and the ache.

When the rhythm stopped, she let out a small cry of protest but was quickly distracted. Ezio was kissing and licking his way down her body, drawing keening moans of pleasure as he left a tingling trail that went deeper than the surface, it went to her very core.

Her heavy-lidded eyes opened; his body was curved over her.

'Oh my God, you are so perfect...' she breathed, placing her palms against his chest, spreading her fingers, feeling the thud of his heart, the satiny texture of his skin.

His face was all sharp, fierce angles, the sybaritic line of his cheekbones drawn knife-sharp by the bands of colour scoring the crests. Her fingertips slid with growing confidence over the hard slabs of his stomach before she slid lower, pausing for a moment in her carnal exploration as he sucked in a sharp breath, her tongue caught between her teeth.

Then she reached the hard column of his erection and tightened her fingers, feeling the throb of his silky-smooth shaft.

'Later...not now... Now I need to be inside you, Tilda,' he rasped. 'I need to have you tight around me.'

Kneeling over her, her face between his big hands, he rained kisses on every inch of her skin before he finally claimed her mouth. As he kissed her with a wild passion she equally matched, she felt as though he'd drain her.

Resting on his elbows, he lowered himself slowly and teasingly, first against her belly and then the mound of her sex, making her back arch. Only his hands on the crest of her hips kept her grounded.

His powerful chest was heaving, as though he was fighting against some invisible barrier to draw in air, the barely repressed raw wildness in his face exciting her more than she would have thought possible. The danger in him was an aphrodisiac, yet his touch as he ran a thumb down her cheek was so gentle, tender, a sharp contrast to the passion.

Fighting the urge to take her right here, right now, he battled to contain the madness that was consuming him. Those little throaty sounds coming from her parted lips, and the wanton glow in her green eyes, were sense-and self-sapping.

This was a kind of madness he had never experienced before.

Still kissing, he reached for the trousers that lay in a heap on the floor beside the sofa, pausing only to swear when his fingers did not immediately locate the foil package in the pocket, and grunting when he did.

She'd have begged him to take her, but her vocal cords wouldn't work; she was just a mass of craving, screaming nerve endings. But it was OK; she didn't need to beg or plead.

There was no pain, just a blissful sense of relief as her body expanded and adapted to accommodate him.

He sank into her, slow and careful, feeling the pulsing of her tight body around him, aware that this was all new to her. He always satisfied his lovers—it was matter of pride for him, and he gained pleasure from their enjoyment—but this was different.

This wanting to make it good for her was more... The emotion that he had excised with surgical precision from the sex act was back...not that this complication mattered to him in the slightest at that moment. All that mattered was Tilda, her heat, the rightness of being inside her.

Her head tucked into his shoulder, where he breathed words of encouragement, and other words which she couldn't translate but still excited her. Clutching his sweat-slicked back, she met his thrusts, sinking into herself with him until nothing existed as the pressure built inside her.

She felt aware of every individual nerve ending, floating feet above the ground at the same time, then as her muscles clenched around him she found herself striving for something just out of her reach, encouraged by the throaty, raw and often indecent coaxing in her ear.

Then she was falling, flickering lights behind her eyelids as nerve endings fired, the heat bathing every contracting muscle in her body as she felt him thrust into her one last time before he collapsed on top of her.

She enjoyed his weight for a few moments before he rolled off her. Wedged in the narrow space between him and the back of the sofa, she turned onto her side and curled against his body.

After a moment he started to stroke her hair. She sighed and kissed the damp skin of his chest. 'What are you thinking about?' she asked when their breathing patterns had slowed.

Ezio was avoiding thinking; if ever there was a moment for living in the moment, this was it.

'I am thinking that we should do that properly in a bed.'

'I think I like improper,' she said, her cheeks heating at her own audacity.

'*Theos*, I was definitely getting that impression too, *yineka mou*. Let us go and explore the improper possibilities a bed offers.'

CHAPTER TEN

'RELAX, HE'LL BE FINE,' Ezio said, placing his hand on the small of Tilda's back. He had adapted his stride to her heels and the disparity between their inside leg measurements as they walked towards the car. 'And don't look back.'

She flashed him a look. The last time he had said 'relax' had been earlier that morning, when he had revealed that they were having lunch in Athens at a world-renowned restaurant as the guest of Saul and his wife.

He had chosen his moment pretty well. Tilda had been quite mellow, having woken up to a naked man who, it turned out, *was* the sex god the tabloids called him, looking as though he wanted to eat her.

The next reveal had been made after he had doubled down on the 'sex god' thing and stopped her detaching herself from the post-coital warmth of his body, reminding her that Sam's induction day didn't start until eleven-thirty.

She hadn't needed that much persuading.

'There might be a few others at lunch...' He had dropped this additional information while stroking her back.

The rest of the information had had been extracted

slowly, and when Tilda had the full picture of what her day would entail she had leapt out of bed. The full guest list for the *casual little* lunch party made it obvious that that it would be neither casual nor little.

Sitting at the table with them would be a UK government minister and his wife, a well-known journalist and his husband and a couple of highly placed Greek officials, and she assumed their partners, along with the inventor of an eco-fuel and, last but not least, an actor-director of award-winning films. His equally successful beautiful wife was away shooting on location.

'How could you do this to me?' She didn't wait for a response; she'd had plenty of time to get ready for a meeting with a headmaster, but now this... Now she had to find an outfit that was acceptable for *both* occasions. She had finally settled on understated. She glanced down, experiencing a quiver of uncertainty at her choice.

The shift she was wearing was a smoky-grey silk mixture, high at the neck with a high waistline, tiny pleats stopping it from being figure-hugging.

The fabric was butter-soft and it was classic, short but not indecently so; she could live with the amount of leg it revealed.

Navy rather than silver, and soft suede rather than leather, the heels she wore today were similar in style to the ones that Ezio had removed last night... The memory sent a rush of warmth through her body and stoked the phantom feeling low in her belly. It was as if, even though he wasn't inside her, her body was reluctant to let go of the feeling.

Her thoughts drifted... If she'd had an ounce of sense, she wouldn't have let it happen. She knew she was heading for massive hurt; the measure of her madness was she'd make the same choice again—she'd take that reckless step into the unknown.

There had been moments during the morning when she'd felt as though she were still falling and a sense of unreality would hit her, almost as if she were living someone else's life.

She felt lighter, somehow, as if the responsibilities that had been resting on her shoulders had lifted. She knew it was only temporary but she was going to enjoy it while it lasted... She was going to enjoy Ezio and explore this hitherto unexpected sensual side of her personality that he had revealed.

She hardly recognised the person she was becoming, the things she was feeling. It was if some invisible protective film had been peeled away from her skin... The image of long, brown fingers peeling layers of clothing off her skin that appeared in tandem with the thought sent a surge of heat through her body.

A moment later, the heat was surging again!

'You look very beautiful.'

'God, you make me sound like a trophy wife!'

His brows lifted at her spiky response. 'You and those compliments...why do you deflect them? And *trophy*? You are no one's trophy. You are your own woman.'

Blinking at the compliment, she wondered, did she really *deflect* them?

She was her own woman, but surrendering to him and her own sensuality had given her another sense of power. Who would have thought that surrender could be so liberating?

Once inside the car, it purred to life.

'Is it far?'

'No, not far.'

'Do you think that he, Saul, is he testing…?'

'I think this is lunch.'

She flashed a look of irritation at his perfect profile. 'I don't see how you are so calm. This matters to you— it matters enough to marry me!'

'Relax or people will think we have just had a lover's tiff.'

'Is that why you slept with me, to make things look more realistic?'

She knew she'd made him angry, but she couldn't bring herself to apologise. After all, it was a legitimate question, it wasn't as if he lacked anything in the ruthlessness department.

'You think I manipulated you into my bed?'

She shook her head and lifted her chin. 'No, you didn't take me anywhere I didn't want to go.' She sensed some of the tension in his powerful shoulders slacken.

'You took me some places too.' *Life-changing places,* said the voice in his head, which he determinedly ignored. 'Don't over-think this. We are enjoying quite spectacular sex for six months. I don't see a bad side, do you?' he said, the comments meant for himself as much as her. His eyes swivelled sideways for a split second before he added, almost against his will, 'I slept with you because I couldn't *not* sleep with you. I hate these social things too—just be yourself at lunch.'

'Have you known Saul long?'

It was hard to make ordinary conversation with Ezio words *couldn't not* playing on a loop in her head.

'In a way. Years ago, I applied for a job with him. Let's just say that my background did not do me any favours. He started with nothing, and he's justly proud of the fact—and also fond of reminding people of the fact. He sent me packing.'

'So taking his company is your way of payback?'

'Is that what you think?' He shrugged and then thought, why shouldn't she think that? 'There is no *taking* involved.' He was paying a good price, or he would be, if Saul could move past his ancient feud with George Baros. Did either of them remember what had started it? Probably, and they had spent the years since polishing their enmity. 'I do not allow emotion to get in the way of good business. Revenge is the flipside of sentimentality; I don't allow either to cloud my judgement...unlike Saul. but I understand his suspicions.'

'But you said he was paranoid.'

'He is, but as they say, just because you are paranoid does not mean there is no conspiracy. A man who trusts too easily is a fool.'

'Do you ever trust anyone? Sorry, I didn't mean...'

'No offence taken. I don't even trust my own instinct sometimes.'

The plan had seemed so safe—*she* had seemed so safe—and now the goal posts had been shifted. Outside the office, his PA was something very different, and without warning. In his bed, she was all his dreams and fantasies made real.

If he hurt her, he'd hate himself...but would it stop him hurting her? Ezio knew himself well enough to doubt it. Tilda aroused his dormant protective instincts, but the irony was, the only thing she needed protecting from was him.

'Why were you looking for a job?' she asked, puzzled.

'My father does not do second chances. He kicked me out, so between them Saul and my father are responsible for my success. They wouldn't give me a job, so I made my own. I started my own company and in four years was in a position to buy out the family firm.'

He down-played the achievement but Tilda, who knew all about his meteoric rise, knew better. 'Your father sounds…'

'Oh, he is worse, much worse!' Ezio's laughter held no humour. 'He made my mother's life a misery, and as they say the apple doesn't fall too far from the tree.'

He could tell from her expression that she had heard the warning. He owed her that much; he didn't want her thinking that he was something he wasn't.

He felt a sudden wild urge of longing for his life as it had been—ordered, calm and he not responsible for anyone but himself… He felt protective of her now; he felt… He wouldn't even let himself think the word buried deep in his heart. He would always revert to type; he knew this.

'You're dying to ask what I did that was so bad to make my father sack me, aren't you?'

'No!' she lied.

'I fell in love.' The cynicism in his voice was bitter enough to sour sugar. 'It turned out the love of my life was only interested in pillow talk. She passed on the secrets I spilled to a rival company. I was a ridiculous young fool.'

'She was the one you…?'

'Yes, I proposed to.' *You started this, Ezio, so there's no point moaning that she has run with it.* He was going to have to rein in this impulse to open up to her.

One sentence, but it explained so much. Her emotions high, she felt her eyes fill with tears. 'Oh, God, that's…'

'A learning experience that has stood me in good stead.'

Tilda didn't know which one she hated most—the fa-

ther who'd discarded his son, or the woman who had
used him. Both had made him the man he was today...
Because of his trust issues, he had built a ten-feet wall
around his emotions.

'I feel sorry for Saul.' Maybe because he could be Saul
in thirty years' time. 'None of his children have any interest in the legacy...which of course plays in my favour;
if they did, there is no way he'd be selling. This is his
way of making sure that what he created carries on and
he can still be a part of it.'

His bleak outlook brought a frown to her brow. 'But
your children might not feel that way...'

'A father—me...?' His rich laughter had a hard edge.
'Can you *really* see that, Tilda?'

She could, and the image in her head of Ezio playing with a dark-haired baby broke her heart. She nursed
the secret hurt to herself and said with quiet sincerity,
'You've been good for Sam, you've helped him a lot. I
think you'd make a good father.'

The restaurant was not large, and outside there was nothing to suggest it was anything special except for the up-
market cars in the car park. Inside it was all exposed
brick and industrial furniture, with some probably very
expensive modern art on the walls.

All the tables were full. Tilda did not feel over-
dressed—though perhaps under-jewelled. They were
met by the *maître d'*, who obviously knew Ezio. As they
walked through, conversation stopped and heads turned,
eyes following the progress of the tall, dynamic figure
she walked beside. It was a bizarre experience for Tilda,
but she supposed a normal day at the office, or on this
occasion outside it, for Ezio.

They were led outdoors where there was a series of intimate courtyards, clearly much coveted by A-listers. Saul, it seemed, had commandeered an entire courtyard for the lunch party.

The *maître d'* left them at the ivy-covered arch that led into their courtyard and gestured with a smile, adding, 'You are the last to arrive.'

'Oh, God… I feel sick.'

'You're hyper-ventilating.'

'No, I'm taking deep, calming breaths.' *Just too many and too fast.* She squared her shoulders and tried not to think of Ezio being a perfect father. 'I'll be fine.'

He laid his hands on her shoulders. 'You don't look fine. You look like you have something uncomfortable shoved up—'

'Ezio!'

His grin appeared. 'Better, but you still don't look like a woman on her honeymoon.' He bent his head and kissed her long and hard. As he drew back, she felt the hair she had spent an age arranging in a really sleek knot tumble free.

Her mouth opened in a silent 'O' of shock.

'Now, that is *definitely* better. If I had a table here right now to bend you over…!'

He gave her a gentle push towards the table, just at the same time as she promised Ezio, in a voice that upheld her drama teacher's opinion that she had excellent projection, that she would kill him.

Hair spilling down her back, she saw the faces at the table looking their way, and her sense of humour kicked in; she started to laugh.

Ezio smiled as soon as he heard the contagious deep, throaty sound. He knew she had the room in the palm of her little hand… He thought about being in the palm of her hand himself and it took him a few moments to follow her to the table.

Their host stood behind her chair and Tilda spoke to the entire table. 'Sorry about that. I spent hours on my hair and…' She nodded to Ezio.

'I prefer it loose,' he said with one of his 'devil on steroids' grins that had every female at the tables sighing into their wine glasses as he took his seat.

Introductions were made and Tilda settled back into her seat, her eyes meeting Ezio's across the table. He winked. The man was shameless, she decided, but he had helped her out—which didn't mean she wasn't going to kill him later… Her lids lowered, hiding the gleam there as she added silently, *or something?*

Ezio sat back, feeling very much a passenger and quite enjoying the experience as he watched his wife charm the table.

Men watched her and envied him. Women envied her a little, but responded to her natural warmth and the fact that her interest in what they said was utterly unfeigned.

She was the genuine article in a room of imitations. She shone and he felt…*proud?*

He had very little interaction with Saul until they were about to leave. The older man leaned in and said quietly, 'I know I offended Tilda, but I hope she has forgiven me and she enjoyed the flowers? Oh, and tell her that I've had a word with Murphy, and he is really interested in her idea.'

'That wasn't too bad.'

'Belt up.' Ezio backed up until he heard the car's warning bleep. 'You were the star turn and everyone there, including me, knew it.'

'Don't be stupid!'

'There you go with rejecting those compliments again… What I want to know is, how did Saul offend you? And how do you know Doyle Murphy?'

'Offend…? Oh… He phoned and, well, he sent me some flowers, and I phoned to thank him but he was fishing, and he asked me if I minded that you slept around and I… I said you didn't, or wouldn't. I had my fingers crossed, but I must have been good, because he apologised. I always knew you'd, well, not be celibate, but I just never thought you'd not be celibate with me.'

'And you are OK with that?'

'You know I'm very OK with that, Ezio, and I don't need any warnings. I know this is just sex.' Sadly, for him it would never be more. He was the wrong man for her, she knew that, but being with him felt so right.

Aware that the dissatisfaction that settled over him was an irrational response to her pragmatic little statement, he drove on in silence for a few minutes.

'And Murphy?' The Irish former racing driver turned entrepreneur was not someone he had ever worked with.

'You read his autobiography…? He cared for his mum who had cancer, and his three brothers and sisters, so Saul thought… I asked Saul for some advice. I thought I might start a charity that would help…'

He listened to her animatedly explain the ideas that were literally bubbling up in her.

'So you went to Saul?'

'He is on the boards of several charities and—'

'So am I.'

'You were busy and I…well…in six months' time I am going to have money and not much to do. I can hardly go back to work for you, can I?'

He said nothing, unwilling to own even to himself that the idea that *somehow* she would remain in his life was even in his head. 'So you have been planning ahead.' For a life without him.

His life would be without Tilda... The bleak, dark future seemed to stretch out into the distance.

'So do you think it's good idea?'

He fought the infinitely childish impulse to retort *would it matter what he thought,* and nodded. 'I think anything you do will be successful and if you need any help, which obviously seems doubtful, let me know.'

'There he is!' Tilda bounced in her seat when she saw her brother, who was talking to an older boy. When he caught sight of them he waved, said something to the other boy, who laughed, then jogged across to where they had parked.

'How was it?'

'It was...' Sam began deadpan then he grinned. 'Amazing!'

The tension left her shoulders as she sagged in relief.

'Tell us about it.'

After five minutes, she was really regretting asking the question.

She took advantage of a lull by inserting, 'Maybe I should have asked you what you didn't like about it.'

'Nothing, only...'

Tilda twisted round in her seat. 'What?'

'The thing is, nearly everyone boards, and if you're going to be in the chess club and other stuff, well, the day boys miss out on a lot.'

It took a few seconds, but when she processed what he meant she was shocked. 'You want to board?'

'I'd be home every weekend.'

Ezio glanced at Tilda's face. 'How about we discuss this later?'

Sam went straight to the pool the moment they arrived back. From where she sat with Ezio under the shade of a group of lemon trees, she could hear him splashing. She nodded her thanks to the housekeeper as Sybil set down a tray of iced tea.

'I can't believe he wants to board.'

'But you're going let him?'

'It feels like if I was enough…a better…he wouldn't want to go. He's always been… You think I smother him, don't you? You think this will be good for him.'

'Is that what you think?'

She nodded. 'I suppose so,' she admitted with a rueful shrug. 'I'm going to have to let him go, aren't I?'

'You don't have to, but I think you will, because you always put Sam ahead of yourself.'

Before she could respond, Sam appeared dripping with a phone in his hand.

'You two are trending!'

'Don't be stupid,' Tilda said.

'No, *really!*' he insisted, waving the phone while dripping on Tilda's shoes.

'He's right,' Ezio said quietly.

'Let me see,' she snapped, holding out her hand to Sam for the phone.

The image on the screen made her freeze in shock. The blossoms floating around them and the shaft of light filtering through the trees gave the photo an other-worldly quality. Her face was between Ezio's hands and they were kissing. They looked like two people in love, but Tilda knew that this description only applied to one…

She was in love with him and always had been. It was like suddenly noticing an oak tree growing in the middle of her living room: it had always been there; she'd just been walking around it.

'Watch it!' Sam warned, rescuing his phone from her limp grasp. 'That's my life there,' he reproached, jogging back in the direction of the pool.

'You have gone very quiet.'

'You knew?'

'Jake sent it to me, yes.'

'And you didn't think to tell me?'

'It's a good photo, Tilda.'

'Yes, Jake is very good.' *And I am an idiot.*

'He never did take the photo *with* your glasses. I've noticed you have not been wearing them. Have you mislaid them?'

Her green eyes flicked guiltily from side to side but, before she could decide whether to lie or tell the truth about her need for glasses, Sam appeared like a whirlwind and grabbed the towel he had left crumpled on the floor.

'It's OK, she doesn't really need them, it's to make her look older and make bosses take her seriously,' he informed them cheekily.

Ezio waited until Sam had vanished before speaking. 'Is that true?'

She shrugged and found herself wishing that she had her glasses to hide behind.

'So they were props! It's no big thing. I looked young.'

'You are young.' Had she really thought the glasses

made her look older? He felt a surge of anger that she'd even felt the need to change her behaviour for her bosses.

'As I said, I looked younger than I am, and it's hard to be taken seriously. I got used to them, they made me feel more confident, and now... I don't need them.' The realisation made her smile.

'I can see that,' he said, looking at the lovely warm woman smiling at him.

'I thought I might work from here for a few days,' he threw out casually, and watched the initial surprise on her face morph into a guarded expression. 'If there are any issues with Sam, I should be here.' It was an explanation about the emotions he was wrestling with he could accept. It made total sense when he factored in that, by the time Sam was settled, this thing would have burnt itself out and he could step back into his life pre-Tilda.

It was a totally logical decision.

'Do you think there will be issues?' she said sharply.

'No, but if there is you might need someone to blame, and it will rather defeat the object of this exercise if I leave my bride before the honeymoon is over. Saul is a man of his generation and very traditional.'

Was it traditional to marry four...five times? she wondered as her shoulders slumped. 'Do you think he has spies planted?' she sniped, gnawing delicately at her full lower lip and drawing his eyes to the lush outline. 'Sorry; I used up all my sparkling charm at lunch. My face was aching with smiling. And when I don't sleep much, I'm cranky.' She closed her eyes... *Did I really just say that?*

'Neither did I, but me? I'm hungry.'

She gasped and her eyes flew wide.

'I hope you've used plenty of sunscreen.' The words were innocuous but the expression in his dark eyes was not. Her stomach went into instant free fall and as she squirmed a little in her chair she was painfully aware of the ache between her legs.

'Always—but actually, I tan quite easily. I got my mum's eyes—she was half-Irish—but my dad's colouring.'

He nodded. Even after the short time exposed to the sun her smooth skin was already tinged with a golden glow that made the green of her eyes even more dramatic.

'I noticed,' he said, thinking of the faint demarcation lines hidden under her clothes he had enjoyed discovering last night, and the tasty gold dusting of freckles on her skin dark against the protected, vulnerable pale parts of her slim body.

The image sent a fresh streak of heat through his already aroused body.

The best way to stop this obsessing about sex, or at least sex with one particular woman, was not to deprive himself of it, he decided, privately likening the deprivation to someone who was dieting but could think of nothing else but food.

The logic might not survive scientific scrutiny but Ezio was not feeling scientific; he was feeling the sort of desperation that he had never experienced in his life.

It had always come easy for him. Women had not often refused him, and the possibility of them doing so had not concerned him; the idea of rejection had never bothered him.

And now it did.

He had broken his own rules, and the hell of it was she couldn't wait to do it again. It wasn't her vulnerability that should have put her off-limits, it was the fact that he was *aware* of that vulnerability that made warning lights flash.

'I know you're worried about Sam boarding—'

She cut across him. 'I know you don't want to play happy families, Ezio, you just want sex…but it just so happens that I do too, so it's all good, isn't it? We don't have to pretend.' If only that were true, she thought with a sigh

'That sounds cold, Tilda.'

'You were pretty cold to your girlfriends.'

'I really don't think they were looking for kindness. They were looking for sex, a headline to help a career, or a chapter in their tell-all biography, and not necessarily in that order.'

His analysis was probably pretty accurate but she also found it chilling. 'But didn't you ever want…*more* than that?'

'Like *love*?'

'How about liking…friendship?'

'If I want friendship, I'll get a dog,' he said, not even believing himself as he looked ahead. Sam would soon be gone, and soon Tilda would be too; she was building her life without him. *It's what you wanted, isn't it?* Ezio mocked the voice in his head.

CHAPTER ELEVEN

HE TOOK THE steps up to his office two at a time, aware as he dialled into the video meeting with the board that the sight of him without a tie was going to raise a few brows. He hadn't had time to change; the traffic getting to the suburb where the parents of Sam's friend lived had been snarled up for miles.

The boys had not noticed. The spontaneous trip away to the mountain cabin and the construction of a very smoky fire seemed to have made them both happy. Sam had been nagging to go and experience '*off-grid* life', as he put it, ever since Ezio had mentioned his trips up there with his grandfather.

He'd been relying on Tilda refusing permission, but rather to his surprise she had given the plan the green light—but then, Tilda had been a little distant this last week. If that distance had extended to their bedroom, he might have suspected she was cooling off, but she wasn't. She was still the most exciting and uninhibited lover he had ever had.

And that was what mattered, wasn't it? The sex was incredible and she was not clinging…what more could he want? He ought to be actively not wanting more. *More* involved the sort of complications that would turn his life upside down, and his life was just one long complication.

He was constantly dodging and burying his feelings, but they refused to stay buried... He sighed, caught the scent of her perfume in the air and tuned out of the meeting for a full thirty seconds before coming back, like a man coming up for air, with a curse that turned the air blue.

It was a productive meeting *after* he had cut short all the congratulatory remarks that threatened to take up half the allowed time.

'Thank you for your good wishes! Yes, I'm married, yes, it is business as usual—so let's move on, shall we?'

After that, they whipped through the agenda at a speed that seemed to fluster some members, but Ezio didn't see much point hanging around. There were places he'd prefer to be and people...well, *one* person...he'd like to be with.

He knew where she was. Halfway through the meeting, he'd seen the distant figure of his temporary wife on the path that led to the private beach, wearing something long and floaty that he imagined himself removing. His groin was still heavy from the testosterone-charged surge he had been helpless to control.

Helplessness was not normally a feeling he suffered, but there were exceptions. A specific one came to mind, along with an image of him lying helpless while Tilda, her clever little hands and even cleverer mouth slowly seduced him.

He'd married Matilda and he'd got Tilda, and Tilda, with her green eyes and sharp tongue, didn't let him get away with a thing—she challenged him on everything, sometimes he suspected just for the hell of it.

The thought should not have made him smile but it did…she had clearly spent the last four years disapproving of him and now she didn't have to hide it. His little puritan with the hungry eyes… She was a mass of contradictions.

Seeing himself through those eyes was not the most comfortable feeling in the world for someone who didn't care about the opinion of others.

His phone bleeped. It was head of Sam's academy, asking if he'd agree to be involved with a fund raiser, and the hell of it was he heard himself agreeing.

Three weeks married and he had probably reduced the salary of half the hacks on the continent, he decided, self-mockery tugging one corner of his mouth upwards.

Tilda pulled the silk kaftan over her head and laid it on top of the bag containing her towel before she kicked off her flat woven sandals. The sand was hot under foot as she ran down to the water's edge and stood for a few moments, training her senses to the sound of the waves and trying to shut out the chaos in her head.

After taking the pregnancy test, the initial relief had worn off and she was aware of a troubling sadness that she couldn't shake. Obviously *not* being pregnant was a good thing, but there was a small part of her that felt… Oh God, she didn't know how she was feeling—not panic, at least, which was how she'd been feeling all week.

She was just late, not pregnant, and she didn't have to tell Ezio, who was always so incredibly careful with her in that way.

'It's a good thing!' she yelled at the ocean.

But not a happy ending. There could be no happy endings for a woman who had fallen in love with Ezio, she had finally accepted that. She wanted to be the mother to babies Ezio didn't want…not with her, at least.

Unless that woman's idea of happiness was seeing the man she loved lose interest, cheat or move on.

Her chin firmed. It would be hard to feel sympathy for a woman with such self-destructive impulses, she concluded as she waded in deeper until the warm water lapped around her waist before she dove into and under the first wave.

She thought back to how her dad had taught her to swim on their Cornwall summer holidays. His '*water baby mermaid*', he had called her. The water she swam through now bore no resemblance to the icy, toe-numbing Atlantic dips of her childhood. She enjoyed the embrace of the warmth as, head-down, she struck out.

She paused when she reached a point that was not too far out and began to swim parallel to the shore. Coming to the end of an imaginary lane line, she duck-dived, as sleek as a seal, and swam back. The monotony of the action slowly emptied her mind and finally the strength in her legs.

Flipping over onto her back, she lay there, arms spread, just giving the occasional kick to stay afloat. Eyes closed, she could still see the filtered sun overhead through the paper-thin covering of her eyelids, a hazy glow.

It was tempting to stay that way, but she knew the dangers of exposing herself to the midday sun. She flipped back and, treading water, pushed the hanks of saturated hair from her face.

The villa probably didn't have a bad angle, but the view of the white marble walls from this vantage point was pretty spectacular; the modern, sea-facing lower level that led out to the gorgeously groomed terraces and the spectacular infinity pool was probably seen at its best from the ocean.

The only person who had a better view than her at that moment was the person on the small red sailing boat she could see on the horizon. She waved, even though she knew he couldn't see her, and struck out for the shore.

If Ezio had been in his office in the square tower, he'd have been able to see her. The thought made her lose her rhythm and go under. Swallowing a mouthful of salt water, she surfaced, coughing. If she was honest with herself, the reason she often chose the sea for her swim in preference to the infinity pool was the excellent view of it Ezio had from his eyrie. She liked the idea of him watching her. She loved the idea of him not being able to take his eyes off her...*while it lasted.*

No, she would not go there. She was determined to extract every last second of pleasure from being with him, and she already had a lot of memories stored away to look back on and probably cry over later.

By the time she walked out of the shallows, her legs were shaking. She was reflecting on her levels of fitness, or at least lack of them, as she walked up the sand to the spot where she had left her bag. She gathered her hair in her fist and, deftly twisting it into a rope, squeezed out some of the excess moisture.

Dropping on her knees beside the towel, she slung her hair back and automatically tightened the clip, holding one earring in and then going to the other.

'Oh, God!' she cried, desperately patting her bare ear as though it could materialise.

* * *

From where he stood watching, at the point where the cypress trees met the sand, Ezio watched her increasingly frenzied fingertip-search of the immediate area.

By the time he reached her she was walking, head bent, trying to follow her own footprints in the sand that were fast disappearing as it dried.

'What is wrong?'

She straightened on the sea edge and spun round. Ezio was standing there looking gorgeous. She felt a surge of irrational relief, as if him just being there could make things all right.

She watched as a sudden breeze caused the strands of well-cut dark hair to blow flat against his skull, and the hem of the black T-shirt he was wearing flutter and lift, revealing a slice of flat brown belly. Then, as the wind direction shifted, it was pulled tight against his body, revealing the sinewy strength of his powerful shoulders. Had she wanted to trace the corrugated ridge of muscles across his washboard-flat belly, she could have.

The initial weird flutter of misplaced relief when she'd seen him was swiftly replaced by a much more sane dismay. She had lost her earring!

'What are you doing here?'

His hooded eyes moved in a slow sweep up her body, from her feet to her face.

'Have you lost something?'

'Yes.'

'Are you going to tell me what?'

'Just being a bit of a drama queen is all,' she said, not quite meeting his eyes.

'You are many things but not a drama queen.'

He watched as she blinked to clear the tears that pooled in her emerald eyes, biting down hard on her quivering lip.

'I lost it,' she croaked out.

Her distress touched him in a part of his heart he'd thought was dead. He walked across and placed his hands on her shoulders, aware of the warm smoothness of her skin as she continued to shiver violently as he pulled her into his body.

'Calm down...look at me!' he said, cupping a hand under her chin and gently turning her tear-stained, tragic face up to his. Something tightened in his chest as he studied the purity of her features. 'Good...now, lost what?'

He could see the muscles in her throat work overtime to contain a sob that was fighting to escape. 'My earring.'

'Your mother's earring,' he realised, pulling her in tight against him.

'Yeah—stupid, I know.' She gulped. 'Not like it's worth a million dollars.'

'It's worth more to you.' His hands slid down her arms and, as he pushed her away from him and looked down into her face, he felt something kick hard in his chest.

He had never embarked on any project without weighing all possible outcomes, but he really hadn't seen this one coming, recognising the swell of protective tenderness for what it was. So much for his *perfect* solution—'no down side' he'd told himself, beyond the fact that he'd be losing the best PA he'd ever had.

There were other PAs, he'd told himself.

There was no other Tilda.

A fresh wave of heat seared through his already

aroused body as his eyes slid over her slim figure, the black Lycra concealing enough to excite the imagination and revealing enough to entice the senses. The stark black was the perfect foil to her pale gold-tinged skin, and the swimsuit itself cut high on the thigh emphasised the slim length of her slender legs. It clung to her narrow ribcage and narrow waist, showed off the delicate, carved perfection of her collar bones and displayed her tight, high, perfect small breasts.

She'd hidden all that, but it wasn't just her physicality she had been concealing. His PA had always had a mind and an opinion of her own but she no longer felt the need to be subtle.

'It's just, I don't have much left that was Mum's. She didn't have much jewellery, but the rest… While we were at the funeral someone broke into the house and took it.'

She lifted her head as Ezio released a string of curses. He looked pretty awesome mad, and he was mad at that moment.

'I know,' she said when he paused for breath. 'Utter callous bastards… Apparently they had quite a thing going—they read the funeral notices and knew when the house would be empty.'

'They were caught?' Ezio asked grimly.

She nodded. 'Yes, but not much was recovered, which is why…' She twirled the remaining earring, a gold stud with a small baroque pearl-drop. 'Ah, well, it is what it is…' She attempted a chuckle, fell short and produced something approaching a strangled croak. 'I must have looked crazy, crawling around like that! My own fault for wearing them, really. I should have kept them safe, but Mum always said, what was the point saving things for "best"?'

As she sketched inverted commas in the air, she realised that the concept probably meant nothing to him.
Pretty things, like pretty women, were all disposable to
him. What did he hold precious? she wondered.

'You mother sounds like she had a healthy outlook
on life.'

A slow, reflective smile lit up her face. Lost in the
memories, she didn't notice his sharp intake of breath.

'She did. Mum was always a "glass half-full" person,
and she'd have said it is just a thing…things don't make
you happy.' Her slender shoulders lifted in a shrug. 'It's
gone,' she said, sounding a lot more philosophical than
she felt. 'I could have lost it absolutely anywhere…prob-
ably when I was swimming.'

'You're a little mermaid.'

He watched her eyes fill with tears. 'What…did something happen on your trip to Athens?'

Nothing, except I know I'm not carrying your baby.
She had convinced herself, and she'd been so convinced
that when the test had come up negative she had repeated
it twice before she believed the results—not pregnant,
just late.

The tears began to leak and she brushed them away.
'No, it's just my dad used to call me that… Oh, hell, I
don't know what's wrong with me.' She did—she loved
him.

'Oh, Tilda, I'm sorry.'

'Heavens…' She sniffed. 'You have no need to be
sorry, you're just—' She closed her mouth over the 'perfect' she had been about to say and belatedly became
aware that the thin wet Lycra of her swimsuit offered
very little concealment of her nipples, which had sprouted
to pebble-hard prominence. She half-lifted her arms to

cover herself, before the utter ridiculousness of her self-consciousness hit her.

This was a man who had seen and explored every inch of her body.

'What…?' She watched as he kicked off his shoes.

'What are you doing? You're wearing your clothes…'

'If I find your earring—'

'That's not possible…it could be anywhere.'

'You have freckles,' he said, brushing a finger across the gold-tinted skin of her nose. 'If I find it you owe me…'

'Owe you what?' He already had her heart and soul; there wasn't a hell of a lot left, she thought dismally.

His wicked grin glimmered on his bronze face. 'Oh, I'll think of something.'

Standing on the shore, a hand shading her eyes, she watched as he waded in until the water was chest-deep before he dived under. He was down so long that she had actually started to wade in herself when he reappeared, his dark hair saturated. He raised a hand and dived straight back under.

It was a process that he repeated, and actually she lost count. She had called out for him to stop several times but, if he'd heard her, he'd ignored her.

She was contemplating swimming out to him to put a stop to this craziness when he reappeared but didn't go back down. Instead, he struck out strongly for the shore.

He stood up and started to wade towards her, making her think of some sea god rising from the waves. Then as he got closer she saw the glint of something in his hand.

She jumped up and down in the shallows.

'I don't believe it! I don't believe it.'

She waded out to meet him and snatched the earring

from his fingers. He caught her by the waist and swung her around.

Held high above him, she curved down and took his face between her hands, raining kisses on his wet brown face. 'Oh, thank you. I have no idea how… It was impossible… Oh, you beautiful man, I *love* you!' The laughter faded from his face. 'Not literally, obviously.'

The look vanished but she sensed caution in his eyes as he planted her back on her feet. Together they walked up the sand and reached where her possessions lay. Tilda went to bend to retrieve them and stopped as she felt his hands on her breasts, cupping and kneading them through the fabric as he stepped in close, allowing her to feel the full strength of his arousal as he pressed into her back as his thumbs traced the bold projection of her aching nipples.

Her back arched as he continued to massage her breasts and slide his tongue up the length of her exposed neck. He turned her round and she lifted her passion-glazed eyes to his face, mesmerised by the mask of primitive need she saw. He looked almost in pain as he took the earring from her fingers and with elaborate care put it back in her earlobe, leaving behind a million whispering, silken threads of painful sensation.

'It's a miracle.'

'I think you're a miracle,' he rasped, and her heartbeat escalated.

He kissed her then, not fiercely, but with deep, drugging kisses that left her feeling limp and languid. Dizzying desire swirled through her as he picked her up and carried her up the beach to where the pines met the sand. There he laid her down gently in the shade.

He knelt there, drinking her in before he slowly slid

the straps of her swimsuit down her shoulders. A few seconds later, she was naked.

'You're beautiful.'

'So are you,' she whispered back, watching through closed eyelids as he stripped off his tee shirt, pulling it over his head to reveal the sleek, hard muscles of his torso. A moment later his wet jeans were gone too.

Just looking at him, standing there shamelessly aroused, took her to the brink.

Ezio brought her back to that place several times as he spent time moving down her body, touching her everywhere, his mouth and fingers finding secret places and nerve-endings where she hadn't known they existed.

When he did slide between her parted legs, his kisses tasted of her.

'*Theos*, you are so tight and wet,' he groaned, moving slowly until, urged on by her cries, the urgency pumping through him, he thrust in hard, continuing the carnal onslaught until her muscles tightened around him and he let himself go.

It wasn't until a few moments later as their sweat-slicked bodies lay entwined that he realised what he had done.

Tilda sensed his withdrawal.

She rolled on her stomach to look at his face.

'I'm sorry,' he said, self-recrimination written into the drawn lines of his face.

'What for?' He was about to tell he'd slept with someone... She was so convinced that when he did explain, despite the seriousness, she almost laughed.

'I didn't use protection. It was...there is not much point saying sorry, is there?'

Tilda pulled herself up into a sitting position.

'It happened, and I am at least partly to blame, but, well…' she said, 'really, it isn't *that* time of my cycle… Well, actually, I'm already really very late, so the likelihood is not zero but low. You might have noticed that I've been—'

'I noticed.'

'That's why I went into Athens today—not for retail therapy. I bought a test and it was negative. I'm not pregnant, so you can relax, and as for the future, well…'

He cut across her. 'But you thought you were?'

'I was a bit worried,' she admitted. 'Though you've always been very…considerate.'

'Not today I wasn't.'

'No, well, I suppose these things happen.'

He was suddenly on his feet, dragging on his clothes. 'Not to me they don't!'

An icy stone inside her chest, Tilda jumped to her feet and began to pull on her wet swimsuit. She had got the fabric as far as her waist when he turned around. His eyes dropped to the coral-tipped peaks of her breasts before he turned away, murmuring something under his breath.

'Are you going to tell me what is going on here, Ezio?'

He turned back and she couldn't believe that this was the same man who had made love to her so tenderly a few minutes ago. His face was like stone.

'I'm not pregnant.'

'But if you were it would be my fault. You're right—it could happen again. I don't want that responsibility. I am not father material. I'm too selfish…too flawed.' About the only thing in his favour, the only thing that made him better than his own father, was the fact he didn't want to hurt her.

Her relief had highlighted his disappointment at the

fact that he had tried to bury for so long—that a part of him craved family, connection, all the things he poured scorn on. Now the irony was *she* didn't want those things either when all he could see was her body growing big with his child. 'All of this is a result of, well, *proximity*. You were there and… Honestly, this is an exercise in futility,' he said. 'You think it's going some place, but it isn't.'

'You're not your father, and I'm not that woman who broke your heart. I wouldn't do that to you, Ezio.'

But I'd do it to you, he thought, bitter self-revulsion showing in his eyes as he delivered his cruel-to-be-kind killer blow. 'I loved *her*, Tilda.'

She reacted as if he'd struck her, but it was the only way he could think of to push her far enough away for him to save her or himself.

'So this…!' She gestured down at the hollow they had created on the ground, cold now, but moments ago warm from their body heat. 'It was just a technical exercise, no heart, no emotion. I don't believe that… What scares you so much about emotions, Ezio?'

She turned and fled then, not caring how she looked, just not caring about anything. Like a wounded animal, she locked herself in her room and cried… It was dark outside when she stopped.

And her mind was set.

She packed her bags, washed her face and went to find Ezio.

'I'll leave in the morning.'

He looked up from the blank computer screen. 'That is not necessary. I am flying back to London tomorrow.'

'Fine, but I'm not staying here.' Where everywhere would remind her of their short, doomed affair. The idea filled her with horror. 'I'm going to see Sam in the morning. I want to tell him in person what's happening. I'll find somewhere nice near the school. Will you say goodbye to him?'

CHAPTER TWELVE

THE TOP-FLOOR APARTMENT was too big for one, but when Sam came home at the weekend she'd be glad of the space. The pool in the basement had sold it to her, and she'd tried to sell it to Sam without much success.

Knowing he was anxious about her reaction, she had struggled to hide her hurt when he'd expressed his wish to spend a few weekends with Ezio at the villa.

'Isn't that what happens to kids when their parents divorce?'

'This is different. Ezio is not your parent, Sam.'

'Neither are you,' had been his hurtful but totally logical response.

She just hoped that he'd get used to it in time.

She was piling some laundry into the washing machine when there was a buzz at the door.

She pressed the button that connected her to the keyed entry lobby.

'It's Ezio. We need to talk.'

'No, there is nothing—'

'It's Sam.'

She buzzed him up and waited for the knock on the door. When it came, she took a deep breath, painted what she hoped was cold neutrality on her face and opened the door, stepping back before his imposing presence appeared in her hallway.

He didn't waste time on small talk. 'Sam is missing.'

She felt her knees give and grabbed a nearby chair. 'What do you mean? How do you know this and I don't?'

'When you changed your number, presumably to block me, you failed to give the school your new number.'

'Oh, God...missing as in...?'

'As in gone from his room. Nobody knows where he is. The school contacted me when they couldn't get hold of you...the kids are searching the school grounds and buildings. They're holding off on calling the police.'

Her hand went to her mouth and panic slid through her like ice. Her brain froze all she could feel was fear. 'This is my fault! I brought him here, let him think we were a family and— Oh, my God! What am I going to do? We need to call the police! Why is no one calling the police?'

His hands went to her shoulders. 'You are going to breathe and then you are going to come with me... I think I might know where he is.'

'Then why aren't you there, finding him?' she exploded, pushing his hands away.

'Because I thought you might like to come along.'

A frown of instant contrition crossed her pale face. 'Of course you did. I'm sorry.' She flicked a conciliatory look at his face, noticing the pronounced edges of his cheek bones and some interesting shadows under his dark, intense eyes. 'It's just when I think—'

'Do not think,' he ordered calmly. 'There is little point torturing yourself with imagined scenarios while Sam is probably right now sitting in the cabin, living off the land.'

'Living off the land?'

'You know, back to nature and whittling... I happened to mention that I ran away there once.'

He closed his eyes, waiting for her wrath, but all he got was a squeeze of his arm.

'Oh, God, I can't tell you how... That's marvellous!' She beamed. 'What are we waiting for?'

He nodded down at her feet.

'Oh, yes.' She ran across the room, shoved her feet in a pair of sandals and was at the door before him.

She struggled to protect her hair form the updraft from the helicopter as it landed.

'Right!' he yelled over the din. 'You get that this can only take us to the...well about a mile off the cabin? But the forester leaves a four-wheel drive in the shed there and he'd left the keys in the ignition for us.'

She nodded and ducked her head as she ran behind him.

Inside she put on the mufflers and sat silently trying not to allow the lurid scenarios in her head to take root. A few minutes in, she became aware of the conversation between Ezio and the pilot.

'Will the rain storm stop us landing?'

Ezio shook his head and spoke into his ear piece. 'No problem,' he said, seeing no point in adding that the road to the cabin might be more of a problem, and taking comfort from the fact that the last time it had been washed out was ten years ago.

By the time they landed, the rain was falling horizontally. She had imagined Greece to be a dry place; she'd not seen anything this bad since she and Sam had tried camping in the Lake District.

'What if we don't find him?'

'We will, and you're not going fall apart.'

She looked up at him and smiled. 'No, I'm not, I'm a little trooper,' she mocked.

'No, you're a wonder of a woman,' he contradicted her, before immediately transferring his attention to the map on his phone. 'The four-wheel drive should be fifty yards that way,' he said when they landed.

It was.

'Right, this might be a bit bumpy.'

She flashed him a tense grin. 'Don't worry about me!'

Theos, but he did; the self-denial seemed futile at the point when he would have walked through a sea of sharks to protect her, and any attempt on his part to deny the fact was by that point redundant.

'Right, *yineka mou*, hold tight.'

Tilda did. The white-knuckle ride lasted what seemed like an age but was probably in reality less than fifteen minutes. At times it seemed as if they were driving along a river bed and there had been some drops that she coped with by simply closing her eyes.

Finally, the cabin came into view—a lot less primitive than it had seemed in her mind.

'There are no lights,' she observed fearfully. It might be the afternoon but the storm had turned the sky night-dark.

'There is no electricity,' he told her as he pulled up in the gravelled parking area that was now a small pond.

She clambered out before he come to help her, landing up to her ankles in water. She sensed him at her side as she ran up to the front door.

Calling her brother's name, she rushed in, pausing as behind her she heard the hiss of flame as Ezio lit a lantern.

'He's not here!'

But something was… She watched as Ezio went across to the table where there stood a large bunch of red roses and a champagne bottle inside an ice bucket, against which was propped a note.

Ezio held it up, his eyes scanning the single page of writing.

'I think you need to read this,' he said, handing it to Tilda.

Dear both,

Ezio is not so stupid so I'm assuming you found this… I just thought you needed a bit of wake-up call. I don't know much, but I do know you are both crazy about each other. So get real, guys, kiss and make up. I don't want to be the kid from a broken home.

Theo's mum and dad are away, so he gave me the house keys. I'll head back to school for double physics.

Oh, and by the way, I didn't shoplift it, Tilda. Theo's mum bought the champagne for me. She thought I wanted to buy you two a present. She thinks I'm very sweet. Also, it cost an arm and a leg, so you owe me.

Love, Sam

By the time she had finished, the tears were pouring down Tilda's cheeks. 'I will kill him stone-dead.'

'Not if I get there before you. Manipulated by a fourteen-year-old. It makes you wonder how scary he is going to be in ten years' time.'

'I'm so sorry.'

'It's OK. That's what family is for, or so I understand.'

Heart beating fast, she stared up at him, not daring to believe… Saying nothing, she locked her eyes on his, not able to believe that anything she could say could bridge the gap that he had built over years of isolating himself.

'Have you moved on, Tilda?'

She shook her head. 'I'm a work in progress.' She sniffed.

'Your brother is right. I am crazy about you, Tilda. I can't believe it took a fourteen-year-old, even if he is a genius, to bring me to my senses. I have never in my life felt about any woman the way I do you… It terrified me… the thought of hurting you *terrified* me… The thought of being a bad father terrifies me still. I couldn't protect my mother, but I thought by pushing you away I could protect you.' He took her chin in his fingers and with his thumb brushed away the tears running down her face.

'I spent a day sitting there, feeling noble and self-sacrificing, then I spent the next day trying to figure out how to get you back. I am such a coward… I was scared of giving you the power to hurt me.'

He moved in closer, taking both her hands in his and raising them to his lips. 'But, Tilda Raven, I give you my heart—it is yours, and you have the power to crush it in your little hand. I want a real marriage. I want a real wife…a family.'

She fell into his kiss, tears streaming down her face. 'I love you so much…it hurts,' she said, pressing a hand to her chest.

'You know that I will never betray you…' He could say that finally, knowing it was true that Tilda was the love of his life.

'I trust you, Ezio, with my life and my heart.'

'You realise that Sam is going to be very smug,' he said, stroking her cheek lovingly.

'Shall we pretend to hate one another?'

Ezio shook his head, his expression darkening. 'I have had enough pretending to last me a lifetime. There is some champagne there with our names on it.'

'Afterwards, I think.' Being loved by Ezio would put more fizz in her veins than a crate of champagne.

She sighed her happiness as his lips claimed hers.

EPILOGUE

'I ONLY ASKED for a new laptop...you had no need to go to this much trouble.'

Sam stroked the beard he was trying to grow with limited success as he looked down at the red-headed baby sleeping in the crib. In the past six months he had grown and now topped six feet, gangly but filling out, as he had started training when he'd got on the school swimming team.

'I think it's really handy. Joint birthday parties with Olivia for ever? Balloons and cake...?'

Sam rolled his eyes and tried and failed not to look enchanted as the baby opened her big, dark eyes and wrapped her hand tightly around his finger.

'Wow, my niece is super-strong! Do you suppose she has super-powers?'

'She has a volume super-power,' said Ezio, who walked into the nursery, looking gorgeous, with dark circles of sleep deprivation under his eyes. 'Especially at two o'clock in the morning. You,' he said, walking across to where Tilda was folding tiny baby clothes, 'Should be asleep. Sleep while she sleeps—that's what all the books say.'

Tilda lifted her head to receive the warm and loving

kiss before she leaned into his body, laying her head on his chest. Her husband had read *all* the books cover to cover, and had driven her mad trying to wrap her in cotton wool during her pregnancy.

'I just like looking at her. She's so perfect and her hair makes me think of Mum…' They had named their baby daughter—who had arrived a few weeks early, small but perfectly healthy—Olivia after her grandmother.

'Right,' Sam said, extracting his finger from the chubby grip. 'I'll be off, but I'll see you at the weekend.'

'Good luck at the chess tournament,' Tilda said, kissing his cheek; it required her to stand on tip toe.

'I don't need luck, I have skill,' Sam said, polishing his chest and looking disgustingly smug. 'Just make the next one a boy so I have someone to play football with.'

'I'll have you know my daughter will run rings around you on the football pitch.' Ezio reached out with his foot to rock the cradle as sounds of grumpy protests emerged from wriggling, red-faced bundle inside.

'Probably, I am pretty awful… See you…' He strolled off just as the baby let out a loud squeal.

'I've noticed that Sam always manages to leave just as Olivia starts to yell!' Tilda observed, expertly scooping the baby out of the crib, a tired, happy glow in her face as she stared down at their daughter.

'He's a genius, that boy.' Ezio came to stand behind Tilda, who laid her head on his chest. 'I still have nightmares about that drive to the hospital.' He sighed. 'I actually forgot how to start a car.'

Tilda tilted her head and smiled up at him. 'You remembered, that was what counted, and I got there on time.'

'Just,' Ezio recalled with feeling. 'You might have mentioned you were in labour two hours earlier.'

'Well, I wasn't due, and it was in the middle of the fund raiser.' Her charity had gone from strength to strength over the past year, but she was taking maternity leave from what had become a pretty full-on commitment. 'I thought it might be Braxton Hicks.'

'Well, it was no practice, it was the real thing...very real... Oh, God, Tilda, you were brilliant, you know that? I could never do what you did.'

'Well, darling, you really don't have the right equipment. But the equipment you do have...' she added with a saucy grin as her eyes dropped down his body '...is pretty much perfect. Is she asleep or...?'

'Put her down,' Ezio whispered. As much as he loved their baby, the moments he had his beautiful wife alone to himself were rare enough not to be wasted.

As they carefully laid her down and went on tip toe from the room, there was a loud explosion of angry baby sobs.

Ezio sighed and happily kissed his wife. They had the rest of their lives to be together.

Together but never alone.

* * * * *

THE MARRIAGE
THAT MADE
HER QUEEN

KALI ANTHONY

MILLS & BOON

To my amazing children,
who called me an author before I'd published a thing.

You are my favourite cheer squad. xxx

CHAPTER ONE

'YOUR MAJESTY, I'M PROFOUNDLY sorry for your loss.'

The words scraped as if fingernails scoring down a blackboard documenting Lise's short and, up until recently, inconsequential life. She splayed her hands on the ancient mahogany desktop, strewn with newspapers all screaming headlines like, *Ready to Rule?* Challenging the reality that even if she wasn't, there was no choice. As she sat behind her father's desk in a study that had been the seat of her family's power for six centuries, those headlines taunted her.

Imposter, they whispered.

Lise took a long, slow breath. Trying to ease the twist of fear choking her since that awful moment thirteen days earlier when the King's private secretary, Albert, delivered the world-ending news.

'Your Majesty, there has been a terrible accident.'

Now, she repeated the silent mantra she'd chanted daily. A reminder of who she was in those terrified times since. *I am Annalise Marie Betencourt. Her Most Serene and Ethereal Majesty, Defender of the Realm.*

Soon to be crowned Queen.

The youngest Lauritanian monarch in three hundred years.

Fraud.

She moved her gaze to the man sitting in the chair opposite her. One who didn't appear as *profoundly sorry* as his words implied. His dark eyes glinted, almost as if he were hungry. A shiver chased down her spine and she pulled her jacket tighter against the midnight caress of desire, the remnants of which still haunted her. Once, this man had made her feel the centre of his *everything*. How she'd lapped up his interest like a kitten at a forbidden pail of cream. Basked in his attention, his flirtation.

It had all fed the gluttonous delusion that she had choices in life. Whispered words intoxicating as a drug, which had led her to believe that she truly meant something to him. Rafe De Villiers. Businessman. Billionaire. Devastatingly handsome with a shade of stubble grazing his angular jawline. Looking dissolute. Disreputable.

Unsuitable.

Yet how she'd hungered for those moments with him, basking in the delusion that this brilliant, charismatic man wanted *her*. Igniting a need burning away common sense, which in other circumstances should have warned her that those seemingly clandestine meetings they'd engaged in whenever he visited the palace couldn't have happened by mere chance. They *must* have been orchestrated by her father.

'Thank you, Mr De Villiers.'

They'd been on a first-name basis once. She'd thought she love— *No.* It had all been an illusion, and there was *nothing* to thank him for. Seeing him now, lounging opposite her dressed in a three-piece suit of elegantly rumpled grey linen as if he had not a care in the world, she was once more assaulted by the gut-wrenching truth. The one that had been forced home in that last, most catastrophic argument with her family... She meant *nothing* to him but a means of accessing power in a blighted deceit concocted by her father and Rafe. One where she'd been halfway fooled into believing they might marry for love.

The humiliation of it all seared like acid in her gut. One more wound to add to the growing list of them inflicted upon her over the past few weeks. It was a wonder she hadn't bled out. Death by a thousand cruel cuts.

Yet she was still standing. Barely.

Rafe pulled up the sleeve of his suit and glanced at his watch, then settled his wolf-brown eyes on her again. She raised an eyebrow. Tried for imperious, although she wasn't sure it worked.

'Am I keeping you from something?'

The corner of his mouth quirked, tugging at the pout of his lower lip. Months ago, she'd been fascinated by that mouth. How she'd craved his lips on hers. Twenty-two and never been kissed. Now she'd missed the chance. Lise blinked away her moment of fancy. Those immature, naïve dreams. She could never forget he remained a schemer. Devastatingly handsome, tempting as Lucifer, but a schemer, nonetheless.

'I have all day for you, ma'am.' His voice was dark and sweet as treacle. So tempting once, to lose herself in every syllable he uttered. 'I was only wondering when—'

A rap at the door interrupted him. It cracked open.

'Ah,' he said, raking a hand through the overlong curls of his black hair. An unruly strand fell artfully across his forehead. Everything he did appeared artful. A study in masculine magnificence. 'Morning coffee has arrived as expected.'

She'd forgotten how well he knew the rituals of the monarch's schedule, whilst she was still learning its dictates. Lise glanced at the carriage clock marking out the interminable hours on the King's desk. The desk that should have been her brother's when the time came, rather than this unnatural sequence of events.

When in his office, at half past ten precisely His Majesty had stopped for coffee. No one ever asked whether *Her* Majesty wanted to do the same. They *assumed*, the pace of change here glacial at best in an institution that had endured virtually unchanged since the thirteen hundreds.

A black-uniformed, white-gloved woman wheeled in a trolley laden with petite delicacies, a royally embossed silver coffee pot, and eggshell-fine cups. She poured Rafe's beverage without asking how he took it. Reminding Lise that he'd spent a great deal of time here with her father, the King, making decisions about lives they'd had no right to make. Such as hers.

Rafe took a mouthful of coffee, tipped back his head, and groaned. That sound of almost carnal pleasure rippled through her, heating her coldest inner reaches.

'I'd have sold my soul for that coffee. Hadn't slept in twenty-four hours when I received your summons… ma'am.'

She tried not to think of what might have kept him up all night, leaving him rakishly dishevelled. In the overcharged atmosphere of gossip-filled ballrooms, rumours flitted amongst the women about his prodigious…talents. Her cheeks burned. She gritted her teeth, loathing how he still affected her.

When had this obsession of hers begun? The plan to trap her hatched? At her coming-out ball? The day she'd been told she wasn't allowed to compete in the downhill skiing championships. That instead she was going to finishing school as if she were some poorly made-up object, requiring honing to be *enough*. She'd barely held it together that night, feeling small and wounded at a party she no longer wanted because it was celebrating her imprisonment and not her freedom. Until she'd looked up at the interminable roll of guests parading down the wide marble staircase into the glittering ballroom, and there had stood Rafe. Brooding over the crowd as if he'd owned it. All dark unruly hair, a fascinating contrast to his perfectly tailored tuxedo. Wild, untamed beneath the civilised veneer.

Then he'd turned prescient black eyes onto her, and everything had melted away. The pain, the crushing sense that she'd be trapped for ever. And he'd smiled, not taking his eyes from her as he'd descended that staircase in the palace ballroom.

Had he seen it then, the naked, hungry hope on her face? The wish that someone would value her for who *she* was rather than the institution she represented? Because no one had cared what she wanted…

His approaches to her after that night had been respectful, careful. With subtle flirting in the brief moments when they'd crossed paths at official functions. Then she'd turned twenty-two. And the attention that had been fleeting had become focussed. Private. The soft words and gentle touches. She'd felt beautiful, *desired*. Like a woman with needs and wants that might finally be satisfied.

More fool her at how deep the betrayal went. But as tempting as it was to immerse herself in the humiliation of it all, she didn't have time to drown. Lise wiped damp palms over her black skirt, the uniform of mourning. Seventy-seven days of it remained, but she would never be free, even though the official grieving period might end.

Her family were consigned to the grave because of her.

'You never complained about His Majesty's summonses,' she said, trying for magisterial. Sounding waspish instead.

'I'm not complaining about yours.' Rafe hesitated, then took another sip from the embossed porcelain, which seemed absurdly delicate in his strong, capable hands. His eyes lingered on the newspapers. Pictures of the horse-drawn funeral cortège. Her walking behind, head bowed. 'Whatever business you have with me can wait. You're allowed to grieve.'

His voice was low, seemingly kind if she could have trusted his intentions as honourable. But to grieve? She wished she could rage, scream, cry…but her recent life had been like wading through snowdrifts, blindfolded. The paralysing inertia of disbelief threatening to freeze her solid.

'The Constitution waits for no one,' she said.

'You're the first Queen in—'

'One hundred and fifty years.'

She didn't need reminding. Her parliament, and particularly Prime Minister Hasselbeck, did that daily. Almost from the moment her family's crypt had been closed. Not only about her obligations, but her shortcomings…

'The country's waited over a century for the rarity that's you. They can wait a while longer.'

Rare, precious, beautiful. She'd heard those tempting words slip from his lips before. Shiny sentiments that had called to her covetous soul. The one that had craved to be loved, until she was shown how tarnished the empty words truly were. She refused to listen now.

They held all the value of fool's gold when the truth was inescapable. Her country didn't want her but had no option but to keep her.

Lise took a trembling breath and tried to rein in her emotions. Sadly, being the spare not the heir, and a female at that, meant her lessons had all been designed to turn her into a beautiful, biddable bargaining chip. No preparation at all for her current predicament. Assessment of her beauty she left to higher powers. The gossip rags extolled all kinds of physical virtues; a sporty figure, blonde hair and blue eyes…

Being a bargaining chip was a given for most female members of the aristocracy in her frustratingly backward country. Useful to forge alliances, seal deals with auspicious marriages. But biddable?

No. If she had been, her parents and brother would be alive today.

'Time's my enemy.' And it had run out. A wedding had been arranged for the Crown Prince long before he'd died. The prime minister thought it expedient to keep the date and the arrangements for her own wedding. The invitees would have been much the same, anyhow. All she needed was a groom. She swallowed down the sick, dark ache. The taunting voice inside and its insidious whisper, *I can't.*

She ignored it. Her duty must be done. No matter how little she wanted what must come next, she couldn't allow her country to be plunged into uncertainty over succession. Not like this, not unplanned. For that, she needed Rafe. Because everyone who learned about the history and constitution of their small, landlocked Alpine country knew that for her to take the throne there was one, simple requirement.

For a Lauritanian queen to rule, she must have a husband.

When she had been nothing more than a pawn in whatever fresh political game they played with no chance of sitting in the seat she now occupied, Rafe was the man her father had chosen. After months of him circling, those meetings she'd at first believed were chance then kidded herself meant something far more, the truth had been revealed in that final, terrible argument with her family. When she'd been *ordered* to marry him.

She'd refused. Refused to follow her family on their yearly break, where she knew intolerable pressure would be put to bear. The King, the Queen and the Crown Prince ignoring that she was a flesh-and-blood woman, not merely Lauritania's Princess. A woman with hopes and dreams of falling in love, who'd wanted desperately to believe she'd meant something to the man in front of her.

It was her deepest shame that because of her refusal, her family had died.

Lise didn't miss the brutal irony the universe cast her way. For now, Rafe was the only choice. Her duty. Her penance.

Rafe had to know what was coming. Yet here they were, toying with one another. She could hardly bear to ask the question of him. But she had her own plans. Her punishment for cutting off her family's lives. Her brother would never get to marry his fiancée or rule the country he was born to. Her parents would never see grandchildren, the future for the throne they'd so craved. She was required to atone for what she'd done.

She'd marry the man her father had chosen for her.

Lise stood. So he stood. Damned protocol. She kept forgetting and ended up with people bouncing about like

a jack-in-the-box. She must remember she didn't move
for people now, people moved for her. And Rafe moved
so well. Nothing unnecessary about him. All long, lean
muscle that his clothes only accentuated. Everything he
did, calculated and perfect. *Calculated*...one word she
must never forget. That was what she needed to become.

'Sit, Mr De Villiers.' He took his time doing so. Rafe
obeyed no one. In a place built on protocol and stric-
ture, he carved his own path. Which was why she'd been
shocked when her father had told her the deal he'd secured, with a man who no one told what to do. Not even
the King.

Lise walked to the mullioned windows, staring over
the towering peaks of the Alps. Swifts wheeled and
soared on the air currents, so blindingly free the jeal-
ousy twisted her heart. She wished she could join them.
Catch a thermal and fly away. But she was landlocked
here as everyone else.

'I require a husband.'

'You don't *want* a husband.' She didn't miss the acid
in his tone. When he'd tried to see her after the argument with her family, she'd refused to give him an audience, even though her father had demanded it. 'Change
the Constitution.'

She clenched her hands into fists, her nails cutting into
her palms. 'That's been tried and failed.'

'In 1863 and 1974. Times change.'

Not in Lauritania. Her country was conservative to
the core. Even worse, her people didn't trust her, as the
headlines in those infernal newspapers attested. The child
conceived as an insurance policy in case the worst happened, with no expectation that it ever would. She was
the country's consolation prize. Second best. Unwanted.

As Rafe knew too well. She'd poured out those childish hurts when she'd trusted him. How cruel of him to presume she now had a choice. 'You know why you've been asked here. Stop pretending otherwise.'

'I think you need to spell it out for me. I'd never presume to know a lady's mind, *ma'am*.'

The formality of him. Lise whipped around, turning her back on the view. She used to love the way he appeared to savour her name on his lips. *Lise*. Like water to a parched man. All lies. She got right to it. There was no prettying the truth.

'I'm asking you to be my husband.' The words almost choked her. Lise glimpsed the mercenary gleam in his eyes. A gleam she'd mistaken for desire, once. Her own foolish mistake.

Rafe steepled his fingers. 'You want me?' His voice was a low murmur, gentle as a caress. Once she'd been desperate to believe anything his alluring timbre promised. That being forced to give up the sport she loved, the freedom she sought, didn't mean her existence was meaningless. But deep in her heart, it had been more. Her own secret craving that, in a duplicitous world surrounded by simpering imitations, this glorious man might love *her*.

But conceding the point was a fatal weakness, even though a whisper of heat flashed over her cheeks. She straightened her spine with all the hauteur she could muster. Later, she'd allow herself to crumble but not today and never in front of him.

'I'm carrying out my father's last wish.'

Rafe's lip curled into the beginnings of what looked like a sneer. 'A fitting tribute for a great man.'

Another shiver skittered down her spine. Or not so great if the rumours she was now hearing were to be believed. She was coming to suspect her family were only human, even though they had pretended otherwise. Sadly, she'd always been held to a higher standard by them.

'I'm pleased you see it my way,' she said. This was payment for what she'd done. And she would pay, for the rest of her life. But she had a few tricks up her coal-black sleeve. She might do a deal with the devil, but she wasn't in the business of selling her soul completely. She waited for Rafe to settle back into his seat, to acquire the look of smug self-satisfaction that had become all too familiar in her life, before she pounced.

'Have you heard of a *mariage blanc*, Mr De Villiers?'

Rafe swallowed down the gall rising in this throat. He'd flown through the night, cutting short a business trip to answer her summons. Sure of what it meant, what he had been waiting for. Now this. *Mariage blanc.* A white marriage. A marriage unconsummated.

'Yes, I've heard of it,' he said, keeping his voice deliberately bland.

'Excellent, that's settled.' Lise sat down once more, her hands twisting restlessly on the desktop, looking decidedly *unsettled.*

'What's settled?' He leaned back in his seat again, trying not to hiss the words through gritted teeth. Indolence was a look he'd perfected over the years. If he appeared not to care, no one could touch him. The aristocracy here had tried, since school, to destroy the upstart farm boy he'd been marked as. No matter that his family had a wealth of their own, although born of hard, physical work rather than lofty inheritance. When his brother, Carl, had died, they'd almost succeeded in crushing him. But he was made of stronger stuff than any of them realised.

Lise frowned. 'Our marriage, of course.'

He sat back, nibbled on some innocuous sweet thing from the plate before him. Took another sip of his now cooling coffee. He never wished to be seen as the pretender, a choice compelled rather than freely made. That would *never* satisfy him. He'd spelled it out to her father, emphatically. The only way he'd marry Lise was if she said yes, without compulsion.

He gave what he hoped was his most neutral look, when all he wanted to do was bare his teeth and snarl. 'What does a so-called *white marriage* have to do with that?'

Her plush lips thinned into a pale, tight line. 'It's what I'm offering.'

Madness. This was not how things were supposed to be.

He'd asked her father for six months to win her. Never doubting it would take him fewer to secure the hand and heart of this woman who he'd wanted to come to him willingly. So she'd believe he'd been her choice alone. He'd been disdained enough for his working-class background. He would not have anyone say the only way Lauritania's Princess would marry him was if she was forced to do so. No. He'd wanted to show them all. Their Princess had *chosen* the commoner above the aristocracy.

Yet what had happened? He'd been called away on a brief business trip a couple of months into the job and her father had pounced. Trying to force Lise into the marriage. A woman who required finesse and tender care. Instead of a happy homecoming, he'd returned to a debacle. Lise, refusing to see him at the risk of calling the palace guards when he tried. The King enraged that one of his subjects would dare disobey a direct command—ignore the fact she was supposed to be his precious daughter.

And him? Everything he'd planned, his careful manoeuvres for *years*, in ashes.

He'd wanted to tear the smug portrait of her father from the wall, chop it to matchsticks and hurl it into the closest fire. Then, in a fit of pique on that fateful day which led them here, the King allowed the Queen and Crown Prince to travel with him in one vehicle. Probably to plan how to force Lise to accede to their command. Not to speak of palace security, capitulating to the act of foolishness. All of them grown fat and lazy on complacency. If the mundanity of a rock fall and car accident hadn't killed her family, Rafe feared he'd have been tempted himself.

How many hours had he sat here negotiating? Asking the King to trust that he knew what he was doing. But like all the rest of them, that man could never believe a mere commoner might know better how to manage the Princess than he did. As they'd never believed Lise could ever love him. And now he was picking up the pieces.

Lise sat dwarfed behind a hideous monstrosity of a desk. Skin pale as the permanently snow-capped peaks around them. Dressed in severe black, the dark lace mantilla over her head an ill-fitting crown of grief. She should be in bright, dancing colours. Decked in all the shimmering jewels he could provide. He'd planned from the moment he'd set eyes on her. A triumph to show the blighted aristocracy here what he could achieve. Being loved by royalty. Taking one of theirs as his own. The man they'd underestimated. Dismissed. Her yes to the proposal was meant to be emphatic. Carefully orchestrated, of course, but unequivocal and full of joy on her part. The King in his infinite arrogance had destroyed it all.

'No sex?' He lingered on the word, and her cheeks bloomed to a fetching shade of rose. He still affected her. Good. Rafe suppressed a smile. 'No.'

He had some cards to play here. Lise *needed* him, for more than one reason. Were things in the country worse than disclosed? Was that why her father had tried to force the marriage prematurely?

Did Lise know?

Her face paled even further if that were possible. Her mouth puckered as she no doubt nibbled the inside of her lower lip. A habit of hers when she worried, and she worried too much.

'What do you mean "*no*"?'

'My meaning's plain.'

'You can't force me to allow you to…' Her gaze darted about the room, never at him. Of course she was nervous of this arrangement. Lise was a woman who sought a fantasy. From the sweeping love stories she read in secret, to the pre-Raphaelite artists she preferred. Each one a homage to the romance she craved.

'Make love to you? I'd never force a woman.'

'There's no love in our arrangement.'

But there could have been. He'd have ensured she loved him when the time came to ask for her hand. From commoner to prince…the aristocracy would never have underestimated him again. The wicked flame alight in his gut burned hotter at the chance lost.

'Have sex, then. No love, merely slick, sweaty—'

'I—I can see you're not interested in a practical arrangement. I'm sorry for wasting your time.' Lise's chest heaved. The pupils of her luminous blue eyes blown wide and dark. 'I'll find other candidates. Alternatives have been proposed.'

Alternatives? Now who was the fool? He needed to tamp down this anger before he overplayed his hand. He could see them all, jockeying for position to become the most powerful man in the country. Those men who thought they knew better. School peers who'd tormented him at the prestigious Kings' Academy for being of the wrong class, even though his family's wealth crept close to theirs. Disdained his younger brother, Carl, whose only dream had been to tend the family herd on the mountain slopes. Bullied so mercilessly he'd refused to return after six months, when if he'd stayed at the school, he might still be alive today...

Even now, Rafe's wealth propped up the institutions and lifestyle the aristocracy so loved. Every drop of fine wine they drank, much of the food they ate, had the De Villiers name attached. His empire built by his own hands through ambition, driven by personal experience and his brother's blood. Yet none of that mattered. To them, he was still the son of a cow herder, as they'd used to mock him each lonely day at that godforsaken horror of a school. Ignore that for generations his family had made a traditional cheese with its own appellation, national protection and of world renown. That with his own business interests, he could buy them all and still be left with billions. Carl had been right. That place and those boys had taught him nothing but contempt. Then when Carl had died, they had heaped only scorn, not solace, on his grief. He would never forget.

Never.

None of his former collegians, the aristocracy here, had any idea how to save the country, which was why he'd been chosen. He'd show them all what he could achieve. The thought of *any* of them touching Lise raged fire in his gut. There was only ever one candidate for her.

Him.

'I've never pretended to be a eunuch. Yet you're consigning me to the life of one.'

He'd planned it. The ring, a diamond the colour of sunshine to match her golden hair. A wedding night where he'd spread her on the marital bed and show her passion she'd never dreamed of. Nowhere in this scheme was a woman who wouldn't touch him.

'You misunderstand. No sex…with me.' She flushed again. Each emotion playing through the colours washing her cheeks. Her face hid nothing. A charming quality for a lover, a flawed one for a queen. She straightened her spine, tried to meet his gaze but her haunted blue eyes didn't rest on his face. Flitting everywhere about the room, other than on him. 'You can, of course, take a mistress. After an appropriate time.'

Was she serious? The tight set of her jaw told him she was. He swallowed down the bitter taste of her offer as if it were poison.

'What would you consider an appropriate time?' He gripped the arms of his uncomfortable chair till his fingers cramped. Better that than giving into his desire to break something, like the clock on the desk, which wouldn't stop its infernal ticking. 'Should I begin after the honeymoon?'

'We need no honeymoon. It's not that type of marriage.'

'Why wait, then? You'll be wanting a lover too. It wouldn't be fair to deny the goose what you're offering the gander.'

'I am not a goose, Mr De Villiers.' Her hands trembled; she placed her palms flat on the dark, aged desktop again. 'You've said enough.'

No, none of this was enough. The absurdity enraged him. 'I wonder. Shall we invite this…brace of lovers to the wedding?'

'Be. Quiet.' Her lips were tight and thin. He wasn't inclined to listen to the tone of warning in her voice.

'What intriguing dinner conversation we'll all have. Though the question, *Darling, could you please pass the salt?* might lead to confusion. I mean, which darling? The spouse or the paramour? I can see us all grappling over condiments in our efforts to please.'

'There will be no grappling—'

'Not between us, no. Not even a clinch in the corner, sadly. I'm a faithful man, so I'd never cheat on my mistress with my wife. It's against my principles. I presume you'd feel—'

'Enough!' Lise bolted to her feet. Chin held high. Colour florid on her cheeks. Here was the magnificent woman they'd tried to train out of her. 'I'm overjoyed to hear how faithful you profess to be. However, there will be no scuffles over the salt and pepper. No cosy dinners for four. In my experience, kings have mistresses, so you're welcome to your own. All I demand is that you remain discreet.'

Her father had kept a varied group of women who catered to his every whim. Rafe wondered whether she was aware that her mother's private secretary had done far more for the Queen than answer correspondence and post letters. Coming from a family where his parents loved each other in the same blinding fashion as when they first met, he found royalty's convenient arrangements sickening.

But love wasn't for him, the only game he'd played and lost. Learned that the daughters of the aristocracy wanted him for one thing, to irk their parents by flaunting the commoner. He'd always been an exercise in rebellion for those women. Rich enough so as not to be an embarrassment, but never enough on his own. He'd fancied himself smitten with a count's daughter. Till he'd proposed and she'd mocked his audacity. He'd learned then, love was for fools. It had no place in his life, leaving him open to its own brand of ridicule. He would not deign to be scorned again.

Power was a currency he understood. It was *everything*.

Love? It made you powerless.

'What about you, Your Majesty?' Propriety and protocol were the armour she wore, so he'd allow her to hide behind it for a little while longer. Time enough to start stripping her down, piece by tantalising piece, when the wedding ring was firmly on her finger.

'I need a husband. I don't need a lover.'

Her admission that there was no usurper lurking in the wings made the primitive creature curled inside him growl in satisfaction. Still, he played her game, for now.

'That's hardly fair.'

'How generous of you to think so.'

'I'm all for equality where pleasure's concerned. In fact, I ensure my partner's pleasure exceeds mine.'

Her dusky lips parted. He'd never kissed her, something he'd regretted. Perhaps he should have been more assertive in his approach. But he'd thought he'd have all the time in the world to seduce, not to conquer.

'There's nothing equal about a constitution which allows a king to rule in his own right whilst requiring a queen to marry.' Her voice was soft, with a tone of defeat. He loathed the flatness of it. He wanted her to fight for what was hers. 'But it's what I face so I'm doing my duty.'

'And when your duty comes to having an heir and a spare or two?'

'You're referring to children, not objects as the monarchy so often treats them.' She raised her chin and stared him down with eyes as cold and brittle as first winter ice. 'For that reason, there will be none.'

Lise's frigid gaze threw a chill down his spine. She was brutally, bitterly serious. This was not where her hopes and dreams lay. He knew. She'd whispered her secrets to him when they'd seen each other, in carefully planned but seemingly spontaneous meetings. She'd begun to open the door to her deepest desires and now that door slammed in his face.

He stared at her, rigid in the chair opposite. Her eyes fixed on the wall over his shoulder.

'What about succession?'

Lise took in a breath, her body shuddering. 'The monarchy dies with me.'

Rafe reared back, the shock of her pronouncement like the frigid slap of a first winter's gale. No. *Never.* He could not accept this. His children and his family's blood should have been destined to rule the country in perpetuity.

'Lise—'

Her eyes narrowed. 'I haven't invited you to use my name.'

She held herself as aloof as any royal he'd ever met. He loathed that she was directing this charade towards him.

'Since you invited marriage, I believe we're past honorifics.'

'Only when I say so, and you haven't agreed to my offer.' Her skin blanched so pale it appeared translucent. The shadows under her eyes stood out, dark and bruised. 'There are two choices, Mr De Villiers. Yes, or no.'

No meant she would be lost to him for ever. Yes, and by a quirk of the constitution he'd be in a cold and empty marriage, but he'd be King.

King.

He could never forget those who'd sneered at him, laughed at his heritage, bullied Carl from school leaving him in harm's way, mocked his brother even in death. Thought he was beneath them because of his business interests rather than being born into the aristocracy. He'd have power over them all. His blood ran thick and hot at the lure of that thought.

'Yes. I'd be honoured.'

Lise's shoulders softened for the briefest of moments before her spine filled with steel. 'The prime minister suggests a sensible date is a month away.'

On the day the Crown Prince had been due to marry. The horror that her government could do this to her. Why did she allow it?

'How convenient.'

'It is.' He couldn't miss the hard edge of anger in her voice then. 'Rather than wasting money and effort on planning another event. The coronation will occur immediately after.'

This country couldn't even give her a day of her own. Proof that they had never seen her as an individual. He clenched his jaw. Perhaps he could offer her something for herself.

'Any preference for an engagement ring?' The yellow diamond he'd thought of had no place here. There was no sunshine in this room. She was locked in a permanent winter. 'I was thinking Ceylonese sapphire. The same, unreachable blue of your eyes.'

She hesitated for a heartbeat then shook her head. 'I need nothing but a signature on the marriage licence. This isn't a time for celebration.'

'I understand. But what do you *want*?'

He couldn't mistake the glitter of tears from a woman who by their agreement was denying herself everything she'd desired.

'A convenient marriage, nothing more.'

He nodded. Unable to say another word lest anger overtake him.

'Thank you, Rafe.' The words were breathy and heart-felt. As he looked at her, he saw the Princess she'd been, before her tone hardened and she became his Queen once more. 'My private secretary will be in touch.'

'I'll await his call.' He stood and bowed. The move stiff and unfamiliar.

Rafe strode out of the study, his footsteps echoing down the marbled halls. He might have agreed to marry Lise, but he refused to honour the rest. He had time now. This was a battle he would win. He'd marry, then execute a fresh plan.

A plan to win his wife.

CHAPTER TWO

LISE STOOD IN her chambers, surrounded by a small group of women. Her hair, curled into an elegant chignon. Her make-up, perfect. A few ladies straightened the skirt of her wedding dress, adjusted the veil then stood back to admire their handiwork. She shut them all out, refusing to look at herself in the long mirror, as they twittered that she should.

Long ago she'd dreamt of this day. With her mother here, helping her dress. Soothing her nerves…although the Queen had never been particularly motherly or soothing, in Lise's dreams her parents could be anything she desired. It was what she'd secretly longed for. Love, not cool formality. Devotion, not duty. A time when she envisaged a future full of joy, love and hope.

She doubted that there would be any joy in this place ever again.

'We're done here. Please leave me.'

The group bowed and drifted from the room, taking their excited chatter with them. A familiar burn stung her eyes. The make-up artist had applied waterproof mascara, so there was no risk of the hours of hard work being ruined by errant tears, which she'd only ever cry to herself.

Alone.

Her father had said, on the only time he'd confided anything to her, that being monarch was a solitary job. She understood that now. She'd refused even a bridesmaid today. The natural choice would have been Sara, her brother's fiancée. Her only real friend. Two young women, battling the palace in their own way. But how could she parade Sara down the aisle on the day Sara was meant to be married herself? With the press salivating over any signs of her friend's grief? It was too much. Lise wouldn't do it.

Anyhow, this was a job she needed to perform without support. Sure, someone was walking her down the aisle. The prime minister took that starring role. Fitting that he should give her away, having previously dismissed her and her desires, just as her family had.

It didn't matter now, anyhow. She smoothed trembling hands over the bead-encrusted satin of her dress. A gown Lauritanian seamstresses had worked day and night to complete on time. Her dress the *one* thing about this wedding she'd had any choice in, and even then, the designer had tried to change her mind. But she wouldn't be swayed. There was nothing to celebrate.

Today was meant to be endured.

A knock sounded at the door. Time to go already? She swallowed the bitter taint rising in her throat and stilled her quivering fingers. 'Come in.'

The door opened and Albert Thomsen, her private secretary, entered the room dressed in an impeccable dark suit. She wanted to run and fling herself into his arms because if anyone in this place had given her guidance and counsel over the years, it was him.

But queens didn't run or fling themselves about. So she waited where she was, for him to come to her. He bowed.

'The prime minister's on his way.'

'Thank you, Albert.' He was a person more like a father than her real father had ever been. A man who'd held his job since the King took the throne. He remained a solid, stable presence since taking over the role as her secretary, easing her into the job. Helping her around any missteps. Praising her minor successes.

People, like the prime minister, had counselled that it was time for Albert to retire. They'd suggested replacement cronies no doubt. But Albert wanted to continue with her, and Lise had no intention of losing her only other friend in this place.

'You make a beautiful bride, ma'am.'

Her heartbeat raised a few notches at the thought of her upcoming wedding. Rafe, all six feet two inches of lean muscle and brooding presence, soon to be hers. It was as if a bird had trapped itself behind her ribs. She pressed her palm to her chest and took a few slow breaths.

He'd never be hers. He was a means to her end.

'I'm not sure the designer agrees.'

'If only it were a happier day for you.' Albert clasped his hands behind his back. Looked at her in that enigmatic way of his that told her nothing but made her question everything. 'It's a courageous choice, ma'am.'

She laughed, a bitter, sharp sound with no amusement in it. There'd been nothing courageous about anything she'd done. Lise nibbled the inside of her mouth.

'You used to call me Lise, once…'

Albert had always been there for her. Providing gentle advice and encouragement. Warm, where her parents' approbation had been a cold wedge.

'That's before you became my Queen.'

'And Annalise, when you were angry at me.'

'Have I ever been angry at you, ma'am? I can't recall,' he said, though his mouth twitched in an almost smile.

'When I took the crown before father's state function.' She'd wanted to try on those precious jewels. Back then, the certainty was they'd be her brother's some day. Never hers. All the diamonds and gold and ermine too much temptation for a teenager. She'd stolen into her father's rooms where it had sat in an ornate wooden travelling box. She'd discovered the crown was big, and heavy. That was when she'd dropped it…

Albert chuckled, his elegant grey moustache quivering. 'No one noticed the mark, and the Crown jeweller repaired it.'

That was a secret they'd kept from the King, for everyone's good, Albert had said at the time. She'd believed people were keeping secrets about her meetings with Rafe once. For whose good was that?

The telltale burn started behind her eyes once more. Would it ever stop? She tried to blink away the tears. Queens did not cry. Of that she was sure.

'What do you need, ma'am?' Albert's voice was warm and kind. Almost her undoing.

'I need to be just Lise, for a little while. Please.'

She glanced at the view from her private rooms. She'd always loved the vista from here. High on a hill above the capital, Morenberg, surrounded by the Alps she loved. The mountains where she felt truly at home. But today they loomed outside, as if judging her.

'You'll always be Lise to me. Even though I call you Your Majesty.'

She turned to him, still standing there, a picture of gravity and stoicism.

'I don't think I can do this.'

'You were born to it.'

'No one taught me the skills.' Nobody thought about her much at all. Her brother was meant to take the throne and she was meant to do her duty, which she'd failed. Spectacularly. What if she'd simply agreed to marry Rafe when her father demanded it? She'd have been wedded off the same as now, and the rest of her family would be alive.

'Some need to learn, and some have it here.' Albert tapped the centre of his chest. 'You've always cared about your people, Lise. No one needed to teach you that. Your instinct will carry you through any mistakes. The rest? I'm here to help.'

'Which I never doubted.'

His lips tilted in a sad smile.

'Have as much faith in yourself as you have in me and you'll do well. Is there anything else you need?'

A way to escape? But there was none. The die had been cast weeks ago. Still, Lise gritted her teeth. She'd wanted to wait till after the official mourning period was over. Three months, that was all she'd asked for. Only a small delay. But no, her government had been clear.

You must secure the Crown.

The silence between them hung all too knowingly in the room. The clock chimed the hour. Dread curdled sick in her stomach.

'Almost time to go,' she said, itching to adjust her veil as the pins fixing it pricked into her scalp. 'I think I need a few moments to myself before the prime minister arrives.'

Albert gave her a curt, well-practised bow and turned.

'Albert?' He stopped at the door as she said his name.

'Yes, ma'am?'

Her moment of being *just Lise* was clearly over. 'What do you think of my decision to marry Mr De Villiers?'

As she'd barrelled from the room after the final argument with her father, Albert had been there. Directly outside. There was no way he couldn't have heard everything she'd said, but his face had told her nothing as she'd run down the halls to her own apartments, her world torn apart.

Albert smiled. 'I've always thought you were a woman of great courage, Your Majesty.'

Rafe stood at the altar of the Morenburg Cathedral. The whispers of the assembled crowd echoed from the vaulted ceiling, melding into an amorphous hiss. Rainbow colours from the centuries-old leadlight stained patterns on the floor like blood spilled on the marble.

He stared down the long red-carpeted aisle to the firmly shut front doors. The scent of the lilies bedecking the hallowed space too cloying. He wondered whether the funerary choice of flower had been Lise's, or whether they too had been pre-ordained. Ordered for her brother's nuptials. The probability they had been galled him. That this day, *his* triumph, was recycled from others. He shook his head. No time to think of that since it was only minutes till the bride arrived. Mere hours till he would be King. The most powerful man in the country.

His pulse quickened, the thrum of excitement coursing through him. In the front seats sat his mother and father. Eyes not quite so wide as they'd been over the past weeks since he'd told them he and Lise would marry. For all the ceremony, his parents remained the humble, unaffected people they'd always been. Now, they'd take their rightful places in society, like him. Their grandchildren would one day sit on the throne. The De Villiers name linked to the Crown in perpetuity. His only wish was that Carl could be by his side, to witness his triumph. The pain of that loss knifed deep; a wound barely healed after all these years.

'You sure about this?'

His best man and best friend stood surveying the pomp in the nonchalant way the finest aristocracy could breed. He'd met Lance at school, his father the British ambassador to Lauritania. An outsider, like Rafe. It hadn't mattered that Lance Astill would inherit a duchy in England when his father died. He wasn't Lauritanian, so he wasn't good enough. Apart, they'd been bullied. Together, they'd been impenetrable. Lance had guided Rafe through the raw pain of Carl's death, becoming like the brother he'd lost. The friendship had lasted when Lance's father was posted elsewhere. It had never wavered.

'Yes.' Rafe's certainty was absolute, unassailable. Coursing through his blood with the enthralling hum of a drug.

'I've a car parked round the corner and this.' Lance reached into his inner suit pocket and pulled out the hint of a silver flask. 'Whisky. Plus a case in the back seat. We can make a dash for it through the door of the sanctuary. Escape. Drown our sorrows for days.'

His mouth quirked in the signature lopsided grin that drove women wild. But his eyes were tight and serious.

'No,' Rafe said.

'You used to be more talkative. She's got you cowed already? No stag night. Now passing up decent whisky. Wives, why would you have one?' Lance gave an exaggerated sigh.

An organ piped hymnal tunes, which echoed from the vaulted ceiling.

'Some things are more important than the whisky.' Rafe's words were almost sacrilege. Once it was always about the whisky and the women. But he hadn't needed to celebrate his last night of freedom. This marriage gave him keys to every door. 'Do you have the rings?'

Lance began an increasingly exaggerated farce of patting of his various pockets, frowning. A lesser man might have been worried. Rafe knew it was only for show.

'I believe I do. Somewhere… Ah.' He reached into his trouser pocket and pulled out two glinting circles of gold. 'Hers is spectacular.'

Lance twisted it in his fingers, eyeing off the workmanship. If nothing else, Rafe's friend had a keen eye for beautiful things.

'Her Majesty refused an engagement ring. The occasion dictated something more than a plain band.' The day required symbols. His great-grandmother's wedding ring, tying Lise to him. The family's past coffers reportedly plundered to have the magnificent token of love made, reflecting his great-grandfather's adoration for his betrothed. A waste in his view. Rafe hadn't wanted to accept it when it was suggested by his parents, given the heirloom was the symbol of a devotion absent in this marriage. However, he couldn't turn down the honour of using it today.

'Must be love,' Lance drawled.

Rafe snorted. Not for him. He'd never allow himself that vulnerability. All 'love' had done for him was turn him into a fool. Never again would he dance to the beat of another woman's drum.

'Careful, my friend,' Rafe said, with a smile meant

for the cameras directed towards them. 'The world is watching.'

He stared down the assembled crowd. Dour, serious-looking people. All the uniforms, medals and emblems they hid behind as if it made them better than the rest. In a short while he'd be set above them all, and there was nothing they would be able to do but bow and scrape before him. The victory would taste so sweet.

Lance glanced up at the cameras assembled to beam the marriage to millions. 'Nervous?'

Rafe shook his head and spoke the unassailable truth. 'I'm where I should be.'

'But is the bride?'

Rafe checked his watch. She was only five minutes late. Not long in the scheme of things. But the curl of tension twisted his gut. He'd wanted no hesitation. No sign that being at his side was other than where she was meant to be. He shook it off. What did it matter when he had a lifetime as Lauritania's King ahead of him?

'I've been meaning to ask, what is that hideous thing on your chest?' Lance pointed to a pale blue and white ribbon. An enamelled, gem-encrusted star with insignia pinned to Rafe's jacket. 'Looks like a vulture.'

'Order of the Raven.'

The country's highest civilian order in the country. Since Rafe didn't have a drop of blue blood in his veins, the decision had been made to confer him with something. For outstanding service to business. He could have laughed. He'd been serving the country for years and it took his marrying their Queen to recognise him.

'You're becoming one of them.'

There was the dull sound of disappointment in his friend's voice. It had been the boyhood promise they'd made after Rafe had saved Lance from a beating meted out by the sons of some counts or other. *Never* become like the aristocracy here. From that day, Rafe had fought back with fists, carrying the pride of his working-class background. Together he and Lance had become a force none of the other boys had been able to reckon with.

'I'll never be one of them.' He fixed his friend with a heated glare. 'I'm better.'

Lance shook his head. 'Always the ambition with you.'

The truth of that cut closer to the bone than it ought. 'If that's how you feel, what are you doing here?'

'Ensuring my oldest friend's making the right decision.' The silence between them lingered ominously for a few beats. Then Lance clapped his hand on Rafe's shoulder, lowering his voice in a conspiratorial way. 'And women. The best man always gets laid at weddings. It's a rule.'

Rafe laughed; the tension broken in the way Lance knew best until the organ swelled in a glorious crescendo as the doors of the Morenberg Cathedral cracked open. Trumpets commenced some suitably wedding-like heraldry. The whispers of the crowd drowned out by the music announcing the arrival of his soon-to-be wife. He turned; his bride stood silhouetted in the door. His heart quickened its pace to racing speed.

Lance chuckled. 'My friend, it looks like you're royally screwed.'

Rafe didn't understand what he meant. Lise crossed the threshold of the cathedral doorway, a shadow backlit by glorious sunlight. The voluminous skirt of her dress filling the entryway, nipping tight at her slender waist. She began her slow procession down the aisle, the prime minister at her arm. But as she walked closer, he re-

alised what Lance had seen the moment she'd stood in
the doorway. When she'd walked into the soft light of
the cathedral nave she hadn't moved out of the shadows.
Her wedding dress was an inky black.

He ground his teeth. The perfectly fitted morning suit
too tight, too hot under the stage lights. Of all the hu-
miliations in his life he'd had none worse than this. He
wanted to tear off the badge of chivalry she'd bestowed
on him only days before, the meaningless trinket that it
was. Symbols? She'd given him one of her own. Not even
a pretence that this was a day to be celebrated in any way.
What she wore was an utter repudiation.

Rafe breathed slowly and reminded himself that the
world watched every expression they displayed. As his
bride approached, he smiled. Wide, doting and fake to
the very core. He glanced over at his parents, who were
beaming as if her slight meant nothing.

'You look beautiful,' he said. Her face was pale and
soft focus behind the black lace-edged veil that fell past
her fingertips, spilling to the floor and trailing behind
her. And to any objective observer, she did. The gown's
bodice fitted to accentuate her slender frame, the elegant
swell of her breasts. All the harshness of the colour softened by a feminine ruffle of dark, sheer fabric round her
neck that dipped in a demure vee exposing a bare hint
of cleavage. The coal-dark satin of the remainder of the
gown shimmering with encrustations of jet beading. Up
close it was an extraordinary piece of workmanship. It
didn't stop the beat of anger drumming in his veins.

The archbishop took his place in front of them as the
music died. 'Are we ready?'

He'd spent his whole life planning for a moment like
this. Four years manoeuvring for this exact day. Yet it

was Lise, not him, who gave a curt nod to commence the ceremony that would seal their future together.

The archbishop intoned a prayer and began. 'We have come together today to witness the marriage…'

With that sentence the hallowed space melted away. The talk of love, joy, tenderness. Of children. Those words should have been a mockery, but somehow weren't. Even the anger burning through him mellowed. Rafe turned to Lise and took her hand in his, as he'd been instructed he should. The tremble in her frigid fingers unmistakeable. Her blue eyes wide and brimming with barely contained tears. And the moment ceased to be about a country, a queen or a king. It centred on the two people in front of the altar, a man and a woman. The vows passed in a blur of false promises. Rafe placed the wedding ring on Lise's slender finger. Her skin soft and delicate as she gently slid the bright gold band on his own with no hesitation.

'… I therefore proclaim that they are husband and wife.'

Rafe raised Lise's veil, uncovering a face as pale as if she'd been cast in moonlight. Her perfect mouth a soft dusky pink. He gazed into the blue eyes searching his face. Pupils wide and dark. The barest blush sweeping across her cheeks before fading away. He raised his left hand to cup her face, which tilted up to him. Her skin, silky and warm under his fingertips, her lips parted. For the briefest of seconds, he believed she wanted this. Him. Then the look passed.

'For pity's sake, kiss the bride,' Lance murmured.

Not today. Their first, real kiss would be in private, not watched by millions. He wanted her to crave it, *beg* for it. For *him*. So he dropped his head and brushed his lips across the smooth skin of her cheek. Relishing her soft exhale as he did.

Rafe turned to the assembled crowd. The coronation came next but that was a mere formality. He didn't need to feel the heavy weight of the consort's crown on his head to know the unassailable truth. It hummed through his blood with a heady roar. Better than making his first billion. Better than drinking the whole case of whisky Lance had stashed in the back of the car outside. For every slight these people had given him, each one of them would know.

The country was his. He ruled them all.

Long live the King.

CHAPTER THREE

LISE TOYED AT the plate of food at the wedding banquet showcasing Lauritania's delicacies, a headache burgeoning at her temple. Other people seemed to be enjoying themselves. Wine flowed freely. There was a sense of festivity she didn't feel. Three hundred or so palace intimates and foreign dignitaries celebrating a marriage she didn't want. A wedding arranged for her brother, not her.

Rafe didn't have any trouble eating as he finished whatever meal lay on his plate. But then, he had what *he* wanted, what her father had promised him. No wonder he could eat, drink and be merry with the rest of them. She brushed away a stray hair that had fallen from her chignon, trying to ignore the sensation of him sitting so close. Gone was the laid-back nonchalance that was Rafe's signature. Today he vibrated, as if filled with some dark energy. In exquisitely tailored morning dress with a silk tie. His over-long hair cut to a more respectable length, but still swept back from his face in that carelessly messy way as if run through by restless hands. Her fingers had itched to touch those glossy black locks as she'd waited for the kiss in the cathedral. The one that never came. Her first and last opportunity. She'd thought for a fleeting moment that today she could steal something for herself. But life wasn't like that, not for her. As she'd gazed into his velvet brown eyes, transfixed by the full curve of his lower lips that would claim hers, he'd turned and kissed her cheek. She would never get to know whether his lips were cool or warm, soft or hard. Whether he was passionate or restrained.

She should have been relieved. A kiss wasn't part of their agreement, even though a kiss was expected, today of *all* days. If he *had* kissed her, it wouldn't really have broken any promises. Now she'd lost her only chance. Though she shouldn't be thinking of chances or kisses. All she hoped was for the day to be over quickly, so that she could return to her rooms, rid herself of her finery. Grieve this sham of a marriage. And steel herself for the next three days allocated as a pretence of a honeymoon, so the country could believe the lie that this was a love match. To give her people some hope built from the tragedy of the past months. And how could she argue against that? Against any of it when she was the cause of the grief? So she was being bundled up and packed off to some unknown destination where there would be more togetherness than she wished to contemplate. Lise's cheeks heated and she took a sip of her wine.

'Your dress is magnificent, Your Majesty.' The prime minister's wife smiled at her. It didn't meet the woman's eyes. No one's smile did. Not even Rafe's when he'd greeted her at the altar and told her she looked beautiful. 'The colour is a brave choice.'

Brave… Why could no one say what they *really* meant?

Rafe stilled next to her, put down his knife and fork. Took a swig of his wine.

Minutes prior to the wedding, a press release had identified the designer as one of Lauritania's finest couturiers. It told the story of the gown with the royal crest and Lauritania's native flora embroidered in beads and crystals on the skirt. So much encrustation that the gown weighed on her, heavy and oppressive, as if she carried the whole country with her.

'It was a way of honouring my family since I'm in official mourning.' The stab of pain above her eye made her wince. She rubbed the aching spot in her temple.

The prime minister's wife brushed her fingers over her jacket sleeve of lemon-coloured silk. Such a cheery shade, which spoke of celebration. It made a mockery of her family's deaths.

'But it's your wedding.' The woman rambled on. 'Surely on today of all days you're allowed to be a little…brighter. After all, you hope to be a bride only once.'

Lise glanced to another table at Sara Conrad. Her brother's fiancée. She was wearing black too. How would Sara feel, watching Lise marry today? Being crowned Queen in her place? The guilt gnawed at her, bile rising to her throat. Lise couldn't celebrate knowing she'd stolen her friend's future. How could she flaunt her marriage when Sara and her brother had lost the chance of theirs?

She clenched her fists in her lap, her wedding ring on one hand and coronation ring on the other, biting into her flesh.

Rafe leaned forwards. 'Are your parents still alive, Mrs Hasselbeck?' His warm hand slid over hers. Squeezed in silent support. The tight band in her head eased a fraction.

The prime minister's wife straightened in her chair, her mouth pinched and tight. 'They are, Mr De Villiers.'

The cut was so plain it couldn't have been a mistake. A few people stopped eating. An uneasy, expectant silence fell over the table.

Rafe's eyes hardened to stone. Face stern, uncompromising.

'Pardon?' He raised one dark eyebrow in a supercilious way. Perfectly regal. Her father wouldn't have done better.

'My apologies, Your Majesty.' Mrs Hasselbeck patted her lips with her white damask napkin, nothing at all apologetic in her demeanour. 'It's all so new, I forgot.'

Lise didn't believe the lie for a minute. How dared the woman? Dismissing Rafe was like dismissing the monarchy itself. Lise opened her mouth to say something, but Rafe cut across her, voice cold as steel.

'You should have your memory checked. The lapse is troubling. It could mean something serious for the future.'

Those words spoke a clear warning. That Rafe wouldn't forget or forgive. Lise shivered. This was a side to the man he'd never shown her before. The ruthless businessman, who would do whatever he wanted because he now could.

The woman dropped her gaze, a conciliatory gesture of sorts. 'It won't happen again.'

'That's pleasing to hear,' he said. The moment passed. The palpable tension settling. People turned away from them and went back to their food and wine. 'But my message is that with the advantage of having both parents alive you shouldn't presume to tell anyone who's recently lost theirs how to mourn.'

A bright kernel of warmth lit Lise's insides, the words a surprise. She shouldn't have enjoyed them. He didn't really care. Rafe simply knew how to play the game of

intrigue too well. She couldn't let her silly heart buy
into the fantasy it meant something more. He was experienced, she was an amateur, and she must never forget.

Whatever she might have hoped for, he would never
love her. In her relatively brief years on this planet, she'd
come to realise no one really did. Her birth had been
deemed a necessity born of duty. She'd not been truly
wanted and, whilst the King, Queen and Crown Prince
had seemed to do much as they'd pleased, she had been
required to do what she was told. And even when she'd
done that, it had never been enough.

The soft strains of a string quartet began, announcing
the bridal waltz. Lise let out a slow breath, let her shoulders slump. The ache in her temples hadn't gone. She
fixed a false smile on her face. Stared out at the crowd.

Lise dreaded this moment. Rafe stood and held out his
hand. She placed hers in his. The warmth of it engulfed
her own chilled fingers. He stared at her with his dark
eyes, almost black in the room aglow for the wedding
luncheon. Her pulse whipped to superhuman speed. Her
head pounded to the same thready, anxious rhythm as he
led her to the dance floor. She needn't worry, she knew
the movements of the waltz. Had suffered through lessons given at her finishing school, when for months all
they had seemed to learn was deportment and dancing.
She placed one hand lightly on Rafe's upper arm, the su-
perfine wool of his coat cool and soft under her fingers.
The muscles underneath hard and uncompromising. He
slid his arm round her back, till his palm sat strong and
hot below her shoulder blade. Drawing her to him.

'Relax,' he murmured, his voice gentle and enticing.
How could she? The space between them too close. She

tried concentrating on the elegant knot of his silver tie. The perfect double-breasted waistcoat of pale grey silk. The way the clothes moulded over his strong chest. She looked up at his face, his gaze intent. His all too fascinating lips curved in a half-smile. She could do this, dance with him. Though her breaths seemed short and sharp as if there weren't enough air in the room. All she needed was to let the man lead. Yet the thought of letting Rafe lead… She had no idea where he'd take her. But the slow, curling slide in her belly took her head to places she didn't want to go. Revisiting the fantasies she'd once had of being held in his arms, made love to, adored.

He moved, his powerful legs brushing her dress. Carrying her with him. They rose and fell in time with the music, in perfect unity. The warmth radiating from his body seeping into her frozen one. A prickle of awareness singing over her skin. She could smell him, fresh and crisp like the Alpine forests mingled with something darker, a primal thing that sang to every nerve in her body. That made her want to fall into him, soak it into the frigid heart of her. Yet she couldn't do that, have him draw her close. Rest her tired and aching head on his chest and take some of his strength. She'd made the decision. The lives of her family had been stolen as a result of her actions. She'd devote herself to the Crown. Preparing her country for a time when the monarchy was no longer required. Nothing else mattered. For tonight she needed to straighten her wedding tiara and get on with it.

More people joined in the dance. The prime minister and his wife. *Sara.* Dancing in the arms of their best man. Looking…happy. Smiling up at Lance whereas the swirling and the sound simply made Lise sick and dizzy. The music too much with the pounding of her head, till the colours blurred and she misstepped.

Rafe steadied her. Stopped. Led her from the floor, drawing her into a quiet corner. Or as quiet as any corner could be with the eyes of three hundred or so people watching them.

'You don't look well.'

'It's nothing.' Heartsick wasn't an illness, was it? 'The waltz has never been my favourite dance with all the spinning. I'm dizzy. It's been a long day.'

Up before dawn to dress, have her hair and make-up done. Trying to numb the pressure threatening to cleave her in two.

'The formalities are over so we can leave soon. No one will ask questions.' His eyes were molten. All liquid chocolate, luscious and addictive. Rafe reached out and slid another unruly strand from her chignon, tucked it behind her ear. The gentle touch of his fingers sent goosebumps sparkling over her skin. 'Then bed for you.'

'It's only afternoon.'

'Indulge yourself.'

Rafe's voice was low and soothing. She imagined her bed now, the plush coverlet of eiderdown. How she wished she could indulge like a normal woman. Sink into it with him. She took a step back as a tempting heat grew between her legs. She couldn't let this overcome her. That wouldn't be honouring her family. She was vulnerable now. Her head throbbing.

She'd master this.

She *had* to.

'I'd like to leave now.'

Rafe stared down at her. He wouldn't miss the looming tears because he missed nothing. He slipped his arm around her waist in a proprietorial way that made something inside her curl with a treacherous pleasure. Motioned to his best man. The pair shook hands. Lance offered final congratulations. Announcements were made. Everyone in the room stood. The men bowed as Rafe led her out, the women curtsied.

The throbbing in her temple increased to a vicious pounding. She massaged the side of her head.

'Anything wrong?'

Everything, and nothing she had any power over.

'Headache. You're right, I—I need rest,' she said as they walked from the ballroom to their private chambers, acknowledging staff as they passed. Together, yet separate. With each footstep the gulf between them widening. It almost felt like relief, yet at the same time she mourned the loss of him. The emotion a confusing mass inside, congealing in her stomach, making her ill.

They stopped outside the door to her room. She looked up at him. So tall, so imposing it was hard not to swoon. Her heart beat a thready, panicked rhythm.

'You need help with your dress,' he said.

Of course, the buttons. Hundreds of them down the back of the gown. She cursed every single one.

'I'll call for my lady-in-waiting.'

Rafe cocked his head to the side. 'There are certain expectations of what will be happening today between husband and wife. One of those is that I'll help you undress.'

What would it be like to let him? The feel of his fingers slipping each tiny button through the loop, exposing her spine to the air. Would the act be perfunctory, or would he torture her slowly? His eyes became dark and heavy lidded, a look that told her everything. Sensual torture was what he had on his mind, she was sure. And she couldn't allow it because she was weak. She needed hours of sleep to shore up her defences against him.

'I find I'm tired of people's expectations. I've performed as was expected of me. Now I'm done.'

Rafe's perfect mouth kicked into a knowing smile. As if he *knew* she was avoiding him.

'Then I'll leave you to your afternoon.' He took her right hand, weighed down with her coronation ring, lifted it to his mouth and kissed. His lips warm and gentle on the back of her hand.

She nodded as he stepped back. So stiff, so formal that something about it made her want to scream and scream till her throat was bloody. Then he turned and walked down the marbled hall to his own door, without looking back.

Rafe strode into his rooms. Dismissed the valet imposed upon him by palace protocol. Tore off his tie, cast it onto the bed. Followed with his jacket and waistcoat.

His wedding night, and they were engaging in this ridiculous charade. Lise still intent on shutting him out, even though she wanted him. He could tell by the high colour of her cheeks, her quick breaths. Dilated pupils and languid blinks of her eyes when he stood too close. It was enough to make him rush her, but patience had been his virtue in business, and he needed it here. He always fought to win, and with Lise it would be a siege. Long and slow.

Something about the thought licked at him deep and low. He'd started today when he hadn't kissed her as he knew she'd expected from the disappointment on her face. Their first kiss was never going to be a chaste peck on the lips. He had bigger plans for that, a seduction that would seal her to him body and soul, unlike their emotionless signatures on an official slip of paper. Children, so his legacy would last. He'd go down in history as the first commoner to sit on the throne.

She'd be desperate enough for him in the end. He'd ensure it. He knew Lise's secrets, what she'd craved— freedom, acceptance—and they were even more important to her now, as Queen, than as the lonely Princess in her gilded tower. He could still give her those things.

He'd been working towards that moment ever since he'd glimpsed her at her coming out ball. When he'd been announced and walked down the sweeping marble staircase. She'd stood at the bottom, gazing up at him, a glowing smile on her face. He'd been struck as a visceral craving dug its claws into him when their eyes met. They'd been introduced, he'd bowed. She'd smiled even wider, still the glorious, natural young woman who had all but disappeared now, worn down in the name of duty. She didn't know him then, but she hadn't judged the entry of a man without a title, *a commoner*.

He'd wanted to steal her away, run so that she wouldn't be crushed by the purpose of others. Still, no matter his desire, she'd been about to be packed off to some hellish finishing school. A place that taught women to aspire to nothing more than advantageous marriages, bent on turning her into a beautiful clone. By some miracle she'd survived without losing herself. There had been nothing careful and suppressed about Lise that first night. In a room of pale imitations, she'd stood out as unique. So he'd waited. He had patience. She'd needed to find her place in the world before finding it at his side then in his bed. He knew enough about the machinations of the palace to ensure it happened.

After waiting so long for this day it had taken all his strength to walk away. Not to take her in a mind-numbing kiss.

He took a deep, calming breath. They had three days away from official duties. That meant he had three days to make inroads on the siege for his wife's body and soul. To tease, to tempt. She'd come to him willingly, begging him by the end of it. If he were a betting man, he'd bet on being in Lise's bed inside a fortnight.

Rafe removed his great-grandfather's cufflinks from his shirt and placed them carefully on the gilt dresser. Precious heirlooms that reminded him how far he'd come from the cursed farm boy of his youth. Taking his family company and their working-class wealth and turning it into billions. He poured a glass of the single malt whisky he'd requested and took a slug, enjoying the peaty burn in the back of his throat. Swallowing down the anger, mostly at himself. The irritations he suffered at his current situation were nothing when compared to Lise's recent loss. Even though her mother was renowned as a cold, ambitious woman and her father as licentious and profligate. Then the brother who'd exhibited meagre promise but descended into reckless pleasure-seeking, no doubt following his father's example. Whatever the truth of them and however Lise might delude herself, they were still her family.

He needed to remember she was deep in grief, and he well knew the cost of that emotion. Plus, tonight they were still playing a role, and, as a seemingly caring husband, he should check on his wife.

Rafe picked up the internal palace phone and requested a delivery from the kitchens to the Queen's room. A peace offering, of sorts. Or perhaps his opening salvo. He walked through his expansive apartments to the door that separated him from Lise. A door for which he now had the key. He smiled.

Let the siege begin.

CHAPTER FOUR

LISE STOOD AT the window, overlooking her city decked with banners and flowers for her wedding and coronation. She winced at the light of the bright autumn day as she downed two painkillers in one gulp of water. She should close the curtains, shut out the sunshine that caused her head to pound, but ever since her family's deaths she couldn't, at the risk of the room closing in on her, leaving her gasping and breathless.

She walked to the bed. Perhaps lying down would help, but on the coverlet lay an exquisite negligee her dressmaker had made as a surprise gift. It taunted her, that fragile piece of wedding-night trousseau. Fine, cream georgette, sheer as cobwebs. Cut in with plunging lace and delicate embroidery. A peignoir lay next to it, designed to allow tantalising glimpses of the wearer. Alluring and seductive. She was used to expensive clothes. Cashmere, silk, the finest of wools. Satin evening gowns requiring a surprising number of foundation garments to hold you in or push you out in all the right places to get them to fit with the perfection envisaged by the designers. But this. Overtly sensual, like nothing she'd ever placed against her skin.

Lise picked up the corner of the nightgown, light as

air. What if she slipped it on for tonight? She could wear things like this to bed, she supposed. But this garment seemed overly decadent. Anyway, she knew that an item like this wasn't meant to be worn to sleep. Goosebumps flourished over her skin. Its purpose was to be viewed through male eyes. Something meant to be appreciated in a sweet burst like fairy floss and then melt away at the first touch.

She dropped the fine fabric, teasing under her fingers. It wasn't for her. It could go the same way as her wedding gown. Taken away to be stored in the royal collection with her mother's clothes and all the other wedding finery before it. Held for posterity to be viewed when she was long dead, and her family relegated to history. It seemed a fitting place to bury it, leaving no trace of the Queen who'd married earlier in the day.

Almost.

Lise twisted at the wedding ring sitting on her finger. It gleamed with the burnish of old gold. She wanted to rip it off but knew she must get used to the constant prickle, since it was there till death. Which was what was engraved on the inner surface, in French. *Jusqu'à la mort.* She shivered. There was something almost macabre about the thought. The finality. Though even she had to admit it was an exquisite piece of jewellery. The wide golden band appeared sectioned, each panel inlaid with delicate, alternating enamelled flowers. Daisies and roses. Impossibly fine workmanship. If circumstances had been different, if she'd been able to believe she'd meant something to Rafe, if they'd loved each other, then this ring would have signified so much. If, if, if. None of those things were relevant to her, to this marriage. She needed to forget the romantic ideals she'd held once before her rude awakening and move on.

All she'd proved to herself was that Rafe didn't love her.

The crack and creak of a rarely opened door disturbed her thoughts. She whipped round, the sudden movement increasing the pounding of her head. Lise put her hand to her temple again as Rafe walked through the freshly opened doorway.

'What the hell are you doing here?'

'Hello to you too, Lise.'

Rafe had changed. Gone was the urbane gentleman from her wedding. Before her stood a man dressed in casual trousers, with shirtsleeves rolled up to show his muscular forearms. The front unbuttoned so she caught glimpses of the dark hair on his chest. All of her tightened, as if she didn't fit her own skin. As if she'd burst out of it as a butterfly splitting from its chrysalis.

She didn't like the feeling. At. All.

'I asked you a question!'

The corner of his lip curled in a mild, indulgent kind of smile.

'Apologies. I thought the answer was obvious. I came to visit my wife. To chat about how she felt the wedding went. The normal intercourse between newly married people.'

He strolled further into the room, looking over everything with an astute, all-seeing gaze. Rafe overpowered the space. His presence bigger than the person, obliterating all else. He stroked a finger gently over the surface of a delicate antique French writing desk. It was as if he were looking for cracks, imperfections. Looking for a way in.

She crossed her arms in a protective move, but she didn't feel protected.

'It was a productive day. I woke up. I dressed. I got married. I was crowned Queen. The end, goodbye.'

'We're far from the end of the day yet.' His voice stroked over her as soft and seductive as the silk negligee on her bed, which Rafe was now looking at with unalloyed fascination. Her cheeks heated.

'It's over for me.' She glanced past his shoulder at the opening to his apartments. Once her brother's, though Ferdinand had vacated them years before. The dust covers only recently removed to accommodate a husband. The shard of pain stabbed to the heart of her, but she ignored it. Lise nodded towards the open space. 'That door's usually kept locked.'

He slid his hand into his trouser pocket, pulled out a key. 'I have this.'

'How did you get it?' She'd requested he be placed in the King's Chambers rather than here. Then he'd be halfway around the palace, well away from her.

'Friends in high places.'

This place was full of traitors. Rafe stood in front of one of the large mullioned windows. She squinted as the pain from all the bright light clawed inside her skull. The tablets she'd taken didn't seem to be working. All she craved was to lie down and sleep away the next seventy-two hours. But no, she had a *honeymoon* to participate in, and nothing about that would ease the pain she suffered.

'I didn't authorise it. Give me that key and scuttle back the way you came.' She waved him out. His smile in response might have been mild as a spring day, but his eyes held all the tempest of a thunderstorm.

'Marriage implies a certain level of…availability.'

Another flush of heat crept to her cheeks. 'You can't just barge in here.'

'I didn't barge. I strolled, with purpose. Next time, I'll knock.'

'There'll be no *next time*.'

'It would be strange if I didn't have access to all areas.'

Lise was about to object, but there was a knock at the proper door of her room. Could no one leave her and her aching head in peace? Lise hated knocks on the door now. She could never forget Albert, ashen-faced, walking through another doorway to deliver her the news...

'Yes!' She might have been a little sharp, but life was sharp. Every day held something designed to cut her. The well-oiled door eased open. One of the servants walked in carrying a tray containing a teapot and cups. She put it down on a small table.

'There's nothing more we require. Thank you,' Rafe said with a glorious smile that made the girl blush as she curtsied and left the room.

He took the embossed silver teapot and poured out a pale golden liquid into two cups. The scent of it fresh and herbal.

'What's this?' She nodded suspiciously at the beverage.

'A family concoction. It can cure anything that ails you, so the legend goes.' He held out a cup to her, took one himself and sat on a couch under the window. She sank into a spindly, straight-backed chair, as far away from him as possible. Rafe took a mouthful of his drink and Lise followed with a tiny sip from her own cup. The brew burst minty and sweet over her tongue; with undertones she couldn't place.

'What's in it?'

'The recipe's a closely guarded secret. My mother knows the blend. She won't give me the ingredients. Is afraid I might commercialise it. Shame. I suspect it would be quite popular.'

'It tastes of things I can't place.' Somewhat medicinal, but pleasant and refreshing. It wasn't the sort of thing she imagined Rafe drinking at all, if rumours of his love of single malt whisky were anything to go by.

'I disliked the stuff as a child. It was forced down my throat every time I sneezed. As an adult, drinking it leaves me nostalgic,' he said, taking a mouthful of his own. For a fleeting moment his gaze seemed distant, the crinkles at the corners of his eyes deepening as if the memory was a happy one. 'My mother sends me a regular supply. To help me sleep when my conscience gets the better of me from making too much money, so she says.'

'How's that going?' Lise took a large gulp of the beverage. The quicker she finished, the faster she might encourage him to go. 'Or let me guess. You don't have a conscience.'

'I have a large hoard of herbal tea, which is now in the palace kitchens hopefully being put to good use amongst the staff… And my conscience is clear.' He chuckled, a warm throaty sound that rolled over her bright, hot and sweet, like the drink in her cup.

She dismissed the sensation, difficult though it was not to simply immerse herself in it and forget her own failings. How nice it would be not to have a conscience, whereas hers tore her to pieces.

'Pleasant for some.'

Rafe cocked his head. 'What could a twenty-two-year-old woman have on her conscience?'

If only he knew. Those hateful words she'd said a constant reminder of the final conversation with her father.

'You can all go to hell. I wouldn't cry if you died...'

But that was her cross to bear. She wouldn't share it with him. 'What thirty-one-year-old man doesn't have something plaguing his?'

'Touché.' He laughed, such a strangely cheerful sound in this space that had no happiness in it. 'But the prickle of conscience suggests regret. That's a wasted emotion. Make your decision, stick to it and accept the consequences.'

If only it were so easy. She'd live a life never accepting the consequences of her decisions. Now, Rafe posed a constant reminder of them.

'So you have no regrets and nothing on your conscience? You sound more like an automaton than a human. Good for you.'

'I've one regret.' Rafe lounged on the floral chintz couch in his typical fashion. Too masculine for this room although he seemed to take ownership of it all the same. 'A very human one. The regret for not kissing a beautiful woman.'

His rich brown eyes skewered her, and her heart rate kicked up, thready and overwrought. It was a terrifying sensation, as if he could see everything she wanted to remain hidden for ever.

'Nothing important, then.'

'Sometimes there's nothing more important than kissing.'

The air in the room grew thick with possibility. Surely he didn't mean her? They hadn't kissed, but that could be put down to part of their agreement. It must be someone else. Someone worldly. Passionate. A woman he could take up with again after a respectable time. The sort of woman he could fall in love with. Not her. Too young, inexperienced…unwanted. That realisation sliced through her, with something almost like pain. The ache in her head intensifying. She rubbed at her temple again, trying not to think about it.

'What's plaguing you, Lise?'

'Nothing.' Nothing she could tell him about. Nothing that wouldn't condemn her, though she didn't know why his good opinion mattered. All she needed was to get away from him and the way he affected her. The pounding heartbeats, which made her head throb ever harder. 'Except this headache.'

'We'd better not let the staff discover your malady, not today.'

'What do you mean?'

'The clichéd excuse for avoiding a husband's advances. *Not tonight, dear, I have a headache.* On the wedding night too. They'll all be wondering about the antics in this room on what's supposed to be the happiest night of our lives.'

She shrugged. 'Maybe they'll assume we both have a headache because they realise it's not the happiest night for either of us and their supposition will end there.'

'I'm not known for my headaches.'

'I applaud your pain-free status.'

'What few people realise…' Rafe leaned forwards with a conspiratorial whisper, his muscular shoulders pressing at the fine white cotton of his shirt '…is that orgasms are a recognised cure. So a headache shouldn't be an excuse for avoiding sex, but an incentive to have it.'

How that three-letter word, *sex*, slipped from his mouth. Accentuated by his voice, deep and tempting, as if it held a wealth of meaning. Once, all she'd dreamed of was a moment when he might hold her, make love to her… A product of her foolish imagination and naïve, romantic dreams. She'd never held any kind of meaning to him. It was the position he wanted, not her. Lise cast aside those thoughts. Rolled her eyes. 'I can see men all over the globe using that line. And there's nothing more to say on the subject.'

'Headaches, or orgasms?'

'The latter.'

'Shame.' Rafe considered her through steepled fingers. 'The tea hasn't helped?'

She peered down into her cup, at the dregs of liquid there. 'With my headache?'

A few random leaves settled in the bottom of the fine porcelain. If someone could divine her future from them, what would it hold? She suspected nothing good…

'Yes. If it gave you orgasms, I'd be the wealthiest man on the planet rather than the wealthiest in Europe.'

Rafe sat back and threaded his hands behind his head as if he was getting comfortable. As if he had no plans to leave. She needed him to go, so she could spend her wedding night trying to forget who she'd married and *why*.

'*If* you were given the recipe,' she said. 'Which you weren't because your mother doesn't trust you and neither do I.'

That seemed to catch his attention. Rafe stopped lounging and straightened. His eyes narrowed. 'In this place I'm the *one* person you can trust. I wish you'd realise that.'

Once, she might have believed it. Not now. She placed her cup and saucer on a side table and smoothed damp palms on her black trousers.

'A trustworthy man wouldn't have feigned interest in me when all the while the deal for my hand was being sealed as a fait accompli.' Her jaw clenched hard. How it galled her, the things his attention made her believe. 'That charade was cruel.'

He narrowed his gaze, assessing and intent. 'My interest was not feigned.'

But he didn't deny the charade. Lise closed her eyes and pinched the bridge of her nose. Tears burning behind her eyelids.

'I can't do this, not today,' she said. More to herself than anyone else but she hoped he listened since she didn't have the energy to fight him. Not now.

'I'm sorry, I've been trying to lighten the mood and you're suffering. Do you need painkillers?'

She looked up at him and shook her head. 'I've taken some. Nothing's working on this headache and right now I'd do anything to get rid of it.'

Rafe raised one dark, strong eyebrow. 'Anything?'

She shouldn't have said that. Not anything, *almost* anything. She pressed back in her chair. The delicate, wooden back crushed into her spine.

Rafe stood. He had a look of predatory intent on his face. Her heart beat faster, which only made her head throb more. Though if she didn't have so much of a headache, she might have been more worried. But her voice seemed paralysed as he walked towards her, every movement languid and slow.

'I understand. It's been a difficult day for you. That's why you have a headache,' he murmured. 'I can help with that.'

He moved behind her. The heat of his proximity was warm against her back. She tried to ignore him standing there, but the feel of his presence trickled down her spine like warm water.

'What are you doing?' She squirmed in her chair, trying

to see what he was up to. Rafe stood out of her eye line. Without him to focus on in front of her, the whole room seemed too light and bright once more. She winced and shut her eyes against it. All she craved was a few moments of peace, for the pain to leave her. Physical *and* emotional.

'You're tense. It's clear in the way you hold yourself. If what I do doesn't help, I'll stop. Let me touch you.' Rafe placed his hands on her shoulders. Firm, warm. Solid and, in the strangest of ways, comforting, as if through his touch he could absorb some of what plagued her.

'You're carrying the weight of the country's grief, as well as your own, on your shoulders. For a few moments, let it rest.' He pressed his thumbs either side of her spine and she arched back at the exquisite ache of tight muscles objecting under his forceful fingers. 'Let me know if you want me to stop.'

His voice was a soothing murmur as he dug his thumbs a bit lower. *Oh, there.* Lise stifled a moan. Rafe didn't stop the journey of his strong, intense fingertips circling either side of her upper back, finding trigger points she didn't know she had. Working them under his clever fingers till they melted away. She'd had massages by therapists after her skiing, but it had been nothing like this. The intensity that made her forget everything. The hurt, the day. All she concentrated on was the pressure of his hands on her spine.

'No.' Her voice sounded far away. He lifted his fingers. 'Don't stop.'

He moved his hands towards her neck, the pressure making her soft and pliable. Melting her. She dropped her head forwards, closed her eyes. The relief exquisite as he dug in relentlessly. Rafe ran his thumb over a tight spot.

'Right there,' he said, and she exhaled. She couldn't remember the last time someone had touched her, someone who might care. Certainly not her family. Yet all she could do was soften under his ministrations.

He left her upper back and slid his hands to her neck, a tremor skipping down her spine as he gentled for a moment, stroking his thumbs up and down as if searching. His fingers firmed on a tender spot at the base of her skull. Who moaned? Was it her? Rafe chuckled.

'Does that feel good, Lise?' His voice was all gentle temptation. She couldn't resist listening to the way her name rolled from his tongue. 'If you allow me nothing else, let me give you this.'

'Yes.' Her voice was a bare whisper as he kept working her tight muscles, softening the knots in her neck. He scraped his fingers across her scalp and eased her head back till it leaned against his hard abdomen. She didn't care about anything. The voice of crippling self-doubt fell silent. The sharp edges of her life blurring and softening. As he gentled the stroke of his hands through her hair, she could purr like a cat. And when he rubbed the burn at her temples time lost all meaning. It could have been moments or hours since she'd been sitting here.

'Please.' Her body had melted like wax under a flame. Rafe ran his hands through her hair as if straightening it, then slid one hand round the front of her throat, cupping her jaw. He leaned in, mouth at her ear, his warm breath a gentle caress as she tipped her head back to rest on his shoulder.

'I'll give you anything you want.'

She didn't know what she'd been asking for. For him to stop? For him to keep going? She couldn't say. Her tongue, thick in her mouth. Her nipples tightened under her top. She wanted Rafe to slide his hand down her chest, ease the ache with his talented fingers.

'Anything. You only need to ask for it,' Rafe whispered, each syllable full of dark promise. Every part of her in a dream as his lips traced the soft flesh behind her ear, the barest of brushes, which set her body on fire.

Anything. He'd give her *anything*…except, he couldn't. She opened her eyes, blinking slowly to focus. Her freedom, her family. They were all irrevocably lost. All she could do now was to ensure that what had happened to her would happen to no one else. She stiffened. Rafe could offer her *nothing*.

'I want you to stop now.' Her voice came out as a rasp, raw and pained.

He stopped. Immediately. She hated herself for missing his touch, an empty, bereft sensation. It proved her weak, as she'd known. One touch and she was ready to throw herself into his arms, welcome him to her bed. He stepped in front of her, looking down as solid and immovable as the mountains surrounding the palace. She wished she could take some of that strength for herself but taking anything from him was a vulnerability he could exploit.

'Of course,' he said. 'You're exhausted, and I'm being selfish. What my bride needs is a dark room, a soft pillow, a warm bed and sleep. I'll ask the kitchens to send dinner to you here. I can look after myself.' He brushed his knuckles against her cheek. Damn him and his gentle voice, his understanding. Because she wanted it, craved it. She closed her eyes, as he stroked her skin again. Shutting out the unbearable tenderness in his gaze. 'I hope you're feeling better, Lise.'

She heard the door snick as he left her alone, as she'd asked. But worse than the caring he'd shown. Worse than succumbing so easily to his touch. Worse even than the terrible sense of loss of his hands on her body…

Her infernal headache was gone.

CHAPTER FIVE

IF RAFE COULD have developed a perfect torture, it would have been the exquisite agony of touching his wife with no early prospect of release. All night he'd had dreams of her, dressed in the magnificent sheer negligee that had lain on her bed. How it would hang on her body, showing tantalising shadows of what lay underneath. Those thoughts had morphed into imagining what she wore to bed each night, which meant all he'd been plagued by were visions of her lying naked on pristine white sheets.

Now he was in a car with Lise, driving the winding roads to his ancestral home in the mountains. The delicious smell of her, like wildflowers and rain. Everything about her taunted him in this closed-in space. Her golden hair, which had slipped like cornsilk through his fingers. All the softness of her that he craved to sink into. Her breathy moans. Those intoxicating sounds he could listen to again and again. Dreams of him over her, buried deep inside her body. The way she melted under his fingertips. All pliant. Willing. *Please*.

He had no doubt she'd wanted him last night. He was hard at the thought.

But he ruthlessly crushed those fantasies, for now. These few precious days away were being sold to Lise

as shoring up the myth of their relationship for a curious public but the reality, for him, was so much more.
Which was why he'd driven here rather than allow them
to be chauffeured in a car with a little fluttering flag
whilst they sat regally in the rear. Sure, there was security following at a respectful distance exactly the way
he'd demanded, much to their protestation, but if there
was one thing they'd learn, he always had his way. Lise
needed reminding that, apart from being Queen, she was
a woman with needs and desires. That she could still indulge in simple pleasures without being overwhelmed
by misplaced guilt.

'Are you feeling better today?' he asked. They hadn't
had breakfast together. She'd slept late and he hadn't
wanted to wake her. But as she'd entered the car he'd seen
the dark smudges under her eyes, ever present, which told
a story all of its own.

'Yes, thank you.' She glanced at him only briefly,
before looking out of the window again. 'Where are we
going?'

He'd told her it was a surprise, and the look on his face
when he had suggested that she didn't much enjoy sur-
prises. Sure, he could have taken her to his mansion in
the fashionable area around Lake Morenberg. The type
of grand home any wealthy Lauritanian must own, yet a
place where he rarely stayed. Instead, he brought her to
where he'd grown up. A simple farmer's cottage on land
that his family had owned for generations. If there was
any place for simple pleasures in Lise's life, then the cottage was the venue to indulge them.

'The first home I lived in.' The home his great-grandfather built for his great-grandmother. Where his father
was born. Where Carl… He tamped down the blunt ache

of his brother's loss, an ever-present bruise. Those feelings left him vulnerable. Never again would he let that wound be picked open. 'My grandparents gifted it to my parents on their engagement. It's quiet. I thought you might enjoy a break away from the city.'

Plus, there was the sense of freedom these wild places instilled. He hoped she'd find that freedom again, to be herself.

To let go.

His pulse throbbed at the thought of her in any kind of abandon, not holding back. Body arched in the throes of passion, his possession. He would get that from her. Claim it when offered, keep it all for himself. Lise looked at him then, and he chanced taking his eyes from the road for a moment, only seeing an innocence in her he knew would turn to caution if she'd ever guessed what he was thinking.

'That's…kind of you.'

Not so kind, when having her in his bed was the end game. Breaking the promises she'd deluded herself into believing he'd made when they'd reached their agreement about this marriage. So long as he could convince her that it was all her idea, his plans would succeed. For in this place, there was no escape. The house was small and the space intimate. Perfect for a honeymoon if togetherness was what you were searching for. He wasn't sure she'd thank him when she saw it.

'We have a stop on the way first.'

They passed the turn-off to his home, and drove further, winding through green pastures dotted with the occasional cow, to a copse of trees. He pulled off the road and parked at the gravel verge. The black SUV of Security stopped well back, but he'd made it clear that they

weren't to follow them into the forest. More protesting.
He'd ignored it. Lise needed to forget about being Queen.
He saw these small steps as one way. But of greater importance, and what her security team didn't realise, was
that he'd care for her better than they ever could. This
was *his* land, *his* home. He'd ruled these mountains, been
King here, even before Lauritania's crown had been
placed on his head.

Rafe left the car and opened her door. The trepidation
on Lise's face was easy to read.

'What are we doing?'

He rounded to the boot and retrieved a small bucket
and knife as she watched, chewing on her bottom lip, a
slight crease forming between her brows. Looking beautifully perplexed.

'Foraging for mushrooms.' Rafe smiled at her as they
walked into the leafy verge. Here he breathed deeply of
the cool autumn air tinged with the crisp scent of nature.
Time slowed. He could travel all over the world, stay in
any of the expansive properties he owned, but only here
was home. With Lise by his side, it felt more right than
it ever had, the realisation a startling one. 'Have you
ever been?'

She shook her head. 'It would have required me to get
dirty, and that would never do.'

'No making mud pies as a child, then?'

'Now you're being silly.' But she gave him the tiniest
of smiles nonetheless, which he took as a win.

'I'm all for giving you new experiences. Mushroom
picking comes first. Mud pies come later.'

Lise laughed, and the glorious ring of it sang through
the trees. He hadn't heard that sound since the times

they'd strolled the palace gardens together before her family had ruined it all.

He craved to hear her laughter again and again, with him the cause of that happiness.

'There's a stream where Carl and I used to play as children and come home filthy carrying frogs and moss. Be careful or we'll go there next.'

'Who's Carl?'

He'd forgotten himself, mentioning his brother's name. Another revelation, that he could lose himself with her, which was a vulnerability he could never afford. Lise was ignorant of the knowledge and the memory he protected, since the pain of Carl's loss had been wielded as a weapon against him in the past, by those richer and more powerful.

He'd never allow that to happen again. Anyhow, there was no one richer and more powerful in Lauritania than himself. Not any more. But uttering his brother's name had been a slip he never made. The only time Carl was mentioned was in the safe haven of family, or with Lance when they'd drunk too much whisky and were intent on reminiscence.

'Rafe?' She wanted her answer. He wouldn't lie to her, but he couldn't respond so forged ahead a little too fast up an incline, deeper into the shade. It was steeper here and Lise didn't really have the shoes for it, pretty little things made for palace halls, not forest floors. She lost her footing and slipped on the leaf litter. He took her hand and steadied her. The slightest tug and she came into his arms easily. The soft press of her body against his as she splayed her hot palms on his chest.

The gleam in her cornflower-blue eyes as he held her told him she was far from indifferent. He ached at the magical feel of her in his arms. Her breaths high and fast. Pupils dilated. He should kiss her here, under the canopy as the breeze skittered through the ochre leaves above them. But he wanted to be somewhere where they could take things to a natural conclusion. In the forest was not that place. Though with a blanket and a picnic...

He wasn't sure where all these romantic notions sprang from.

Lise slid from his grasp, wiped her palms on her skirt as if trying to wipe the remains of him away. Something small and painful scraped inside him as she did.

'Do you know what we're looking for?' Her question about Carl forgotten in a moment where he knew she was as affected by their proximity as he'd been. And he could smile at the change of subject because what he truly searched for was here. Standing in front of him looking beautiful and uncertain.

'Yes. Ceps.'

He turned and strode further into the shade of the trees as she hurried to keep up with him.

'How do I know they're not going to poison us?'

She had so little faith in him. In anyone, perhaps. He'd work to change that, where he was concerned at least. As for the rest of them? They could wallow in her distrust. No one else was worthy of her anyhow.

'Because I've done this hundreds of times since childhood. You're the one who'll try to pick the poisonous mushrooms. I'll make sure what you choose won't kill us both.'

He scanned the leaf litter round the trees. Glimpsed the telltale signs under a break in the canopy. Rafe walked up to his prize. Slipped out a knife and cut the stalk. It gave him the same innocent thrill it had as a child when he'd found his first edible mushroom. The simplest of pleasures that even he'd forgotten over years of becoming hard and jaded both at his business and with his country.

He held up the mushroom. Lise smiled and it was like the sun breaking in the middle of the forest. Warm, dazzling. He basked in it.

'Now it's your turn,' he said, handing her the knife.

'Where do I find one?'

He showed her. Something about Lise here seemed calmer. The lines of stress etched onto her face had smoothed. A tightness relaxed. He suspected the mountains were her place, too. That she felt it as much as he did.

They hunted in silence. He smiled as he watched her. Intent, looking at the ground. She let out a little cheer.

'This!' She pointed, then brushed some leaves away like uncovering buried treasure.

He walked up to where she stood, peered at her find. Slapped his hand to his chest and groaned. 'You're trying to kill us all.'

Rafe spied the pout on her lips, her disappointment. He laughed. 'I'm joking. It's perfect.'

'Not poisonous?'

'No.'

She punched him in the shoulder but grinned all the same. Looking young and happy for the first time in weeks. 'You're mean.'

'You do the honours.' He nodded to the knife and held out the bucket. 'Then find me some more. We need enough for dinner.'

'Who's cooking?'

'Me.'

She stopped, turned. Looked as if she was seeing him for the first time. 'You cook?'

'How else am I going to eat?'

'I don't know.' She shrugged. 'Restaurants. Private chefs.'

His mother would never have stood for that. She believed her boys needed to learn to feed themselves. He'd fought her attempt to drag him into the kitchen as a teenager, but at least had a few meals in his repertoire.

'You can't live on fine dining. Sometimes you want a home-cooked meal.'

He'd never thought he'd need the ability. Yet as Lise looked at him with big, wide eyes in a way that suggested he was somewhat heroic, that simple skill now seemed vital.

She scuffed her feet on the ground. 'I don't know what that tastes like.'

'Then tonight will be full of new experiences for you.' Her cheeks blushed a fetching shade of pink, leaving him in no doubt what new experiences she had on her mind, and they had nothing to do with food. 'But before then we need a few more mushrooms.'

He watched as she continued her search, all so he could cook her a simple meal. Her smiles as she found what she was looking for were all for him and the happiness for what he'd shown her. And Rafe wasn't sure how he'd make it through dinner when all he craved was dessert.

Lise rubbed her hands against her jeans, not completely removing the dirty smudges left by their picking expedition. Their precious cargo stowed safely on the back seat of Rafe's low-slung sports car, filling the cabin with its earthy smell. There, in that small forest beneath these towering peaks, it was as if she could breathe again. The tight band, a constant round her chest, finally easing. Somehow, it was as if the natural grandeur of the mountains diminished her problems. As if she could almost be happy here. Though how could she be happy when her family were lying cold and dead in a grave?

She stopped looking at the view, instead looking at Rafe as he deftly negotiated the treacherous, winding roads that would soon carry the dairy herds down from the tree line to the winter pastures and barns. His hands were relaxed. Long fingers on the steering wheel. Forearms, strong and bronzed in the sunshine. Arms that had wrapped round to steady her as she'd slipped on the loose leaves. The overheated memory of being cradled, safe. It flooded over her, warming like the autumn sunshine spilling through the windscreen. A delicious, hazy sensation that slid inside and had her shifting in her seat.

Rafe glanced over at her. 'It's been a long drive. We're almost there.'

He'd misinterpreted her discomfort. Which was a good thing. If he knew the real reason, he'd use it against her, of that she was sure.

They rounded a corner, turning into a narrow drive that meandered further uphill. Nestled in a tangle of wildflowers and rambling cottage garden sat a two-storey chalet, with steep shingled roof and Juliet balcony up high. The fresh, whitewashed walls and dark timber cross-hatching reminded her of a gingerbread house. Wisps of smoke drifted lazily from a chimney.

'This is lovely,' she said, almost with a sigh. Rafe smiled as he pulled his car around the back to where a building stood. The barn, if she had to guess.

'It's a little crooked and well worn being so old, but this has always been home.'

Rafe tugged their bags from the boot of the car. Lise loved the way the muscles in his arm bunched and flexed as he did. She grabbed the bucket of mushrooms. He walked to a back entry and opened it, guiding her through the mud room into a sunny, country kitchen where she placed the bucket on a bench top.

'How often do you come here?' she asked. The place looked well lived in, the wooden surfaces polished to a shine, no dust anywhere to be seen.

'If I'm not travelling, this is where I try to stay.'

That surprised her. Most of Lauritania's wealthy lived on the lake, or in one of the fashionable skiing areas. This part of the country was only known for summer pastures and farming.

'It's so far from the capital.'

He laughed and the deep, masculine sound rippled through her like an earth tremor. 'I enjoy the solitude. Plus, I've a helipad built out back. If pressed for time I fly.'

Another surprise. It was something about him she should have known, but in all the times they'd been together, they'd only talked about her. How much of himself did Rafe hide?

'You could have flown me here?'

'Of course, but the drive is beautiful, and I thought you'd enjoy it. Next time I'll bring you by helicopter. If you trust me.' Something about the fact he'd again thought of what she might enjoy warmed her insides. She liked him caring, she ached for him to touch her. They were dangers she could not succumb to. Because she didn't trust him. She didn't trust anyone any more, least of all herself...

'Come,' he said, jolting her out of those miserable thoughts. 'I'll take you to your room.'

She followed him through the kitchen and up a wooden staircase, the treads burnished to a low gleam by generations of footsteps. On the top floor, the ceiling sloped with the frame of the house. Rafe dropped his bag outside one door. Toed open another and let her inside.

A fire crackled in the grate of a rough stone fireplace. That, and the sun streaming through the doorway to the tiny balcony she'd seen on the drive towards the house, made the room warm and inviting. Dominating the space stood a magnificent four-poster bed with a comforter of rich burgundy. Plush rugs covered the dark wooden floor. In front of the fireplace sat a deep blue velvet couch she craved to sink into and never leave.

But she realised, looking about her, that the room was undeniably masculine with its solid furniture and bold palette. A man's space. *Rafe's*. She turned, and found him leaning against the door, her bag at his feet.

'I can't take this room. It's yours.' How could she sleep here? In his *bed*. It was too much. Her heartbeat picked up its already hyperactive pace. She needed to distance herself from him, not immerse herself completely.

'It's more comfortable than the second bedroom and has its own en-suite bathroom.' He shrugged. 'I thought you'd appreciate it.'

'I can handle having to walk to the bathroom. If I survived Princess School, I can survive that.'

He raised an eyebrow, and his mouth curved into that warm, slow smile of his that did complicated things to her insides she refused to dwell upon.

'Princess School?'

'Finishing school. It was...' stultifying, depressing, demoralising, '...austere. I shared a room with another girl, and we definitely had to share bathrooms.'

'Strange. I thought it would be palatial quarters, hot chocolate, toasting marshmallows, and plotting to acquire rich husbands.'

'The plotting for husbands was there. Along with lessons in flower arranging, correct placement of cutlery, deportment and how to be the perfect lady. All those kinds of world-saving skills. Exactly what I needed for my job as Queen.'

She gave a laugh, which came out more like a hysterical snort.

'Learning how to be a perfect lady was obviously one lesson you paid most attention to.' He grinned at her.

'Obviously.' Lise laughed harder, but there was no joy there, only disbelief at the absurdity of it all. The futility of those twelve, lonely months. They'd prepared her for precisely nothing. Not her family's death, not her new role leading the country. She laughed till she doubled over, then the laughing morphed into the clutch of grief that clawed her throat, of loss and missed opportunities. That her family never saw any more of her than her value as a bargaining chip. As a wife to someone powerful. It was how her country saw her, too. Only her marriage making her legitimate as Queen.

Lise couldn't stop the tide of pain as it overwhelmed her, threatening to rend her in two. She buried her face in her hands, trying to calm herself. To choke back the sob threatening to break free.

She didn't hear Rafe's steps across the floor. His strong arms wrapped round her again, bringing her to his chest. Holding her so she wouldn't break apart. She buried her face in the hard muscle. Forcing down the tears that she'd never allow to fall in front of him. Trapping the sadness with shuddering breaths. Because Lauritania relied on her to pull the country from its grief. She didn't have time for her own. Still, her hands gripped his shirt to give her something, anything, to hold onto.

'Lise.' His voice was a soft murmur. She didn't deserve this solace. The pain was something she should feel, but she couldn't move away, couldn't let him go. If she did, she might drown in it all. Sink beneath the waves of grief and never surface again. Rafe held her till her choked breaths eased and the threat of tears receded. She rested her head against his chest. Lulled by the steady thump of his heartbeat as he stroked her hair, saying nothing, merely holding her together. It was too easy to stand there in the safety of his arms, letting the warmth of him seep into her frozen places. To soak him in.

To hope for things that weren't for her.

She pushed away from his chest and his hold eased. His expression one of concern before she moved away and scrubbed at her eyes, rubbing at the few tears that had managed to escape.

'I'm fine. Really.' She turned to the view from the glass doors leading to the balcony. At a winding road, the spire of a little church, nestled in the rolling green foothills of the Alps. Looking at anything to avoid looking at him.

She felt Rafe's warmth behind her. His hands, rested on her shoulders. A gentle rub of his thumbs on her neck. Goosebumps shivered across her back and down her arms at his comforting touch. 'It's okay not to be.

You've been through an ordeal. Take some time to grieve, whilst there's no one here to watch you.'

Yet unbeknownst to him, her losses were self-inflicted. Own goals. She shrugged him away. She had no right to his sympathy or the temptation of his touch, which made her want to fall into him and never get up again.

'I don't have the luxury of time.'

'You've a country to run. And you're exhausting yourself. There's no thanks in that.'

Rafe walked in front of her, cupped her face in his hands. 'Asking for help doesn't make you weak. It takes strength to know when you can't do it on your own.'

She wanted help. She wanted someone to rely on, something she'd never really had before. To allow her to feel more like herself. Not the broken woman. Not the Queen. Just Lise.

I'll give you anything you want...

He was asking for that person to be him and part of her, the dark secret heart of her, wished it could be. And those were dangerous, tempting thoughts to have.

Because Rafe was the last person she should ever trust.

CHAPTER SIX

LISE HUGGED HER knees as she sat in the verdant grass staring at the picturesque view over a valley. A little church, a quaint village, all surrounded by majestic Alpine peaks. She'd followed a short and well-worn trail, bringing her to this place with its outlook over the mountains. She'd attempted to call Sara, to check on her friend to see if she was okay, to try and talk too about her own conflicted emotions, but there had been no answer. The phone oddly going to a message bank that claimed to be full.

Lise flopped back and spread her arms wide, staring into the deepening blue sky above her. She should have worn something more suitable than light clothing and a flowing skirt for the walk, as the sun had begun dipping low, the air taking on a crisp early autumn chill. But the thought that she could simply wander away with no plan or agenda had been too tempting. As Queen, she was coming to learn there was always some agenda, always a plan. She shut her eyes, concentrating not on what she had to do but in this single, blissful moment. On the gentle chimes of cow bells in the distance, the tickle of grass under her fingers. The brush of a late afternoon breeze on her cheeks. Simple, honest pleasures that she could allow herself to indulge in.

The sense of some presence, that she was not alone, caused her to open her eyes and turn.

Rafe. Cutting a swathe through the swaying grasses, as he strolled in her direction. Lise's heart fluttered like the butterflies that had earlier been sampling the remaining wildflowers dotted around her.

'Hello, Sleeping Beauty. Did I wake you?' He smiled, and any remaining chill left the afternoon and she bathed in the warmth of him.

'I wasn't asleep, and no prince kissed me, so...'

What was she saying? His dark eyes gleamed in the golden light of a dropping sun and the corner of his mouth quirked into a wry grin.

'That could have been arranged, although you'd have to have settled for a king, rather than Prince Charming.'

'I'm not sure that's how the fairy tale goes.'

Lise couldn't help herself. She glanced at his mouth, the curve of his lower lip that seemed so soft and full, and wondered again what it would be like to kiss him, just once. For real, not only in her overheated fantasies.

'You're Queen, you could write your own.'

She shook her head. 'Life doesn't work like that.'

'In the end, life is what you make of it.' Rafe gestured to the ground next to her. 'May I join you?'

She nodded, and he sprawled beside her, plucking at the grass and flowers as he stared out over the landscape. Its magnificence paling in his distracting presence.

'You've found one of my favourite places here,' he said, pointing to the valley. 'The church is where generations of my family were married...and buried. I started my schooling in the village.'

'And now you rule all you survey.'

The corner of his mouth curled to a wry grin. 'This

is my true home. I always believed I ruled here. The invincibility of youth.'

She stared out over the landscape. Not looking at him because his presence was a palpable thing that slipped under her skin, filling her with the pulse of desire. She craved to lean into Rafe's warmth and strength, absorb some into herself.

'It's somehow easier to think, up here,' she said. She breathed deeply for what felt like the first time in weeks. It was as if here, away from the capital, her knotted thoughts unspooled.

'And what are you thinking about?'

She might not be able to sink into his arms but surely she could share some of her fears? For all his faults and scheming, he had never failed to make her feel…*worthy*. One of the few people who ever did, and in a way she had truly believed. Lise sat up, plucked a long blade of grass from before her and wound it round her finger.

'How can I rule a country when I was never shown the way? My purposes were only decorative. This role requires more than simply smiling and waving or cutting ribbons.' She cast the now crushed strand of grass away and hugged her knees to her chest. Of course, she wasn't simply planning to rule the country, but to move it towards a future without her or a royal family. Never again would someone be forced to take on a role they didn't aspire to simply because of a quirk of birth. To be forced to marry…

'Don't say that.' Rafe's voice was strong and sure. 'You may not have been trained as Queen, but *you've* trained. To push through pain and fear to win. Don't forget your skiing. You were slated to make the European championships. It shows a strength and commitment to succeed that others didn't display. You have a determination inside yourself. No one can take it away from you.'

'You make it sound so easy.'

'Was competition easy?'

She shook her head. It was gruelling and exhilarating and terrifying, but never easy.

'There's your answer.'

She turned to him and looked at his hands, his strong, capable fingers weaving the final touches to a wreath of grasses and wildflowers.

'What's that?'

'I used to have to make garlands for the cows in our autumn village festival, celebrating their descent from the mountains for winter.'

'You're making a cow crown?'

He chuckled and the warm, throaty sound rippled right through her.

'If I'm King of these mountains, *ruling all I survey*, then I need a queen.' Rafe held the wreath up to her cradled in his palms, then reached out and placed it gently on her head. 'And now, I have her.'

Something inside, a hard veneer that she'd shellacked over her heart, softened and cracked a little. The well of emotion, dangerously like hope, threatening to spill over inside her. 'It's so much lighter than the real thing.'

Rafe cocked his head, his gaze intent and assessing. 'You wear both crowns well, Lise. Never forget.'

Over his shoulder, a star winked on in the sky. She hadn't realised how quickly the sun was sinking below the horizon. This moment full of magic, she didn't want it to end. Just the two of them sitting here. Rafe and Lise. King and Queen of the mountains. In the fading light the breeze picked up and cut through her. She shivered.

'Come.' He stood up and held his hand out to her. She slipped her cool hand into his, engulfed by the heat of his palm as he helped her to her feet. How easy this was, to go to him. Hold hands and walk together towards the house as a real couple might. 'It's getting late and, even though the path is well worn, being out in the mountains at night can be treacherous. I also have dinner to make.'

Rafe released her hand as they entered the house. She immediately missed its warmth, the sense of comfort he provided. He kicked off his shoes at the door then moved to the rustic kitchen, with its copper pots and knots of herbs and garlic hanging from the ceiling. Rafe eased a cork from a bottle of wine. Poured a glass and slid it across the counter to her. Poured one for himself and raised it as if in a toast.

'Here's to a simple life. Good food, good wine, good company.'

She turned and toasted too then took a sip of the crisp, fragrant white. 'Well, we have one here. The wine's superb.'

He bowed. 'My latest acquisition.'

'But it's made by the oldest winery in the country.' They were world renowned and had won international awards. The business had been run by the family for close to a century. 'Why would they sell?'

Rafe crossed his arms, his biceps bulging in a distracting way as he did.

'They were crippled by red tape, lack of government assistance and cheap imports. There's been no care taken for the businesses that made our country great. They're being lost to overseas interests. I've been fighting to stop that happening. Maybe we can change the decline together? Reinvigorate the economy.'

'What's wrong with the economy?' Her father had never spoken to her of it, presumably because it had been unnecessary. In her brief weeks as Queen, no one had mentioned the economy at all.

'People have been lulled by complacency. It's time you shook them awake.' Rafe tilted his head, and his eyes narrowed a fraction. He remained a mystery in so many ways. Right now she couldn't read him at all. 'But enough. This weekend's about getting away from all that. We have the good wine. The good company. What we need is the good food.'

He took a wooden board from a hook, set it in front of her with a knife and a bowl of mushrooms in what seemed to be a deft change of subject. 'I've brushed off the detritus. Chop these into slices and we'll eat soon.'

It was as if he'd deflected her question. Part of her felt dismissed, although another part didn't want to contemplate right now what it took to run the country. She wanted to simply take a breath. *Be.* Time enough for the business of ruling Lauritania a bit later. It was only a few days.

'What are we having?' she asked, slicing through the mushrooms.

'Not the cordon bleu of the palace. Something more rustic.'

'I'll let you in on a secret,' she said, taking another sip of her wine before chopping more mushrooms, 'That's the type of food I wish I could cook.'

He raised his eyebrows. 'What did finishing school teach you if not how to feed yourself? It seems like the sort of basic skill a person should learn.'

'Apart from flower arranging and correct placement of cutlery, I'm an expert on theatrical dishes like bombe

Alaska or crêpes Suzette. Of course, if I want to eat anything other than extravagant desserts for the rest of my
life, I'm doomed.'

'Never with me. I'll save you from starvation,' he said
with the flourish of a spatula and a grin that lit a glow
inside her. Reminding her of the breathtaking man she'd
craved with something of an obsession. He was handsome
all the time, devastating when he smiled.

She put her hand to her chest. 'My hero. In a palace
with a kitchen full of chefs, you're the one who'll poach
me an egg if I want it.'

He tossed some butter into a pan and it sizzled as he
seared some sort of meat. Once that was done, she handed
him a bowl of finely sliced mushrooms and he added
them into the pan with an onion he'd already chopped.

'I'm afraid my heroic status is a myth. I've never mas-
tered egg poaching. Veal with mushroom cream sauce is
more my style.' Her mouth watered at the mere thought of
that meal, and an appetite she'd forgotten resurfaced with
a low grumble in her stomach. Lise took another sip of
wine as Rafe drizzled some of his own into the pan and
tossed the mushrooms with a practised skill.

'Impressive,' she said. And he was, in all ways. Commanding the kitchen, no doubt as he commanded the
boardroom. And she realised she'd never really seen him
in anything much other than business clothes. Not like
this, in jeans with a casual shirt, cooking in a kitchen
and looking…human. It was something of a shock to her
system. She placed her now empty glass on the counter-
top and Rafe poured some more wine into it.

'I could teach you.'

'I think I'll just watch.' And she needed to watch him.
This relaxed man, at ease with himself and in charge of

everything around him, was a risk. She'd made commitments to herself. Nowhere in those was allowing him to slide under her skin.

He plated up the meal with a tidy twist of pasta and sprinkle of fresh herbs. Took both plates to an antique table, which carried the scars of many a meal prepared and eaten on its surface. In the centre sat a small cut-glass vase overflowing with wildflowers. A candle, which he lit. It looked cosy, romantic.

Dangerous.

'This is…' *Lovely.* 'Unnecessary.'

'We're having a simple meal, Lise, that's all.'

But there was nothing simple about this. The soft light. The warm room cocooning them. It was as if they were the only two people in the world. A world where they were not Queen and King of a whole country, but simply Lise and Rafe, rulers of the mountains. A tempting fantasy she had to ignore. They *were* Queen and King, and that reality would never change. She reached up and removed the beautiful grass and flower garland from her head as she sat, placing it on the table next to her.

Rafe raised an eyebrow, fixed her with a heated gaze. 'Shame, you looked beautiful.'

She tried to ignore the delicious thrill that ran through her at his words.

'One does not wear one's crown to a private dinner,' she said, in her most queenly tone, before taking a mouthful of food to avoid the moment. The rich flavour of mushrooms burst against her tongue. Lise caught a moan in the back of her throat. Rafe's gaze turned incendiary.

'You approve?'

She nodded, washed the mouthful down with another sip of wine. When had she last enjoyed anything she'd eaten? When had any food tasted more than dust on her tongue?

'We make a good team,' he said.

'How so?'

'Your mushroom-cutting skills are superlative.'

She laughed. 'Who'd have thought that was a skill I needed to learn?' She leaned back in her chair, relishing the food on her plate, the sharp edges of life softened by the wine in her ever-topped-up glass. After she finished, he cleared away and rinsed their plates. Wouldn't let her help. Motioned to the couch that sat squashed and low in front of the flickering fire. He took another board with a slab of cheese and placed it on the hearth.

The light danced in the room, painting his skin gold. Rafe's eyes dark and sultry. She sank into her end of the couch. He sprawled next to her, feet bare and propped on the coffee table in front of them. She'd never seen a man's naked feet. An odd sort of realisation that she'd always been faced with men in suits and polished shoes. Something about that made the evening seem even more intimate.

'I can see why you come here,' she said, trying not to think about any part of Rafe naked. There was no sound bar the pop and crackle of the flames in the grate. She tipped her head back and stared up at the ceiling, the rough-hewn beams and white plaster in between, that had seen his family raised here. The man himself, this place that made him. Something about that was real, and grounding. A connection to the past she seemed divorced from, even though her family had ruled the country for centuries.

'As I've said, the mountains are my home. No matter where in the world I am, it's here I think of.'

He stared into the flames, took a sip of his wine. She watched the masculine bob of his Adam's apple as he swallowed.

She nodded. 'It's why I skied. I could get away from myself. The mountains don't allow any ego.'

'They don't accept mistakes. And they'll be here long after we're gone.'

'It's the one time I could feel alone. Challenge myself.'

He turned to her, his eyelids low and shuttered. 'What have you replaced the challenge with?'

'Isn't Queen enough?'

'That's a duty for others. What about for yourself?'

She remembered that day, the day everything had been set in train. When she'd only thought about herself and nothing else. She hadn't realised, in those moments, what she'd lose.

'There isn't anything more.'

He reached over and placed a hand over hers. She wanted to pull away, but somehow couldn't move, relishing the solidity of his touch.

'To be a good ruler you must allow something for yourself, or you'll cease to care. Not today, not tomorrow, but some day. Then the decisions you make won't come from the good of your heart, and they'll be the wrong ones. For your country. For your people. For you.'

What was he alluding to here? Her vow that the monarchy died with her? Lise shook her head. She didn't know what to take for herself. How was there anything left when everything had been stolen from her family? Where did she even start? With wine, perhaps. Maybe with another sip, a simple choice. She could do that, in the glass that Rafe seemed to ever fill.

The man in question left the couch and moved over

to the cheese board close to the fire and cut off a now molten piece. He slathered it onto some crusty bread and held it out to her.

She shook her head. 'I couldn't.'

Though the glistening, molten cheese and bread looked tempting…

'One bite. My family made it,' he said. 'I'll eat the rest if you don't want to.'

Lise took a bite, teeth crunching in the crisp white bread. The cheese oozing everywhere. She gave a low moan of pleasure at the salty tang, then handed the bread back to him. His eyes darkened as he ate the rest himself.

'It's my idea of dessert,' he said. 'You can keep crêpe Suzette and bombe Alaska to yourself.'

'You don't like sweet things?'

He sat on the coffee table in front of her. Their knees brushing, sending a thrill through her. The fire flickering, glowing like a halo behind him.

Except the man was no angel.

'I indulge in some.' Rafe's voice was soft and smooth, like silk against her skin. He didn't take his eyes from her, as if he were trying to stare deep inside. Into all her secrets. He didn't need to do that; he knew enough of them to be a danger to her. Her heart beat a thready rhythm, and the breath caught in her throat. She reached round him to take her glass of wine, breaking eye contact.

'I'll keep that in mind. Any time I want to cook, it won't be dessert.'

'I didn't say I didn't like dessert, Lise. I'm merely selective in my choice of indulgence.'

He moved away from her now, and she let out a long, slow breath. Trying to forget the feel of him holding her as she fell apart this afternoon. Weaving her a floral crown, holding her hand as they walked to the house. The closeness that didn't feel feigned. In her deepest heart that was what she wanted for herself.

Rafe cut off more cheese, held it up. She shook her head. The room was warm, the couch soft and deep. Everything here cushioned her from the reality outside. The sharp edges of life a bit rounder, burnished smooth. And Rafe. The black curls gleaming in the low light. His hair all unruly as if it never behaved. A lot like the man himself. A passionate man, from all the envious whispers she'd overheard when he'd begun to pay her exclusive attention. A warm flush bled over her. She closed her eyes, to block him out, but it didn't work. Felt the couch dip, the heat of him closer. He slid an arm round her shoulders. She opened her eyes and glanced at the hand casually sitting along the back of the couch near her. The sprinkling of hair. The square-cut nails with perfect half-moons. When had a hand held so much fascination? He eased her closer, till she leaned on the side of him, tucked under his arm.

'Relax, Lise. Close your eyes if you want.'

'I don't want to sleep.'

He didn't feel safe. But neither had skiing on the black runs and that had made her stomach swoop and her heart pound. Never knowing what would come round the next bend. This was a little like that, the thrill of anticipation skittering through her belly. It was what she'd been missing, and she craved it like a drug. When had she stopped taking risks? Perhaps she could accept this, for a little while. She'd so wanted him to hold her, kiss her, before it all. The day of her wedding her only chance. She drank the rest of her wine. Rafe took the glass from her hands and set it on a table, before settling her into him again.

He'd wanted her. He'd made it clear. Why *not* kiss her on their wedding day when he'd had the perfect excuse? When she couldn't have said no, not in front of their guests and the millions watching on television. His answer to that question seemed imperative.

'You could have kissed me in the cathedral, yet you didn't. Why?'

She felt his lips at her hair. The warm breath of his murmur.

'You said it wasn't that kind of marriage.'

He was feigning obedience now? She snorted. 'I don't believe that. Your recalcitrance is renowned.'

He chuckled, and the sound ran like a dark river of pleasure running right through her. 'I wasn't kissing you in front of all those people.'

She turned to look at him. His face, dark and serious. His eyes intent.

'Why?'

'I refused to share what you say would have been our only kiss with the world.' He cupped her jaw with his hand, so warm, so close. His voice a whisper on her skin. 'Because I couldn't kiss you then the way I wanted to.'

His thumb caressed her cheek, the gentle back and forth sprinkling goosebumps over her body. All of her trembling, tight and wanting. How had he wanted to kiss her? Why couldn't it be done before the cameras? She had to know. Now craving their first and only kiss, more necessary than her next heartbeat.

'You could do it now, like you wanted to.'

Rafe's nostrils flared. His thumb stilled for a moment and resumed its slow slide across her skin. 'You claimed it wasn't what you wanted.'

'It's not.' He raised an eyebrow. 'But, I mean, I shouldn't deny you our first and only kiss. It wouldn't be fair.'

'You're asking me to kiss you?'

'Yes. It's no big deal. It's only a kiss.'

The hint of a smile tugged at his lips before his face became serious, intent. Staring deep into her eyes. His, an inky black like Lake Morenberg on a moonlit night. Deep, unreachable, unfathomable. A look that delved into the soul of her. She couldn't have that. What he'd see. She closed her eyes so that she couldn't be impaled by that all-knowing gaze.

'No. If we're going to kiss, look at me.'

It was the demand of a king, and it shook through her like a tremor, cracking at the foundations of everything Lise believed she wanted. She obeyed, their heated gazes clashing. The firelight sparking in his eyes making him seem otherworldly. Unholy. The moment stretched, as if the evening held its breath.

'One kiss,' he murmured, easing closer. Closing the gap between them. His lips soft, with a satisfied curve that screamed to her he believed he'd won. Yet she didn't care. This was better than standing at the top of a run, waiting for the signal to push off and fly as fast as she could to the finish line. It all overwhelmed her. The crisp, wild smell of him. The tight clench of his jaw and flickering pulse in his throat that hinted he wasn't unaffected by this as he eased closer. Giving her time to say no, as his mouth was a breath away from hers. She closed the distance till his lips brushed hers, which she met with a sharp inhale. The shock of that first touch. Then he pressed further. Gentle, coaxing her to life with a bright burst of heat deep inside.

She went with him, her stomach swooping as if she'd

launched down the steepest of slopes. The flame roaring through her as if he'd ignited a fuse. It was okay. This was just a kiss, one kiss as he teased at her. She wanted more, not this furtive play. She sank her hands into his hair. He deepened the movement. Traced his tongue over the seam of her lips in a flicker. She opened her mouth and he claimed it. The tip of his tongue tempting hers in an intimate invasion. She chased it, gripped by a need that overtook her as Rafe plundered. This wasn't just one kiss. This *consumed* her.

He eased her back onto the couch and she offered no resistance, wanting and wanting. Rafe settled between her thighs. The hardness of his body hot between her legs. The heart of her turned molten. Something inside twisting higher and tighter. She rocked against his body. Craving this. Craving him. The voice in the back of her head whispered *no*. She didn't deserve the pleasure. But it was drowned by a deepening of the kiss, the exploration of his tongue, as if he sensed her withdrawal from him. How could she ignore it? This wicked thrill as she raced downhill into the chaos of it all. Pressed underneath Rafe, being kissed by him. Could she come like this alone? She might. She could. To the left, slightly. If she could just… Lise shifted restlessly. She needed him close. Closer. *Inside her.*

Rafe rocked into her, grinding his body on hers. His mouth claiming. This was no kiss. It destroyed her and she didn't care. She wanted to destroy Rafe in the process too, as the course he'd set ran out of control. An avalanche of sensations burying her.

She tore her mouth from his. 'Rafe. I want—'

'Tell me.' His voice was all command and the thrill of its mastery shuddered through her.

'I need you.' Who was the woman who said those words? The breathless, desperate woman whose voice whispered months of longing, heartbreak and desire. His mouth descended on hers again. She felt the taut curve of a smile against her lips. It could have been one of triumph, or something else. She didn't care. In this moment she lived for the dissonance of his hard body against hers.

He eased a hand under her top, the warmth of it still a shock even on her overheated flesh. The trace of his fingers across her skin. He moved up, slipping his hand behind to release her from the constraints of her bra, all the while kissing as if his life would end if he didn't plunder her.

She wrapped her legs around him, unable to control the rock as she moved her body with his. Chasing the liquid heat between her thighs. The feel of him burning through her. Starting low and igniting the fire. His hand slid further, moving the cup of her bra aside, teasing her nipple with a gentle roll between his fingers. She started as if shocked, but he'd trapped her mouth and the low groan from it, as if taking it all for himself. She craved nothing between them, squirming beneath his body, needing more, needing to be close. Her hands under his shirt now, the hard muscles under her palms, the hiss as she curled her nails into the flexing muscles of his back. Hands bunching the shirt at his waist reflexively. He pulled his lips away from her and she whimpered, not wanting any part of him to leave her body.

'Take it off me.'

The gravel voice scored across her, as rough and raw as she felt. She clutched the bottom of his shirt and pulled it up over his shoulders. He lifted for a moment and sat back, discarding the clothing onto the floor. His body golden in the firelight. Hard muscle, with that intoxicating sprinkle of hair across his chest. His eyes on her, all dark heat. Nostrils flaring and he was primal, like some wild untamed thing reserving his passion all for her.

'Now you.' Again, a command. He gave her no time to follow it. His hands gripping her top and easing it over her head. Taking her bra with it. She lay, exposed. He hissed, his gaze raking over her as her nipples ruched tight and needy in the night air.

Under his scrutiny, she shifted uncomfortably. The promises she'd made herself pricking at her consciousness now that the fog of Rafe had lifted a fraction. She shifted an arm, to cover herself, and he grasped the hand and pinned it above her head. A flood of heat roared through her at the dominant move. She couldn't breathe, every inhale a brief suck of air because he stole all the oxygen from the room.

'This is the dessert I prefer.' His eyes held hers. 'Look at you, laid out for me like a feast.'

His hand drifted low, easing up the hem of her skirt. She should stop him. Push him away because of the promises she'd made. To herself.

'Rafe.'

His name came out high-pitched. A breathy plea. He released her trapped hand, and his free fingers trailed her stomach. Lower and lower till they teased the edge of her underwear. Her hips bucked into him. Wanting, craving his fingers to ease the burn that bit with the edge of pain.

'Shh… I know. I'll take care of you.'

No one ever had and she wanted it, wanted him to make everything better. He slid his fingers underneath the edge of her panties. Gentle, teasing lower and lower till they found the spot she craved. She arched, head thrown back. Gasping as he circled. Everything centred on that point between her legs. The craving that consumed her. The noises she made. Moving her hips in time with the inexorable swirl of his fingers as he drew on her slick, desperate flesh.

And any thoughts of promises were blinded in the bright light of pleasure that gripped her body and began an inexorable spiral tighter. He lay on his side now, beside her, stroking her. Murmuring she didn't know what because language was meaningless in the face of this. The deep dark tone of his voice inflaming her as much as his fingers did. Then he drifted his hand further, to the entrance of her body. Slid inside. One finger. Withdrew. Two. Touching some place deep inside. Making her trembling and frantic. Every nerve screaming for the release only he could give her.

'Please, please, Rafe.'

'You deserve kisses, everywhere.'

'I need more.'

Through fluttering lashes, the haze of arousal, his triumphant smile cut through. She didn't care. Everything centred on his touch. The heat of it scorched her. Burning between her thighs. She clutched them together because the ache threatened to overwhelm her. Rafe bore down. Eyes all fire and dark desire. He took one nipple in his mouth. His tongue swirling. When she thought he couldn't ignite more heat inside her, she realised how wrong she was. Then her left nipple. His tongue making a slow trail down the centre of her stomach. Soft kisses and licks. Lower and lower still. Her hips squirmed, he gripped them with strong, warm hands.

'Open for me.'

Her legs relaxed. He kissed her inner thigh, up and up.

Till he was there. *There.* His breath warm at the apex of her thighs. The touch of his lips, light and gentle. Then his tongue. She arched back. Light exploding behind her eyes. The pleasure. He didn't stop the slow slide, the tease driving her wild. Everything centred on him, between her legs. A finger now, easing inside. And nothing could hold back the brutal pleasure that built and built and roared over her as she held her breath, clenched her hands tight and rode wave after wave of trembling ecstasy.

He moved over her, his weight pressing her into the couch. His lips on hers, the salt sweet of her own arousal. The thrum of desire still coursing through her. Rafe had broken her apart. She'd been lulled by a belief that a kiss with this man could be so simple, when Rafe was anything but. A cold thread of recrimination wound through her veins. Dark, destructive. The desire that had overwhelmed her, flooding her with an intoxicating warmth, disappeared as if she'd been doused with frigid water.

Before she could push Rafe away he stopped, broke the kiss, gazed down at her with dark eyes burning hot like the fallen embers in the fireplace.

'I want you. To be inside you,' he murmured, and his voice slid over her like midnight velvet. 'What do you want?'

It would be so easy to whisper the word, *you.* He had the power to make her forget everything, but she hadn't earned that right.

She never would.

'Off. Please.' Her hands splayed on the warmth of his naked chest, the crisp hair teasing under her fingertips, but she didn't push him away. He was the one to move. Lifting from her. Sitting back on the couch as he dropped his head and raked his hands through his hair.

'Lise.' Her name on his lips was like a groan. Impassioned. Pained. Stabbing through the very heart of her. All this interlude had proven was that she was weak. Once again, her self-interest had guided her.

What sort of Queen was she if she couldn't keep vows to the dead?

'I can't… I *can't.*'

She stood, naked in body and soul. Rafe would see right through her if he looked hard enough. He always had.

Lise didn't stop. Didn't collect her clothes. She turned and fled up the stairs.

Rafe stood in the country kitchen, gulping down a strong, black coffee, Lise's grass and flower crown withering on the benchtop. How magical she'd looked crowned in flowers, like the hopeful Princess he'd known her to be before life overtook them both. It had seemed like a new beginning, till everything fell apart again.

He glanced at the staircase, at the clock ticking away the hours on the wall. The cold of a brisk, mountain morning nipped at his exposed skin. He'd not slept last night. Listening for any sound from Lise. Alert to every creak and crack of the ancient floors, which in his fevered fantasies meant she was coming to him to finish what they'd started, all the while drowning in the frustration of lust and desire unfulfilled. He'd had plenty of that over the years since he'd first set his sights on Lise but now… Cataloguing those moments on the couch, the taste of her pleasure, the sound. The scent of her arousal that he couldn't wash away.

That he never wanted to.

He could have gone to her, but the memory of that tortured look on her face as she'd said, *'I can't,'* stopped him. He'd rushed her. Rather than taking one step forwards he'd tried to run a marathon. He was a man renowned for his patience and strategy and he'd failed in all ways last night, overcome by the craving to make her *his* in every way. All he was left with this morning was the burn of regret, when he'd spent his life after Carl's death ensuring that he regretted nothing.

The clock chimed nine. He didn't believe Lise was still asleep, and they couldn't avoid what had happened the night before. He needed a reset so he could understand why she refused anything that might give her pleasure. So they could begin again.

He poured a cup of coffee for her, as she preferred. Plenty of milk. Sugar. Then walked up the stairs and knocked at the door of her room. Silence. He knocked again, then opened the door a sliver and peered inside.

The fire had died overnight, the room gripped in a morning chill. But that wasn't what caused the shiver to run over him. It was Lise, huddled in the corner velvet couch, staring into the dead fireplace. Her shoulders bare.

'You should be in bed. It's freezing out there. I've brought you a coffee.'

He came into the room. Lise didn't move as he rounded the couch. She wore a pink slip, her nipples tight against the silken fabric. Her skin pale and white as midwinter snowfall. How long had she been sitting here, staring into the fireplace? He glanced at the bed, the covers in disarray, twisted and knotted like his. As if she'd not slept at all.

She wrapped her arms tight around her knees, as if she was trying to protect herself against something. Rafe walked towards her. Lise's focus remained intent on the dark, dead fireplace as if the secrets of the universe could be divined there. Her nose a little pink, her eyes swollen. Whatever gripped her, it wasn't a conversation he could have like this. He picked up a folded rug from the arm of the chair.

'You need something to keep you warm.'

'No.' He barely heard the word; it came out on a breath.

As he sat on the couch, she pressed herself further into the corner, away from him. He placed her coffee on a side table, gut twisting in concern. 'What's wrong, Lise?'

Her recent life had been full of too many tears. He wished there were a way to obliterate the pain that burrowed deep inside her.

'I told you. How this marriage had to be. I told you.'

It still didn't make sense. How could she maintain the desire to live life untouched after last night? For those brief moments spasming in ecstasy under his ministrations, she'd been *his*. Completely, enthusiastically. Yet now, she was further away from him than ever.

'Things change. There's no crime in passion.'

'What if we had sex? What if I fell *pregnant*?' She spat out the word as if the thought of having his child was an insult. 'It's what you want, isn't it? The "heir and a spare or two"?'

He'd inured himself to most rejections over the years, but that statement still twisted like a knife under the ribs. The poisonous words crept into his consciousness. The sneer, the rejection, the laughter. *'Rafe, what we've had is a little bit of fun—but marry you...?'* None of the women of Lauritania's aristocracy had wanted any permanence, not with him. The commoner. No matter those families were now close to bankrupt. That he owned them, owned everything they had. They still pretended they were better than him. Why should he think she would be any different? She was more than a mere noblewoman. She was the *Queen*. He gritted his teeth, tamped down the twist in his gut. Those memories, those thoughts, had no place here. He'd moved past them. He had.

'Would it be so bad if you had a baby?' Rafe loathed his question, what it revealed of him. It was what he craved, cementing his family on the seat of his country's power for generations to come.

A shudder ran through her. 'I don't want a daughter brought into the world I inhabit. I'll never do to a girl what was forced upon me as Queen.'

He ignored the slice of rejection. She hadn't been allowed to find her own way, that was all. And he of all people understood Lise's need to make a place for herself, to carve her own path. Time to remind her she could.

'You can be the catalyst for change, so you're the last Queen this happens to. We can do it, together. Bring Lauritania into the twenty-first century.'

'You have so much faith in me.'

'Because I know you. You're in your rightful place. Ruling the country is exactly where you should be. You're wasted anywhere else.'

He edged closer to her, still with the blanket in hand. Her knuckles blanched white as her hands gripped more tightly round her bent legs.

'I'm an impostor,' Lise said. 'I failed my family.'

She shivered, goosebumps peppering her skin. Lips, pale and dusky. Why sit there in the cold? They could have carried on last night. Spent it together, pleasuring each other till dawn broke and they slept from exhaustion, truly spent. They could have been warm in bed right now and yet she'd refused it. Refused comfort. It was as if she were punishing herself.

And the realisation came like dawn breaking over the mountain peaks. Lise punished herself for living.

He was a fool for not realising it before, because he understood all too well. He had a choice. To leave her paralysed with grief or to share a little of himself in the hope it would help. Give her something that granted a power few had over him. Rafe stood to stoke the fire. Collect his thoughts on a story etched into his soul.

Only his family and Lance knew how deep the pain scored. People at school had taunted his memories, but to them Carl was soon forgotten. His brother's only use being the vehicle by which to hurt Rafe in his grief.

'I understand why you feel like this,' he said.

Rafe jabbed at a few bright coals still hiding in the hearth, coaxing them to life. Wishing he could do the same with Lise as easily. He added a few more logs till the fire crackled bright and warm then sat down again.

'You've no idea,' she whispered.

'Every day for the past fifteen years I've wished I had no idea what you're feeling.' He could never escape the things he rarely talked about because the memories were too painful. Rafe lifted the blanket he held and passed it to Lise. 'I want to tell you a story about two brothers. But before I do, you need to be warm.'

His offering didn't seem enough. Yet she wrapped the blanket, crocheted by his grandmother, round herself. The wool would prickle against her soft skin, but at least she wouldn't sit there shivering, uncovered.

'I'm not an only child. I had a brother once. He was a year younger than me.' Rafe loathed talking about him in the past tense, because he carried Carl with him every day. 'He died in an accident when I was sixteen.'

The pain of the memory impaled him. He draped his arm over the back of the couch. His hand lay tantalisingly close to the gentle curve of Lise's neck. She chewed on her bottom lip, but there was a flicker of recognition on her face and something else. A spark of something brighter, like hope that there might be burdens they could share.

'Carl?'

Rafe nodded, swallowing down the emotion at hearing Lise say his name.

'When I went to the Kings' Academy, all the sons of the aristocracy loathed me. Our family wasn't poor, but our money came from physical work, not exalted inheritance. I sullied their hallowed halls.' Teachers had told his parents he was destined for bigger and better things than a farming life but all he'd learned at that school was hatred and prejudice. 'Bullying was rife and brutal, but I taught myself how to fight back. Then my life became less about the farm and more about studying, to be better.'

To beat them all. And he had. Topping every class. Then he'd met Lance and they'd become an unassailable force. The boys at that school had only hated him more. He hadn't cared. In his last year he'd been dux of the school, had received an outstanding achievement award from the King himself.

'Carl did not fare as well. He was a gentle, quiet boy. I think he liked the herd better than people.' Even Rafe had taunted him about that, something he regretted to this day. 'The bullying was relentless. Carl didn't understand why the boys would never be friends with him. He failed his classes, begged to be sent home. My parents removed him from the school. If only he'd remained...'

Rafe hesitated, the pain blunting only a fraction, even after all these years. He glanced a Lise, a slight frown marring her brow. She reached over and squeezed his hand, that small comfort giving him the impetus to continue.

'It was during term time. We'd lost two of our best milkers. Carl was going to hike the mountain pastures to try and find them. Night fell, and he didn't come home...'

'And nights on the mountain can be treacherous, even if you're on a well-worn path,' Lise said. He nodded.

'I received a call at the school that night. Was sent home to join in the search.' Rafe dropped his head. The memory of a crumpled body at the bottom of a steep slope would haunt him for ever.

'We found him the next morning. Carl was taken to hospital and died a few days later without regaining consciousness. The damned cows made their way home themselves.

'I wanted to leave school. My parents wouldn't listen. If I'd protected him from the bullying. If he'd remained a student rather than returning home. If...' Rafe dropped his head. Closed his eyes. Trying to ignore the burn that stung the back of his nose.

'It was an accident. It wasn't your fault.' Lise's voice rang out firm and clear.

He knew that now. Back then, he'd believed that had he protected his brother, Carl would have lived. The truth lay somewhere in between. Carl had not been cut out for the Kings' Academy, bullying or no, and the way he'd loved wandering the mountain pastures there had always been a chance he'd come to grief. Though in those years afterwards Rafe had blamed himself with a savagery that had almost torn him apart. Till his parents had hauled him aside, told him they loved him and that, with his grief and rage, they feared losing not one son, but two. From that point on he'd decided he couldn't change the past, but he could try to change the future.

He cleared his throat of the emotion choked there. 'Like your family. A mountain pass. A rock fall. So why blame yourself? Blame Security for allowing them to travel together.'

Lise trembled, the look on her face once again so bereft he thought she'd fall apart. No more of this distance. He couldn't stand it, not when they both needed each other. He drew her into his arms. She came to him without resistance. He held her close as she curled into his chest, her skin cold against him. He wrapped the blanket tighter round her. Soothed his hands over her quaking body.

'Ferdinand never got his chance,' she said. 'He was going to be married. Sara…'

She clung to him. What could he tell her—that her brother was a serial philanderer and that her best friend had had a lucky escape to be rid of him? No. He wouldn't hurt her any more than she already was, he wasn't that cruel. Better that she believe the illusion for now, that her brother and his fiancée were a grand love, fated to be rather than cursed from the beginning.

'Sara's a young woman with her whole life ahead of her to live and love.' *Like you*, but he didn't voice those words. She wouldn't appreciate the truth of them, that, whilst the pain wouldn't disappear, she *would* carry on. She had to come to the realisation herself. 'All we have are these brief moments. Sometimes to remember. Other times to forget.'

He stroked his fingers along her jaw, rewarded by her parted lips and soft exhale as he did.

'I can help you with the forgetting,' he murmured, threading his fingers into her hair before he could think that it might not have been wise, considering her earlier reaction. Drawn to Lise in ways that defied logical thought. It was as if, after last night, he couldn't *not* touch her. Craving to ease her pain.

She pulled her head back and looked up at him with her cool blue eyes. What did she see when she did that? It was as if they opened the door to his soul, that celestial colour. Then she shook her head. Disentangled herself from him. Yet again he had to let her go when all of him shouted *no!* That what she needed was closeness, not distance.

'There's never any forgetting, Rafe. Not for me. Your presence will always make me remember.' She stood, holding her back straight, her head high. The crocheted blanket slid from her shoulders. Even in a scant slip of nightwear, looking pale and fragile, she still had the bearing of a queen. Lise turned and headed to the door of the room. As she reached it, she hesitated. 'You should have realised. That's precisely why I married you.'

As she left the room, he knew in those moments he'd been summarily dismissed. There were undercurrents here he couldn't understand and needed to get to the bottom of. But an unshakeable knowledge spread over him with a bone-cracking chill.

She'd married him as part of her penalty for living.

CHAPTER SEVEN

THREE DAYS AWAY, and they'd returned to the palace with its timetables and strictures. Lise was torn. For a brief time she had found a measure of peace, away from the capital. Those days were like an oasis of calm in the middle of a wasteland of grief. She hadn't wanted to leave the tranquillity of Rafe's home in the mountains, where she might once have pretended they were simply a man and a woman united by shared grief, and not who they truly were. A man who wanted power from a beneficial marriage and a woman forced to marry by her constitution. No matter what Rafe had shared with her, that was their truth. They were who they were, and life wasn't all glitter-covered fantasises but full of harsh realities. Living with the dark, twisting ache that she didn't deserve any meagre shred of happiness.

Yet her pain had dissipated to a background hum in the fog of passion in Rafe's arms. All she could think about was what he'd done to her. The exquisite sensation of his mouth on the heart of her, the way she'd broken apart under his wicked tongue. Her craving for more, for *everything*. The heat rose in her chest, and she was sure the blush bloomed over her face.

'They call this informal?'

Her stomach swooped as Rafe walked into the dining room. He'd taken a call for business and hadn't followed her to breakfast, so she'd thought she'd have longer to eat without him. At least in the mountains she could walk the narrow cattle trails to escape. To create a little space, since being back in the palace allowed her none. Here, togetherness was everything. The illusion of Queen and King working together for the good of the country.

The man in question glowered as he looked at the expansive table, set in full silver service for two. Lise sat at one end. A place for him lay at the other where a patch of sunshine hit the table. In front of the setting lay perfectly pressed newspapers. If it weren't so real, it might have been comical.

'We're serving ourselves. Here, that's almost considered to be camping.' The laden buffet could have fed a family of ten, rather than the two of them. Though she hadn't eaten much of the magnificent meal set out on the sideboard. Since they'd returned to the palace her stomach had recommenced twisting itself into complicated and uncomfortable knots.

Rafe snorted. 'I'm not sitting so far away we need to phone each other to speak.' He strode to his end of the table, grabbed the cutlery and newspapers and placed them next to Lise. 'It's ridiculous.'

She nodded to the end of the table he'd vacated.

'That was my father's place. He liked to read the paper in the sunshine.' Lise sipped her coffee. 'My mother sat here because she said the sun ruined her skin.'

'I'm not your father.'

The memory of the King, sitting at the end of the table poring through the papers, sliced like a shard of glass. But her father wasn't here any more and, no, Rafe was most definitely *not* him. No man of her family would have worn jeans to the breakfast table. Even very fine jeans, that hung low on the hips and showed off the distracting vee of a man's torso. Nor would they ever have worn a business shirt with the sleeves rolled up. Rolled-up sleeves would have been sacrilege and meant showing muscular arms. If they'd even had muscles, which she wasn't convinced of, but Rafe most definitely did. The magnificent swell of his biceps when his shirt was removed, his powerful chest. The corded tendons straining as he'd dropped his head between her legs and...

'Lise?'

He was standing at the sideboard now, plate loaded with food. He probably needed to eat quite a bit, to keep his energy up for...all the things she refused to think about at this moment because she was becoming quite obsessed with ideas of Rafe permanently shirtless.

'I'm sorry. Yes?'

The corner of his mouth tilted in a lopsided grin as he strolled back to the table. Could he tell what she'd been thinking? No doubt. She'd bet the Crown jewels he knew *exactly* what had been distracting her. He placed his plate on the tabletop.

'I said, to me, an informal breakfast suggests something like breakfast in bed.'

Swoop. Her stomach dropped once more and her heart took off at a race. The feeling more intoxicating than slaloming cross-country through trees. And more dangerous.

She nibbled a bread roll and took another sip of coffee. 'I'm sure breakfast in bed has never been served in the palace. It's not done.'

Rafe hadn't sat down. He moved towards her, and she was forced to tilt her head up to meet his gaze. 'Use your magisterial powers to order breakfast in bed and make it so.'

Could he see the desire that curled slow and hot through her belly? Winding deep and low on a seductive journey that made her thighs clench together and her nipples bud and prickle in her bra.

'For both of us?' Her voice came out as a breathy whisper. It sounded like an invitation when she meant they could both dine alone in their respective rooms, didn't she?

'Perhaps you could join me? My bed is bigger. A perfect place to consume a sumptuous meal.' Her breath caught when he dropped his head to hers. His lips at her ear, his words caressing her throat as he murmured, 'More room to indulge in…eating what I prefer.'

She closed her eyes, memories cascading over her like a flood of warm water. Rafe, holding her hands above her head. Pinning her with his dark and heated gaze.

'Look at you, laid out for me like a feast.'

He could spread her out, here on the table. There was no one to see them…

A subtle cough behind her jolted Lise from the addictive fantasy. Rafe whispered into her ear, 'Breakfast in bed tomorrow.'

It wasn't a request and the decadent promise in his voice threatened to liquefy her bones, till she slid off the chair and melted in a puddle on the floor. She was sure none of that was at all regal of her. Queens didn't melt or swoon.

Rafe didn't seem likewise affected. He turned to the butler who stood behind them and raised his eyebrow in a supercilious way even her father would have been challenged to replicate.

'Yes?'

'Coffee, Your Majesty?'

'Thank you.' Rafe nodded and sat to eat as his coffee was poured. Rifling through the newspapers spread out in front of him. She hated the papers now, talking about her on the front page, every day...

'The narrative reads well.' Rafe took a long sip from his cup. Closed his eyes for a moment as if savouring the drink, then concentrated on the news again.

'What do you mean?'

He turned one towards her. A picture of them in Rafe's car returning to the palace. Both of them smiling at something. She couldn't remember the moment, but there it was, caught on camera for everyone to see, with words about a 'romantic escape' and 'new era'.

'Running a country's like running a billion-dollar company. Shareholders are most confident when the management's working together. Your people are most happy if they believe we are.'

Of course, with him, everything reverted to business. Even their relationship, such as it was. Fodder for the hungry masses. This thing between them, nothing more than an illusion of happiness. She was just another deal to him.

'I'm pleased we can give everyone the pretence.' She scrunched the napkin on her lap. Tossed it to the table. Swallowed down a different sort of ache, a sharp kind of hurt that sliced away inside. Paring away pieces of her. That was always her value, as part of the business of the Crown, not as a flesh and blood woman. Never that. She stood, wanting to escape the tightening inside her. 'I think I'll go for a run. Or a swim.'

Rafe stood as well. 'It's not a pretence for me. I hope one day you feel the same.'

'Yes, if I did it would help fit with the narrative you're so fond of.' She waved her hand over the papers on the table. Hating that this was what her life had become.

'There's a lot to being a monarch that's deliberate and calculated.' He caught her fingers, traced his thumb gently over the back of her hand. Beyond her control a thrill of goosebumps shimmied along her arm. 'It doesn't mean you don't deserve to feel something real.'

'I'll keep that in mind.' She slid her hand out from his, confused. He could be so passionate, all consuming. Then so businesslike and circumspect. It was hard to pin down who the real man was.

Another of the palace staff came into the room and Rafe slipped his arm round her waist. Dipped his head and gently kissed her cheek. Her skin tingled where his lips had touched but this was all for show. It meant nothing.

'Why don't I come for a swim with you? Show you exactly how I'm feeling,' he said. His lips traced the shell of her ear and a blast of heat whooshed through her. Rafe's body hard and uncompromising against hers. She imagined him slipping into the water. Pushing her up against the side of the pool. His muscular body slick against hers. The pleasure of it all. Touching her. Not stopping till she screamed his name.

But she needed to make some order of all this. The confused, jumbled kind of sensations he invoked. She slipped from his grasp. Pulled away. Gestured to his plate. 'Please, finish what you're eating. I may take a while to decide what I'm doing.'

He smiled, the warm indulgent tilt of his lips the same one that had greeted her on that couch in the mountains in front of a crackling fire, right before they'd kissed,

and her world had tilted on its axis. She wasn't sure it
would ever right again.

'Of course,' he said. 'I'll come and find you when
I'm done.'

She turned her back and walked away, wishing she
didn't want him to do so, all the while hoping that he
made the wait worth it.

A run hadn't helped clear her head, not even jogging
through the topiary garden, one of her favourite places
in the vast palace grounds. In desperation she'd tried texting Sara but there'd been no response, the silence louder
than words. Lise's thoughts once again twisted and knotted, impossible to unravel. Guilt over her friend's loss.
Confusion that Rafe might understand her because he'd
been through punishing grief himself, but could she really trust him? She walked down the corridors of the
palace towards the pool, bathing suit in hand. A swim,
she'd do that now. And maybe he'd join her. A whisper
of pleasure slithered through her at the thought. Treacherous body of hers. It knew what it wanted, and he was
at the top of its wish list.

As she approached the competition-sized indoor pool,
Albert stood near the doorway. She raised her eyebrows.

'I thought you'd like to know that the prime minister
is here, talking to His Majesty.'

Lise frowned. There'd been no official appointments
in her diary, this being her first morning back in the palace. Everything had been scheduled for the afternoon.
Anyhow, she was the Queen. Shouldn't the prime min-
ster be talking to her?

'Did Mr Hasselbeck say why?'

'He said the King would know what it was about. But His Majesty appeared...surprised.'

Albert was an astute judge of people, but she knew how fine an actor Rafe could be. The blood chilled in Lise's veins. There was no way anyone should circumvent her, and that was what was happening here. 'Where are they?'

'The study, Your Majesty.'

Her study. The other end of the palace. 'I think I should be there. How long have they been talking?'

Albert nodded. 'About fifteen minutes, give or take. Were you planning to change, and should I alert them to wait?'

She looked down at her clothes. If they couldn't handle a bit of spandex and sweat, then to hell with them. She took off at a jog. 'No, and no need to follow,' she shouted over her shoulder. Protocol be damned. There'd been more than enough secret chats about her in that study, with Rafe involved. No more.

As she ran through the corridors staff stopped, bowed, curtsied, stared. She tried to acknowledge them but had to be quick. Something was going on and she needed to find out what. It was the thing that had pricked her consciousness for a while now. There was a reason her father had demanded she marry Rafe. She didn't know why, but he'd wanted Rafe close.

As she approached the door to her study, she skidded to a halt. Took a few moments to catch her breath, check her hoodie was zipped up to a respectable level. Inside she heard Rafe's growl.

'How the hell did you let it come to this?'

She threw open the door. No knock, because she was Queen and there wasn't a door in this palace she had to knock on before entering. Two faces turned to her. The prime minister, who looked her up and down as if she had something nasty stuck to her shoe, and Rafe, whose gaze slid over her slowly, palpable as a caress. Hasselbeck stood. Rafe just sat there behind the desk, looking at her. His thunderous gaze softening to something no less stormy, but more heated.

Lise wanted to shout at them both, but she reined in her temper, barely.

'I would have thought, Prime Minister, that if you were calling on the palace, I should have been advised beforehand,' she said, trying to insert a chill into her voice commensurate with the ice permanently running through her veins. She eyed a red folder on the desk, open. Papers scattered across the dark desktop. Her desktop, behind which Rafe was sitting.

The usurper.

'My apologies, Your Majesty. There were a few matters I needed to discuss with His Majesty. I didn't wish to trouble you.'

Which likely meant he didn't think a woman could manage or understand what he was trying to say. He'd always dismissed her when she was a princess. She wouldn't stand for it, as Queen.

Though come to think of it, Hasselbeck looked decidedly sweaty. She didn't invite him to sit again, so he didn't. He glanced at Rafe, who said nothing, damn him. No rebuttal at all. Although he did have a slight smile on his face as if he was enjoying the scene. Of course, he should be standing too, and the lack of concern for propriety rankled her. But she'd deal with him later. She had her whole life to do so, as the cursed wedding ring on her finger perpetually reminded her.

'Did your conversation concern personal business with my husband, or business about Lauritania?' Hasselbeck fidgeted. She didn't need him to spell out the answer because, from his discomfort, she knew.

Lise wasn't the tallest of women, especially without heels. Still, she drew herself as tall as she could, given the circumstances.

'Anything that concerns my country, concerns me,' she hissed, but her eyes were on Rafe. He didn't have the good grace to look uncomfortable or chastened. He looked entertained. At least Hasselbeck appeared nervous, his neatly trimmed moustache quivering.

Rafe eased from the chair, then moved to the front of the desk. His eyes so dark they were almost black. He turned to the prime minister. 'Do you want to explain this, or shall I?'

Hasselbeck looked from one to the other then bowed. 'I'll leave you to discuss the situation, with my profound thanks.' He began to back away.

'You haven't been dismissed yet,' Rafe said. The prime minister stopped at the door, eyes narrow and loathing written all over his face. He turned to Lise and the look on his face chastened a fraction.

'Ma'am?'

The request for permission mollified her only a little. 'You can go. But make sure this *never* happens again.'

The prime minister nodded, opened the door and fled. She knew the rotten scent of treachery when she smelled it, and it didn't leave the room with the prime minister. It stayed and clung to Rafe.

'You're glorious when you're magisterial,' he said. 'I think the man cowered.'

Rafe's voice was liquid heat. It was tempting to let it

trickle through her and warm all her cold places, but she wouldn't let him distract her. Lise whipped around, the suppressed anger bubbling in her blood. Rafe didn't appear apologetic, and she hated that he stood in the room as if he'd always meant to be here.

'I'm the Queen. Over seven hundred years of history stand behind the role I now hold. You've been King for mere days. Why are you meeting the prime minister without me?'

Rafe didn't cower. He stood there all dark and brooding, his shirt stretched tight and far too distractingly over the muscles of his chest. He crossed his arms and his biceps bunched. Something heated slid inside her belly. Anger, that was all it was. Something to warm the frozen heart of her.

'His arrival was as much a surprise to me as it was to you.'

She clenched her jaw. The schemer in Rafe was coming through again. She didn't believe him, and she wouldn't be distracted by his brooding masculinity.

'I should have been called immediately.'

'I agree.' He raked a hand through his hair. Blew out a long, slow breath. 'Unfortunately, I became preoccupied with what he had to say.'

'Which was?'

'Did your father or brother ever discuss finance with you?'

'No,' she was forced to admit. She'd always been an afterthought if they'd thought of her at all. She'd formed the view long ago that if she wanted more, she had to make her own way. Even when she'd tried, it had to be attractive types of charities. Abandoned kittens and puppies because everybody thought they were cute and worth saving. Not the meatier issues of domestic abuse and homeless teenagers, which had been her true passion. Those she'd had to sneak around to see, in secret. Not any more.

Rafe ran a hand through his hair again, leaving it messy and dishevelled. 'You might want to take a seat.'

'I'm sure I've had worse news.' She'd never sit down to take bad news again, even if her knees trembled and her stomach churned. She was made of stronger stuff.

Rafe nodded. 'For some time, the country's fiscal position has been…precarious.'

He'd mentioned economics on their pretend honeymoon, then avoided the conversation. Everything in her stilled. 'How precarious?'

'The prime minister advised me that by the end of the year the government may not be able to pay the public service.'

She sank to a seat in spite of herself. This was something her father must have known of. Her mother, her brother too. How could she have been kept ignorant? Especially Rafe, when the perfect moment had arisen only days earlier. But then he hadn't wanted anything to ruin the perfect weekend of attempted seduction, had he?

'The government's plan includes support from me, provision of financial advice and a number of austerity measures.' He shuffled some papers, placed them into the red folder and handed it to her. 'It's all in here.'

She looked at him, leaning on the desk. One foot crossed over the other. The only thought swirling through her head was that he didn't seem surprised. At all.

'How long have you known?'

He hesitated, his mouth thinning to a taut line. He was

thinking, and that told her all she needed. She'd bet the kingdom on him having known for—

'That the treasury has been in financial trouble? About five months.'

Bingo. He'd been told at about the time he'd begun seeking her out in earnest. At the time she'd thought he might be interested in her.

'That the economy's at risk of collapse,' Rafe added. 'About twenty minutes.'

The flame of humiliation and then hatred burned bright. She wasn't sure who she hated now, but since her father was dead and Rafe was here...

'My father offered you a princess, didn't he? To get your co-operation and assistance in digging Lauritania out of this mess.'

'Lise—'

'No. Stop right there.' She held up her hand. 'I *know*. My father needed your help, so he offered me as your reward.'

It was clear now. The desperation to get her to marry. The fury when she refused. Why couldn't her father have trusted her with the information? To save the country, she might have accepted the plan.

'Is that what you all saw in me?' she hissed, the pain of realisation too much to bear. She blinked away the hot sting of tears, 'A financial cost of doing business? Something to be traded?'

He cocked his head. Regarded her. Those dark eyes of his all-knowing.

'I saw a passionate young woman. A woman seeking permission to be herself.' His voice ran soft and silky across her skin. 'Something you should never have had to ask for.'

She hated that he knew so many of her secret desires, the old hurts. That he could read her so well. Even though she shouldn't think this way, he still called to her on some deep and hopeful level. That his seeming passion for her hadn't been faked. She crushed those sentiments. Stood, holding her head high.

'I'll take that report and read it. Decide how to manage the situation.'

'It gets worse.'

She stiffened her spine. She would not crumble. She wouldn't. 'How can it be *worse*?'

'Read the report, Lise.'

The betrayal stabbed deep. Her family dead, her country in ruins. She grabbed at her chest, unzipped her hoodie. She couldn't breathe.

'I'll need to assemble the best financial minds in the country—'

'I am the best financial mind in the country.' It was said with no humility, but no hubris either. Still, Rafe was the last person that she wanted to talk to, even if he was the best at everything he did.

'I'd like a wider choice.'

He pushed away from the desk. 'It shouldn't be anyone who helped to cause the situation.'

She nodded. The suggestion seemed sensible, but she hated that he'd thought of it first. She picked up the red folder from the desktop then headed for the door.

'Remember, Lise. You don't have to do things alone. I'm—'

'What?' She whipped round, gripping the folder tight in her hands. 'Here to help? Or the truth, here to keep more secrets? Because that's what everyone's been doing.

Hiding things. And why wouldn't they? I'm the Queen nobody wanted.'

'Do you really believe you're so hard to love?'

She turned and left the room without answering, the question still spitting like a vicious cat in her ears. Because the answer was clear. People only loved what she represented. No one had ever truly loved her.

Rafe sliced through the cool water, pushing harder and faster till his muscles screamed. He'd been a fool not to call for Lise immediately. He'd allowed his own arrogance to ignore the obvious, that she would see the meeting with the prime minister as another betrayal. Whatever fragile trust he'd been hoping to build, it had been smashed in one morning.

He hauled himself out from the edge of the pool, chest heaving from fifty brutal laps to burn through his fury. Fury that he wasn't in the water with Lise right now, fury at himself because the perfect opportunity to discuss this had arisen on their weekend away and he'd selfishly kept the truth hidden. But most of all, fury towards a prime minister who should have briefed his Queen. That man was one to watch, and carefully. He'd seen Hasselbeck's spark at Lise's cold rage. Fear for his own job no doubt, but a silent glee with her anger at Rafe as well.

Rafe knew the government didn't rate her, and they barely tolerated him. He scrubbed a towel through his hair. Rough-dried the rest of his body then lashed the towel around his waist. The lot of them were vermin. Rats who'd grown fat whilst the country suffered. It had all worked well with a complacent, lazy king. Lise was an unknown, and people knew his reputation too well. If they worked together, the things he and Lise could achieve were mind-boggling. One crack, and people would try to tear them apart. He refused to accept that. He'd be written into the history books as the commoner King who saved the nation. *Everyone* would know his name. He'd accept nothing less.

His phone rang from the table he'd tossed it on before diving into the water. He snatched it and swiped to answer before checking who'd called.

'Yes!'

'Hello to you too, Your Majesty.' Lance's amused voice clipped at him. 'I'm guessing married life is going swimmingly?'

Rafe took a slow breath. His friend was one of the few people with whom he could be completely honest, however even this was a stretch. He went with the anger still crackling through him.

'Why the hell are you calling so soon after my wedding?'

'Why are you answering?' Lance chuckled. 'Haven't you got better things to be doing? That beautiful wife of yours, for starters.'

Regaining broken trust, though he'd never tell Lance, even if the man was his best friend.

'What do you want?'

'I've a favour to ask in person. It's a delicate situation.'

Rafe pinched the bridge of his nose. The universe conspired against him. Still, if his friend needed a favour Rafe would always answer the call. One thing he and Lance had promised each other all those years ago whilst at school was that when one of them asked for assistance, the other would honour the request. Neither of them had failed their boyhood promise yet. He wouldn't be the one to start.

'When do you want to meet?'

'Tonight. Around eight.'

'I'll arrange it with Security. We can have dinner.'

'Thank you, my friend. I promise that I won't intrude on your wedded bliss for too long.'

'You'd better not,' Rafe growled, and disconnected the phone to Lance's laughter.

He took another deep breath to tamp the anger down before walking out of the swimming pavilion, through the palace and towards his rooms, the marble floors cold beneath his feet. He didn't care that he was half dressed, didn't give a damn about propriety. He needed to find Lise and start the dialogue to regain her trust.

As he passed one of the hundreds of anonymous doorways in the place, he saw her. Pacing across a conservatory overlooking a perfectly sculpted topiary garden. In her hands she held the red folder, flicking through it with restless energy. Dressed not in the exercise clothes that lovingly covered every inch of her exquisite body, leaving nothing to the imagination. Driving him close to distraction, which had meant he couldn't stand when she'd burst into the room but had remain seated to get his body under control lest he disgrace himself. No, now she paced in a demure, high-necked, long-sleeved black dress. Once again steeped in the colour of mourning, a deep frown marring her brow. She seemed so pale and fragile, trying to absorb the news. Without thinking, he stepped into the room.

Lise whipped around at his approach, wide-eyed with surprise. She looked at him, over his torso, down his body. It wasn't a cursory survey either. Her eyes snagging on his chest, lingering on his abdomen, finally hitching on the knot of his towel. He walked slowly towards her because she seemed as skittish as the deer who inhabited the wilder mountain regions here. Ready to run at the first sight of trouble.

'What are you doing dressed like that?' Her voice was a soft rasp against his skin.

He shrugged. 'I've been swimming.'

'Could you not have…?' She flapped her hand about in front of her. She wasn't looking at him now. Her eyes were everywhere else. The bloom of red creeping up her throat.

'What?' he asked. Knowing exactly what. Despite all her righteous anger, he affected her, and desire was something he could work with.

'Nothing.' She held her head high in glorious defiance of everything he knew she still felt for him. Passion such as they'd experienced didn't die easily and sometimes anger only inflamed it.

An addictive thought.

He turned his mind to something more mundane before his own desire for her became apparent. 'Lance will be visiting tonight, around eight.'

Something whispered across her face. Her eyes widened a fraction. She chewed at the side of her bottom lip. 'It's nice to have a friend. Say hello to him for me.'

'You're welcome to join us.'

She shook her head. 'I need an early night.'

What they needed was to be in bed together. Burning away the emotion and fury with their bodies. Not this cold war.

He nodded to the folder she held before her. The red clutched against her chest like a garish wound. 'Have you finished reading?'

He'd been given a summary and could only guess the horrors it contained.

She dropped her head. The knuckles on her hands gripping the folder whitened. 'They want to rationalise the public service.'

This he knew. A gross suggestion that punished the innocent whilst those responsible still grew fat, rewarded by their own negligence.

'Sacking twenty thousand. As a start,' she whispered, then her voice firmed, 'I'll sell the Crown jewels before I destroy the lives of twenty thousand people.'

'You can't do that. The country needs its symbols.'

She raised her chin, looking every bit the monarch she'd been crowned. He wished her people could see her like this. Then they wouldn't doubt her, they'd exalt her.

'People can't eat diamonds and those precious symbols won't keep them warm in the coming winter.'

'We'll find another way.' He only hoped the alternative was better. It had to be. She seemed unmoved.

'How long will it take to assemble a meeting of experts to discuss this?'

'I've already given some acceptable candidates some thought. Hopefully only a few days, considering the urgency.'

She pulled herself upright, her mouth tight and hard as she stared him down.

'Then make it so.' He might have smiled at the very words he'd used with her only hours earlier being tossed back at him, as if he were one of her minions. But he didn't think she'd appreciate any mirth. Not now. She tapped the folder in her arms. 'I'll spend the evening considering this. I don't want to be disturbed.'

She stalked from the room. Damn it all. He hadn't improved anything. Rafe watched her leave, the click of her low heels echoing on the marble floors.

They were now further away from each other than ever.

CHAPTER EIGHT

LISE SAT ON the couch in her room, the cursed red folder on the table in front of her. A barely touched dinner to her side. She took a deep shuddering breath, but the trembling wouldn't stop. She was cold, so cold. How could no one have told her? What were they thinking, that they could hide the coming disaster? She buried her face in her quivering hands. Pressed her fingers hard into her eyes, trying to push back the tears that stung her eyelids. If only her family had confided in her. She might have married Rafe if the importance of their union had been disclosed. She could have helped save the country in that way. Then her family would have lived. All ifs, buts and maybes.

She stood and looked out onto the darkening valley. The lights of the capital blinking on as dusk fell. All those people out there, living their lives. Hoping, dreaming and her government was demanding she decimate them. No. Never.

But she didn't know what to do. Everything in that cursed report sounded so urgent. Budget emergencies led by poor decisions and some even poorer speculative investment of Lauritania's funds, and here they were. The country's fate was in her hands, yet none of them trusted her with it. Her actions would affect thousands. In her time at finishing school, with the palace tutors, managing a country's economy had never figured in her education. She hadn't even known how to manage a bank account until Albert taught her, a life skill he'd said every person needed to learn. She'd been locked in a pretty tower, given nothing to help her negotiate life other than being told she'd have an auspicious marriage and her husband would look after everything from then on.

The ache welled in her chest. Gripped her throat till she couldn't breathe. She clutched the back of a chair. Weeks of fighting to hold onto control and it came to this. People who didn't even know it yet were relying on her to make the right decisions. Twenty *thousand* people. She fought the first sob that tore from her throat, the tears that flowed freely down her cheeks for the first time since she'd been told of her family's deaths, but she couldn't hold it in any longer. If no one trusted her, how could she *fix* things? It broke out with a rush, the grief, the fear. An avalanche she couldn't hold back. Sobbing in a way she wasn't sure would ever stop.

The door adjoining creaked open. A cool rush of air flooded in from Rafe's rooms. She straightened, wiped frantically at her eyes and nose but there was no hiding these tears as she tried to choke down the agony cutting her in two. As the whole atmosphere of the room changed, she knew without looking that he was now bearing down on her.

'Leave me alone.' Her voice scratched out too rough and raw to hide how she'd weakened. She turned her back so he couldn't see, shoulders hunched over, wanting to curl into herself and disappear.

'Lise, I heard you.' That voice. So soft, so gentle. Wrap-

ping around her like a goose-down comforter. She sensed
the warmth of him, standing behind her. For a moment she
imagined he could take it all away. The pain, the fear. If
only she could lean in, accept some support. She wouldn't
need long. Warm herself from all the cold…

No.

Her parents and her brother were lying dead in the
family crypt. They'd never be warm again and neither
should she be. She wouldn't succumb to this, or to a man
who made a career of temptation. And like everyone else,
he mistrusted her. If he didn't, he would have told her
everything when he'd had his chance.

She whipped around, chewing at the inside of her
mouth to stop her lips trembling. Pointing to the door
between their rooms. 'Out!'

Rafe stood there unmoving. Dressed in a perfectly
pressed business shirt and trousers. Black hair raked
back. Dark, brooding features. Looking for all the world
like the King he'd become by their marriage. Yet what
she hated most, more than seeing the man she'd married
looking as if this were the role he was born to, was the
tenderness in his eyes. They promised things she could
never accept.

'You're crying. Let me—'

'No.' No one should see her weakness. Certainly not
him.

'Lise. I keep telling you, you're not alone.' That deep,
low voice was a soft burr against her skin. She ignored
it. In truth, she *was* alone. Sara wasn't responding to
her texts and Rafe…her emotions were too tangled to
know how to deal with him. Instead, she raised her head
high. Another tear escaped, sliding down her cheek. She
scrubbed it away.

'I asked you to leave. Will none of my subjects actually obey me?'

Rafe held up his hands in mock surrender. 'I've never been known for my obedience.'

It had been the one flaw in her plan for this marriage. A belief he'd listen to and accept what she'd demanded. An error of judgement born of desperation to carry out her father's final wishes and assuage her guilt.

'I wish I'd married someone who was.'

He crossed his arms. His biceps bunched under the fabric in an all too tantalising way. Reminding her of what he'd looked like with his shirt off this morning. His arms, beautifully defined. His chest, the smattering of hair coalescing in a dark line bisecting the ridges of his abdomen and disappearing below the towel. Wrapped around those narrow hips. Water sparkling on his skin like diamonds. She dragged her eyes from the belt around the waist of his trousers. Tried to look at his face instead.

'You'd better get used to it,' he said. 'I'm with you until death. It's a promise I intend to keep.'

She glared at him. That reminder etched for ever into the inside of her wedding band. 'I'm the Queen, I'm sure I can arrange an execution if I put my mind to it.'

'Happily for me, capital punishment was abolished by the constitutional amendment of—'

She threw up her hands. 'Don't talk to me about my own constitution! What good is being Queen if you can't take the head of someone who's annoying you?' His beautiful lips curved into a sensual smile. It peeved her that he wasn't in the slightest bit concerned about her threats, hollow though they were. 'Why aren't you more afraid of me?'

'I've told you before, you're magnificent when you're

being magisterial.' His eyes were dark and sultry in his handsome face. He began to stroll towards her. 'Irresistible, in fact.'

She moved, placing an armchair between her and him, but that didn't seem to offer protection. His steps were languid, almost careless, but that heated gaze of his was fixed on her.

'Lance will be here soon,' she said. Rafe stepped around some furniture and her stomach flipped as if it were filled with a flock of swallows that roosted in the palace ramparts. Every part of her skin too tight in her clothes. She scratched at the high neck of her dress. Her body melting and softening as he bore down on her.

Rafe checked his watch. 'He can wait.'

Worst of it all, she still wanted him. Craved the man who was edging closer, backing her into a corner from which she didn't want to escape. She glanced at her bed. So tempting for him to tumble her on it, thrust his hands into her hair, hold her tight and kiss her again. Let him bury himself in her and subdue her fears with cries of pleasure. But she'd made a promise to herself. She was worth nothing if she couldn't uphold it.

'I—I'll have you locked in...in the dungeons.'

His smile was pure predator. Oh, how she wanted to succumb. Let herself be devoured. He was in front of the chair now, a single step around it and he'd be right there. He raised an arrogant eyebrow. One touch and she wasn't sure she'd say no to him.

'I don't believe the palace has any,' Rafe said with a smile.

On a delicate table next to her bed sat the internal palace phone. She nodded towards it. 'All I need to do is to press the duress button. You'll find out about the dungeons soon after.'

'If that's what you need to protect you from yourself.' Rafe gave a deep, mocking kind of laugh. 'You're afraid of your feelings. And with me, there's nowhere for you to hide.'

She stopped her retreat. Firmed her spine and stood tall in the face of his taunts.

'There are *no* feelings where you're concerned.'

A muscle in the side of his jaw twitched as he took another step towards her, close enough now to touch. 'Prove it.' His voice was smooth and hard. Silk over steel. 'Kiss me, then make that claim again.'

Recollections of their *only* kiss burst into her consciousness like a firework. Heat crackled over her, but she wouldn't back down, not whilst he stood there and mocked her. She closed the gap between them. Cupped her hands to the warm skin of his jaw and pulled him down to her. His lips parted, his breath hot as he brushed his lips against hers and the thrill of that soft touch rushed to her core. Their mouths fused as he slid his arms round her and dragged her body against his, no space between them as he angled his head and their tongues touched. Twined together.

She speared her fingers into his hair and gripped, whether to pull him down closer or push him away, she wasn't sure. It was as if her world exploded in a conflagration of need and panting breaths that caused her heart to race and turned her core molten. This was more than a kiss; it was a battle of desire and erotic promise. She trembled as he pressed her to him, the evidence of his arousal bold and impossible to miss.

Lise was lost in sensation. His hair caught in her fingers, his mouth moving over hers. Their bodies, melding together. She flexed against his hardness and there was a groan. Her? Him? She couldn't be sure. Then he stopped and pulled his mouth away. Looking down on her, his eyes fierce as she let him go. He stood back. Lips still parted. Breaths heaving like her own. She craved to be in his arms again, fused together with no distance between them. Proving that not only was she craven, but a liar as well. Except in this moment, only a step from her, Rafe was as far away as he'd ever been.

He glanced over her shoulder towards the door of her room, his gaze distant. Then he frowned and turned his attention to her once more. Eyes glittering in the low light of the evening.

'Anything to say, Lise?' His lips curled into a wicked smirk, but she didn't react. Trying to give nothing away when everything inside her seethed with emotion. 'Because that felt a *lot* like feelings to me.'

She attempted to ignore his look of triumph, as Rafe brushed past her and strode from the room.

Rafe throttled the neck of a dusty wine bottle as he stalked around the bowels of the castle. He'd ostensibly come to find the palace cellars to select a vintage for dinner, but in truth he couldn't face Lance, not with anger and unrequited desire still careering out of control through his blood. He needed to regain his famed control, which was rapidly shredding because of a kiss, which once again proved Lise was not the Ice Queen she pretended to be, but a woman on fire.

What kind of monster did she think he was, leaving her to cry? And it had been more than simple tears. The agony of the sounds had had him rushing through the door between their rooms before he could even give what he was doing much thought. The brokenness of it all. Perhaps he should have backed away, but he was never a man to be shy and she'd needed *someone* to comfort her, even though Lise was desperate to run from herself.

He checked his watch, realising that in his introspection he'd forgotten the time. Taking stock of his surroundings, he found himself in a cavernous storage area, piled with all kinds of forgotten treasures. An ostentatious statue of Bacchus stood in the corner and the gleam of burnished wood and gilding peeked from under dust covers. He turned at the sound of footsteps.

'Where are you?' That male voice. The clipped British accent. 'Ah. Store Two. This looks interesting.'

'Lance.'

His friend strolled through the doorway, holding a glass half full of red wine. He looked around the space, eyes narrowing to settle on the bronze in the corner. 'That is the ghastliest statue. I've a client who'd love it. Do you think the Queen would sell?'

As he'd journeyed through the lower reaches of the palace Rafe had seen corners stuffed with discarded objects. The palace itself was full of them, rooms shut off and never used.

'She might. I could talk to her.' Lance had an eye for quality and was one of the finest antique experts in Europe. He'd know what was worth something and perhaps they could divest themselves of some of the unwanted treasures gathering dust.

'I'm not sure that'll go well.' Lance snorted. 'What are you doing down here? In the doghouse already after four days of marriage? That's a stellar achievement. I don't believe even I'd have done better.'

'I was getting wine for dinner.' Rafe gestured to the bottle.

'As you can see, I already have some.' Lance held his glass to the light, which shimmered through the ruby liquid, then took a hefty swig. 'This is a lovely drop. The Queen was most gracious when we couldn't find you. She asked staff to check your suite. Strange to have your own rooms considering you're married…'

Lance was many things, and thirsty for information was one. He didn't peddle in it, necessarily, but had a rampant curiosity. Rafe wouldn't give him any more to pique his interest, or he'd never hear the end of it because his friend had always liked to bring him crashing back to earth.

'That's the way it's done in the palace.'

Lance cocked his head. 'If that's the story you want to tell.'

'What other story would there be?' His voice sounded distant, unconvincing. Swallowing down the lies to his best friend was more difficult than he thought.

'Whilst considering whether to mount a search party Lise and I had a lovely chat. She mentioned Carl, like she didn't believe he was real.' Rafe's heart stopped for one beat, then picked up its pace. A sharp ache and then anger, stoked inside. Even though he'd bared his soul to Lise, she thought it was an untruth? Rafe didn't know why that realisation knifed him deep inside.

Anyhow, Carl's name shouldn't be mentioned in random fashion. His memory should be carefully handled, with respect.

'I assured her that, whilst you might be a cad, you weren't known for lying,' Lance said. 'Not about that, at least.'

Rafe tried to sound disinterested. 'Thank you for your support.'

'You haven't spoken about him in years.' Lance's eyes narrowed.

'Did you tell Her Majesty that as well?'

'That's for you to divulge.' He looked sharp as a hawk. The pause went on for a few seconds too long. No doubt he was waiting for Rafe to fill it. Rafe stayed silent. 'Though, speaking of cads, *I've* never been relegated to a palace storeroom.'

Rafe looked at the rough-hewn ceiling and thanked the change of topic.

'As I said, I was finding wine for our dinner.'

Lance raised an imperious eyebrow. 'Hmm. The palace has a cellarmaster for that sort of thing. The staff are intrigued. I believe I heard something about…dungeons. There are all kinds of whispers going on upstairs.'

Which was what Rafe hadn't wanted. He thought he'd seen a shadow under the door of Lise's room just before he'd left. People were watching and listening to them, of that he was certain. 'There's nothing to be intrigued about. Lise is playing her own game.'

'Is this one of those grown-up games like doctors and nurses? Or should I say, jailer and captive?' Lance's mouth twisted into a wicked smirk. 'Though I would have thought being the jailer was more *your* style. Of course, for an exquisite young woman like Lise, I can see why exceptions could be made. She really is delicious company. Even I—'

'Lance. Enough.' Rafe's voice was a low hiss. He stormed towards his friend and Lance threw back his head, roaring with laughter.

'How the mighty has fallen.' He raised his glass in :

mocking toast. 'Drop the jealous husband act. You've always had your life so carefully planned, pardon me if I'm not entertained by this turn of events.'

'You know my thoughts on love.'

'I wasn't talking about love, were you?' Lance cocked his head. 'How quaint.'

'Remind me, why are you still in the country and how can I have you deported?'

'You're King. Call Security.'

'I expected you to escape after the reception, being allergic to weddings as you are.'

Lance began peering under dust covers. 'I've been checking out the wildlife. It's most distracting.'

That was the friend he knew. Lance loved women and women loved Lance, only none of them could pin him down. 'You had something sensitive to discuss.'

'Yes. Down to business.' He slipped a piece of paper from the inner pocket of his suit jacket. 'Someone wants to leave the country and can't access their passport.'

Rafe raised his eyebrows and leaned forwards. 'What are you up to and is it legal?'

'Looking out for your interests, and it's perfectly legal. You have enemies.'

'I had enemies at school.' Rafe snorted. 'They're still there, the same bullies. What's new?'

Lance looked serious, a state of being Rafe knew his friend tried to avoid although he was a serious man deep down. His friend might have carefully cultivated the image of a rich and lazy dilettante. He was none of those things.

'They're consolidating. The Queen's an unknown. People are taking sides.'

A chill ran through him. Rafe had suspected as much,

though the thought that people were choosing sides already was concerning. There was a lot to do to save the economy. He needed cooperation, not frustration.

'The little bird I'm helping doesn't want to be used as a pawn in someone's game. If you sign this form, I'll have a replacement passport tomorrow and we'll be gone.'

'Why didn't you ask Her Majesty, since she's such a fine new friend?'

Lance handed Rafe the paper. Rafe looked at the name. Raised his eyebrows. 'Sara Conrad?'

He shouldn't be surprised. The Crown Prince had kept mistresses, even during his engagement. It was a well-kept secret, but Rafe had a way of finding these things out because knowledge was power. He wondered now whether Sara had ever loved Ferdinand, contrary to Lise's romantic delusions about her brother's relationship with her friend.

'Now you know why I didn't ask Lise. I'll leave her to her grief, uninterrupted.'

Rafe agreed. Lise was so mired in her own sadness she mightn't understand others moving on. 'You and Sara?'

His friend had a reputation, which he upheld with impunity. When younger, Rafe had tried to keep up, until he'd realised it was a fruitless endeavour. Lance took things to an entirely different level.

'You know how aristocrats do things. She fears plans are afoot to marry her off again.' Aah. That was why Lance had helped her... The sour taint of bile rose in Rafe's throat. No matter the truth of Sara and Ferdinand's relationship, a woman's fiancé had only recently been placed in the ground. That she'd be married off again disgusted him. 'People are trying to create new allegiances.

I'm helping a damsel in distress and thwarting an attempt at a power block.'

Rafe rubbed his hands over his face. Their argument in Lise's suite, the shadows at the door. If their enemies thought there were cracks, they would hammer deeper wedges into them.

'Have you a pen?'

Lance whipped one from his pocket. Rafe took it, scrawled his signature on the page and handed it back.

'Thank you, my friend. Do you need me to leave so you can make peace with Lise?' Lance downed the last of his wine and clapped Rafe on the back. 'I've heard making up is half the fun of a fight.'

Rafe shook his head. 'Dinner's waiting and I refuse to disappoint the chef.' Even more importantly, he wanted to hear more about the 'whispers' Lance claimed to over-hear. Time for Lise, later. He'd eat some food, tamp down his anger. Let Lise think she'd won for tonight. But to-morrow? He was having a conversation with his wife.

CHAPTER NINE

RAFE STRODE FROM the dining room back towards Lise's suite. He'd wanted to talk over the calm of breakfast, where she couldn't hide. Yet she hadn't been in the dining room this morning. She'd been breakfasting in her own room, so the staff told him.

In bed.

It seemed an age ago when he'd made that suggestion to her, hardly crediting it was only yesterday. How life could change in twenty-four hours. He should be there with her right now. They could be feasting on each other as he'd intended, rather than sitting down to the luxurious breakfast he'd had, which tasted little better than sawdust on his tongue. A poor substitute when all he craved to taste was her. The fire of anger burned a little too brightly in his gut as he made his way to their rooms. More at himself than anything else. He had greater finesse than this, and yet around her all his plans and good intentions crumbled to nothing.

Breakfast in bed.

They both knew what he'd meant. Lise's pupils had flared wide and dark when he'd mentioned it. Her lips parted, breaths quick and shallow. She'd wanted him as much as he did her. Arousal joined the irritation ham-

mering at his cold, calculated self-control, the two fresh
emotions now a heady and dangerous mix that had him
thrumming, not at all conducive to polite conversation.

In other circumstances they could have burned it away
together. Not now. He reached her bedroom door and
knocked. Perhaps a little too firmly. Took a breath to
calm the driving pulse beating low and hard.

'Come in.' Even though her voice was muffled slightly
by the wood, it was firm and clear. She should be worried. Perhaps she hadn't seen the scurrilous online gossip
in the tabloids yet? He thrust open the door and entered.

Lise stood near the window, framed by the view behind of the lake and capital she now ruled. Looking as
regal as any monarch he'd ever met, with her chin held
high and spine stiff. She wasn't the tallest of women,
but in that pose it still seemed as if she looked down at
him. That she appeared entirely unaffected irritated and
enthralled him in equal measure. He wanted to break
through that cool veneer. Like before, marvelling at the
passionate treasure underneath after he'd stripped her
back to her truest self.

Rafe strolled into the room trying to appear nonchalant when every part of him stretched taut, primed for
the spears of battle. Even today, she wore black. A dress
of some sort, high-necked, below the knee. Belted at her
slender waist. Skimming over the swell of her breasts,
the curve of her hip. Yet it could have been the sheerest
lingerie, the way the impeccable fit called to him. He
barely understood this need. How his craving for power,
establishing his legacy, was being overborne by another
craving... For her.

'Sleep well, Lise?'

She glanced at the unmade bed. A tray still there, with

food half eaten. Visions flickered through his head like a stuttering film reel. Lise, naked and glowing in the soft light of a fire. Body arched and gasping as he tasted her. Head thrown back as she came. The breathless whispers as her fingers gripped his hair. *Rafe, Rafe*...

And that beat deep inside took up a relentless pace, riding him hard. His famed control fled where she was concerned. Yet she seemed entirely unmoved, though her gaze didn't leave him, following every footstep as he moved closer to her. A polite distance, but still close enough to see her throat convulse as she swallowed.

'Yes, I did. And I can highly commend your suggestion of breakfast in bed. An inspired idea.' She sauntered towards that bed with a taunting sway of her hips. Picked up a piece of bread slathered with jam and bit into it. Consuming the morsel slowly, licking a stray crumb from her lips once finished. Minx. 'Did you sleep well too?'

'As I've said before, I'm not afflicted by poor sleep.' Although his night had been plagued by dreams of being buried in the wet heat of her body. Wasted fantasies when they should have been playing them out together.

Lise raised a supercilious brow. He'd seen that look before, proving she was her father's daughter in some ways at least. 'Your clear, unblemished conscience.'

No, she was not doing this. He had nothing to feel guilty for. He raised a brow to match hers. Time to end what he'd started the night before.

'I never took you for a coward.'

She turned her back on him to stare out of the window. 'I'm not, I'm—'

'Which is why you threatened to call Security and have me locked in a dungeon.' No more lies. It stopped today.

Lise whipped around. 'I told you to go. You don't listen.'

'I do—'

'You're no better than the rest of them!' She stabbed the air in front of her with her finger. '"*What's the point competing in the downhill championships since you can't win?*" "*Why learn about running the country when you won't need to?*" "*Who cares about your thoughts on the subject since you must marry?*"'

The words had taken on a mocking tone. She shook her head, then looked directly at him, her gaze cold and piercing. '"*When you claim you want me to leave, you really mean stay.*" No, Rafe. You might hear what I say, but you don't listen to what I want.'

Her wrenching sobs from the evening before still rang in his ears. Not a sound he would easily forget. 'I will not ignore another person in distress, especially not the woman I married. How many times do I have to tell you, you don't need to do this alone?'

She looked down at her twisting fingers then seemed to check herself, grasping onto the back of a chair instead. Her fingertips blanched white. 'I don't deserve any sympathy.'

Rafe didn't understand. If she wasn't deserving now, when would she ever be? He moved towards her. Slowed his breathing. Tried to gentle his voice. 'You needed my support. I understand you're afraid—'

'Your arrogance is astonishing.' Her eyes narrowed. 'You know *nothing*.'

Oh, no. This, he would not accept. He'd transformed his family's humble though successful business into a billion-dollar empire. Perhaps she needed reminding of how much this country *owed* him. And he'd take it, in the end. It was all his due. People would *never* forget the De Villiers name.

'My arrogance, as you call it, is well placed.' His jaw clenched, the taunts from the Kings' Academy searing into his consciousness. Leeches of the aristocracy were prepared to take what he offered when they were at risk of losing everything. His money to save their skins. Particularly those families whose sons had disparaged him at school. Who had bullied Carl till he'd left. 'The De Villiers group props up most of Lauritania's oldest companies, almost destroyed by complacency and lack of government support. There's nothing made here that you eat or drink or wear that doesn't have my name behind it. So, say again that you don't need me, and I'll walk from this room right now.'

He'd taken a risk, calculated but a risk, nonetheless. She said nothing, which was telling, and a small victory. The country needed him, but he wanted her to admit that *she* needed him too. The continued silence made him grit his teeth till he would be silent no more.

'As I thought, you can't. Now, for last night...' He took a slow breath, trying to tamp down the growing maelstrom inside. Perhaps it wasn't the best time to have this conversation, with both of them on edge. But he was never one to run away from a fight. 'To the rest of the world, we must be seen as one. An unassailable force. Nothing less is acceptable.'

In truth, nothing else would save the country.

Lise hadn't moved, her face unreadable except for the tug at her lower lip as she worried her teeth over it.

'To whom is it unacceptable? The one who concentrates daily on the *narrative* in the papers?' She lifted her chin at him. 'You know what I see when I look at you? A man absorbed by self-interest.'

He refused to acknowledge the prickle at the base of his skull. Something like a conscience. No, he wouldn't allow that to go unanswered. Rafe shook his head. 'You look at me and you're terrified of your feelings.'

'Is that so? When you look at *me*, Rafe, what do you see?' She waved her hands up and down her body. 'The Princess I was or the Queen I've become? Or is it the woman who told her father in their last argument that she wouldn't cry if he died? That her family could go to hell? That I renounced all claims to the Crown?'

Rafe stilled, as if someone had frozen him solid on the spot. She'd renounced her line in succession to avoid marrying him? She wanted him *that* little? The chill of her admission invaded him to the core. 'Did anyone else hear you say it?'

Lise's lip curled to a sneer. 'Oh, don't worry, Rafe. As you know, under our constitution I must sign a formal acknowledgement of renunciation. I can't lose my job simply because I say I don't like it any more. Quitting's not that easy. Your position as King is safe.'

She misunderstood his intentions. Any hint of destabilisation now would be disastrous. This argument had to be defused and yet they were both itching for a fight, the air electric between them. He shook his head. 'That's not what I meant.'

She threw up her hands. 'Why doesn't anyone say what they mean?'

Lise wanted honesty; he'd give it to her.

'It's difficult because honesty has been used as a weapon against me.' Rafe took a slow breath. 'For example, there's a reason I don't talk about Carl. When I tried after his death, his memory was used to taunt me by boys at school. The only time I've spoken about him to anyone other than my family or Lance was to you.'

Lise's eyes widened. 'Do you think *I'm* going to hurt you like that?'

He didn't respond because his answer might give her even more ammunition against him. She knew more ways than most to damage him if she thought about it hard enough.

'What I'm trying to explain is that we all say terrible things, and especially to our parents. Things designed to hurt that we don't mean. You think when Carl died, I didn't blame my mother and father for sending us to that school? Had your parents lived, they would have forgiven you as mine did. It's what families do.'

'If they love you, yes.'

Lise chewed on her bottom lip, the look on her face lost and broken. He didn't know how to respond because he suspected she was right.

'We need to stop fighting amongst ourselves. Those in power await your missteps. You offended their aristocratic pride by choosing me over one of their own. They'll punish you for it.'

She raised her chin, her gaze cool and magnificent as the snow-capped mountains that surrounded them. 'Let them try.'

'They already are.' Her eyes widened a fraction. Staff were talking about last night, as Lance had suggested. Salacious snippets for the press. Most, outrageous, but the hints of truth were there. Enough to have people questioning what was going on in the royal bedroom. 'Check this morning's Internet gossip pages if you don't believe me. None of that is good for the country.'

Lise hesitated a moment, then nodded.

'You're right. We're at cross purposes and the country's running out of time. But I have requirements of my own…' He stepped forward, opened his mouth to try and convince her once again that he was on her side. She held up her hand in a stop motion and the words died. 'No more secrets.'

'Agreed. I'm your greatest supporter in this place.'

Lise continued to stare him down.

'Then prove it.'

Rafe had been right. She hated it, railed against it, but couldn't dismiss his good judgement. The more reputable papers kept a dignified silence on the subject, but the tabloids had been full of titillating stories about their relationship. Even she could admit some of the headlines were quite clever. Things like, *Who's the King of the Castle?* Or Albert's particular favourite, *Dungeons and Dragon Queen.* She pored over each one, assessing the damage to the Crown over the days since. It terrified her, the way the stories took on a life of their own. Small truths turning into giant fictions.

The sourness of bile rose in her throat. All at the knowledge this was self-inflicted. She and Rafe tried to make up the lost ground. Out amongst the thankfully adoring public where everyone was all warm greetings and not entirely worried smiles. There, at least, they worked as a team. In private too, there had been a small thaw and, she had to admit, this way was easier. Seeing again the man she'd admired once. The one who had made her feel as if anything was possible. But there had been no more meaningful touches. No touching at all.

Rafe had been kind, attentive. Respectful and distant in a way. And each time he was close, she *wanted*.

Her head still told her he was wrong for her. Her body cried he was wrong in all the right ways. It drove her mad. The churn of anxiety in her belly mixed with the curl of desire. Swirling and twisting her into tighter knots. She craved like a drug the sweet oblivion his body could provide. The floating bliss. The forgetting. During the day she could throw herself into duty. Meeting her people, hearing their concerns, and even solving some of them. She'd begun to enjoy that sense of achievement when once she'd believed there was nothing about the role she'd wanted or could much contribute to. Then at night Rafe invaded her dreams, till she woke all slick and wet with his name gasped from her lips.

There was no off switch to this need. It simmered barely below boiling point, overflowing when she least expected. Even today, as they worked to save the country with him commanding the room. A picture of rakish perfection in his bespoke suit. His hair curling in that careless kind of way that tempted her to reach out and sink her hands into the midnight darkness of it. Brush it away from his forehead when the unruly strands fell—

'Your Majesty?'

She snapped herself from the daydream. Realised she'd been staring at him. The corners of his mouth tilted in a soft, knowing smile and her heart tripped a beat. Now a room full of eminent financial experts waited on her next words. Sworn to maintain confidentiality about the true state of Lauritania's economy until some credible solutions could be seized upon in the hope of solving the country's woes. They'd spent the day working through options, and here she was fantasising.

'I suggest cutting parliamentary travel entitlements,' she said, though it would cause a riot amongst parliamentarians. 'Flying first class is a luxury they can forgo.'

Lise stifled a yawn, her eyes watering as she did. She needed coffee and a moment to herself. One where she might breathe without the weight of expectation crushing her. 'Ladies and gentlemen, perhaps we could take a break. I'm sure everyone would like some time to stretch their legs, check their phones. We can get back to saving the country in twenty minutes. Some refreshments will be served outside.'

There was murmur of assent. People bowed or curtsied as they left through open glass doors onto a secluded patio, leaving her blissfully alone. She turned away from the garden view, to look at an imposing portrait on the wall. The past few days being watched over by a painting of Lauritania's last and greatest Queen, Marie. Was it a deliberate decision to use this room? In the palace, rarely did anything happen by coincidence. Lise stared up at her great-great-grandmother, dressed in an exquisite, bejewelled gown. A monarch who'd ruled the country successfully for over seventy years. What advice would the woman have for Lise now, when her parents had given her none?

'You look like her.'

The soft burr of Rafe's voice whispered over her. She hadn't heard him come into the room again, but he was close. The awareness of how near he stood shimmered down her spine.

She studied the Queen's portrait. Marie's expression distant, serene.

'Which part?'

'Her eyes.' The same blue as her own, so lifelike it was

as if they looked straight into the heart of her, almost like a judgement. A reminder to Lise that she must not fail here. Rafe moved to her side. 'There's a steel in them.'

'Me? Steely?' She shook her head. 'No.'

He clasped his hands behind his back. 'You've never been on the receiving end of your wrath.'

'Neither have you.'

'When you threatened to take my head or lock me in the dungeon—' he raised a knowing brow and placed his hand to his chest '—I feared for my very existence.'

He seemed so earnest, yet his eyes glittered wickedly. She laughed. 'I don't believe that for a moment.'

Rafe turned to look at Marie's portrait again, his gaze lost in it. 'You might be surprised.'

'What do you fear?'

His attention left the painting, all of it now directed at her as if peering deep into her soul. It was an uncomfortable sensation. The corner of his mouth kicked up, 'Queen Marie has never been forgotten, and neither will you.'

There seemed to be such honesty in his words, but it was no answer to her question. 'You think?'

He cocked his head. Fixed her with eyes that weren't distant or serene, but hot and compelling. 'I know.'

Heat whispered over Lise's cheeks. She found it difficult to accept his praise, especially when he was a master of palace games. The gentle compliments she'd fallen for once, losing herself completely to his words. Though Albert had said similar things about her, and she trusted what he'd said…

'I thought you'd be outside, mingling.' She waved her hand towards the open doorway. The murmur of voices and clink of cups on saucers floated into the room. 'With your adoring crowd. They like what you have to say.'

He had such command of everyone here. All the experts looked to him. Listened as he kept discussions on track, grabbed an odd idea before refashioning it into a brilliant solution. He was a true maverick. Watching his mind work was…

Thrilling.

When had she come to think of him this way, to rely on him? It seemed as natural as her next breath. He spread his arms wide and took a bow. 'They'll have enough pieces of me over the coming days. However I find the only person I wish to take from me, is you.'

It was impossible to catch her breath when he said things like that. The heat in her cheeks increased. 'I'm not sure that's a proper thing to say.'

'I'm not really one for being proper. But for now, there are other things on my mind.' He walked over towards a table in the corner, where a large pot of freshly brewed coffee stood. He poured some, added a lug of milk. One and a half sugars, exactly how she liked it. Rafe walked towards her holding out the cup. She accepted it and took a grateful sip. He'd asked how she took it only once. Every time since, each cup he'd made for her was perfect.

'You look…tired,' he said.

He wasn't wrong. The long, lonely nights worrying about how to fix the disaster left by her family seeped into her bones till they ached as if they were going to splinter.

'We're keeping the same hours. I'll be no more tired than you.'

Rafe scrubbed a hand over his unshaven jaw, the stubble a tantalising scratch under his fingertips. 'That may be, but I want to make sure you're looking after yourself. As your husband, I believe it's part of my job description.'

He stood closer now. The top button of his shirt undone, no tie. A smattering of dark hair hinted at the open neck of the pristine white shirt. On that strong chest, where he'd held her in the mountains, and she'd been lulled by his soothing heartbeat. What Lise wouldn't give to rest there again…

She shook her head. 'I need to fix this.' The choking frustration at the failure of her education threatened to throttle her.

He glanced outside at the milling group of people, then dropped his voice. 'And you will. The suggestion of reducing the size of the public service by natural attrition was all yours. You're taking on some of the austerity yourself. Selling the royal yacht.' It seemed an unnecessary extravagance, given that Lauritania was landlocked and the yacht had to be moored elsewhere. 'And Lance will be for ever in your debt for offering to sell antiques of value currently unused in the palace storerooms. Fiscal policy can be learned. But you have something that can't be. Humanity. A desire to build up the country's people, not take away.'

Lise drained the dregs of her coffee. Winced. 'I'm not unique in wanting those things for Lauritania.'

Rafe took the cup gently from her hands and placed it on the table.

'You care about inequality. Look at the organisations you supported.'

Her heart missed a few beats and Lise placed her hand to her chest, as if that would steady it. 'How do you know about them?'

She'd kept her involvement in some of the 'grittier' charities, as her father had called them, quiet. Seeking no accolades or plaudits for her work. She'd hoped if she kept her patronage private, her father would let her continue.

He hadn't.

'People who have a keen interest in our country were watching and appreciated what they saw.'

Her father had told her to leave any support to her brother, but Ferdinand hadn't been interested in funding shelters for young people or women escaping violence at home. That recollection tempered the flutter of surprise at the thought anyone paid much attention to what she did. The organisations she'd wanted to help most had suffered in her enforced absence. She dropped her head and twisted at her wedding band. 'Not everyone liked what they saw.'

'Your father was wrong for thinking you should stick to only saving stray puppies and kittens.' Lise stopped toying with the ring on her finger and looked up at him. Rafe and the King must have spoken of this, all those times they'd discussed her future without her. She tried to muster some semblance of anger or indignance but the flame of it guttered out and died in the warmth of Rafe's approval.

'They're worthy causes,' she said. Though she'd never been allowed to own a rescue kitten or a puppy, for all the public support she'd given them. Only pedigreed animals were allowed in the palace.

'They are.' Rafe nodded. 'But you wanted to do more. People noticed. Like when you were forced to give up competitive skiing. Everyone heard what your father had to say, that you were concentrating on your formal duties since you'd come of age. What people saw was your quiet acceptance of the role being formed for you.'

Not the role she wanted. Never that. What she'd wanted didn't matter.

'Maybe the tantrums happened behind closed doors,' she said. Though they hadn't. Not then. Her moment had been reserved for a day when the illusion of a hopeful future with a man she might love had been crushed under the King's handmade shoe.

'Perhaps. But you were headed for a world championship to represent your country. Tantrums would have been forgiven, in that instance.'

She shook her head. A strand of hair fell from her chignon. Rafe reached out, hesitated a moment—a pause between breaths—then slipped the unruly piece behind her ear. A shimmer of pleasure skittered down her spine.

'I know the people found it unfair you couldn't finish what you started,' Rafe said.

'What people?'

She'd only ever heard what her family had to say about her failings, not about her successes.

'Your loyal, obedient subjects, of which I am one.'

'Oh, no, now you're being too much.' She snorted. 'You've never had an obedient day in your life.'

Rafe moved close and she could smell the citrus of his aftershave and the cool undertone like the autumn breeze in the mountains that she would associate with him for ever. Then he leaned down and murmured into her ear, 'I can choose to be if I wish. Most people aren't worthy.'

'And I am?'

'There are people who saw you as an integral part of Lauritania's future, not a footnote to it.'

'You have such faith in me.' The crown they'd placed on her head at her coronation had been too heavy. As if it didn't fit. As if the role of Queen wasn't meant for her at all. Now, with Rafe's support, she was beginning to believe it was.

Beginning to believe that this role might be one she could turn into her own...

'You have a passion and drive Hasselbeck and his cronies don't understand. They want everything to stay the same, which requires a compliant monarch. You'll never be that, and she's your reminder,' he said, nodding to the painting of her great-great-grandmother on the wall. People began drifting back into the room and taking their place at the grand table that dominated it. Rafe took no notice of them, his only attention to her, as if not another person in this place mattered.

'They're afraid you'll believe in yourself. And when you do, they fear the Queen you'll become.'

CHAPTER TEN

RAFE WOKE IN the darkness and checked his phone. Three in the morning. He turned. Under the door to Lise's room cut a sliver of light. Strange that she'd be awake this early. He rolled out of bed, went to the walk-in wardrobe, and threw on a pair of pyjama bottoms, no shirt. He knew Lise enjoyed seeing him half dressed. Any tantalising lick of her gaze over his bare skin gave him hope that soon this cold war between them would end. And he needed it to end. Being close to her and not touching. Not kissing. No silken skin sliding over his as they immersed themselves in the heady pleasure of each other's bodies. It had begun to consume him, till Lise was all he could think about. His silent obsession. The meagre taste he'd had would never be enough for the addict he'd become.

He walked to the door between their rooms and knocked without an answer. Knocked again, louder this time. No sound came from the room beyond, so he opened the door and went through.

A lamp glowed in the corner. The bed turned down but not slept in, the sheets pristine. He checked the expansive en-suite bathroom, but nothing. She hadn't slept here. Lise had been tired over dinner. Pale skin, dusty shadows under her red-tinged eyes. Yawning when she'd thought he'd not been looking. She'd drunk coffee. Espresso. Strong. Not her usual preference. Looked worn and frayed at the edges after days of trying to bring Lauritania back from the brink.

They would succeed. Failure was not an option. So he tried to stitch her together as much as he could, when it appeared as if she might unravel. But she hadn't yet. Lise had been underestimated by her family, her government and, in the past, by herself. Now she was working harder than anyone to keep it together and no one could doubt she was growing into a force to be reckoned with.

He walked back to his room and dragged on a shirt before padding barefoot down the chilly halls of a disappearing autumn, in search of her.

Rafe wanted to spend the cold, snow-covered season in bed with Lise, keeping each other warm in the best of ways. On bleak days of wind and sleet they could take time being wrapped in each other. A fantasy, perhaps, but he believed they'd made inroads. She seemed freer, happier. Like the hopeful Princess she'd once been. It was a pleasure to witness.

As he moved through the palace everything lay dark and quiet. Paintings of Lise's ancestors glaring down at him as he looked for her. He didn't care. To hell with all of them. They hadn't cared for Lise. Her father, mother, brother. Leaving her to fix the mess they'd neglected without any preparation. He strode to the pool where she might have gone for a swim, as he knew she sometimes did from the night staff who kept a hidden watch for her safety from darkened alcoves. Sadly, the pavilion sat empty. Moonlight shimmering on the water through the glass above. He travelled back past their suites towards the study, which was the only other place he thought she might have gone if she'd remained in the palace.

As Rafe reached the room a streak of light shone from underneath the dark oak. The door lay open a crack, so he pushed his way in. Lise slumped over her desk, head on her arms. Asleep. The computer screen on, a royal crest sliding lazily across the lock screen. An empty tea-cup and pot sat abandoned in a corner. The fresh herbal smell made him smile a little, that she drank his own family's concoction.

On the desktop were scattered papers covered in her elegant, looped script. Notes. Scratchings. Ideas. He didn't look too closely though, transfixed by her face. Her pale lashes feathered on even paler cheeks.

'Ahh, Lise.' She was dressed for the bed she'd not slept in. A robe wrapped round her, grey and soft. He reached out, stroked her hair. Brushed a few silky strands from her forehead. She didn't stir, other than a long, slow breath in and out.

It couldn't be comfortable lying there, which told him how exhausted she was. She needed to sleep late. As it was the weekend now, Lise could. They didn't have anything that couldn't be moved. A meeting approving the final arrangements for the Queen's Ball was all that stood in her way in the early morning. He wanted her to sleep late with him, but she'd unlikely accept that yet, as much as he wanted to tuck her into his body and keep her safe. Instead, he'd settle for taking her to her room. Rafe moved in close, manoeuvred one arm round her curved back, another under her legs and scooped her slender frame high into his arms. She stirred then. Protested in a sleepy kind of way as her body stiffened into consciousness. He held her close. Stilled for a moment as she squirmed.

'Shh…' he murmured. 'You fell asleep at your desk, love. Lay your head down.' He waited a heartbeat. Two. Absorbed the sleepy mumble of something that made no sense. He waited another second as Lise draped an arm over his shoulder, snuggled her head into his neck, and he relished the feel of her in his arms again.

In sleep, Lise's body told the truth of her and him. He moved silently towards her room, accepting a moment in time with her in his arms. Carried her inside where the temptation to curl up with her almost overwhelmed him. Reaching her bed, he bent over to lay her on the covers.

As he did, Lise gripped him tight, and clung to him with a whimper of distress. *'No.'*

He straightened and she nuzzled into him, her breath ghosting across his neck. Rafe stood for a few moments, letting her settle back into sleep. She grew heavy in his arms again. He rested his head against hers, breathing in the scent of wildflowers, which he'd come to think of now as her own. She needed to sleep long and soundly, yet she didn't want him to let her go. The solution was obvious.

He manoeuvred into the bed with her still in his arms. She opened her eyes then. Confused, still mostly asleep the way they looked at him dreamy and unfocussed. Rafe lay back, taking her with him.

'Rest now,' he said as he stroked his hand over Lise's side. Absorbing her long, contented exhale as her head nestled into his shoulder, her hand over his heart.

He reached out and turned off the bedside light. A lassitude stole over him. Borne by tiredness, sure. He and Lise had both been working long and hard. Still, it was more. Something strange and foreign that he took a while to recognise. A bone-deep contentment that he was finally where he should be again. She might hate him in the morning; he would deal with her disapprobation then. But having her in his arms again? That was worth it.

Lise's heart pounded as she grappled to find purchase on something, anything. She had to hold on. She couldn't let go, yet she couldn't recall why. But she was falling.

Falling.

She gasped, trying to suck in the air that never seemed enough. Trying to breathe but the breaths wouldn't come. Clutching onto the first thing she could reach.

'Lise. Shh… I have you.'

The rough caress of a voice. Where was she? Lise opened her eyes. Blinked at the soft light of a new day. In her bed, on her side, with her hands clenching around clumps of a man's T-shirt.

'You had a bad dream.' Rafe. She couldn't release his shirt, her hands clamped in place over the scrunched fabric. Bad things happened if she let people go. 'I found you asleep at your desk and tried to put you to bed. You held onto me.'

She remembered now. Numbers. Too many numbers that screeched at her in urgency and hurt her eyes as she tried to sort through finances that made little sense. She'd put her head down on her desk for only a few moments. To rest. Then she'd woken cradled safe like a child in strong arms. Weightless, being carried. Till that sensation of being let go and she grabbed on tight.

The shivering started, a quake through her body. 'I'm cold. Rafe, why am I always so cold?'

He wrapped his arms round her, drawing her close to the hard heat of him. 'I don't know, but I'm here.' He dropped his forehead to hers. Holding her till the shivering subsided and she was lax and soft in his embrace. She lay there, his body warmth sliding over her. Aware now of their legs and feet entwined. The bulk of his muscles and jut of strong bones. Soaking in the pleasure of it all as he held her tighter to his body. The care he'd taken, demanding nothing for himself. Every part of him raw and male and uncompromising as she lay flush against him. Especially...

Oh.

He shifted and the hard length of him pressed into her stomach.

Yes.

She pulled back to look at him. His dark curls unruly across his forehead. The shadow of stubble peppering his jaw. Lise smoothed her hands over his chest, where his shirt sat crushed by her fingers. Mapping the defined landscape of his body. His eyes scanned her face, dropped to her lips. She reached out and traced his jaw, the roughness teasing her fingertips. They reached his mouth and he nipped at them. Heat rushed through her, the desire overwhelming, here in his arms. The scent of him all fresh and crisp and wild like the cold air of his craggy mountain home. It made her crave to simply give into the relentless need throbbing through her with every heartbeat. To claim a wildness, a freedom for herself once more. She canted her hips into him, and he pinned her with an incendiary gaze.

'Be sure,' he growled, feral and raw. The sensual warning rippled through her, an exquisite ache blooming deep inside. As their bodies rubbed together, he tipped his head back, closed his eyes and moaned, the salacious sound setting her ablaze. She pressed her lips to the strong column of his exposed throat. Breathed in the musky scent of his skin.

The only time she felt warm was with him. The only time the crippling guilt had been silenced was in his arms, her fears annihilated by his lips and hands. There was something about him that made her want to laugh again. Made her feel strong and capable, like the Queen she'd been crowned rather than the lost Princess who'd first taken the throne. None of this had been easy, trying to save the country, but this glorious man, he had faith in her, believed in her. And she'd begun to believe in herself too, that maybe she didn't have to burn everything to the ground, but simply change what didn't work and keep the rest. And why, in the process, shouldn't she take something for herself? Stop fighting and give into pleasure for once?

'I'm sure.'

His gaze was intent, hot. Boring into her as if he could see her soul. 'Do we need protection? I have none in this room.'

He'd thought of that, her refusal to fall pregnant, when she would have forgotten everything for him in this moment. A rush of heat flooded her, like being immersed in hot water. She gripped his shirt hard. Shook her head. Her cycle was regular and her period due any day.

'No. It's a safe time.'

'My health checks are clear.'

'I trust you,' she whispered, realising the blinding truth of her words in this moment. She hadn't thought she'd trust anyone again, but somehow Rafe had slid his way through her defences.

Then her world flipped, and she lay underneath Rafe. Pressed deep into the mattress. His hips cradled between her thighs. The hardness of him *there, right there.* Her hands moved under his shirt, running over the tense muscles of his back. She slid them down his spine, relishing the quiver of flesh under her palm. The whole of her burning up in the bed.

He kissed her neck and she trembled, his teeth scraping the sensitive flesh at the junction of her shoulder. She slipped her hands beneath the waistband of his pyjamas to his backside, the muscles flexing and releasing as he rocked against her. Both fully clothed yet it was as if they had nothing on. The curl of pleasure tightening inside. His fingers circled her nipple through the soft fabric she wore. She writhed underneath him, trying to get closer as he dropped his head and sucked before pulling away. She whimpered in protest.

'You need something, Lise?'

The feel of him, hard and strong as she ground into him. 'Too many clothes.'

She tugged his shirt over his head, and he tossed it on the floor. Mouth on hers, teeth clashing as he plundered her. No finesse, no softness but a taking. She gave back, her tongue curling with his, their panting breaths filling the room. He raked her thin robe from her shoulders then lifted her top. Lise shrugged both off, she and Rafe tangled in each other as they wrestled out of the remaining clothing until they were deliciously naked. Hands roaming and searching. Goosebumps peppered her body.

'Getting cold again? I'll keep you warm.' Rafe stroked his hands lower, teasing her inner thighs. 'Open for me.'

His voice a rough demand that sent another shiver through her. She relaxed her legs, breaths coming in short gusts. Squirming against his clever fingers, teasing her close to where she needed, but not close enough. The sensation in her body empty, unquenched. Rafe traced his lips along the shell of her ear, murmuring about her perfection, how responsive she was for him as the maddening stroke on her inner thighs continued. Then one hand left its ministrations. She groaned. The sound was greeted with a wicked chuckle, which rumbled through her.

'Patience,' he murmured, the breath tickling at her ear, 'will be rewarded.'

The fingertips of his right hand brushed her nipple. She arched her back, catlike, craving more contact than these frustrating teases. Her reward was his thumb and forefinger, rolling the too sensitive flesh between them.

She writhed. Desperate. Wanting him to fill the emptiness inside her. He didn't move. Other than to keep up the torture of her nipple, each touch sending electric shocks between her legs. His free hand continuing to stroke her inner thigh, driving her mad.

She shifted against him to try and get his hands closer. Moaning unintelligible things. 'Please, please, Rafe.'

'I love it when you beg for pleasure,' he said, voice harsh and strained. The weight of his own desire, bold and heavy against her leg as he tormented her. That frustrating hand of his dipping low to slide between her legs. He stroked, gently at first. Driving her higher and higher. She wasn't cold now. Her body a furnace. All she needed was relief. She chased it with mindless determination.

He rose above her, the blunt head of him between her legs. Slowly, so slowly, easing inside as he held her gaze.

'Whatever you need,' he whispered. 'I don't want to hurt you.'

Rafe's voice rippled through her as he gave her what she craved. She burned for him as he slid deep into her body. Her spine arching at the exquisite pressure, the fullness.

'You aren't. Please. Please, Rafe.'

He stopped and stared, looking deep into her eyes. The muscles of his neck straining as he held himself still above her, but there was something else. Something passing across his face. Myriad emotions that washed over him then were gone, heated things that spoke of desire and possession and something else that made her breath catch.

'Tilt up,' he murmured, stroking a hand down her body, under the swell of her backside. 'Wrap your legs round mine. Move with me.'

She did, joining him in the rhythm of their lovemaking, as he filled her over and over till the fire ignited inside her. Building to something exquisite, irrevocable. She moved with Rafe as she let it take her, hurtling her towards the edge.

'Come for me, Lise, for *me*.'

In this moment, she didn't care about duty or responsibility. Only the feel of him against her. Rough against smooth. Hard against soft.

'*Rafe!*' She shouted his name without shame. Gripping him as the waves of pleasure crashed over her. Her cries reverberating through the room as Rafe captured her mouth in a deep, unrelenting kiss.

Rafe circled the edge of the maelstrom as Lise fell, his body taut and primed only for her. Nothing prepared him for the beauty of her in ecstasy. The glorious flush of pink painted her skin. Her body rigid and panting, possessed by the pleasure of their joining. His mind blanked of anything bar the silken grasp of her body. He kissed her trembling lips, her breaths hard and fast as he thrust into the dark, wet heat at the centre of her.

Finally Lise was his.

Her hands tangled in his hair, the pleasure excruciating. They moved in a dance he knew too well but was nothing like he'd experienced before. Surging forwards, not so gentle now. This all-consuming desire to win, possess, pleasure. Something more than sex, a craving that only she could sate.

The noises she made, soft, mewling sounds. The gasps, the slide of bodies. Her softness under his palms. His own moans as the grip of her drove him wild. The prickle at the base of his spine, the heaviness that told him he was close, so close.

He ran a thumb over her nipple. Took it between his fingers and rolled as she moaned loud and long. A flutter deep inside her and he knew she was close again. He craved her pleasure once more. Pushed her harder, faster. She met him stroke for stroke.

Her body stiffened and grabbed him tight as she arched back. There was no holding on, the edge rushed up and he hurled himself over into the storm that was his wife.

As everything fell back into place around them, she softened into him. Relaxed as he stroked his hands over her silken skin, as the tremors subsided.

'We'll spend the day in bed,' he murmured. His voice unfamiliar to his own ears. Rough and full of lust. A promise of things to come.

'The whole palace will have heard us.' Lise whispered the words. He wasn't sure why, when only moments before she'd screamed his name.

And he craved it. The acknowledgement that they were together now, not just on paper, but in truth. Rafe traced his lips over the shell of her ear. A growl, full of heat and possession so she could never forget this moment.

'Let the whole palace know you're mine.'

CHAPTER ELEVEN

THE COLOUR AND light of the palace's grandest ballroom swirled around her. People in their finest dresses and most opulent jewels glittered under the glow of pendulous chandeliers. The monarch's annual ball was one of the most anticipated events on Lauritania's social calendar. Lise looked around at the decorations, flowers. The food and wine. All she saw was the rivers of money lost on frivolous things when the country's finances were on a knife edge. Still, the country looked forward to the ball as if it heralded a new beginning. This year, the date signifying the Queen and her people out of official mourning.

Lise took a moment to herself, sipping at her glass of champagne, the bubbles tingling in her mouth. *'Little bubbles of happiness'* her mother had called them when Lise was introduced to the drink for the first time on her sixteenth birthday. Still, she wasn't convinced joy was found in the sparkle of this fine vintage. What did soften the sharp edges was Rafe. She peered over the top of her glass at her husband. Strange how that word now fitted as comfortably as old clothes. Though nothing about him could be described as old, or comfortable. Certainly not the dinner suit exquisitely crafted to mould every hard line of his body. A body that seemed perfectly honed to pleasure hers. Like this afternoon, when she should have been preparing for the ball. Instead, trying on her trousseau, which hadn't quite made it to the palace collection, despite her initial intentions. She'd wanted to surprise him tonight. Instead, he'd found her in her room. Slipped the cobweb-fine silk and embroidered confection wordlessly over her skin, laid her out on the bed. A flood of heat coursed through her. He'd been insatiable as he'd kissed down her body and she'd threaded her hands through his unruly curls. Her cries ringing through the bedroom as he'd feasted…

'Your Majesty.'

Lise turned. Put on her formal smile. Ignoring the sliver of disappointment that she couldn't immerse herself in the memories of the indulgent afternoon any longer. But the night was drawing to a close. Soon she could be in Rafe's arms again.

'Prime Minister.'

Whilst it probably wasn't the done thing to think about Rafe making love to her whilst talking to Hasselbeck, her body wasn't so keen to keep her libido in the box she attempted to push it back into. Every part of her flushed, hot and needy. All for Rafe. Always for him. His power to make her scream was only matched by his ability to make her laugh again. He'd firmly entrenched himself as her obsession. Her counsel, her rock of support.

'Your announcement regarding Lauritania's financial woes seems to have been a success.'

Hasselbeck's words weren't meant as a commendation. She dragged herself back into the conversation when he was the last person she wanted to speak to. He'd never rated her, and it was something she wouldn't easily forget.

'People will understand the difficult decisions if everyone shares in them. Those who have the most should proportionally bear the greatest burden.'

The prime minister's face pinched, as if he'd sucked a lemon. He wanted her to fail. She knew it. She glanced at Rafe once more, now holding court with the British ambassador. In complete command of everyone and everything around him. He looked up, their eyes met, and he winked. Another rush of heat licked over her, no doubt pinking her skin. One more black mark on her queenly abilities because queens probably shouldn't blush. Though Lise wasn't sure she really cared any more about what she should and shouldn't do in her role as monarch. She was turning it into her own in ways she'd not thought possible, and Lauritanians seemed to be happy with their new King and Queen…

The prime minister followed her gaze in Rafe's direction. 'It seems marriage to His Majesty suits you.'

The media had been fed carefully crafted stories about their relationship. The breathless reporting of a happy union buoying the people. To Lise, that reporting now felt real. She touched her neck where a scrape from Rafe's stubble lay hidden under concealer. The make-up artist smirking as she'd obliterated the evidence of the afternoon's lovemaking. She loved Rafe's marks of possession on her skin. Owning every part of her. She trembled at the ripple of recollected pleasure.

'It does.'

Hasselbeck leaned in, almost conspiratorially. Lise tried not to shrink away. People were now watching them, and she didn't need any talk of instability or a rift between her and her prime minister, not when her whole country's future was at stake. She pasted a fake smile on her face and gulped some champagne.

'You know he went to school with my son? The De Villiers family always had grand aspirations. His Majesty was the most ambitious, even then.'

She forced out a laugh, when she really wanted to hiss that Rafe was worth a thousand times more than anyone else in the room. They paled when compared to him.

'There's nothing wrong with aspiring to be better. It's a noble endeavour,' she said as Hasselbeck's attention flicked over her shoulder. At the same time, the back of her neck tingled with a familiar warmth.

'Talking about me?'

Rafe's voice was cool and distant. Full of disdain. She looked at him, stiff and formal. Gone was the relaxed, smiling man who'd been charming dignitaries only minutes earlier.

'We were just saying what a supportive consort you are for the Queen. It's pleasant to see some happiness in the palace.' Hasselbeck smiled, showing too many teeth. 'Indeed, Lady Conrad appears to be finding fresh happiness too if rumour is correct. With the best man from your wedding… His Majesty's friend.'

Lise reeled. Sara, with… Lance? She had no doubt he was a charmer, that much had been evident from her meeting with him in the castle. But he was a player too, by Rafe's account. She couldn't imagine Sara in the slightest bit interested in someone like that.

Though an expression flickered across Rafe's face that seemed…knowing. He placed his hand on the small of her back, flexed his fingers.

'Yes,' Rafe said. 'She had a desire to see England and His Grace offered her a seat on his private jet.'

Lise's champagne flute almost slipped from her grasp.

How did Rafe know when she didn't? She downed the last of her drink then placed the glass on the tray of a server walking past.

'How convenient for Lady Sara,' Hasselbeck said with a sneer.

'Most,' Rafe replied. 'I'm sure you'd agree everyone deserves occasional respite from the demands of duty or family expectation. Now, the hour is late. It's time Her Majesty and I retired.'

Lise tried not to show any emotion as Rafe guided her towards the exit, her stomach clenching in the twin emotions of shock and hurt. Their formal departure was announced. She smiled at the crowd from muscle memory alone. Rafe had agreed to no more secrets between them. Yet she'd been trying to get in touch with Sara since the wedding and had heard *nothing*. What was going on? She felt bloodless. Frozen. As if every part of her were hewn from ice. As they left the ballroom Rafe removed his hand from her lower back and the freeze intensified.

'What the hell was that?' she spat.

'Not here.' Rafe quelled her with a frigid glance then smiled at a member of staff, who bowed as they passed.

She tried to muster the disdain that had come so naturally to the rest of her family. If he wanted indifferent, she could do that. Lise allowed the chill to seep through her veins again, obliterating all the warmth Rafe had brought to her life.

She'd asked for truths and had been fed a lie by omission. What else had been going on when she hadn't been paying attention? She'd find out or be damned trying. As Lise walked to their rooms, she wondered whether she could believe anything Rafe said, ever again.

* * *

Rafe strode through the palace halls to their suite, jaw clenched. As they reached the entrance it was all he could do not to fling back the door and stalk inside. Instead, he allowed Lise to sweep past him in her dress of ethereal grey, dotted with crystals that glittered with every move. She'd asked, *'What the hell?'* Yet after overhearing her conversation with the prime minister, he could well ask the same.

Aspiring to be better?

What had she meant by that?

Lise moved to the window staring out at the view, her gown and jewels sparkling in the lamplight. Her mother had been renowned as an icy beauty, remote and untouchable. Right now, Lise was her mother incarnate.

This was not how the evening was meant to end, in some pointless cold war. Cold was not what he looked for when it came to Lise. He tugged at his bow tie. Shrugged off his jacket and tossed it onto a chair. Undid the tight top button of his shirt so that it didn't throttle him. How she'd dazzled the ballroom, finally out of mourning black. Tonight, all eyes had been on the young Queen and all he could think was that this magnificent woman was *his*, in every way.

Yet she seemed to believe he was on some *noble endeavour* to *improve* himself. As if he wasn't good enough. Rafe clenched his fists, relaxed them, and flexed his fingers. There would be an explanation, there must be. He and Lise hadn't been apart since their first time of making love. Each night spent in bed together, a passion and hunger for each other that wouldn't be denied. Each day working to save the country. They were building something, as he'd known they would. Something solid and untouchable. Hasselbeck and his cronies could keep their grubby intrigues away from it.

He tried shaking away the dark simmer of anger that bubbled in his gut. She turned to him, the diamonds fire against her throat. A stark contrast to her glacial gaze. He took a steadying breath, not trusting himself to say anything in this moment. Instead, he removed his cuff-links and placed them on a bureau, began rolling up his shirtsleeves.

'When were you going to tell me about Sara?' Lise's voice was low and cool like the autumn chill whistling under the eaves. It was a surprise that she appeared unaware Sara had left Lauritania. Necessitating him making his own disclosures to hide Lise's shock and stop the prime minister fishing for trouble between them.

'There's nothing to tell. She wanted to leave the country and needed a passport. I signed her application. She went.'

'You signed her passport application? She's *my* friend. My brother's fiancée...' Something about Lise's face crumpled, before she stiffened her spine and smoothed out her expression into frigid disdain. 'And you decided I didn't need to know?'

He shrugged.

'You were grieving.' And surely if Sara wanted Lise to find out she would have said something herself. 'And I thought—'

'I *demanded* no secrets from you.' Lise clenched her fists, the whole of her tight and shaking. 'Yet you kept this from me. I had to find out from Hasselbeck, a man who's determined to humiliate me. How could you?'

'How could *I*?' This conversation was skidding off track in ways difficult to control. Rafe held up his hands, trying to placate her. To stop her vibrating with barely controlled fury. All the while his blood surged with the furious adrenaline of his own growing outrage. 'You seemed to be fine friends, laughing at my attempts at… *self-improvement*.'

She stalked towards him.

'I could hardly entertain a pitched battle with my prime minister on the floor of the palace ballroom,' she hissed. 'But let me ask you this, since your ambition is renowned. Would you have married me if I were simply Lise Betencourt? Would you have loved me if I were a mere commoner? Not the Princess or the Queen?'

It was as if he'd been doused in iced water. Love? When had that word entered their discussion?

'We have passion and purpose.' More than either of them could have hoped for at the beginning of their marriage. Love? That was meaningless. He moved towards her, slow and steady. Trying to suppress the urge to shout. To make her see. 'But we are who we are and can't change that fact. So your question's meaningless.'

She threw up her hands. 'It means *everything*. You wanted the Crown. The country. The power. Never me. *Never* me.'

Lise curled into herself then. It looked as if she were being sawn in two. 'But that's fine because you became King and one of the most powerful men in Europe.' Her voice faded. Quiet and defeated. He hated that tone. Better she rage and scream at him rather than this, devoid of emotion as it was.

Rafe stepped forwards, closer now. Close enough to see the sparkle of welling tears before she blinked them furiously away. 'Lise—'

'Don't use my name.'

'Why?'

She jabbed her finger at him. 'I am not and have never been Lise to you. All you ever saw was Her Most Serene and Ethereal Majesty. Defender of the Realm. Annalise Marie Betencourt. Queen of Lauritania. And that's exactly whom you shall have, from this moment onwards.'

His jaw tightened. He breathed through a furnace of heat raging in his gut. He would get through to her in the end. 'You're chasing shadows, things that aren't real, whereas this, how we work together, *that's* something honest and truthful.'

'You want to talk about truth now?' She raised her chin and glared at him. 'I see you for who you are. The ambitious farm boy who coveted the Crown and acquired it.'

Rafe jerked back. And there it was. He couldn't have taken a more direct hit if she'd slapped him. He'd always believed Lise was different from the rest. That in him she saw something more than his history, his past. Yet in the end what they might have shared was meaningless. The words he'd overheard tonight with Hasselbeck were *her* truth. Lise was still Lauritania's aristocracy, and he was the common dirt upon which she trod.

'You go too far,' he snapped. The pulse roared in his ears. 'Ask yourself one thing whilst you sit there on your lofty throne. Where would you or the country be without me? You'd be nothing more than a mouthpiece for the prime minister.'

Lise narrowed her eyes, hard, cold and unreachable. 'Better than a puppet of yours.'

He shook his head. How could he have been fooled? No matter the alluring wrapping, they were all the same, these blue bloods. Only one of their own was good enough. He'd always be the outsider.

'If that's what you believe there's nothing more to say.' He bowed deep and low, like the commoner he was. 'Good evening, Your Majesty.'

Rafe snatched his great-grandfather's cufflinks from the bureau and stormed from the room, slamming the door shut behind him. He'd never be enough for the government, for the people, for her. Lise wanted to be Queen on her own? She could do it and to hell with how heavy the crown sat on her head. He grabbed the solid iron key from the side table, shoved it in the keyhole of the great oak door between them and twisted.

The lock tumbled closed with an emphatic, satisfying click.

CHAPTER TWELVE

LISE STARED OUT of the window of her study. Autumn now firmly taking hold of the countryside, the trees turning gold. Soon the frost would start, the creep and clutch of winter gripping the mountains. But it was always winter for her. Especially now.

She hadn't seen Rafe for two days. He hadn't come to any meals. No light shone out from under the door of his adjoining room at night. The *locked* door. The ache of it twisted hard in her stomach. The hurt still as sharp as the night of the ball. His lack of honesty when he'd promised no more secrets. When she'd realised that yet another person couldn't love her. But there was more. Her memories of his widened eyes, the visceral pain on his face as he'd reared back at her words.

'The ambitious farm boy who coveted the Crown...'

She loathed being cruel and wasn't proud of what she'd said because she knew what those words would do to him. She'd asked him once did he believe she'd hurt him and now she knew the answer in his silence that day was *yes*. For she *had* hurt him in the end. Coldly, deliberately. As he'd hurt her too, although that didn't excuse her own actions. He'd never wanted Lise Betencourt. He'd wanted the Crown, the Queen. Status, nothing more.

She realised now the trap she'd laid for herself. Somewhere deep inside she'd hoped that he could love her, as she'd fallen in love with him. Because that was why she was standing here, with her heart aching as if it had taken a mortal blow. She was in love. Try as she might to fool her head otherwise, she couldn't. Love had caught her when she'd least expected it. When it wasn't hers to wish for.

But why? She wasn't sure any more. She'd spent so many years believing no one could love her, it seemed to have become self-fulfilling. Yet she understood now that, before loving another, she needed to learn to love herself. Lise pulled her jacket tighter, hugging it to her body. Whilst she didn't like herself for what she'd said to Rafe, she'd come to realise one thing. She was *worthy*. Of the many things Rafe might have said to her, on one, he'd been correct. She'd survived, become stronger as a person. Grown as Queen. It was a role she didn't disdain any longer because a person sitting on the throne could do great things, great good. That was something Rafe had taught her. A painful lesson, but she finally recognised her worth as a woman. Didn't she deserve to live a life full of joy and love, for herself?

Her marriage was hollow, sure. Fantasies that it was something more scoured clean away. So, what was left? She couldn't divorce. The stability of the country and the fragile steps to repairing the economy relied on Rafe and her together. *Jusqu'à la mort. Until death.* Rafe had warned her all along with those words engraved on the inner side of her wedding ring. A ring that sat like the weight of the planet on her finger.

She lifted her hand to look at the exquisite gold and enamel band. As she did, a part of the intricate design snagged on the wool of her skirt, and something pulled free. A golden panel like a tiny door, upon which one of the delicate, enamelled flowers lay embellished. Lise peered at it, because there was something engraved underneath the panel, on the body of the ring.

Mon coeur. My heart.

Pulse racing, she tore the ring from her finger. She'd thought the panels were merely a part of the intricate design, not hiding any message. She flicked open another with her fingernail.

Mon ame. My soul.

Then another, and another.

Mon debut. Ma fin. My beginning. My end.

She twisted the ring between her thumb and forefinger. The whole message laid out for her to see. The secret she'd worn every day since Rafe had slipped it on her finger.

My heart, my soul. My beginning, my end. Until death.

Her eyes blurred with the sting of tears, which slid onto her cheeks. Those words. How she'd always dreamed of a man thinking of her this way. The kind of soaring passion she craved. But what of it? The ring was a family heirloom, that much she knew. Still, why give her something so deeply sentimental if it meant nothing?

She pressed her hand to her aching heart. Unable to move or breathe. Could the message on the ring be…a start? What if…? She didn't know, her thoughts a tangle once more. She looked at the ring again. Being in love made you vulnerable, meant that you could be hurt. What if, like her fear of being unloved, Rafe feared that loving her would mean he'd be hurt again?

Which was exactly what she had done.

She heard it then. A gentle knock. A respectful cough.

Lise wheeled around, brushing away the tears that marred her cheeks. *Albert.* For a moment, she allowed the sting of disappointment at seeing her private secretary, rather than her husband.

He entered the room, face full of sympathy. 'I have some news about Lady Conrad.'

'Yes?' She'd asked Albert to find out what had gone on, since Sara hadn't responded to her attempts. What was another rejection to add to the ever-growing list? Lise dreaded what he might say but needed to hear it all the same.

'The English tabloids report a whirlwind romance and engagement. I haven't been able to speak with her myself. I'm sure she'll be in touch when she can. She's likely afraid you'll be hurt, so soon...after.'

Relief mingled with confusion and dismay. Rafe had said something similar.

You were grieving...

Something cracked inside that she was not sure would ever come together again. Even though their betrothal had been arranged, Lise had always trusted that Ferdinand and her best friend loved each other in some way. What else was she kidding herself to believe, which had no basis in truth? She took a slow breath to steady herself.

'Thank you, Albert.'

He nodded to the ring, still gripped in her now quaking fingers.

'I'd heard a rumour of its wonders, but thought it impolite to ask,' he said in almost reverent tones, holding out his hand. 'May I?'

Lise hesitated. She didn't want to relinquish it, still not having come to grips with the words' meaning, if anything at all. But Albert was like a father to her, so she dropped the ring into his palm. He turned it round, inspecting the enamel flowers. Reading the messages. A soft smile playing on his face.

'The Crown jeweller was asked to ensure it was sound prior to the wedding. That it was fit for a Queen.' He looked up at her, tears once more flowing freely down her cheeks, and a tiny frown creased his brow. 'Is there anything else I might do for you, Lise?'

He was allowing her to be the woman, not his monarch.

'I made a mistake, marrying him.' Her voice cracked. Thinking it was one thing, admitting it to someone like Albert... 'Rafe wanted to be King. He didn't want me.'

'How could he *not* want you?'

That was the crucial question. 'I—I don't know.'

Albert looked at the ring, snapped the little enamel doors firmly shut, hiding its secrets once more, then he handed it back to her. The golden band sat warm and heavy in her palm. 'A man who gives a woman this—'

She shook her head. 'It was apparently his great-grandmother's.'

'He could have had a new ring made. One with no messages at all, yet this was the wedding ring he chose.' Albert reached out and closed her fingers around the ring, engulfing her hand in his. 'You need to believe you're deserving of what it says.'

She was trying to, but there was so much still to repair it seemed insurmountable. 'I wasn't...kind to him.'

'People who are afraid often aren't.' He let her go, clasping his hands behind his back. 'Do you know why I stayed on as your private secretary when I could have retired?'

She shrugged. 'I assumed you loved the role.'

He sighed. Shook his head. 'I saw how your family held you to a different standard. That was unfair. I am immeasurably proud of the girl you were and the woman you've become. So I stayed for you. Lise, you might now be my Queen, but you've *always* been like the daughter I never had. I remain because I love *you* and I'm here for as long as you need me.'

'Albert.' More tears flooded her eyes. When would they ever stop? She walked towards him, engulfed him in a hug. He returned it in a heartfelt embrace.

When they pulled apart, he withdrew a handkerchief from his pocket and handed it to her. She gave a tremulous laugh, patting at her eyes.

'Oh, dear, you're going to be with me for ever.'

'It will be my greatest privilege. Now go and claim what you want. What you deserve.' His smile was gentle and kind as he bowed and took his leave.

She placed the ring on her finger once more, its weight now a comfort rather than a curse. She loved Rafe. She *deserved* that love. He'd once said she could rewrite the fairy tale and she would. Their time began now.

She would fight for Rafe to love her.

Rafe lay on the bed staring at the limewashed ceiling. He hadn't run here. He didn't run from anything. It was more to regroup. Coming to his mountain home, to contemplate the habits of a lifetime. Two days were all he'd allowed himself. To hike the high pastures and remind himself of who he was, because he'd lost his way, and a chance with Lise in the process.

Shame sat heavily on him, a weight almost too much to bear. Lise had been right. He'd wanted the power. But the power of a king didn't change who he was. A farm boy. And he *had* been ashamed of his heritage, he recognised. If he hadn't he would never have been driven to the position he was in now. Forgetting the truth of himself. The things he'd learned from his parents in these mountains, about hard work and never shirking your duty, reminding him of the kind of man he was meant to be.

The ambitious farm boy who coveted the Crown. Yes, he was all those things, and the crown that he'd so craved was a hollow one. He wasn't proud of how he'd got here. Lise had once thought she was the fraud. Yet she was the one who'd tried living true to herself, in the end taking up a role she'd never wanted because of her duty to her country. The only fraud was him. The crown on his head hadn't made him better than anyone. They still saw what they wanted to see. The pretender. When this…the old house, the history of his family, was enough. It always had been.

He'd kept a secret from her, a small one perhaps, but she'd demanded complete honesty and he hadn't given it to her, only feeding her insecurities. Leading to an argument that played into both of their fears. His regret in that regard was deep and complete…

The shrill ring of his phone had him leaping from the bed to a side table where it lay vibrating. He checked the screen, but the number wasn't Lise's. It was the prime minister. He gritted his teeth. The man would pay for hurting Lise. His days in his job were numbered. Rafe swiped to answer.

'What do you want, Hasselbeck?'

'Her Majesty.' Hasselbeck's voice was too quiet, strained. 'She's missing.'

It was as if Rafe had broken through ice on Lake Morenburg and plunged into the frozen waters beneath.

There wasn't enough air in the room. He couldn't fight his way through it. He gripped the sideboard to steady himself. Took some slow breaths.

'How the hell do you lose the *Queen*?'

Steadily the shock morphed into a trickle of fear. She'd said once before she'd walk away. If she'd left, it would serve them all right, especially him since there'd been no one there to protect her from the cruel lies she whispered to herself.

'Have you tried her phone?'

'It's turned off.'

She didn't want to be found. He strode to the window. Looked out at the winding thread of road leading down the mountain to a tiny village that lay a few miles below. A car trundled along, sunlight glinting from the windscreen. Travelling towards the church whose spire he glimpsed, nestled in the valley. The church his parents had married in, where Carl was buried, where he'd been christened. Where life was going on. How could that be when here it felt as if time had screeched to a terrifying halt?

The edges of the phone cut into his hand. He loosened his grasp. 'I'm coming.'

Rafe checked his watch. If his helicopter hadn't been out of commission for servicing, he could have called his pilot to collect him. Driving, he could be back at the palace in an hour, although it might take longer. The car he'd been watching slowed as a herd of cows meandered across the road, then stopped. He ran his hand through his hair. If they didn't want to move, they could block the only road's exit for some time, and he didn't have a four-wheel drive to traverse cross-country.

'There's nothing you can do if palace security has had no success.' Hasselbeck's voice was terse and sharp.

If those words were meant as criticism, he deserved it. It was no worse than the self-flagellation he'd mete out to himself, until Lise was found safe. Time to end this call and go. Outside the little car had managed to get through the road-block of cows. 'I'll be there in…' It disappeared around a bend and reappeared, closer. Tourists no doubt. This was a popular time of the year in the mountains after all.

Yet the vehicle didn't take the well-worn path, it turned into the road that led to this place. His home.

'Here,' he murmured to himself. Through the trees there was a flicker of movement as the car travelled closer and closer. A tiny flare of hope lit inside. It couldn't be anyone else. Could it? The car pulled to a jerking halt at the front of the house. Its door opened.

Lise. Her golden hair gleaming in the soft light. She glanced up at him and the memory of her coming out ball came rushing back. When she'd looked at him standing at the top of the stairs, with a gentle smile that speared the heart of him sure as Cupid's arrow. He'd wanted to possess her then. Now…

'What?' Sharp frustration in Hasselbeck's voice brought Rafe to his senses.

'Her Majesty's arrived.'

The sigh of abject relief filled his ear. 'I'll send Security.'

'You will listen, Hasselbeck. No security. She's safe with me.' Safer than in a palace full of enemies. Enemies whose job security would be addressed, once he'd repaired the damage he'd done to her on his own. 'I'll bring her back when she's ready.'

Not before. He hung up, tossed the phone on the couch,

and took the stairs to the lower level two at a time. If she
was never ready to return?

So be it. He would take her wherever she wished to go.

Lise placed her hand on the door handle. It wasn't locked
as she turned it, so she pushed the door open and walked
inside. Rafe stood in the entrance. Hair an unruly mess
of black curls. Delicious stubble grazing his jaw. Dressed
in low-slung jeans, a dark T-shirt gripping his muscular
body, no shoes. Her legs weakened as he towered in the
space. Was his gaze heated as his brown eyes fixed on
her? It was hard to tell as she wasn't sure right now what
was reality and what was wishful thinking.

'Lise.' Her name came out as a whisper, like a bene-
diction on his lips.

'You were on the phone,' she said. He stood back as
she moved further into the hall, shutting the door gently
behind her. 'My absence has been noticed?'

'You've aged the prime minister a hundred years.'

'They'll regret having a queen to serve.'

He shook his head. '*Never.* They should be praising
the heavens.'

She wanted to rush forward into his arms, beg him to
love her, but she held back, as did he. His hands by his
sides, fists clenched.

'How did you get a car?' he asked.

For now, a polite conversation was enough. At least
they were talking again, without recrimination.

'I sneaked into the palace garages and took one,' she
said, and couldn't help a grin of pride. His eyes widened,
and then the corner of his own perfect mouth tilted.

'I didn't know that sneaking was in the repertoire of
a queen.'

'You'd be surprised what queens can do if they put their minds to it.'

'One thing I've never done is underestimate your abilities.'

He'd always had so much faith in her, even when she'd had none in herself. She dropped her head, scuffing at the floor with her dainty shoe.

'I wanted to find you. There are things I need to say.' She looked up again and he took a step towards her. 'Apologies to make.'

He shook his head, reaching out then hesitating. Running a hand through his hair instead. 'No. There's so much I should have said to you, but I didn't want to add to your pain when I believed you'd had enough. That wasn't my choice to make, especially when you demanded more. I should have remembered you were stronger than anyone realised. Than *you* realise.'

She shrugged. 'You wanted the Crown. I'm not so naïve as to ignore its allure.'

'To my shame, I craved the power over everyone who believed I was less, believing it would somehow make me better. I was wrong.'

'If you're shamed, I am too. I hurt you. I'm no better than those aristocrats at your school who disparaged you, bullied Carl. For that, I'm sorry.' Lise worried at her bottom lip, hoping her apology would be enough. 'The things I said were cruel.'

'They were true.'

She looked at him, standing strong and proud. He had every right to be, given all that he'd achieved.

'You're no farm boy.'

'I am. I've embraced my heritage.' Rafe held out his arms to the sides. 'That's who stands before you. A man, not a king. I should have believed that I was worthy of you. Instead, I was a coward. Afraid of giving you the power to hurt me like no other could, because you alone have that power, Lise.'

She stepped forward, close enough to see the pulse beating strong and sure at the base of his throat. The warmth of his body seeped into hers. The scent of him, like the fresh mountain air that reminded her of freedom.

'As you have the power to hurt me. Because love, when combined with fear, has the power to wound as much as it does to heal. You claimed I could rewrite the fairy tale. I want it. I *deserve* it. To be loved by the man I married. You deserve it too.'

Rafe's mouth opened. Closed. His throat convulsed in a swallow.

'I've protected my heart for a long time.' His voice sounded raw, pained. 'And you were prepared to renounce your claim on the Crown to avoid our marriage.'

She placed her hand over her heart, which thudded in her chest. 'All I wanted was a choice.'

His gaze dropped to the wedding ring that sat on her finger; he cocked his head, the question on his face obvious.

'It's what I wanted for you too. What I asked your father for. A *chance* to offer myself.'

Love filled her, brimming inside. She hoped that what she would say next was enough. It was like standing at the top of a mountain, a steep, snowy slope laid out before her. The thrilling race of her heart in the moments before she pushed off and let herself fly, trusting it would be the perfect run.

'I've spent a lifetime believing that no one truly loved me and yet here I am, standing before you, offering myself to you. Lise Betencourt, woman and Queen.'

Rafe shut his eyes and dropped his head. His shoulders rose and fell before he seemed to gather himself and look at her once more, with a heated gaze piercing into the soul of her.

'In that time we spent together, Lise, when you whispered to me your hopes and dreams for your future, I recognised the incredible woman that you *are*. Now all that I want is a chance to prove myself worthy of you.'

That was when she truly saw it, blazing in his eyes. Naked longing. A softness, she realised now, that was reserved only for her. It was like looking in a mirror, because what she saw in Rafe reflected deep inside herself. A need that would never be sated.

Her perfect match. Her other half. Stepping towards her with his heart as open as her own.

'Rafe, you were always worthy of me.'

Those words were like a balm to his soul. What a fool he'd been, thinking love wasn't for him. He'd been halfway there before he'd realised how much Lise meant to him, then wondered how the journey had started. He'd hurt her when the simple words *I love you* would have given Lise immunity from her fears that others played upon. Her insecurity all caused by him, because he'd been afraid to tell her the extent of feelings he'd refused to acknowledge, in case she rejected him. After all that, self-protection still hadn't saved him. It had only hurt Lise more and that was his deepest regret. The one that almost cleaved him in two and left his heart bruised and bleeding.

'I'll gratefully accept your love as the priceless gift it is, then try to return it a thousandfold. I've done a terrible job of showing you how I feel. I should have protected you and all I did was to hurt you more.'

'We're both good at hurting each other. Do you think we'll be as good at loving each other?'

'I don't accept failure willingly, Lise. I do everything I can to avoid it. In this, I *won't* fail because loving you is easy.'

'You were all I ever wanted. All I still want,' she said. 'Despite our rocky beginning I find I'm still a romantic who believes in happy endings.'

He laughed, the first moment of happiness in these blighted few days. 'I want to hold you now, to prove this is real.'

They fell into each other. Rafe reaching his arms round her, drawing her to his body. She nestled against his strong chest as a voice inside whispered, *She's mine, she's home.* But Lise deserved more.

'Sadly our engagement lacked any romance. It's not like I'd planned.'

'You had a plan?' She pulled back a little, eyebrows raised. 'If I were an ordinary woman, how would you have proposed?'

He pressed his lips to her hair, inhaled the scent of her. Wildflowers, a reminder of spring. Rebirth and renewal.

'The same way as if you were Princess or Queen. Because the royal and the woman are one and the same. I would have brought you here. Into the mountains. To my real home.'

She shook her head. 'My father would never have agreed.'

He couldn't help the wicked smile that broke free. He dropped his mouth to her ear, so that his breath would caress her throat. 'I could have plucked you from the palace gardens in my helicopter.'

His hand stroked up and down her spine. 'I'd have stolen you from them.'

'A jailbreak.' She shivered. He didn't believe it was from the cold. 'Sounds thrilling.'

'Then I'd get on my knees.' He dropped to the floor in front of her. Took her hands in his. Her fingers were warm against his own, 'And say… Lise, you are my heart, my soul…'

Lise smiled and he was struck silent for a second. He could bask in that look of joy for ever.

'My beginning, my end,' she said.

'You know.' He kissed the ring on her finger, such a precious symbol of all that lay ahead for them. 'The daisy and the rose. These flowers have a meaning. True love. Love at first sight. What a fool I was not to realise, when I married you.'

'I only discovered the secrets of the ring today. And I began to hope. To find the courage to fight for what I wanted.' Tears welled in her eyes then, dripping to her cheeks. Her sadness had felled him. At least these were tears of happiness.

'What would you have said next?' she asked.

He looked into her face, this brave, beautiful woman. Offering her the truth of his love. 'Will you marry a humble farm boy?'

She looked down at him, deep into his eyes. He was once again lost to everything bar the heat of her gaze. 'Yes. I'd be proud to marry him. In fact, if I wasn't married to him already, I'd marry him again.'

'Perhaps we can, in the little church in the valley.'

'Where your parents married?'

He nodded. 'And where Carl is buried. A ceremony for us alone.'

Rafe stood and wrapped her in his arms once more. She melted into his embrace.

'I'd love that,' she said, voice muffled against his chest. 'So, what now?'

He released his hold on her a little. Stroked his palms over her hair and then cupped her face in his hands.

'We live happily ever after.'

'As simple as that?' She smiled and it was like sunrise over the mountain tops, blazing and bright.

Rafe smiled too; he couldn't help himself. 'It's what always happens at the end of a love story.'

She sighed. 'I suppose we should get started on an heir.'

The thought of making love to her again coursed through him like a shot of schnapps. Fiery and intoxicating. But she deserved more, she deserved *everything*.

'I thought you wanted the monarchy to end with you.'

She shrugged. 'I've come to realise the good it can do, that *we* can do. I find I'm not so keen to destroy centuries of my family history out of fear of failure. With you by my side I feel capable of anything.'

He stroked his thumbs over her cheeks, soft and warm under his fingertips.

'*Never* again will you be placed under pressure to perform your role,' he said, his voice firm. 'That includes children. We have a constitution to change first, so there's plenty of time. I have more important things to think about.'

'More important than the country and the Crown?' she asked.

'Yes.' Rafe dropped his head, till his mouth was a mere breath away from hers. 'I have my wife to kiss and there's *nothing* in the world more important than loving her.'

EPILOGUE

Two years later

THE LIGHTS WERE low in their suite as Lise sat gazing into the blissfully sleeping face of Lauritania's newest, three-month-old Princess. Named after the country's longest-serving Queen, their little girl, Marie, had arrived in a squalling rush a month early, but tiny and perfect. Lise cradled her close. Dark lashes brushing delicate pink cheeks. Love overflowed in Lise's heart, a well of feeling that threatened to overcome her as she nestled Marie safe in her arms. The love she and Rafe shared had seemed miraculous enough. She had never imagined she could contain more of the emotion. Their baby proved her wrong.

They had made all kinds of promises when they'd renewed their vows, in a private ceremony. Just the priest and each other, in the little village church. Vows to love, to honour, and then a silent promise that there would be no children until the country's constitution had changed. Rafe stood by their decision, never questioning it until she did. In the end, Lise was tired of others guiding her actions. Because what she and Rafe shared made her strong. She trusted herself, confident she could guide Lauritania through the coming years ahead. Rafe's love had given that to her. As a team, they were *invincible*. Nothing was impossible with her husband by her side. He believed in her, and she believed in herself. Marie was proof of that. Their daughter planned, wanted, adored. All of it achieved through love. Passionate. Unassailable. Eternal.

As if she'd conjured him, Rafe walked into the room, devastatingly handsome and still in a suit despite the late hour. Campaigning to the last, no doubt, for the most important vote of their lives. He stopped as he took them in. Mother and daughter. His lips curved into a tender smile.

'Now there's a perfect scene. My two beloveds.'

He came to her and stroked his hand through her hair. She tilted her head to him. He bowed down and brushed his lips over hers, the thrill at his touch as fresh and intoxicating as the first time. Rafe then moved to drop a gentle kiss on their baby's head. The little girl stirred, took a deep breath, and sighed before nestling into Lise once more.

'No word?' she whispered, almost not daring to hope.

He shook his head. 'Not yet.'

'If we fail today, we'll keep trying until we succeed.'

Even though change came slowly to Lauritania, the constitutional debate and vote seemed to be going later into the night than she'd expected. But she would never give up on this. Marie was destined to be Lauritania's next Queen. And she *would* rule the country on her own terms, without the need to marry. Lise's speech to support constitutional change had been a statement of fact and intent, of how lucky *she* had been in love, for sure, but promoting a fervent desire to give their firstborn choices without limitation. Rafe's campaign had been no less forceful, with all the passion of the protector he was.

'Your people adore you. Adore our daughter,' Rafe murmured. 'When have we ever failed?'

There was only truth in his words. Success had mounted on success. The country's economy turning around. After Hasselbeck had lost the support of Parliament, they had a new prime minister who worked with his Queen rather than against her. Lauritanians were ecstatic at the young, vibrant royal family leading the country to a grand renewal. Now, every day was filled with happiness and hope. Yet their work was not yet complete.

'I want *everything* for our child.'

'And she'll have it because she has us. Does she need to be put down?'

Lise looked down at the baby's peaceful, sleeping face once more. 'Yes. But it's hard to let her go.'

'I know.' Rafe held out his hands, raised an eyebrow. Lise smiled as she relinquished Marie to him. He gently took his swaddled babe into his arms, an unfailing cocoon of safety he provided to their child and to her. She stood and Rafe watched, his gaze turning molten as she stretched. He'd worshipped her through every phase of her pregnancy. The morning sickness, her rampant hormones with their crying jags, in the aftermath of her fast and furious labour. And now, the ample curves of new motherhood.

'As beautiful as your mama,' he whispered into their daughter's dark shock of curls, just like his own.

'More like her father.'

He grinned, and it lit a fire of joy inside her to see her two most beloved like this. 'Heaven help us all.'

'If she's like her father her country should call itself lucky to have her.' And they did. The people adored Rafe too, the man who was their King. Praised his brilliance at helping guide the economy into recovery. His love and care for the country and their Queen.

He gently placed Marie into her bassinet, then held out his arms. Lise walked into his embrace as he brushed his lips against hers once more and then deepened the kiss. She threaded her fingers into his hair. The emotion flowing between them, through them, like a bright and living flame.

A knock sounded at the door and her heart rate spiked. Rafe broke the kiss and rested his forehead on hers, his breath gusting over her lips. 'It will all be well. How can't it be when we have each other?'

She drifted her thumb across his lips, and he kissed its tip.

'Come in,' she said and turned as the door opened to Albert. Rafe squeezed her hip in support, and she swallowed but didn't move away. Their physical affection as strong for each other in public as it was in private. A mark of their reign. They stood together as one on this as they did on everything. Albert beamed at them both.

'The vote was unanimous. No dissenters. Congratulations, Your Majesties, and to Her Littlest Highness. The constitution is changed.'

Lise shut her eyes against the fresh sting of tears as Rafe gave his thanks for the news and Albert took his leave. She opened her eyes to flashes outside. Then the boom and crack as fireworks burst out all over the city. She and Rafe went to the window and flung it wide to the drifting sound of cheers rising across the capital.

All for them and the little girl who was Lauritania's distant future.

'I had no idea they'd be so happy,' she said, wiping at the tears slipping down her cheeks.

'They are because they love you. Though never as much as I do,' he said, his voice rough and raw. 'And for this moment, I have a gift.'

Rafe reached into his pocket and pulled out a ring.

'What's this?' she whispered, as an oval yellow diamond twinkled in the low lights of the room.

'You said you didn't need anything for our engagement, but this is more. An eternity ring.' He slipped it onto her finger, then took her trembling hands in his own sure grip. 'You are the sunshine of my life. A source of endless happiness. I hope this ring will remind you that I love you more each passing day. That you were destined to be my for ever, from the moment I set eyes on you.'

Lise looked up at him, this man she adored beyond reason. Good and kind and honest…and *hers*.

'I never need a reminder because that certainty is here.' She placed her hand in the middle of her chest. 'I hold your love in my heart, where it's always with me. Always safe. No one can ever take that away.'

As the capital continued to celebrate, the sky lit in showers of rainbow sparks around them, Lise slid her arms round Rafe's neck.

'I look forward to my for ever with you,' she whispered. 'There's nowhere I'd rather be.'

He smiled at her, soft and warm. Eyes alight and burning with adoration, mirroring what she carried for him, within herself. Then he dropped his head to hers and murmured against her lips, 'Let me show you eternity, my love.'

* * * * *

COMING SOON!

We really hope you enjoyed reading this book.
If you're looking for more romance, be sure to
head to the shops when new books are
available on

Thursday 13th October

To see which titles are coming soon, please visit
millsandboon.co.uk/nextmonth

MILLS & BOON

MILLS & BOON®

Coming next month

HER CHRISTMAS BABY CONFESSION
Sharon Kendrick

His words were as emotionless as his expression and Bianca couldn't deny a twist of pain as their coldness washed over her.

But what else had she expected? Joy? Excitement? Surely she hadn't anticipated Xanthos would behave in the way would-be fathers were supposed to behave. Get real, Bianca.

"You're not suggesting I planned this?"

"I have no idea," he drawled, dark eyebrows shooting upwards. "Did you?"

"Please don't insult me!"

He nodded, as if her anger and indignation were in some way reassuring. His gaze rested upon her face. "What do you intend to do?"

"I'm k-keeping my baby, of course!"

"Good."

The word took the wind right out of her sails and she blinked at him in confusion, before reminding herself that she didn't need his approval. But that didn't prevent the sliver of hope which shot through her, like sunlight breaking through a dark cloud. "I know you never intended to be a father—"

"No, you're right, I didn't." His words effectively killed off that brief flash of optimism. "So what do you want from me, Bianca?"

Continue reading
HER CHRISTMAS BABY CONFESSION
Sharon Kendrick

Available next month
www.millsandboon.co.uk

Copyright © 2022 by Sharon Kendrick

MILLS & BOON

THE HEART OF ROMANCE

A ROMANCE FOR EVERY READER

MODERN

Prepare to be swept off your feet by sophisticated, sexy and seductive heroes, in some of the world's most glamourous and romantic locations, where power and passion collide.

HISTORICAL

Escape with historical heroes from time gone by. Whether your passion is for wicked Regency Rakes, muscled Vikings or rugged Highlanders, await the romance of the past.

MEDICAL

Set your pulse racing with dedicated, delectable doctors in the high-pressure world of medicine, where emotions run high and passion, comfort and love are the best medicine.

True Love

Celebrate true love with tender stories of heartfelt romance, from the rush of falling in love to the joy a new baby can bring, and a focus on the emotional heart of a relationship.

Desire

Indulge in secrets and scandal, intense drama and plenty of sizzling hot action with powerful and passionate heroes who have it all: wealth, status, good looks…everything but the right woman.

HEROES

Experience all the excitement of a gripping thriller, with an intense romance at its heart. Resourceful, true-to-life women and strong, fearless men face danger and desire - a killer combination!

To see which titles are coming soon, please visit

millsandboon.co.uk/nextmonth

LET'S TALK
Romance

For exclusive extracts, competitions
and special offers, find us online:

 facebook.com/millsandboon

@MillsandBoon

@MillsandBoonUK

Get in touch on 01413 063232

For all the latest titles coming soon, visit
millsandboon.co.uk/nextmonth

MILLS & BOON
A ROMANCE FOR EVERY READER

- **FREE** delivery direct to your door

- **EXCLUSIVE** offers every month

- **SAVE** up to 25% on pre-paid subscriptions

SUBSCRIBE AND SAVE

millsandboon.co.uk/Subscribe